W9-BPP-862

CROWN JEWEL

CROWN JEWEL

A SIMON RISKE NOVEL

CHRISTOPHER REICH

MULHOLLAND
BOOKS

Little, Brown and Company
New York   Boston   London

Mulholland Books / Little, Brown and Company
Hachette Book Group
1290 Avenue of the Americas, New York, NY 10104
mulhollandbooks.com

First Edition: March 2019

Mulholland Books is an imprint of Little, Brown and Company, a division of Hachette Book Group, Inc. The Mulholland Books name and logo are trademarks of Hachette Book Group, Inc.

The publisher is not responsible for websites (or their content) that are not owned by the publisher.

The Hachette Speakers Bureau provides a wide range of authors for speaking events. To find out more, go to hachettespeakersbureau.com or call (866) 376-6591.

ISBN 978-0-316-34239-1
LCCN 2018960229

10 9 8 7 6 5 4 3 2 1

LSC-C

Printed in the United States of America

To Liz Myers and John Trivers
Friends
Amicus certus in re incerta cernitur

CROWN JEWEL

CHAPTER 1

Lyceum Alpinum Zuoz
Engadine, Switzerland

The men were watching again.

There were two of them, up by the monastery on the hill overlooking the athletic field. They stayed in the shadows of the gallery, popping out to take a photograph, then ducking back again. The boy could tell they thought he hadn't spotted them.

But he had.

He always did.

"Look out!" someone shouted. "Robby! Tackle him!"

Robby returned his attention to the scrimmage in time to see the scrum half—it was Karl Marshal, the best player on the team—lower his shoulder and plow into him. Robby's feet left the ground and he landed flat on his back, his wind knocked out of him, sure he'd never take a breath again. The other players ran past, laughing.

"Might as well make a mud castle while you're down there."

"Only one you'll ever have."

He heard a whistle. Karl Marshal had scored a try.

Robby climbed to his feet and wiped the dirt from his face. When he'd regained his breath, he set off down the field, limping at first, then shaking it off and running as fast as he could. He was small for a sixth former and thin, with pale skin, a mop of curly blond hair, and questioning blue eyes. His size didn't bother him. His father was tall. One day he'd grow. He might not be as big as the others yet, or as strong, but he was no quitter. One of his teachers had remarked upon his determination and called him "Das Krokodil." For a few days, the

3

nickname stuck. He liked being called "Krok." A week later, everyone had forgotten it.

He caught up to the game in time to run into a ruck. He got knocked down two more times, but he caught a pass and almost tackled Karl Marshal. Robby was practical. He knew it would be foolish to expect anything more. Finally, the whistle blew. The scrimmage ended.

Walking back to the athletic center, he glanced at the monastery. It was nearly dusk, the gallery cloaked in shadow. The men were nowhere to be seen. Robby wasn't concerned one way or the other. People had been watching him his entire life. The best thing to do was simply to ignore them.

It wasn't until later that night as he got ready for bed that he thought about the two men again. He realized that this was the fourth time in the past week or so that he'd seen them. One had a large nose that looked like an eagle's beak and black hair. The other was bald and never took his hands out of his pockets. Robby had exceptional vision. It ran in the family. It bothered him that they stayed so far away. Farther than the distance prescribed by the school for journalists and photographers. This was odd, Robby concluded, in his methodical manner. "Rum," Mr. Bradshaw-Mack, his English teacher, would say. "Very rum, indeed."

Robby went to the window and peered outside. Down the hill, the lights from the village of Zuoz glowed warmly, a spot illuminating the tall, rectangular spire of the Protestant church. A crescent moon sat low in the sky and he could just make out the silhouette of the jagged peaks all around. The Piz Blaisun, the Cresta Mora, and, further west, near St. Moritz, the Corvatsch.

He closed the window, secured the lock, then crawled into bed. His roommate, Alain, was reading an *Astérix* comic book his father had sent him from Paris. Robby wished he had a father to send him comics, or, preferably, a book about rugby, which was his favorite sport. It was hard to be too sad, though, because he'd never really known his dad, and besides, he had a wonderful mother.

Robby picked up his phone and considered calling her. The more he thought about the watchers, the more they bothered him. He refused to use the word "scared," because people like Robby were not allowed to be scared. It was a question of setting the right example. He heard Alain snore and decided against calling. Good manners were part of that example, too.

Robby turned out the light and laid his head on the pillow. There was math first period tomorrow, then history, and rugby again after school. As he drifted off to sleep, his eyes opened for a second, even less, and he thought he saw a shadow in the window. *The watchers.* Maybe it was just a dream or a figment of his imagination. Either way, the image didn't register. He turned over and fell into a deep slumber.

It had been a long day and a twelve-year-old boy got very tired.

Chapter 2

Les Ambassadeurs
London, England

Simon Riske did not like losing money.

Seated at the center of a card table in the high rollers' room at Les Ambassadeurs, London's most exclusive gaming establishment, he peeked at his cards, then lifted his eyes to the dwindling stacks of chips before him. He wondered how much longer his bad luck could continue.

"Well," said Lucy Brown, seated at his shoulder so she could view his cards. "What do we do?"

"What do you think?"

"Both cards are different."

"So they are."

"Neither match the cards in front of the dealer."

"And so?"

Lucy screwed up her face and Simon allowed her a moment to figure things out.

It wasn't normal for players to discuss their hands, especially when large sums of money were at stake. But Lucy was young and blond and pretty, and upon sitting down, Simon had explained to all present that he would be teaching her a thing or two about poker. The other players—all male—had taken a peek (some discreet, some not so) at Lucy's black dress, her figure, and her blue eyes. If anyone had voiced an objection, Simon hadn't heard it.

"Fold?" said Lucy.

"Fold," he said, sliding his cards to the center of the table.

"Darn," said Lucy.

Simon had a more colorful word in mind. Instead, he offered his best "not to worry" smile and signaled for a drink: a Fanta for Lucy and a grapefruit and soda for himself. Alcohol and gambling were as combustible as matches and gasoline.

It was an ordinary evening at Les A (as the club was known to habitués). Downstairs, a lively crowd milled about the gaming tables, the atmosphere one of a posh Georgian country house. The play was spread evenly among roulette, blackjack, and baccarat. Slot machines were the province of the lower classes and strictly verboten.

But the real action took place in the private rooms on the second floor.

It had been Simon's plan to observe from afar while explaining the rules of the game to Lucy. The idea vanished approximately five seconds after he witnessed a player win a five-thousand-pound pot on a weak hand. Being a modest and unassuming sort, Simon had reasoned that he could do better. That was two hours and twenty thousand pounds ago.

"Another hand," said Lucy, cheerily. "Our luck's bound to change."

Simon looked at her expectant gaze, her adventurous posture. Lucy was twenty-three and gifted with what some might, in the polite confines of Les Ambassadeurs, call a curvy figure. Like most women her age, she liked showing off her assets. Simon's relationship with her was purely platonic, somewhere between father and friend. It was nebulous territory. In fact, he was her employer. Lucy worked as an apprentice in his automotive repair shop, where she was learning to restore vintage Italian sports cars, primarily Ferraris, with a Lamborghini thrown in here and there. In a sense, she was his own restoration project. But that was another story.

As for himself, Simon was dressed in a black suit and white open-collar shirt, both fresh from the cleaner. His nails were neatly trimmed and he'd spent ten minutes scrubbing them with steel wool to clean the grease from beneath them. He collected cuff links, and tonight, for luck, he'd chosen his favorites, a pair he'd been given by MI5, the British security service, as a thank-you for a job undertaken on its behalf a year earlier. His eye fell on his puny stack of chips and he scowled. So much for talismans. His hair was in the sleekest order, cut short so in need of a brush, never a comb, which was the polite way to say that it was receding faster than the Greenland ice shelf. Unlike the man a few places to his left—a wan unsavory sort who'd taken too much of Simon's money—he'd shaved and treated himself to a splash of Acqua di Parma. His bespoke lace-ups were polished, and only his beryl-green eyes shone brighter.

But all his finery couldn't disguise his true nature. Simon had spent too much time on the wrong side of the tracks to ever be a real gentleman. Some things you could never wash from beneath your nails.

"Well?" Lucy demanded, her lip thrust out petulantly.

"That's plenty for tonight," said Simon. "We've done enough damage."

"But you still have some chips."

"The idea is to leave with a few in your pocket," he said. "More rather than less."

Lucy appeared crestfallen.

"There's just enough to buy us a fancy dinner," he continued. "How about the Ivy?"

"That's for old people."

"It's the princes' favorite place."

"Exactly."

Simon considered this, realizing that "old" for Lucy meant anyone over twenty-five. "How about fish-and-chips at the pub round the corner?"

"I'm not hungry." Lucy crossed her arms and pouted. It was an inviting pout and Simon felt sorry for her boyfriend.

"One last hand," he said. "But I mean it."

Lucy brightened, clutching his arm and scooting closer. "We're going to win. I know it!" She kissed his cheek and Simon said that was close enough and scooted her back a few inches.

It was then that the tenor of the evening took a dramatic turn.

Simon ponied up his chips. The cards were dealt. Simon's were as miserable as usual. The players called and raised and called again. The dealer tossed out the last cards.

And that was when Simon saw it again. A flick of the wrist. A rustle of the sleeve. A flash of white. The player two seats to his left—the unkempt man who'd been winning the entire evening—was cheating. Twice now—Simon had caught it. The man was good, a professional, or "sharp," in the parlance, but Simon knew a thing or two about cards himself, and about unfair advantages.

"What is it?" Lucy nudged him, sensing something amiss.

"Nothing."

Lucy held his gaze and he gave her the subtlest of looks—eyes harder, jaw steeled—and she looked away, knowing better than to ask any questions. If he ever had a daughter, he hoped she'd turn out something like Lucy, though he'd never in his life allow her to go out dressed as she was.

Simon signaled to the server. "Jack Daniel's," he said. "Straightaway."

Lucy tugged at his sleeve. "You said only a fool drinks while gambling."

"Did I?"

Lucy nodded urgently.

"That was before we lost your annual salary."

"Maybe we should go."

"Nonsense," he said. "Not when we're just starting to have fun." He turned to the dealer. "Five thousand pounds…no, make it ten."

The dealer shot a discreet glance at Ronnie, the casino boss, who stood at the door. Ronnie was a friend. He and Simon played on the same rugby team on Saturdays during the fall. He was forty, tall, and dapper in a white dinner jacket, red carnation in his lapel. A black Clark Gable with the same gambler's mustache and rakish air. Ronnie nodded, shooting Simon a cautionary look, then left the room.

Ten stacks of chips came Simon's way.

The server arrived with his cocktail. Simon stole it off the tray and downed it. "Another," he said, returning the empty to the tray, flipping the server a fifty-pound chip for good measure. "And one for my friend, too."

Lucy took a judicious step away from Simon. She'd worked with him for three years. She knew his moods. She knew when a bomb was about to go off.

Simon noted the cheat shift in his chair, the corners of his mouth lift in anticipatory delight.

The dealer called for bets. Simon ponied up five hundred pounds, the minimum.

There were two ways this could go. He could wait and take matters into his own hands, or he could act now, expose the cheat, and let Ronnie sort things out.

Simon preferred the first choice. A confrontation in the alley followed by a full and frank exchange of views. He would take back his money and the cheat would pick himself up off the ground and get to the hospital to look after his missing teeth and broken bones.

But, of course, there was Lucy to think of.

The game progressed. For once, Simon had a decent hand. He called and raised and called and raised.

The dealer turned over the last card, known as "the river." An eight of spades.

Simon was holding two kings and an eight of hearts. The eight of spades gave him two pair. His best hand all evening.

The room went quiet, the only noise the *clack clack clack* of the roulette ball skipping across the wheel in the outer room.

The player next to Simon tossed in his cards. "I'm out."

"Raise two thousand pounds," said Simon.

The man next to him tossed in his cards. "Out."

"Call," said the cheat, picking up four blue chips and tossing them into the pot.

It was the moment of truth.

"Two pair," announced Simon. "Kings and eights."

Simon's eyes went to the cheat, who coolly deflected the gaze. To his credit, the man didn't flinch. One hand went to his kingdom of chips, fingers racing between spires, touching each in turn. It was a distraction, a motion to lure the eye. He lifted the cards off the table. Fanned them deftly. And in the downward motion he made the switch. A flick of the wrist. A rustling of the cuff. A flash of white, though this time his motion was so expert that even Simon, eyes trained on him, did not catch it.

"Full house," the cheat announced, spreading his cards on the table.

Shouts went up. Exhortations of amazement and disbelief.

"Damn," said the player to Simon's right. The other players simply shook their heads.

And as the cheat extended his hands for the pot, Simon lashed out and grabbed one wrist, closing his fingers around it in a vice. Their eyes met. Instead of protesting, of calling out Simon, the man stood, wrenching his hand free, the violent motion knocking over his chair. He stumbled backward, head turned, plotting a way out.

Simon was up, too, and a half step behind. A dozen people ringed the table. All remained glued to the spot, their expressions as immobile as their feet. The cheat shoved the man nearest him hard enough to topple him into the woman behind him. The two fell unceremoniously to the floor. He dashed through the gap between them and out the door, heading toward the staircase that descended to the main floor. Simon gave chase, leaping over the two, pausing at the top of the stairs before vaulting the balustrade and landing in the center of the blackjack table eight feet below. He jumped to the floor, cutting off the cheat's path. Seeing his escape ruined, the man slowed. He started left, then went right, then stopped altogether.

Simon crashed into him before the man could make it a step. Simon led with his shoulder, aiming for the sternum but striking the man's collarbone, feeling it crack as they hit the floor. The man grunted, his face inches from Simon's, and Simon saw that he had bad teeth and worse dental work, and his breath reeked of the brandy Alexanders he'd been drinking all night.

But if Simon expected him to give up, he was mistaken. A knee to the groin signaled his resistance, followed by a head butt glancing off the bridge of Simon's nose. Stunned, breathless, and momentarily paralyzed, Simon was unable to stop the man from climbing to his feet. In desperation, Simon threw out a hand and grasped hold of his ankle. Unfortunately, it was the wrong ankle and belonged to a horrified Asian woman. The woman screamed and her cry roused Simon. He was on his feet as the cheat navigated his way through the crowd of gamblers.

By now security had mobilized in response to the incident. Two men in maroon jackets blocked the only path out of the casino. The cheat spun and pointed at Simon. "It's him," he said in accented English whose origin Simon would only place later.

The guards hesitated long enough for the cheat to lash out with a cosh, striking the first man squarely on the jaw, dropping him, before backhanding the second, the cosh caroming off his temple. His route to the entrance clear, the cheat bolted. He grabbed at the door handle, pulling it toward him, unaware that Simon was close behind. In England, exit doors pivot outward. The door didn't budge. At that moment, Simon had him. He grabbed the collar of his jacket and yanked the man backward. Ready for a blow, he ducked as the cosh cut a path above his head, noting that a nail extended from the business end of the leather cudgel. Simon thrust an open palm upward, landing it on the man's jaw, snapping his head backward. His other hand latched on to the man's wrist. He dropped to a knee, wrenching the wrist and the arm attached to it, with all his might. There was a pop—loud as a champagne cork—as the shoulder dislocated. The man cried out. The cosh dropped into Simon's hand and he spun it so the nail was facing outward. It was a killing weapon.

"No!" a man shouted. "Simon, stop!" It was Ronnie, the casino boss, emerging from his private office across the floor, barreling toward him.

Simon didn't hear him, or didn't want to. He wanted to punish the man, to hurt him badly. Turning, he lashed out toward the cheat's undefended face.

A woman screamed. It was Lucy. He saw her from the corner of his eye.

The nail stopped a millimeter from the man's eye.

"You got lucky," said Simon, throwing the man against the wall. "Say thank you to the lady."

The cheat said nothing. His silence riled Simon all over again and he hit the man in the stomach. "I won't ask again."

The man fought for his breath, his eyes cursing Simon. His gaze shifted, focusing on something…*or someone.*

Simon began to turn as a fist slammed into his kidney. It was a professional punch, knuckles first, delivered with force and accuracy. A second punch followed to the opposite side, harder still.

Simon bent double at the waist, tears fouling his vision. That was that. He was officially out of the game. TKO.

He dropped to one knee, aware of a commotion around him—Ronnie going after the cheat and his secret accomplice—but not much else. He tried not to move, the pain exquisite and relentless. He heard Lucy shout, "Stop him! Don't let him leave! Come back, you fucking thief!"

They left Les Ambassadeurs an hour later. Simon walked out the front door, pushing it, not pulling, under his own power. His car was brought up and he held the door for Lucy, declining her offer to drive. Once behind the wheel, he made a circuit of Sloane Square and headed east toward Lower Grosvenor Place.

"You're not taking me home," said Lucy. "Not after all that."

Simon kept his eyes on the road. He was in no mood to take orders. His side ached like hell. He'd washed up and used the men's room. As expected, there was blood in his urine. It wasn't the first time. If it persisted, he'd see a doctor. His head throbbed and there was a noticeable knot above the bridge of his nose. Hoping to keep it from swelling, he'd pressed an old fifty-p coin against it for a minute, then given up. Que será, será. But it was his pride that hurt worst of all. He'd brought the operations of London's best gaming house to a halt only to allow the cheats who'd robbed him of twenty thousand pounds to escape. The loss was hypothetical. The cheats hadn't been able to pocket their ill-gotten gains. Ronnie had returned his original stake. Somehow, the thought did little to console him.

"I'm too excited to sleep," Lucy went on. "We absolutely must do something. Where shall we go?"

"It's eleven o'clock," said Simon. "You're twenty-three years old. You have work tomorrow. If I hear you set foot outside your door before six a.m. tomorrow, you can find yourself another job."

Lucy looked at him as if he'd slapped her. "What?"

"You heard me."

"You have no right," she exclaimed. "I can do whatever I choose."

"Feel free."

Simon continued across town, thankful that traffic was only bad, not miserable. All the way Lucy carped and complained, but he said nothing more until they arrived at her flat. "Here we are. Go upstairs. Get into bed and go to sleep. It's been enough of a night for both of us."

Lucy unclasped her safety belt. She motioned as if she was going to start up again, then thought better of it. "Not fair," she said, then climbed out of the car.

To her credit, she did not slam the door.

Maybe she was finally growing up.

Simon waited until she was inside and had disappeared into the vestibule before slipping the car into first and making a U-turn. His home and business lay in southwest London, a stone's throw from Wimbledon. It was a thirty-minute drive in the best of conditions. Tonight, it would be double that. But traffic didn't play into Simon's thinking. Not a whit.

He was too jacked up to go home. Nothing revved his juices more than a little physical violence, even if he had been on the losing end of it. All measure of good sense had gone out the window the moment he'd given chase to the cheat. At that instant, his world had boiled down to him versus the bad guy, good versus evil, though it was a question of his ego run riot, not anything so grandiose as maintaining the universe's order. Mess with me and you're going to pay. It was as simple as that. It was not a motto by which to live any kind of successful life. But at that moment, Simon hadn't cared about mottoes, or, to tell the truth, *anything,* except catching the thief and inflicting punishment upon him.

Two hours later, those same wild and ungoverned impulses raced through his blood. If he'd been hard on Lucy, it was because he feared she shared his affinity for mayhem. He couldn't control himself, but he could control her. He was a hypocrite. So what?

Simon pointed the car north toward Covent and the City. He rolled down the window, enjoying the warm, fetid air, the scent of the River Thames hidden somewhere inside the exhaust and grit of central London. He was navigating to that part of the map where borders lay undefined and lands undiscovered, to the dangerous and beckoning area labeled "Where Dragons Lie."

Simon Riske headed into the night.

CHAPTER 3

Eight hundred miles to the south, on the rocky shoreline of a postage stamp–size country, in a casino far larger and far more famous than Les Ambassadeurs, a team of twelve professional criminals entered the Casino de Monte-Carlo between the hours of nine and ten p.m. Nine were men and three women, at least to look at.

Every casino in the world deployed facial-recognition software. In cases of suspected cheating, customers' faces were compared against photographs contained in criminal databases, both national and international. Prior to arrival, the team members had spent hours altering their appearances. They employed the finest in makeup and disguises: hairpieces, facial prostheses, false mustaches and beards, contact lenses, dental implants. A professional makeup artist with twenty years' experience in the motion picture industry oversaw their transformation. It was not the team's first visit.

At ten p.m., after the last of the team had entered, each member moved to a predetermined workstation in the high rollers' rooms on the casino's second floor, where the game of baccarat was played. Each player began with a bankroll of ten thousand euros. They played quietly and conservatively. They did not drink. They did not seek the attention of the beautiful women drifting in and out of the rooms. They did not on any occasion speak to the dealer. And never ever did they place wild or outlandish wagers. Nothing was remarkable about the players except one thing: they won.

And they won.

And they won.

By two a.m., the last member of the team had departed the premises. Once outside, members dispersed according to plan after discreetly turning over their winnings. Their combined initial stake of one-hundred-twenty-thousand euros had grown to four million.

A little after two, a thirteenth man entered the casino. His name was Ratka. Just Ratka. This was not his real name. He had taken it from a false passport he had used many years ago. In fact, the passport was so poor in quality it had attracted the attention of a border agent in Geneva, Switzerland. At the time, Ratka had just escaped from a prison in Orbe, in the mountains east of the city. During his flight, he had killed a guard and blinded another with his own fingers. He was arrested on the spot and returned to another, more secure facility. He escaped again but took on the name inscribed in that passport. Sometimes it was necessary to remember a mistake in order to prevent repeating it.

Ratka was forty-nine years old. He stood an inch over six feet tall. His hair was black, abundant, and swept off his forehead to reveal a violent widow's peak. His face was doughy and pale, cleaved in two by a large crooked nose very much like a hawk's beak. His eyes were narrow and deep set and so brown as to be black. He wore a blazer and an open-collar shirt left open to display a gold cross nestled in his chest hair. He was not an attractive man, but he radiated a dark energy.

Like the other members of the team, Ratka climbed the stairs to the second floor and made his way to the *salle de jeux*. He had not come to gamble, or at least not to win. One of the team had claimed that a dealer had recognized him and possibly another member. The dealer was a longtime casino employee, but not a friend of Tintin, who was in their pocket. Ratka needed to see the man to decide on a course of action. So close to the end—in spitting distance of more money than he had ever imagined possible—he could not allow anything or anyone to jeopardize their hard work.

Ratka found a seat at the dealer's table. He ponied up a thousand euros and played a few hands. He won. He lost. He was as helpless to the fates as the others at the table. All the while, he kept his eye on the dealer.

Time had given him an unbreakable faith in his ability to know a man's heart. He needed only a few minutes to ascertain if a man was hard or soft, if he was loyal or traitorous, if he could be turned or if he could not.

The dealer was a black man. His name was Vincent Morehead and he was a native of Saint Croix, the Virgin Islands. All this Tintin had told them. Morehead was single with no family, either in France or at home. Not that any such sentimental considerations entered into Ratka's decision-making. If you were not a Serb, he had no feelings for you.

After a while, it came time to reshuffle the shoe. The dealer offered it to Ratka. Ratka ran the cutting card along the deck, but his eyes remained on Vincent Morehead. He slid the card into the deck. Morehead pulled the shoe back across the baize tabletop. Their eyes met. In that instant, Ratka knew that Morehead knew, not only about the two men he'd recognized, but possibly more.

Ratka played awhile longer, then left the table, tossing Morehead a twenty-euro chip for his trouble. He ignored the dealer's "Merci, monsieur."

Outside, Ratka walked the short distance to the Café de Paris and took a seat in a booth at the rear of the restaurant.

"Well?" asked a colleague.

Ratka stared at the man. "Well," he said.

Chapter 4

The club was called Libertine, if it had a name at all, and it occupied the underground premises of an abandoned abattoir and meat market in King's Cross. It was a dank, cavernous space dominated by towering brick arches that divided the club into three areas: dance floor, bar, and pitch-black netherworld that all were advised never to set foot in. The music was too loud, driven by a relentless backbeat, and meant to turn even the most docile guest into a frenzied partygoer. Spotlights raked the entire floor like klieg lights policing a concentration camp.

It was a bad place in a bad part of town frequented by bad people. Simon felt completely at home.

"What'll it be?"

"Brandy Alexander," said Simon.

"No Jack?" The bartender was tall, raven-haired, and direct in her gaze and her manner. Her name was Carmen. She was Spanish, from Madrid and proud of her Castilian lisp.

"Not tonight."

She leaned in, dark eyes on his, confident in their desired effect. "Mixing things up, eh?"

He motioned her closer. "Carmen?"

"Yes, Simon?"

"Get me my damned drink."

Carmen's face dropped. *"Cabrón,"* she said.

Leaning an elbow on the bar, Simon turned and surveyed the room. It was a busy night, even for Libertine. The dance floor was packed edge to edge, decidedly more women than men. There wasn't a suit or a tie to be seen, so he loosened his own and stuffed it in his pocket. Score one for the enemy.

Carmen returned, slamming the drink on the bar as if it were a court summons. "Brandy Alexander for *Señor* Riske."

"Salud." Simon raised the glass and drank half of it in a go. His eyes watered, and after a moment, the throbbing in his forehead went away. He thought back to the poker table and wondered how many times the cheat had slid a card from his sleeve to win a hand—the answer was "Too many"—and how he'd missed it. The more he thought about it, the more he marveled at the cheat's prowess and his preparation. Not just the practice required, but his foreknowledge of how they ran the game at Les Ambassadeurs. Then there was the matter of his drinking. He had to have quaffed four or five brandy Alexanders just while Simon was at the table.

Simon looked at the frothy concoction set on the bar in front of him. It was too sweet for his taste, but there was no doubting its potency. How the man had maintained his sleight of hand after downing several of these was beyond him.

The DJ was playing Pet Shop Boys and Soft Cell, music from his salad days in Marseille. He finished the drink and ordered another. Effective, indeed.

"'Bout time."

"Excuse me?" said Simon to the blond woman who'd placed a very pretty hand on his arm.

"That you took off that tie." She was his age, coiffed hair, with a touch of pink lipstick, plenty of mascara, and a little black dress that might even embarrass Lucy. A diamond the size of a grape adorned her ring finger, and she wore pavé bands above and below it to let you know she played her games in better circles than you. She touched the knot on his forehead and her lips puckered in a measure of sympathy. "Darling, what happened?"

"Work."

"What do you do?"

"This and that."

"You're too smart to be a bouncer, and besides, they don't wear Zegna suits."

"You noticed."

"Not just the suit."

"I'm flattered."

"My name is Tania."

"Hello, Tania."

She waited for his name and when he didn't give it, she tried harder. "Buy me a drink?"

Simon waved Carmen over. "The lady will have a—"

"A gin martini. Boodles, please. Ice-cold with three olives." Carmen responded attentively, and Tania reached out to her as she was leaving. "By the way, what is the gentleman's name?"

"Riske with an *e*."

"Sounds dangerous. Does he have a first name?"

Carmen regarded Simon with a barely concealed scowl. "When he looks like that, does it matter?"

"Know her, do you?" asked Tania.

"In passing."

Tania ran a loving hand along his arm, her beautifully manicured fingers dancing higher and higher. "I don't suppose you're going to tell me what really happened to you?"

Simon put a hand around her waist and drew her close. Her eyes were blue and sparkled nearly as much as her jewelry. But behind the makeup and the jewelry, he saw that she was tired and lonely, and he liked her the more because of it. "Maybe," he said. "If you can convince me."

Tania pressed herself against him. "Oh?" she said. "Have any ideas?"

"A few."

CHAPTER 5

Vincent Morehead changed out of his uniform and walked to the employee entrance at the rear of the casino, making his usual stop in the kitchen.

"Early morning pickup," he called across the service counter.

Gigi, a young sous-chef from Dakar, arrived carrying a white paper bag. "You have the best fed dog in town," she said. "There's filet, lamb, and foie gras, ground up together just like he likes it."

"Peter Tosh is very grateful." Peter Tosh was Vincent's two-year-old black mutt, whose natural dreadlocks made him a dead ringer for the famed reggae artist.

"I'm free Saturday," said Gigi. "In case he'd like to thank me in person."

Vincent took the bag. "I'm fairly certain he would."

"'Fairly'?" Gigi put her hands on her hips in mock anger.

Vincent smiled. "Saturday. Good night."

"Sleep well."

Vincent tucked the bag underneath an arm and left the building. The employee exit opened onto a deserted landing next to the Fairmont parking lot and looked over the famed chicane of the Monaco Grand Prix. Vincent did not own a car. He lived two kilometers up the hill, just over the French border. Normally, he enjoyed the walk. The fresh air was a relief after being cooped up inside for nine hours. He spent the time planning what to make himself for supper. (Employees were forbidden from helping themselves to leftovers.) Tonight, however, his appetite had left him. Darker thoughts held his concern.

He set off up the hill, walking faster than usual. He'd identified two of them for certain. It was their eyes that gave them away. The eyes and the way they handled the shoe. The "shoe" was the rectangular device that shuffled the eight decks of cards and from which hands of baccarat were dealt. One of the men always grabbed it from the top and dragged it toward him with no regard for the tabletop. He had enormous hands, and one—the left—had a nasty scar running across it. The other man used both of his hands on the shoe, his touch as delicate as if he were handling nitroglycerin. His hands were as tapered as a pianist's.

Vincent had seen both of the men at least three times. Except for their eyes and hands, their appearances couldn't have differed more. One day blond hair, the next brown. One day glasses, the next none. One day a mustache, the next a beard. Vincent had devoted his entire professional life to the gaming industry. It was not the first time he'd spotted cheats. But these...*these were a cut above.* They were professional criminals. They frightened him.

At this time of night, the streets were deserted, the only sound the pitter-pat of his leather-soled shoes. He continued past the botanical garden, checking over his shoulder at regular intervals. The more he pondered his position, the more frightened he grew. Naturally, he'd told his shift boss, but nothing had been done. When he'd asked to speak with the investigator sent by the company's board of directors, he'd been told to be quiet. And then, tonight, he'd spotted the two men again.

Vincent was in a quandary. Whom should he obey? His boss or the Boss? He took a breath and asked for guidance. The answer came freely. Every person—man, woman, or child—had only one Boss.

Vincent lengthened his stride, his fear leaving him. First thing in the morning he would go to the police. It was decided.

"Hey you—black boy."

Vincent froze. The voice had come from behind him. He turned. He recognized the man. He'd been at his table just prior to closing. The man with the widow's peak and the nose of a hawk.

"Yes?"

Vincent felt a rush of wind behind him. Something very hard struck his head. Darkness enveloped him.

CHAPTER 6

A fingernail etched its way down Simon's bare chest.

He woke.

Tania lay beside him, propped up on an elbow, studying the lattice-work of scars crisscrossing his torso. Another nocturnal companion had once commented that it looked as though he'd been worked on with a saw, a shiv, and a soldering iron.

"Work, too?" she asked.

"Pleasure."

"Liar." She stopped at a dark circular lesion on his shoulder. She sat up, the mood broken. "This is a bullet wound."

"Is it?"

"And so is this." The second was on his hip, a gulp away from a more important area.

"It can't be," said Simon.

"My first husband was a soldier. He had a few just like these. Is that where you got them? Military?"

"God, no."

The inquisitive hand continued its tour, tracing a berm of scar tissue below his ribs that had bleached bone white over the years. "My second husband was a surgeon. These wounds were not tended to by a professional."

"You can say that again."

The hand slipped under the covers and probed a more sensitive area.

Simon's eyes widened. "I'm afraid to ask what your third husband did."

23

"I don't have a third husband," said Tania, her fingers proving very skilled indeed. "Yet."

Simon gasped.

"And so?" she demanded archly. "Answer my questions."

"Never."

Tania straddled him, pinning his wrists to the bed. She was surprisingly strong for a lithe, naked woman half his size. "This is your last chance. Confess."

Simon struggled, or pretended to. He enjoyed these games. "You'll have to do worse things than that if you expect me to talk."

She kissed his neck, her breasts grazing his chest. "I don't expect you to talk, Mr. Riske."

"You don't?"

"No," she replied, with relish. "I don't."

"Then what do you expect me to do?"

"Why Mr. Riske, I expect you to—"

Simon's phone buzzed. Tania looked at it.

"To what?" asked Simon, willing the phone to its own special circle of hell.

"To—"

The phone buzzed a second time and she snatched it from the nightstand. "D'Art," she said, reading the name off the screen.

The phone buzzed again. Simon told her to answer it. Tania sat up, tucking her hair behind her ear and assuming her best secretarial posture. "Good morning, Simon Riske's office. Mr. Riske is currently occupied with an important client. May I take a message?"

"Do pardon me, ma'am," came a ruffled baritone voice. "I'm sorry to disturb you...your...um, oh, good Christ, is he there?"

Simon, who'd heard every word, gently took the phone. "Tell me this is important, D'Art." He threw off the sheets and walked to the window. Peeling back the curtain, he saw that it was a sunny morning with a few billowy white clouds low in the sky. "I'm listening."

"Heard you lost twenty thousand pounds last night."

"He was cheating. And where'd you hear that?"

"Toby Stonewood."

"Lord Toby Stonewood?" Lord Toby Stonewood, Duke of Suffolk, was one of the richest men in England and the owner of Les Ambassadeurs.

"One and the same. He requests a moment of your time."

"Regarding?"

"A private matter which he would like to discuss with you face-to-face."

Simon looked toward the bed, where Tania lay all too invitingly. She had put on her oversized reading glasses and was politely checking her own phone. Simon liked the professorial look. "How's this afternoon? Say, two?"

"How's this morning? Say, *now?*"

Simon's dreams of playing school with Tania were fading fast. "Now?"

"Unless you'd like to tell Lord Toby to come back later yourself."

Simon studied the curve of Tania's back, the nape of her neck. The problem with having sex with an absolute stranger was that it was never very good the first time. The second time, however, was always vastly improved.

"You have an hour," said D'Art.

Simon turned back toward the window and spoke under his breath. "Give me an idea how serious this is. One to ten."

"Eleven," said D'Artagnan Moore.

"I knew you were going to say that."

CHAPTER 7

Vincent Morehead came to.

He lay on a cold floor. It was bright and as his eyes focused he saw a great multicolored glass chandelier above him. He blinked furiously, and for a moment he thought he was back in the casino, or in the lobby of a fancy hotel. He didn't know which. No hotel in the city had anything so ornate.

Someone was standing near him. A shoe was inches from his face. He gazed up and recognized the man who'd sat at his table before closing. The man who'd called him "black boy." Another man stood beside him. Vincent spun his head and saw that he was encircled. He was too groggy to count how many there were. *Eight . . . ten . . . twelve?*

Vincent pulled himself to his feet, only to stumble into the arms of one of the men. The man shoved him and Vincent stepped back into the center of the circle.

"Why . . ." he began, and though it was difficult to form words, he knew why and was afraid.

It was then he saw that the men all held lengths of pipe, some longer, some shorter. Lead pipes. The big, hawk-faced man tapped his pipe on the floor. The others followed suit.

"*Tigars,*" they began to chant. *Tee-gars.*

The room echoed with the word and the percussive taunts.

"*Tigars.*"

The first blow struck Vincent in the calf and knocked his leg out from under him. He fell to the ground. A man dashed at him, swinging the pipe at his head. Vincent raised a hand to protect himself. The pipe shattered his forearm. Before he could scream, another blow struck his ribs, then his shoulder. He collapsed on the floor, no longer aware of anything except the bright light above him and the agony that held him in its relentless grip.

"Tigars."

Blows rained down. He writhed and screamed and prayed to be saved. Not to live, but to die and be spared such pain.

"And so," came a commanding voice, echoing across the room. "What have you done to our new friend?"

The chanting stopped. The blows ceased. The circle parted.

A man Vincent had not seen earlier but knew from sight stepped closer. He crouched and took Vincent's jaw in his hand, lifting his head so they could look at each other face-to-face.

"I hear you are an observant one. Too observant, perhaps. You guessed our game. Bully for you."

"Won't...talk...swear," Vincent managed. He was crying. He couldn't help it.

"You can be sure of that," the man replied, to a chorus of laughter. "You are a strong one, aren't you? Won't do you any good. One man alone cannot prevail against a dedicated force. I'd ask you to stand, but that would be rude of me, given your circumstance. Let's settle for sitting up."

Vincent only half understood the words. The world was fading in and out, pain the only constant. Arms grasped his torso and shifted him to a sitting position, and when he howled in complaint they held him there. "No," he said. "I won't...tell...I..." His thoughts slipped away. He remembered being on a beach at home, feeling the warm sand sift through his fingers. His eyes rose to the colorful glass chandelier. Murano glass, he thought hazily. He'd visited the factory once.

"...problem with you boys," the man was saying to the others, "is that you don't hit hard enough. In my day, we had plenty of practice. We learned how to cripple a man, how to blind him. Mostly, we just knocked their brains out. To do real damage, like we used to do to the tough guys

27

who wouldn't talk, you need leverage and torque. You have to hold the pipe like so." He shrugged. "Well, maybe, it's better if I just show you."

Ratka threw him a pipe, and the older man twirled it deftly before taking firm hold of one end.

Leverage and torque, thought the older man as he drew back his arm and took aim. Leading with his hip and then his shoulder, he brought the pipe around in a wide, whiplike motion and with all his might struck it against Vincent Morehead's temple.

"And that, my friends," he said, standing over the lifeless body, "is how you do it."

CHAPTER 8

Simon arrived at the headquarters of Lloyd's of London fifty-nine minutes later.

"What took you so long?" With a grunt, D'Artagnan Moore rose from a couch running along the wall of his office.

"I hope we didn't entice you to break any laws," said a handsome, ruddy-faced man with thinning gray hair, also standing.

"No more than usual," said Simon, with a polite smile.

Moore crossed the room. He was a bear of a man, six and a half feet tall, three hundred pounds, with a shaggy black beard tickling the top of his bow tie, the rest of him adorned in the finest Highland tweed, despite the fact that the weather people had forecast a day of record heat.

"Had a good night, did you?" asked Moore, sotto voce, as he shook Simon's hand. "She certainly sounded lovely."

"I made it here, didn't I?"

"And you'll be glad you did."

D'Artagnan Moore was a registered insurance broker, one of the most respected in the trade. His clients included shipping companies, art museums, airlines, vineyards, and other entities, public and private, offering products, services, and commodities that defied ordinary classification. It was barely ten, but he held a tumbler of scotch in one of his hands.

"Thought you waited till the sun was above the yardarm," said Simon.

"My client is suffering a bout of nerves. Have to keep him company. Shall we?" D'Artagnan Moore led Simon across the office. "Simon Riske, meet Lord Toby Marmaduke Alexander Stonewood, Duke of Suffolk."

"It's a pleasure, Your Grace," said Simon.

Toby Stonewood's handshake was dry and firm. "Not sure if I should be afraid."

"I'm sorry if things got out of hand last night," said Simon.

"You did what anyone would have…and with reason."

"Only sorry we didn't manage to snare him."

The Duke of Suffolk was tall and distinguished, the picture of the ruling classes, dressed in a double-breasted navy blazer with shiny gold buttons, white shirt, and a rep tie reserved for old Etonians, alumni of the poshest and most revered of British preparatory schools. A latter-day Wellington without the cockade hat, though if the tabloids were to be believed, he shared a similar reputation with the ladies.

"No luck tracking him down?" asked Simon.

"A clean escape, I'm afraid. And call me Toby. None of this 'Your Grace' nonsense. Can't stand it."

Simon considered this, offering an agreeable smile. He'd worked with the wealthy and the more than wealthy for the past fifteen years. Smile aside, he'd learned better than to think of himself as an equal. Distance was to be recognized and respected. "Toby, then."

Pleased, Stonewood placed his empty glass on the side table. "How did you spot him?"

Simon dragged over an armchair from D'Art's desk and set it so that it faced the couch. Simon's past was a closely guarded secret. Something about his having been a member of a criminal organization tended to frighten away prospective clients. "Let's just say I have some experience with his type."

"As well as a sharp eye. You were a policeman, then?"

"Not exactly." He let the words linger and the suggestion of the truth with them.

"We have cameras to keep an eye on all of our tables," said Toby Stonewood. "Especially on players who win a bit too much and a bit too often. I think our security chief calls it 'defying statistical averages.' We didn't catch it."

"Sometimes a human eye can see things a camera can't."

"Did you know he was cheating the entire time?"

"I knew I was losing too much. That put me in a bad mood."

"Whatever it was," said Lord Toby, "your eye or your intuition, I need it."

The nobleman scooted to the edge of the sofa and fixed Simon with an earnest gaze. He explained that Les Ambassadeurs was not the only gaming establishment he owned. He was also the principal shareholder of the Société des Bains de Mer, the corporate entity that owned the Casino de Monte-Carlo, perhaps the most famous casino in the world, located in the principality of Monaco.

"I only wish our losses were limited to twenty thousand pounds," Lord Toby went on. "Unfortunately, they're far worse. I must ask that you keep what I'm about to tell you in this room."

"You have my word," said Simon.

"And he knows how to keep it," said D'Art. "Lloyd's of London's trust in Simon is unmatched."

Lord Toby Stonewood stared at Simon long and hard, his flint-blue eyes unblinking. "Over the past nine months," he began, "the casino has suffered losses on an unimaginable scale, nearly all of it from our baccarat tables. As you know, baccarat is almost entirely a game of chance. Over time, it's weighted with a two percent advantage to the house. In theory, it is impossible for us to lose over any extended period…a day, a week, a month. Now, of course on occasion a high roller will put together a streak and take home ten, twenty million. But those are one-offs. Usually, he'll come back and lose it. Still, *somehow* we've managed to lose nearly two hundred million dollars."

"Cheating," said D'Art.

Toby Stonewood nodded. "There's no other answer."

"What did your security staff say?" asked Simon.

"Couldn't find it. Believe me, we've tried. I spent days with them in their operations center studying live feeds, tracking players we suspected. We have it all: facial-recognition technology, cameras to spot card switching, radio tracker in our chips. Even so, we came up empty-handed. It just appeared that too many people were winning. Nothing illegal in that. We brought in an expert in this kind of thing. Rooting out cheats."

"And?"

Toby shifted in his seat, his complexion gone gray. "Yes, well," he said uneasily. "He disappeared the next day. Turned up a week ago tangled in a fishing net off the coast of Villefranche."

"Are you still losing?"

"On a daily basis. If this continues, the casino will be bankrupt in a month."

"Close down the tables," said Simon.

"Not an option," said Toby. "We might as well shut down the entire place."

"How can I help?"

"Come down. Take a look around. That's all I ask."

"But I don't know a thing about cheating on this scale."

"You spotted the man at your table last night."

"One man. And I missed his partner. You have a larger problem."

"And we're taking active measures to stop it. You offer a kind of different skill."

D'Art leaned forward, putting a hand on Simon's knee. "Give Toby a listen. The timing couldn't be better. Monaco's hosting the International Boat Show next week. The town will be overflowing with tourists, most of them wealthy and ready to drop a few thousand at the casino."

"I wouldn't know where to begin," said Simon.

"There's to be a Concours d'Élégance the last two days of the show…for cars, of course. Plenty of Italian contraptions like the ones you fix up. Cover doesn't get any better."

"D'Art's right," said Toby. "You'd fit right in. Bring one of your cars. There's a time trial, as well. Bit of fun. I'll pay the entry fee. We'll put you up in a suite at the Hôtel de Paris. All expenses on the house."

"Damned good grub, if I do say," boomed D'Art.

"I'm fine with a ham and cheese," said Simon, shooting his friend a look.

"Figures," said D'Art, disparagingly. "Along with your Tennessee sour mash. Americans."

"I don't mind a croque monsieur, myself," said Toby, keeping the peace. "Allow me to sweeten the pot. We'll bankroll you with one hundred thousand dollars to play the tables. Keep whatever you make."

"That's not necessary," said Simon.

"And a success fee," added Toby. "How does one million dollars sound?"

"Success defined as?" asked Simon.

"Hard proof of cheating…and whoever's behind it." Toby Stonewood sat back on the couch, arms crossed, worry etched into his face. "If you can track down the money, so much the better. I'll give you five percent of anything you find. Mr. Riske, this has got to stop."

Simon looked from one man to the other. He wondered how much Lord Toby Stonewood had offered the expert who'd washed up in a fishing net. Success fees were nice, but you had to be alive to collect them. A million dollars was no good to a dead man.

"Well?" said D'Art.

Simon had already made his decision. "Deal," he said.

He was a gambling man. He never turned down a bet on himself.

Chapter 9

The drive to the shop passed in a blur. Window open, music blaring, Simon tapped his hand on the wheel in time to the beat. He was listening to the Clash and singing along to "The Magnificent Seven."

He crossed Blackfriars Bridge, skirting Waterloo Station and Battersea Park before heading into the more peaceful residential confines of South-fields. Nothing lifted his spirits like a new assignment, especially when it dropped into his lap out of the blue. It wasn't the paycheck at the end of it (though he was never one to turn down a chance at earning a hefty sum) so much as the opportunity to immerse himself in an unfamiliar, often foreign field. And then to test his newfound prowess under adverse, even perilous, conditions.

Monaco. Larceny on an organized scale. A time trial thrown in for good measure. And a million-dollar success fee at the end of it. What wasn't to like?

His good mood vanished a few seconds after he turned down the alley to his shop and found a car blocking his parking spot. The overflow lot sat adjacent to the alley. He activated the gate opener and parked between two automobiles protected by body tarps.

The automobiles were Ferraris, each worth in excess of five hundred thousand pounds. The expensive ones he housed inside the shop 24/7. His own car was a VW Golf R, pearl-gray with Recaro seats and Pirelli low-profile tires. It was a high-performance gunner masquerading as an everyday Joe. Just as he liked it.

Simon let himself out of the gate. A ten-foot fence topped with razor wire surrounded the lot. The gate was secured and, according to the salesman, capable of withstanding a frontal assault by an armored tank. *God forbid,* thought Simon, *a tank in southwest London.* He lived a stone's throw from Wimbledon. The stewards of the All England Lawn Tennis and Croquet Club would surely be appalled at the thought.

A beat-up sign above the work entrance read EUROPEAN AUTOMOTIVE REPAIR AND RESTORATION.

His pride and joy.

The car blocking his spot was a black Daytona Spider, '70 or '71, a sleek two-door with Borrani spoked wheels, a long sloping hood, and concealed headlights. It had cost twenty thousand dollars the year it was made—expensive, but not exorbitant. Today it would fetch three million. Expensive, but not exorbitant.

But not this one. At least not today.

Simon bent to examine the front fender hanging askew, noting that the paint was scratched and that a turning lamp was missing. He rounded the car and winced. The right rear quadrant of the car was crunched like an accordion and the rear tire was bent inward.

"Hey!" An angry voice pierced the midmorning calm. "Don't touch that car!"

"Get away from there!" came a second voice. "Scram!"

Simon looked over his shoulder as two young men rounded the corner of his shop, running in his direction. One was slim, short, with black curly hair and an olive complexion. The other was tall, buff, and blond, his cheeks flushed red. Both were dressed in torn jeans and T-shirts that looked as though they'd never been washed.

"Did you tell me to scram?"

"That's our car," said the bigger one.

"My car," the shorter one added.

"Yours?" said Simon, approaching the owner. "Doesn't look like you know how to drive it. What did you hit? A parked car? A building?"

"He drove over a curb and hit a stanchion, then—"

"Shut up, Eric." The shorter man stuck his hands in his pocket and bowed his head sheepishly. "Are you him? The guy that owns this shop? Risky?"

"Riske," said Simon. "The *e* is silent."

"Then you will fix my car. I need it no later than tomorrow at one."

The taller, blond man took up position behind his friend. "One o'clock."

Simon crossed his arms. "Is that right?"

"I realize it's a rush job. I am willing to pay accordingly."

Simon kept his comments to himself. Rude, demanding, and narcissistic weren't unknown character traits of individuals who owned this type of automobile. "I'm booked," he said.

"What do you mean?"

"Full up. All slots taken. Besides, we don't do minor body work. I can give you the name of a shop in Islip that—"

"No," interjected the shorter man.

"—should have it done in about three weeks," Simon finished.

"Three weeks?" The blond one, Eric, put a hand to his forehead and bent double as if someone had kicked him in the gut. "You're a dead man," he muttered to his friend.

The owner of the car continued, unfazed. "It must be you. No one else."

Simon looked at the man more closely, then examined the car. A piece of the puzzle fell into place. "Have we met?"

"You restored both of my father's automobiles. He says you are the only person allowed to touch his cars."

"Besides you?"

The short man grimaced. "We will come to that later. Right now, let us concentrate on the matter at hand. You will fix the car, Mr. Riske. No one else."

"Your father is?"

"Rafael Harriri. I'm Martin, his oldest son."

Simon was as principled as the next man, but there was something about the name of a former client and a billionaire, not necessarily in that order, that shaped his thinking. "Come with me." He unlocked the door to the shop floor, motioning for them to go ahead. "Hurry up. And don't touch a thing."

The floor was buzzing with activity. A dozen Italian sports cars in various states of disarray were spaced across the floor. There were ten Ferraris and two Lamborghinis ("Lambos" in the trade), though it was difficult to tell which was which, or if some were even cars at all. Doors were missing, interiors ripped out, hoods standing at attention, the engines either missing entirely or half dismantled. Three cars had been stripped of paint and their dull metal husks resembled the hulls of long-abandoned ships.

Simon surveyed the lot, taking note of where each car stood in its long and tortured path back to life. The cost to restore them ran anywhere from a hundred thousand to a million. It was worth it. Once he'd finished his work, the combined value of the vehicles under his roof would top fifty million dollars. Not bad for some flimsy metal, a little rubber, a few strips of decent leather, and an internal combustion engine.

Simon dropped off Martin Harriri and his friend in the waiting room, then doubled back to his office. Lucy Brown stood, arms crossed, blocking the door. "I didn't go out."

"Wise decision."

"You're wearing the same clothes."

"Am I?"

"You haven't been home." Anger curdled to disgust as she thought through the accusation.

Simon used the opportunity to slide past her and enter his office. How was it that women always knew when you'd been fooling around?

Lucy followed closely. "So, where were you?" she demanded.

"Get the two guys in the waiting room some tea," he said. "Tell them we're looking at the car and that I'll be back to speak with them in a while."

"You didn't answer my question."

"Now, if you please, Ms. Brown." He rounded his desk and sorted through the mail—bills, as usual—making a point not to look up. Finally, she took the hint and, with a huff, departed.

"And don't give them your phone number!" he added, a second too late.

Simon picked up the phone and called Harry Mason, his chief mechanic and floor boss. "Meet me out back. Need you to look at something."

"I'm busy."

Simon rubbed the back of his neck. Harry Mason was pushing seventy, a short, irascible Irishman with a perpetual scowl. He patrolled the floor looking as though someone had stolen his last bottle of scotch. He cared about two things in life: cars and soccer, though not in that order. Simon knew that Harry was seated at his desk with his face buried in the sports page of *The Sun,* reading about his beloved football club, Arsenal.

"How's the new manager doing?" Simon asked.

"Not good enough," responded Mason with fire, taking the bait. "He'd better light a fire under their asses if he wants a top-four finish."

"Put down the paper and meet me out back. Now."

After he filled his mug with coffee, he left the office and found Mason giving the black Daytona a once-over.

"Who the hell managed to do this? Those two knuckleheads in the lounge?"

"You mean our newest clients."

"We don't do repair work."

Simon knelt to examine the front fender, waggling it like a loose tooth. Taking hold of it with both hands, he gave a terrific yank and the fender came free altogether. Standing, he handed it to Mason. "Today we do." He ran a hand along the crumpled chassis. "How long to fix this?"

Harry Mason crossed his arms over his belly. "Bang out the metal, sand it down, prime it, then put it through the paint shop."

"I didn't ask what needs to be done."

"Week."

Simon took hold of the passenger wing mirror, which was bent at a right angle, snapped it off, and tossed it onto the front seat. "Think Adriano has any of these in stock?"

"Why would he?"

"We'll need to fix that ourselves."

Harry Mason grimaced.

Simon squatted to study the front wheel, then lay down on his back and slid under the car. "Harry, take a look at this."

"For Chrissakes," said Mason. "Must I?" There was much moaning and griping until Mason slid beneath the automobile beside him.

"New struts?" asked Simon, the light from his phone illuminating two fractured metal rods attaching the wheel to the suspension.

"Didn't that numbskull brake at all before taking it over the curb?"

"I'm betting our client had had a few too many."

"I thought their kind didn't imbibe."

"He's Lebanese."

"His problem, isn't it?"

"Do we have any replacements?"

"We do."

Simon slid out from under the car and got to his feet. When Harry Mason was slow to free himself, Simon lent him a hand and hoisted him to his feet.

"You've got something on your jacket," said Mason.

Simon studied the stain. Oil. A great big gob of it. The jacket was a write-off. He swore under his breath. "Add it to the bill. He can afford it." He removed the jacket, crumpled it into a ball, and dumped it in the trash. "So?"

"So what?" asked Mason.

"How long for all of it?"

"A month. We're full up as is. I can put someone on it next week."

"I need it tomorrow."

"Are you daft? New paint alone takes two days to dry."

"I'll drive slowly."

"Drive? Where? This isn't your car."

"I'll be entering it in the Concours d'Élégance in Monaco next Saturday. Steam clean the engine, detail the chassis top to bottom, and renew the leather."

"The entire shop will have to work on it all night long."

"I'll be right there with them. I'm going upstairs to shower. Our new clients are in the reception area. Tell them our specialists are examining the car top to bottom and that I'll be along in thirty minutes."

Simon's flat occupied the second floor of the building. Entry was gained through a pair of reinforced steel doors, one off the shop floor, the other at the top of the stairs. His real job demanded that he protect himself as well as his cars, even if he wasn't worth anything close to the least expensive of them.

In the daytime, he worked as an investigator, problem solver, and all-around busybody. His clients included corporations, wealthy individuals, and the occasional law enforcement or intelligence agency. He was the man you went to when you couldn't go to anybody else. If that sounded ominous, it shouldn't have. Ninety percent of his cases involved nothing more perilous than surfing the Internet, slipping some banknotes into the hand of the right person for a bit of information, or following the odd Joe here or there. The steel doors were for the other ten percent.

One day he'd think of a proper title. Something with just the right amount of intrigue. For the time being, his business cards gave his name, email, and phone number. His reputation told prospective clients everything they needed to know.

Simon locked the door behind him and crossed the living area to his bedroom, where he took off his clothes and threw them in the hamper. He busied himself putting shoe trees in his loafers and returning them to their proper position. A full-length mirror hung above his fleet of shoes. He saw a lean, muscled man, broad shoulders, arms too big for his size, torso decorated by the scars Tania had found so interesting. Knife, dagger, shiv, blowtorch (actually a jerry-rigged can of deodorant and a cheap lighter…and yes, that one hurt the most). The circular nubs of ruined skin were bullet wounds and courtesy of the good guys, namely, the Marseille police. There was a reason he'd been in that prison.

The tattoo running the length of his forearm explained it all. It showed a ship's anchor around which a skeleton was draped, some wiggly blue lines that were supposed to be waves, and the words *"La Brise de Mer."* It was the name of the notorious criminal organization founded in Corsica and active across the southern coast of France, the Bouches-du-Rhône and the Côte d'Azur. He came by the tattoo honestly, if the word applied. From ages sixteen to nineteen, he'd roamed the streets of Marseille boosting cars, robbing jewelry stores, and hijacking armored trucks. His actions earned him the tattoo, the bullet wounds, and a stretch in Les Baumettes, a prison celebrated for its lawlessness and barbarity.

The thought of prison and his time there sent an unwelcome shiver down Simon's spine.

He jumped up and grabbed the pull-up bar bolted to the ceiling. He knocked out twenty reps, then hung for a good ten seconds, feeling his muscles stretch and cry out for relief, then gave himself five more.

Time for a shower.

"I have good news and bad news," Simon explained after he'd ushered Martin Harriri and his friend Eric into his office and shown them a place to sit. "The good news is that since I know your father and, if I recall, advised on the purchase of the car, I've decided to fix it."

"And the bad news?"

"I'll need at least a week, maybe two."

"I'm dead," groaned Martin, burying his face in his hands. He sat in a director's chair that had belonged to Steve McQueen during the making of *Le Mans*. Eric sat behind Martin on the sliver of free space available on the couch, a vintage jukebox brushing one shoulder, a stack of olive legal files a meter high the other. The rest of the office was equally cluttered. It was a graveyard of memorabilia, most of it related to Simon's work. The general disorderliness stood in stark contrast to his flat. There was something there for an analyst to look at, but Simon didn't go in for that kind of thing.

"When I was younger," Simon said, "I drove a few cars I wasn't supposed to. You'll survive."

"Were they a Ferrari Daytona?"

"It wasn't the make so much as who they belonged to. Believe me when I say the owners weren't happy with me."

"What happened?"

Simon ignored the question. "Right now, let's worry about you. Give me your father's phone number."

"You can't call him."

"Feel free, then. Tell him the bill will be fifty thousand pounds. I'll need a down payment…say, twenty thousand. You're good for the rest of it."

Martin considered this, then slid his phone out of his jeans. "What are you going to say?"

"Just give me the number."

Simon dialed as Martin read out the digits. Mr. Rafael Harriri, billionaire trading magnate, favorite son of Beirut, and collector of fine European automobiles, answered immediately.

"Rafael? Simon Riske…Yes, it is a surprise…All good with you?" Pleasantries were exchanged with Simon explaining that no, he was not married, no children were on the way, legitimate or not, and that his business was doing nicely indeed. "Listen, Rafael," Simon said when decorum permitted. "I've got a piece of rough news."

Martin sank lower in the chair. An unpleasant keening noise emanated from him as if he were suffering from a painful stomach ailment.

"I'm afraid I'm stealing your Daytona," Simon went on. "Yes, that's right. I'm stealing it."

Martin dropped a hand from his eye. The moaning abated.

"By the purest coincidence, I ran into your son this morning. He pulled up at a light next to me. I didn't recognize him, but I knew the car in an instant." Simon met Martin's gaze. "It's never looked better. Absolutely showroom condition. I realized then and there that I needed to take it with me to Monaco next weekend for the Concours. I got your boy's attention—fine-looking young man, I might add—and, well…he's sitting across the desk from me in my office as we speak. I know it's asking a lot and on short notice, but what do you think? May I take it to Monte? Of course, we'll put it on a truck there and back…No, no, I'll pay the fees. I insist…Good. It's settled, then."

Simon talked for another ten minutes before ending the call.

Martin stared at him, dumbstruck. "Why?"

"Everyone needs a guardian angel once in a while."

"Thank you, Mr. Risky."

Simon winced. "The *e* is silent."

"If there's ever anything I can do…"

Simon stood. "You can start by paying up. Did we settle on twenty thousand pounds?"

Martin took the request in stride. "Do you accept cash?"

CHAPTER 10

Of course it was Karl Marshal who saw her first.

It was during rugby practice two days earlier. Conditioning was finished and the team was practicing ball skills prior to a scrimmage. Coach MacAndrews had taken Robby to one side to tutor him on how to kick a drop goal, a skill that Robby had yet to master.

"Drop. Skip. Kick," said Coach MacAndrews.

Robby did his best to follow the instructions. He held the big ball in his hands, dropped it onto the ground, and kicked it. Each time, the ball dribbled a few meters down the field and he would rush to retrieve it.

"Dammit, man," said the coach, squaring Robby's shoulders toward the goalposts and walking him through the motions yet again. "Do as I say. Drop. Skip. Kick."

Robby made another vain attempt. The ball skidded off the side of his shoe and landed with a splat in the mud. The others laughed but Robby paid them no heed. Years ago, when he was little, that kind of teasing would have left him bawling. He'd been very good at crying. At some point, however, he'd stopped being affected by loud voices and heated remonstrations. Now he viewed the situation from a safe and objective distance. He was a twelve-year-old boy with limited athletic skills who could not kick a rugby ball. With practice, he would learn. The thing was to keep trying. A voice he was sure belonged to his father egged him on. One day, the voice said, he'd kick the farthest field goal that Scottish bastard MacAndrews had ever seen.

"Marshal!" called the coach. "Show the little prince how to do it."

But for once Karl Marshal was not paying attention. He was standing well away from the rest of the boys, looking across the field toward the *wanderweg,* or footpath, that started in the village of Zuoz and led up the hillside past the athletic field, all the way to the peak of Piz Griatschouls, the mountain the boys called the Puke-erberg when they had to run up it each and every week at the end of Saturday morning practice.

No one was thinking about running up the Puke-erberg right then.

To a man, they were looking at the same thing that had captivated Karl.

That "thing" was a woman, who at that moment was drawing alongside the field and was no more than twenty meters away. Or, Robby thought, about the same distance as a decent punt.

It was not uncommon for people to walk past the field during practice. You could set your watch by Frau Baumgartner, the headmaster's wife, who passed by when the bell tolled three o'clock on her daily trek to the monastery (to combat her thrombosis) and returned when the bell tolled four. In fact, so many people trafficked the *wanderweg* at all times of day that no one paid them any attention.

Until her.

The woman was tall and blond with a figure to satisfy every teenage boy's desires. She was wearing tight blue jeans and an open-necked shirt covered by a quilted down vest. The shirt was of interest because it fluttered in the late afternoon breeze and afforded them a telling view of her cleavage. Finally, the woman was beautiful. There was no other way to put it. She was not merely sexy or pretty. She was jaw-droppingly, gut-wrenchingly, drop-dead gorgeous.

Or, as Karl Marshal more succinctly put it later, "She was heinous."

No one spoke to her that first day. The entire team, including Robby, froze in their tracks and stared. She didn't say anything either. In fact, it seemed that she didn't even notice they were there. She glanced over their heads at the school buildings that stood on the hillside behind them but didn't register their communal and, to be honest, rude stare. Even Coach MacAndrews was struck dumb. He forgot to yell at Karl for failing to pay attention, though a few seconds later (upon coming to his senses), he did grab him by the ear and order him to knock out twenty burpees.

She came each day thereafter, always during practice, always wearing the quilted vest, her shirt buttoned just as the boys liked it. If they were scrimmaging, she would stop to watch and, by her rapt attention, appeared to know something about the sport.

It was Stavros Livanos who first spoke to her. And it was because of him that they learned she was not Swiss at all, or French, as many of them guessed, but German.

"Hey!" he'd shouted. "Wanna play?"

And when she didn't respond, he repeated the question in German.

"Hey du, möchst du mit uns spielen?"

Stavros was Greek, but he'd grown up in St. Moritz and spoke with an Engadiner's *bergschnur.*

"Nein, danke," she answered. *"Sie Buben sind viel zu stark und zu schnell für mich."*

No, thank you. You boys are much too strong and fast for me.

She spoke perfect high German. Moreover, Robby recognized the accent as being from Hesse, the region in central Germany where his own family came from.

It was at that moment that he fell hopelessly in love with her.

He was not alone. Since that first sighting, the mysterious woman was the subject of conversations from morning till night. Had she moved to the village? To whom did she belong? There was no chance someone so goddess-like could be unattached. Was she perhaps the rakish art teacher Signor Marelli's mistress? Or a famous actress hiding out from the paparazzi? Or had a billionaire established residence nearby, and she was his companion? There was no shortage of guesses.

In the boys' locker room, a challenge was issued. Who among them was brave enough to ask her?

Karl Marshal spoke up immediately, vowing to ask that very afternoon. Stavros Livanos promised to beat him to the punch. In seconds, every boy was shouting that it would be him. There had never been a room full of braver men. But ninety minutes later, when her blond head appeared behind the soccer goal and she came into full view wearing that vest and that shirt, with the wind behaving as instructed, and she walked alongside the field, no one said a word. Not Karl. Not Stavros. Not anyone.

Instead, it was Robby who, emboldened by their Teutonic kinship, asked.

"Guten Tag," he said in a firm voice. *"Entschuldigung. Wie heissen sie?"*

Good afternoon. Excuse me. What is your name?

The woman stopped and, seeing that the scrimmage had come to a halt and that the entire team was hanging on her response, grinned. It was a warmhearted, approachable grin, and every boy on the field smiled in return. Coach MacAndrews, too.

"Mein Name ist Elisabeth," she replied.

My name is Elisabeth.

And then she did what she did that caused Robby's heart to burst from his chest and his feet to become glued to the ground.

"Wie heisst du?" she asked.

What's your name?

"Robert," he replied, with the bearing and diction he'd been taught his entire life.

"Allo, Robert," she said. *"Es hat mich sehr gefreut ihnen kennenzulernen. Bis morgen dann. Tschuss."*

Hello, Robert. I'm very pleased to meet you. Until tomorrow, then. Bye-bye.

Robby nodded, unable to come up with anything resembling an answer. It was no wonder he'd forgotten a thought he'd had only ten minutes before, when he'd gazed at the monastery and realized that he had not seen the two strange men since Elisabeth first arrived.

Chapter 11

Paris was behind him, as was the wait at the Channel tunnel, the industrial plain of the north, the furious traffic surrounding the French capital. He was in open country now, old France, the France of the Three Musketeers and Jean Valjean and Joan of Arc. It was the France of a thousand villages and hamlets, of rolling hills captained by church spires, of wheat fields recently harvested and medieval forests never touched, of towering limestone cliffs and lazy meandering rivers. He drove with the windows down, the wind warm and thick with the invigorating scent of tilled earth.

It was an eight-hundred-mile trip better broken up into two days with an overnight stop in Beaune or Dijon. He wasn't averse to a nice meal and a glass of decent red, and both cities offered numerous appealing opportunities. But Toby Stonewood had been adamant about getting started as quickly as possible and Simon had required a full day to ready himself for the job.

The past twenty-four hours had given him a crash course in the dark arts of expert cheating, and that, along with D'Art's plea that Simon not let Lloyd's of London down, had left him consumed with seeing the job through to a successful end. And so it would be a one-day drive: the kind where your butt becomes glued to the seat and everything beyond your window melts into a blur.

Everything except the silver Audi fastback that had been following him at a safe distance for the past two hours.

*   *   *

Simon's preparations had begun just after one o'clock in the afternoon the day before, when he presented himself at the front door of a modest country estate in Surrey, the kind of place that Jane Austen aspired to, an hour south of London. He was expected, and the large man who answered the door frisked him a little less roughly than he might have before leading him upstairs into a dimly lit, leathery office.

"Well, well. If it isn't Mr. Posh himself. Fifty quid says you left one of your fancy cars at home."

Simon squinted to see through a pall of cigar smoke thick as London fog. "Hello, Eddie. Considered opening a window?"

"I pay top dollar for my Cubanos. I like to enjoy them. Now sit down, stop complaining, and tell me why you're slumming."

His name was Edward Margrave, but he was known as Eightball Eddie, and he owned the concession to sell slot machines to pubs across the United Kingdom. Eightball Eddie was seventy, give or take, a sharply dressed bantamweight with graying hair swept off his forehead, a hearty laugh, and the worst false teeth in London. But it wasn't the teeth you noticed. It was his eyeglasses: oversized black frames with convex lenses thick as a phone book that magnified his eyes to what appeared to be twice their size. He'd explained his condition to Simon once a few years ago, but the crux of it was that even with the glasses, he viewed the world through what amounted to a soda straw.

"Thanks for seeing me," said Simon. "I know you're busy."

"Oh yes," said Eddie. "Queuing at the door, they are. But I do appreciate your manners. You were always polite to a fault. I never forgot that. Others weren't."

Before Simon became an investigator, he'd worked as a private banker at a major international bank in the City. Eightball Eddie was a client who'd followed him into his new line of work. There were two things to know about Eddie. One, he hated leaving his home. Not only was he going blind: he was agoraphobic. And two, he loved gambling. At one point, he'd been a professional billiards player, a hustler on the side, hence the nickname. He didn't just bet on pool. He bet on everything, always, and for large sums of money.

"Go on, then," said Eddie. "You've got me all hot and bothered. You didn't come all the way down here to see if I was still kicking."

"I need your help," said Simon. "For a job. I'm happy to pay a consulting fee."

Eddie waved away the offer. "Wouldn't think of it. Not after all the money you made for me, not to mention the other shenanigans. I should be paying you for what you done."

Simon preferred not to think of the "other shenanigans."

"Baccarat," he said, after he was seated.

"Toff's game," said Eddie. "Requires no skill whatsoever. Fucking chimp can win. What do you want to know about it?"

"Just one thing," said Simon. "How do you cheat?"

Simon left Eightball Eddie's country estate a good deal wiser about the game of baccarat and outfitted with a new understanding of the lengths to which some people will go—and the methods they may use—to earn a dishonest dollar. In his pocket, he carried a list of items required to suss out the person or, according to Eightball Eddie, the persons (no fewer than three and, more likely, as many as a dozen) who were stealing from the Société des Bains de Mer in Monaco.

To obtain the items on that list, Simon traveled north back across the Thames, then due west toward Heathrow, leaving the M4 in Southall and turning up Havelock Road. To his left stood the gurdwara, the monumental temple catering to the city's Sikh population. To look around him, he was in India, not England. Storefronts advertised fabrics and spices and money remittance services in Punjabi, with the English translations below. Pedestrians wore turbans and saris. Even the air smelled of curry and spices.

He continued past Manor House Grounds and found a parking space on a leafy street of row houses. The business entrance was at the rear. A teenage boy in a hoodie, cell phone in hand, answered the door. "Hello, Simon."

"Shouldn't you be at school?" Simon asked.

"I passed my A levels in May," said Arjit Singh.

"You're only fourteen."

The boy shrugged, eyes going to the phone in his hand.

"And now?" asked Simon. "Off to Oxford?"

"I'm going to the States. Caltech."

"Not alone?"

"I have family in Fullerton, wherever that is. I'll live with them." He opened the door all the way and allowed Simon to pass. "Dad's in his workshop."

Simon passed through the kitchen and opened the door to a steep staircase leading to the cellar. A rotund man in a dark lab coat stood at a workbench, a stainless steel attaché case open before him. Like all Sikhs, he wore a turban and kept his beard long and neatly groomed.

"I think it presumptuous of you to expect me to drop everything the moment you call and devote myself to your odd requests," said Vikram Singh.

"And how are you today, Dr. Singh? Or is it professor? I always forget."

"Behind on a number of projects. You are not my only client."

"Just your favorite."

"Hardly."

"I pay cash."

"Your saving grace."

Simon approached the engineer and gave his shoulder a friendly tug. "Congratulations on Arjit's being accepted at Caltech."

Singh said in a morose tone, "It isn't MIT, but it will have to do."

"You're not serious?"

Singh shook his head dismissively. By the look of anguish clouding his features, Simon knew he wasn't simply playing down his son's accomplishment. He meant it.

"Everything you need is here," said Singh. "If Mr. Margrave's assumptions are correct, you should have little problem identifying the culprits."

To Simon's eye, the case's contents looked modest and unimpressive. Singh removed each item and explained its name, function, and operating instructions. The tools were not designed to help someone spot a cardsharp, but to flush out a disciplined and technologically sophisticated team of professionals. When he'd finished, Simon no longer thought the devices were either modest or unimpressive.

"Da hag?" he asked—the two words of Punjabi he knew.

"I won't bother correcting your pronunciation, but you said that you love me."

"How much?" repeated Simon, sticking to his mother tongue.

"Twenty."

"Twenty thousand pounds?"

"And that's with the cash discount."

Simon took the roll of bills Martin Harriri had given him that morning and pressed it into Singh's hand. Easy come, easy go. "And Vikram," he said in parting, "Caltech is amazing."

That was twenty-four hours earlier.

Simon's eyes returned to the rearview mirror. The silver Audi was still there, maintaining a neutral distance behind him. British plates. Lone driver, at least as best as Simon could tell.

"No one will know about this," Lord Toby had stated, as gravely as if swearing an oath. "Just the men in this room."

Simon studied the car in his rearview a moment longer, then downshifted and floored it.

It was time to find out if Lord Toby Stonewood was a man of his word.

Chapter 12

Simon yanked the wheel to the right, crossing two lanes of traffic and taking the off-ramp for Voiron. The Audi sped past, as Simon expected it would. Any professional would do the same. If the car's presence was in any way related to Simon's assignment, there would surely be another car farther back. Mounting an operation to cheat a casino out of hundreds of millions of dollars was a feat requiring impeccable planning, discipline, and execution. Setting up a "three-car follow" was a piece of cake in comparison.

Simon guided the Daytona into a service station. The Ferrari's V12 engine gave him fifteen miles a gallon tops, and its small tank demanded that he stop frequently. Taking his time, he cleaned the windscreen, checked the tire pressure, then walked into the mini-mart. It wasn't his practice to leave a client's car unguarded, even for an instant, but circumstances dictated otherwise. He picked up a soda and chips, moving as deep into the store as he could while still able to keep an eye on the road outside. A minute passed. He spotted a Renault gliding off the highway and driving past the service station. A lone man in the cockpit: dark hair, sunglasses, vigilant. Simon exited the mini-mart as the Renault returned for a second look. The timing couldn't have been better. Seeing Simon, the driver jumped on the gas pedal and disappeared around the corner. It was a mistake on his part and gave Simon the proof he needed.

He was being followed.

Simon climbed into the Ferrari and returned to the highway. It was his turn to put a foot on the gas and he took the car well over the speed limit, enjoying the engine's confident growl as the needle stormed past 120 miles per hour. It wasn't long before he spotted the silver Audi in the slow lane ahead of him.

Years had passed since the last time he'd been followed. Back then it was the Marseille flics, and he'd make a game of leading them on wild-goose chases through the city and the surrounding hills. It was a point of pride that he could outdrive them.

"Let's have some fun," Simon said to himself.

He zipped past the German coupe without a backward glance.

Game on.

Barely a minute later, the Audi reappeared in his rearview. Simon eased off the gas, daring the Audi to come closer, but the driver slowed, not yet willing to give up all pretense.

"Have it your way."

He accelerated once again. The Audi matched his speed.

In the distance, a sign announced the exit for Grenoble, a small city at the base of the French Alps. Simon's route called for him to continue south through Avignon and Aix-en-Provence before dipping down to the coast and following the autoroute to Nice and then onward to Monaco. There was another route, however, a back way through the mountains. Though longer by several hours, it was more suited to his current purpose.

At the last instant, Simon guided the car into the left lane and headed in the direction of Grenoble. The Audi followed as Simon passed through the city and left the highway altogether, beginning a long, curvy ascent into the Alps. The road narrowed from four lanes to two, slimming further to a winding track barely wide enough for a car to pass another. Every ten or fifteen minutes, he'd arrive at a village or hamlet and reduce his speed as he navigated past a bakery and a butcher and one or two general stores. The peaks of the surrounding mountains came into view, many covered with snow. The air grew cooler. The wind picked up. It was on a long series of hairpin switchbacks that he spotted the Renault lower on the mountain.

He arrived at the Col du Ciel, elevation eight thousand feet, and was forced to slow to a crawl. A tractor dragging wagons of freshly cut and baled hay occupied the lane ahead. The Audi drew up behind him. He checked over his shoulder. The driver was dark-haired and swarthy, aviator sunglasses shielding his eyes. A stream of oncoming traffic scotched any chance of passing the tractor. In a minute, the Renault pulled up behind the Audi. A mouse and two cats waiting to pounce.

Then the tractor stopped altogether, its rear signal indicating that it wished to turn across lanes.

Simon had made a mistake. He was caught in a box. He could not drive forward. He could not retreat. A guardrail ran along the right-hand side of the road, and beyond that a vertiginous precipice, a fall of a thousand feet. A stone wall bordered the other side of the road.

Simon looked in the side-view mirror as the driver of the Audi climbed out of his car. He kept his hand close to his leg, but the pistol was evident all the same, as was his intent.

Simon was trapped.

Oncoming traffic cleared out and the tractor began its laborious turn. Simon had no weapon, nothing with which to defend himself. He popped the clutch and put the car into first gear, his heel digging into the gas pedal. The Ferrari's rear wheels spun madly. Rubber burned road. Smoke rose into the air accompanied by a terrific screech. Taken by surprise, the driver reacted instinctively, jumping back a step. It gave Simon the moment he needed. Dropping the clutch, he shot the Ferrari forward, ramming the trailing hay cart, sending bales flying and filling the air with dried grass.

The road was clear.

Away.

Simon's relief was short-lived. The Audi closed in rapidly, the Renault lagging behind it. It was not their proximity that rattled him, or the realization that the driver had wanted to kill him. It was the man's identity. He looked remarkably like the devil who'd rescued his larcenous colleague in Les Ambassadeurs with an expertly placed punch to Simon's kidney.

This wasn't about Toby Stonewood.

It was about revenge for losing a large sum of ill-begotten money.

Simon drove aggressively as the road began its descent from the mountain pass, one curve following another. The Ferrari was a high-performance automobile…*in its time*…but it was no match for a late-model German sports car. The Audi stayed on his tail, closing in perilously on the short straightaways. Simon could not keep his distance for long. On the next section of straight road, the Audi could ram him. Controlling the Ferrari would be problematic. Either he'd crash into opposing traffic, leaving him defenseless against a determined man with a pistol, or careen through the flimsy guardrail and plummet down the mountainside.

He found neither option appealing.

A sign announced the village of Diablerets-les-Monts. Simon brought up the map on his phone, darting glances at the screen. Five hundred meters ahead, there was a turnoff to the right that required him to make a hairpin turn before straightening out, like Bo-Peep's staff. By the look of the terrain, it either ascended or descended a slope.

Either way, he had to make a move.

Simon threw the car into third gear, redlining the rpms. The Ferrari shot ahead. A distance of ten meters opened between him and his pursuer. The road veered left. A stone wall climbed the opposite side. To his right the slope fell into a grassy cleft. He glimpsed a stream and forest and several wooden huts.

He spotted the turnoff and continued to accelerate. He was going too fast. There was no chance he could hold the turn. Surely he'd end up off the road, dead in a ditch. None of it mattered. He had one chance and he had to take it.

When he was certain that he could not make the turn, that he would crash through the red and white wooden railing, he braked very hard and spun the wheel to the right. The rear of the vehicle slid out. He held the steering wheel tightly, fighting the car's urge to straighten. No power steering. Only will and muscle. He threw the car into second gear and floored it. The Ferrari straightened out. The nose dove and Simon guided the car down a steep dirt track.

Behind him, the Audi started its turn even later. Too late. It failed to negotiate the hairpin curve. The car splintered the guardrail and tumbled down the hill, turning over several times, coming to a stop on its roof.

The Renault blew past ten seconds later, unaware of what had happened.

Simon ran to the Audi. The driver was conscious but groggy, bleeding profusely from a gash in his forearm. Simon freed him from the car and dragged him into the grass. There was no time to look for a first aid kit. He took off his shirt and tore off a sleeve, using it to fashion a tourniquet around the man's upper arm.

"What's your name?" Simon asked as he worked.

The man muttered a few words in a language Simon didn't recognize, but the gist of it was easy enough to understand. He was not expressing his thanks. Simon patted him down, fighting off the man's perfunctory attempts to stop him. He opened the man's wallet and took out the driver's license. Goran Zisnic, age twenty-eight, resident of Split, Croatia. "I'll keep this," Simon said, slipping the license into his pocket. He dropped the wallet in the grass. "Stay put. I'll call an ambulance."

Simon returned to the Audi and located the pistol. He didn't like guns. He dropped the clip, flicked the bullets one by one into the stream, then threw the weapon into the woods.

"I don't ever want to see you again," he said, giving Mr. Goran Zisnic a not-so-friendly pat on the cheek. "Ciao."

He was fairly certain they said that in Croatia, too.

Simon caught up to the Renault in the next village. Rounding a curve, he spotted the car parked next to a convenience store a hundred meters further on. He slammed his heel on the brake, nearly giving himself whiplash and narrowly averting bloodying his nose on the steering wheel. Quickly, he backed up so as to be out of sight. There was no place to hide, no side streets to conceal his approach, so he jogged along the edge of the road, doing his best to keep out of the man's line of sight.

He needn't have worried. The driver was engrossed in a phone conversation. The window was open, and judging by his tone of voice, he was angry. Simon grabbed the phone out of his hand and tossed it away. The driver protested, but the shout was muffled by Simon's hand on his throat. When the man went for his gun, Simon caught him by the wrist and wrenched it violently. The ulna snapped like a dry twig.

The man whimpered and Simon used the opportunity to slip the man's wallet from his jacket. Ivan Boskovic, age twenty-six, also from Croatia. Quite the Balkan party. He took the pistol and stuffed it in his waistband.

"Ivan, I'm going to keep your phone so you don't call any of your friends and tell them what happened. Your buddy is back about ten kilometers. He had an accident. Don't worry, I sent a doctor to look after him. Keys, please?"

Ivan Boskovic was a quick learner. Knowing he was in the presence of a superior foe, he handed over the car fob without protest.

Simon jogged back to his car. Along the way, he dumped the pistol into a sewer grate and chucked the car fob who knows where.

It was another three hours to Monaco.

He floored it.

CHAPTER 13

The clock showed the time to be ten minutes past six as Simon guided the car off the Grande Corniche and down the winding road into the principality of Monaco. Traffic slowed and he needed twenty minutes to make the descent to the hotel—a distance of a half mile. The French word for a traffic jam was *bouchon,* or cork. If that was the case, this cork belonged to a bottle of Lafite Rothschild. Every car in sight was a Bentley, BMW, or Porsche, all polished to a showroom buff.

He kept the windows rolled down, the air warm and pleasant against his skin. He'd visited Monaco on several occasions during his time working as a private banker. He looked at the attractive men and women strolling along the sidewalks and they brought to mind his former clients. The people he'd served for years, as not only a financial advisor but much more.

He saw them here now, dawdling on the steps of the hotel in tan poplin trousers and untucked Lacoste shirts and Italian loafers and Swiss watches. The outfit went for women, too. (No Rolexes allowed, thank you, unless it was the stainless Cosmograph Daytona worn by Paul Newman that had recently fetched a million dollars at auction.)

He heard them speaking French and Italian and German, laughing with an aloof, resentful manner. It was difficult to manage the travails of owning homes in three countries and garages filled with exotic automobiles, of caring for snotty children who only called when they wanted money or favors, or both. He smelled them, too, citrusy colognes and flowery perfumes and their unbearably strong mints to camouflage their smoker's breath.

In a way, these people had been Simon's family, and he'd come to know their foibles better than they did themselves. His duties began at safeguarding their money and quickly ran to matters nonfinancial. For a deposit of one hundred million dollars, the client received not only the finest financial advice but a personal concierge to cater to his or her every whim.

He reserved tables for them at the finest restaurants and found them rooms at the right hotels—the right rooms, mind you. Every five-star palace had a few rooms where you wouldn't put your drunk Uncle Harry. Simon made airline reservations, planned safaris, arranged for jewelry to be appraised and art to be authenticated. Once he was charged with tracking down a bracelet lost in Paris the week before. The client had no idea where. Simon found it. He recommended the right doctor, and if the client didn't have time to visit, he procured a prescription for the right pharmaceutical, invariably Xanax for women and Viagra for men, and he could provide the number of a discreet agency to help put the latter to the test.

In short, he did everything he was asked to the best of his ability. He stopped at murder. And yes, he'd been asked to arrange that, too.

The Place du Casino was shaped like a horseshoe, with the casino at its head, the Hôtel de Paris to the right (as one approached), and the Café de Paris with its esplanade of open seating facing it across an expanse of lush grass and topiaries. The Casino de Monte-Carlo, built in the mid-1800s atop a dramatic promontory overlooking the Mediterranean, was a grand Beaux Arts castle, painted an eggshell cream with ornate balconies, Grecian statues on recessed plinths, and a wrought iron porte cochere to welcome its guests. The entire area was a monument to wealth and the overwhelming magnificence of money for money's sake. Then again, thought Simon, what was one to expect when you crammed sixteen thousand millionaires into one square mile of territory?

A line of cars crowded the curb in front of the Hôtel de Paris. Valets in cream jackets rushed here and there, welcoming guests, ferrying luggage, and moving the cars to the garage. Simon surveyed the scene impatiently.

It had been an eventful drive and the prospect of waiting another ten minutes was unacceptable. He revved the engine—a caress of the accelerator was enough—and all heads turned toward the Ferrari. A valet at the front of the line abandoned his charge—a tall red-haired woman in a flowing electric-green outfit—and hurried toward Simon.

Simon got out of the car and handed him the keys. "Riske. Checking in. I have a few bags in the trunk."

"Yes, sir," said the valet, snapping to attention. "The reception is up the stairs and across the lobby to your left."

Simon slipped a hundred-euro note into the valet's hand. "Keep it safe."

A shriek and the red-haired woman stormed up the line of cars, hands waving. "*Che Cosa!* You steal my valet," she said to Simon. She was Italian and upset. "Give him back."

Simon held his ground. "Possession is nine-tenths of the law."

The valet kept his head down and continued removing Simon's bags from the trunk.

"I am Contessa Maria Borghese. You cannot take him from me."

"I'll send him back as soon as he's finished," said Simon. "You can tell him who you are yourself. I'm sure he'll be impressed."

The Contessa stepped closer. "You…you…are no one. *Teppista americano!* He only likes the car."

"At least I have something going for me. Arrivederci."

Head thrown back in contempt, the woman spun and returned to her car.

"Ouch. That hurt." A navy station wagon had pulled up behind him. A trim blond woman in a black leather jacket, T-shirt, and jeans stood by the driver's-side door, a spectator to the event.

"I get it all the time," said Simon.

"I'm not sure she's entirely correct."

Simon noted that the station wagon's license plates were German. KO for Köln, or Cologne. He had not detected an accent.

"You are here for the Concours?" she asked. "Showing or driving?"

"Driving. The time trial."

The woman cast her eye over the Daytona. "Is this your car?"

"A friend's," said Simon. "More of a client, actually."

"You," she said, looking at Simon with the same critical eye. "You belong with a Spider. The old one. Nineteen sixty-five, I think."

"A little above my pay grade, but thank you. I agree." Simon smiled. The model was his favorite. He had a picture of one on his office wall. "I take it you are here for the Concours as well, then."

"Me?" She dismissed the thought with a shiver. "Never."

Simon discerned that she really meant "Never again." The woman was his age, give or take, with golden skin and light brown eyes and high cheekbones that gave her an authoritative air. She was nearly as tall as he, with a sharp straight nose and slim, sharply defined lips. A striking woman rather than a beautiful one. He decided that he must get to know her.

"The name is—"

"Will you excuse me?" she said, looking past him.

"Simon," he rushed to say, but it was too late. She was gone, walking to the head of the line, shoulders set, chin raised to face any challenge. He kept his eyes on her, feeling something spark inside him. Something not entirely welcome.

After a moment, he walked into the lobby, crossing the floor to the reception. The hotelier appeared to be expecting him. He informed Simon that he'd been given a suite on the third floor and repeated Lord Toby Stonewood's promise that all expenses were on the house, including anything from the hotel's restaurants and room service, as well as items in the hotel's shops, but excluding the jewelry boutiques.

"Naturally," said Simon.

The hotelier smiled and, in a slip of professionalism, vouchsafed that he must be "a very good friend of the hotel."

Someone chuckled and Simon noted that it was the blond woman from outside. She had taken up a position further down the desk and had overheard the remark.

"The hotel likes the car, too," he said.

"Obviously," replied the woman in a near perfect imitation of the Contessa.

They laughed.

Simon accepted the key and was accompanied to the elevators by the hotelier. It was not an establishment where one showed oneself to his or her room. The blond woman arrived in the company of another hotelier a moment later. She stood close enough to Simon that he could smell her perfume—something light and woody. He felt a desire to step closer. An elevator chimed. Its doors opened. She looked at him and he looked at her. Striking, to be sure, but there was something else that drew him to her. Something infinitely more attractive. It was her character, he decided, her confidence and bristling air of competence. She was an army of one.

"After you," said Simon.

"A gentleman," she said before entering the elevator.

From this woman, it sounded like the ultimate compliment.

"The name is Riske," he said too loudly, not giving a damn. "Simon."

"Good evening, Mr. Riske."

She made no effort to offer her name. The doors closed and Simon glanced at the hotelier. "Do you know her?"

The hotelier offered a cryptic smile. He'd been asked the question before. The answer was yes, he knew her name, and it was none of Simon's business.

The room was the size of a basketball court, with ceilings high enough to put in a regulation basket with room left over for a twenty-four-second clock. He had declined the hotelier's offer to send a valet to help him unpack. He opened his bag and put away his clothing, then arranged his toiletries in the bathroom. One washcloth to either side of the sink upon which he placed his toothpaste and aftershave and skin cream, and of course his floss.

A white envelope from the Monaco Rally Club waited on the desk. Simon examined the contents: passes, schedule, guidebook, tickets to the gala dinner and to the lawn event to be held at the Sporting Club. And more important, as far as Simon was concerned, information about the time trial Saturday, including a map of the course. A meeting for drivers was set for the next morning at nine.

Simon showered and put on fresh clothing. One shirt ruined, another dirty. He'd have to take up Toby Stonewood on his offer of free shopping at the hotel's boutiques sooner than expected. It was the cocktail hour so he chose a patterned shirt, trousers a shade too light for October, and a navy blazer. The boat show was in town. He wanted to fit in.

On the way out of his room, he stopped at the minibar, which wasn't mini at all: it offered full-size bottles of spirits as well as beer and soft drinks. A certain bourbon from Tennessee was missing. *Snobs,* he thought, though he knew that D'Art Moore would applaud the omission. Instead, he made himself an espresso with the nifty coffee machine and added three sugars to satisfy his sweet tooth.

There was a packet of Fisherman's Friend mints on a glass shelf, next to some nuts and napkins. Just the sight of the mint-green packaging provoked a smattering of butterflies. Not knowing who he might run into—hoping it might be *her*—he popped a mint. His eyes watered at the industrial-strength lozenge and he spit it into the sink. It wasn't the taste that repulsed him but the memories it summoned. Memories of smoking a pack of Gauloises a day and drinking too much Pernod. Memories of another life, when his name was Simon Ledoux and his hair was long enough to pull into a ponytail and he stole cars the way other people— *honest people*—brushed their teeth.

Feeling nauseated, he stepped onto the balcony. He closed his eyes and breathed in the scents of jasmine and wisteria, willing away the images of guns and glass vials and half-naked women with sleepy eyes and crooked smiles. The fresh air failed to do the trick. He felt a machine gun bucking his shoulder and smelled the cordite in the morning air, hearing the shell casings tinkle as they danced on the street. It was all coming back. The exhilaration of driving the wrong way down a one-way street with a police car close behind. The unfettered freedom of being on the wrong side of the law. Hovering above the memories, a seductive voice promised him that this time it would be different. This time, he would get away with it.

Why not give it one more try?

After all, Ledoux, you were damned good at it.

And you loved it.

Maybe you still do.

He was sweating when he went back inside and had to change his shirt. Again.

Chapter 14

The team arrived at its headquarters in the eastern Swiss Alps in late afternoon. They came in three cars, each taking a different route into the country. The first to arrive came from the south, through Milan, then through the lake district, skirting Lake Como, before turning east at the border, remaining in Italy until the last moment and crossing in time to take the Bernina Pass. The second came from the north, traveling through Zurich, following the main touristic route to St. Moritz, past Sargans and Chur, finally heading east into the mountains at Thusis. The last car came from the northeast, transiting Munich, heading south through Bavaria, past Garmisch, before cutting the corner of Austria and entering Switzerland at its easternmost finger, the mountainous Romansch region, a country unto itself.

No stops were permitted. Gas tanks were topped off prior to departure. Bathroom breaks were verboten. The members of the team carried their own snacks. Under no circumstance could they risk being photographed. No country was more aggressively surveilled than Switzerland.

The egress, or "getaway," if one were to be necessary, had been well planned and would be nigh impossible to track. It was their arrival that threatened to jeopardize their long-term freedom.

The fact that police would identify their vehicles was a given. It would take time, but images from every camera leading into the valley would be collected and scrutinized. Cars belonging to visitors would be cross-checked against those belonging to residents. License plates, registrations, bills of sale would be analyzed. Like a noose closing around a doomed man's neck, the circle would get tighter and tighter. It would take days, weeks, even, but the vehicles would be identified. Make no mistake.

And when they were, authorities would find that all had been purchased legally and for cash, each in a different corner of Europe. Berlin, Madrid, Budapest. The identifications of those who'd purchased the cars were doctored and entirely false, thus illegal.

Another roadblock.

More time.

The progress of the authorities would slow.

Eventually they would give up.

After all, if the team was successful, there would be no victims to save, no villains to hunt.

One by one, the cars arrived at their destination. Few team members had seen a place as grandiose. None had set foot inside one, unless it was a police station or a prison. They called it a mansion, a palace, a fortress, a keep. It was none of those things. It was a chalet. It even had a name. The Chesa Madrun.

It helped immeasurably that the chalet had an underground parking garage. Their orders were strict. Once they arrived, they were not to leave the premises until the day itself, not even to set foot outside and smell the glorious alpine air. Others were watching. Others were laying the groundwork. They were the strike force, the "tip of the spear," or, to borrow an unfortunate German synonym, the *einsatzgruppe*.

There were four of them in all, not counting the woman. All had experience in this type of thing, if not the act itself. They were thieves, robbers, extortionists, blackmailers, and bombers. It went without saying that they were killers. All had done time in a maximum-security facility of one nation or another. They knew that in Norway a convicted murderer lived alone in a neat room hardly different from a youth hostel, with a single bed, a duvet, a hot plate, and a television. And that in Turkey, a common burglar was thrown into the general prison population with none of those things. They preferred Norway. None had been convicted in Switzerland or for that matter had ever set foot in the country.

They were individuals who had spent a lifetime outside the law. Men who were accustomed to living with the police on their tail and keeping their cool all the while.

Inside the chalet, the team members settled into their living quarters. The kitchen was amply stocked. Before long, a group meal was prepared. Spirits were high. Until now, everything had gone according to plan. There was no reason to suspect that would change. Soon each of them would get their hands on more money than they'd dreamed of earning in a lifetime.

There was an atmosphere of laughter and comradery when the woman arrived. The men took one look at her and the room went quiet. They knew who she was by name and by relation, but none had expected her beauty.

"So," said the woman, "did you bring the goddamn *plastique?*"

CHAPTER 15

There was no time to waste.

Simon set the stainless steel briefcase on the bed and keyed in the six-digit combination. Wall-to-wall gray foam provided safe housing for a variety of electronic devices, ranging from small to smaller to smallest. With thumb and forefinger, he freed a rectangular steel object, not dissimilar to a Zippo lighter in size and weight. The device was smooth on all sides save for an on/off switch easily activated by a thumbnail.

Simon clicked it. A green light appeared. The device paired with an in-ear receiver that he plucked free and placed in his right ear. A low-frequency thrumming was immediately audible.

"The first rule of cheating at any card game," Eightball Eddie had said, "is that you have to see the cards. Card counters remember the sequence of cards as they appear in a game. Edge counters differentiate between face cards and number cards by the pattern printed on the top of each card. The aim of both is to gain a mathematical advantage over the house of two to ten percent that will play out over a succession of hands. Neither of those methods works for baccarat. Baccarat's a game of pure luck; the skill is in the betting. Therefore, the only way to cheat is to see the cards before they're dealt. To do that, someone has to have a camera to scope them out either as they are being put into the shoe and shuffled or, more likely, afterward, when the cards are being cut."

Enter Vikram Singh.

It turned out that cameras, both still and video, emitted a low-frequency audio signature when activated. The rectangular steel device in Simon's palm was a highly sensitive microphone, in effect a camera hunter, designed to detect that sound. Upon identifying that audio signature, it transmitted a signal to the earpiece. From there, it was like a game of hotter/colder. The closer Simon got to the camera, the more rapid the pulse. If the pulse became continuous, it meant that he was within thirty centimeters, or twelve inches, of the camera.

"You won't see it," said Singh. "Lenses can be made as small as the head of a needle with a Bluetooth transmitter the size of a grain of rice."

"So they can see the cards?" Simon had asked both men. "Then what?"

Eightball Eddie had scratched his head. "Too smart for me. All I know is someone is telling them how they should bet."

But Vikram Singh knew the means, if not the method. "Once they know the sequence of the cards, they can plug it into an algorithm that predicts the order in which they'll be dealt to both players, the *punto* or the *banco*."

"So who's doing that?" Simon asked.

"His partner or partners. I have no idea how big the team is."

"One guy takes the pictures…"

"And transmits them to a second person close enough to receive the Bluetooth signal."

"And the second person…"

"Analyzes the cards and tells his partner when and how much to bet."

"How can I find that person?"

"He can't be far. A Bluetooth transmitter that small just can't throw a signal a long distance."

"Defined as?"

"A hundred meters. Probably closer. With as few walls in between as possible."

Which brought Simon to the transparent ziplock bag holding what appeared to be a few dozen chocolate M&M's. These were his secret weapon and to be saved for later. He wasn't one to go into the enemy's den with guns blazing. If he was looking for them, they were looking for him. He'd do best to keep that in mind.

*　　*　　*

Simon left the hotel a few minutes before nine. It was a warm night with hardly a breeze, humid and still. The Place du Casino was a riot of activity. A steady stream of cars made the circuit past the Hôtel de Paris, the casino, and the Café de Paris, music blaring from open windows, arms extended, cigarettes in hand. Nine months of the year, Monaco was a quiet, pleasant backwater, a secure tax-free enclave where you can plant your flag. "Sleepy" wasn't too strong a word. All that changed during the summer months, when Monaco, like the rest of the French Riviera, became a playground for Europe's rich and infamous. There was a Festival des Feux d'Artifices, performances at the opera house, and concerts under the stars at the Sporting Club's Salle des Étoiles. High-class fare for its high-class residents. The International Boat Show was the showstopper that ended the season on a high note.

Simon dodged his way past a troop of blondes wearing the uniform of a luxury car manufacturer and showing off its newest sedans, all parked in front of the casino steps. He navigated his way through the crowd waiting to go inside, showing his passport before being waved through the main entrance. The law prohibited Monégasque citizens from entering the casino.

If Les Ambassadeurs was a posh nineteenth-century English country home, the Casino de Monte-Carlo was Versailles. Simon crossed the entry hall with its marble floors and towering mirrors and proud pillars rising to a glass ceiling. He'd journeyed back in time three centuries to when Louis XIV was king and faro the card game du jour. Simon's trip was short-lived. An army of slot machines welcomed him back to the twenty-first century. He strode past them and into the gaming rooms, where tables offering roulette and blackjack were crowded to capacity.

Simon, however, was interested in baccarat. He made his way to a quieter room on the second floor and found an empty seat. The tables were crescent-shaped, with room for eight players. He threw a thousand-euro note on the table and received several stacks of chips in return.

Though Lord Toby had offered him a house credit of a hundred thousand euros, Simon preferred to use his own money. For now, anonymity was preferable to profit.

Baccarat was a maddingly simple, unpredictable game. Like blackjack, you were dealt a limited number of cards. The object was for the value of your cards to total as close to nine as possible. Only two hands were dealt, one to the house, or *banco,* the other to the player, *punto.* Players chose one hand, or both, on which to wager.

Play began when the dealer gave himself and the player two cards each, both dealt faceup. Cards two through nine counted at face value. Aces counted as one and face cards as zero. Two and three equaled a five. Nine and seven equaled sixteen but was counted as six. A third card was dealt to each player if his score was too low. As Eightball Eddie had said, "Even a chimp could win."

Baccarat was a favorite of the player who believed in luck as a manifestation of good fortune, something as real as rain or sunshine. Fortune that showered its favor on a player in the form of the right card at the right time. A toff's game, Eightball Eddie had said, "toff" meaning "idiot."

Simon played two hands, betting on the house each time. He won one and lost one. All the while his eye roved from the smiling dealer to his fellow players to the discreetly positioned opaque domes on the ceilings—the "eyes in the skies"—concealing cameras that covered every square inch of the casino floor and sent back images to a central operations room where security professionals could observe play. He was quick to spot the floor bosses, a few walking the floor, others standing with dealers at their tables. To look at, Toby Stonewood ran a tight ship. It would not be easy to pull a scam in front of so many prying eyes. And yet the casino had lost millions. Hundreds of millions.

Simon collected his chips and stopped at the bar for a drink. He ordered a double bourbon and tipped lavishly, carrying the cocktail to a room where betting minimums were higher. He found a seat at a table requiring a minimum wager of five hundred euros. It was uncommon for tables to go higher, unless it was a private game or after prior consultation with casino staff. He arranged his chips and asked for an additional five thousand euros.

The game had officially gotten serious.

Simon played for an hour, finding himself up a few thousand euros. The shoe passed from player to player. When the cards ran low and it came time to shuffle, a pre-shuffled stack of eight decks was placed into the shoe. The dealer offered the cutting card to a sharply dressed man who'd been winning on a regular basis and was up fifty thousand euros. With his slicked-back hair and hooded eyes, he certainly looked the part of a sharp, or a cheat. If he had a camera up his sleeve, he would use it to record the flutter of the cards as he ran the cutting card along their edge.

Simon watched as best he could without staring, his attention directed inward as well, hoping to hear the pinging that would indicate a camera in use. To his disappointment, the man jabbed the cutting card into the deck without ceremony. Camera or not, he had made no effort to preview the cards.

There was no joy to be had at this table.

It was then that Simon heard a hoot of excitement from an adjacent room. Collecting his chips, he headed toward the merriment. A crowd had gathered around another baccarat table, also with a five-hundred-euro minimum, where a balding man with rimless spectacles and a pencil mustache held the shoe. An enormous pile of chips sat before him. In short order, Simon watched him win three consecutive hands, letting his wager ride each time. Ten thousand euros grew to forty thousand in five minutes' time.

There were no seats free so Simon moved as close to the man as possible. If he had a camera, Simon figured he should hear it now. No pinging came from his earpiece. Another hand was dealt. Another win. Eighty thousand euros. By now every player at the table was betting with the winner. You always followed a streak. The only thing Simon noticed, if it was anything at all, was that the man seemed to be concentrating intensely (far more intensely than a game of luck would demand) and appeared to be staring at the cards in the shoe. Was he counting them? Or doing something else?

Suddenly, the man looked directly at Simon, catching him in flagrante, staring right back at him. Simon smiled awkwardly, but it was too little, too late. Without delay, the balding man pushed his chips to the dealer, who issued him a marker to take to the cage for payment. It was a jarring decision. He left the table seconds later.

Simon had no idea what the man had been doing, but he'd been doing something. He didn't know if the man thought he was a floor boss or security, but there could be no doubt that Simon's presence had rattled him. He waited until the man was out of sight and followed. The main hall was a swirl of activity. Simon stopped at the head of the stairs, surveying the scene. He spotted his man leaving the cashier's cage and heading in the direction of the front door.

Simon studied his purposeful gait, his hunched shoulders, his air of anxious flight. He decided to follow the man. He had no reason, other than that the man had won six hands in a row and Simon had come all this way to find the individuals who were stealing from the casino. True, he had not picked up any electronic signal indicating the presence of a camera, but anyone who wins six hands in a row is guilty of something, even if it's just being too damned lucky.

There was another reason. He was no surveillance expert—a "pavement artist," in the words of a favorite author. Given the crowds out and about, it might be a safe time to practice.

With a renewed sense of purpose, Simon hurried down the stairs and across the main hall, halting outside the front door. The Place du Casino was in full swing. A line of cars leading all the way up the hill made their slow circuit. It was a pleasant evening. There wasn't a table to be had at the Café de Paris. Simon looked to his left and spotted the man. He was dodging past several couples, arms linked and taking up the sidewalk. The man was headed down the incline to the port.

Simon slipped his hands into his pockets and followed, sure to keep a safe distance. Keeping the same driven pace, the man continued to the bottom of the incline, not once looking behind him. He crossed the

Boulevard Albert 1er and walked along the port, presenting himself at one of the guarded entries. He showed a badge and passed through the gate. Simon jogged ahead but lost the man as he disappeared into the canyons of giant ships.

He pulled up, deciding he'd done as well as could be expected. It was doubtful the man belonged to any gambling ring. Why would anyone who owned a boat worth tens of millions need to cheat? On the other hand, Simon couldn't ignore the small voice inside him telling him that he'd been witness to wrongdoing.

It was after eleven. He yawned, feeling the events of the past few days catching up with him. It would be wise to log some rack time. The attractions of the city could wait. He set off back up the hill, looking forward to slipping his feet between the sheets and picking up his book, the latest Philip Kerr novel set in World War II Berlin, and simply relaxing.

Then he saw her and all thoughts of bed, book, and slumber vanished.

Chapter 16

Simon followed her, telling himself it was for no other reason than that he was also going to the hotel. His natural stride was longer, and in due course, he passed her, offering a nod, no more. A gentleman didn't force himself on a woman, even conversationally.

He looked at the port, lit by row after row of fairy lights strung across the docks with impeccable care. He recalled reading that all yachts less than two hundred feet in length had been banished to a port down the coast for the duration of the show. The smallest yacht moored was 250 feet, the biggest too big for any private individual. He made an approximate count of the vessels and decided that the fair value would come to something close to six billion dollars.

"Here you are again. The valet thief."

Simon looked over his shoulder. It was her. "I only steal from those who can afford it," he said. "Or deserve it."

"A regular Robin Hood."

"I'd prefer John Robie."

"'The Cat.'"

"You know him," said Simon, pleased.

"Of course I do. But you're not quite that handsome."

"Who is?"

"And I hope you're not after my jewels!" She laughed and he slowed so she could catch up. "Do you have one of the big ones?" she asked, looking down at the port and the boats.

"I beg your pardon?"

"Some are so enormous. I really can't imagine."

"You don't like the big ones?" Simon asked.

"I prefer a more moderate size. Something manageable."

"But not too small?"

"Of course not," she said as if her pride were insulted. "But with a wide beam. For comfort."

"Width is important. The bigger ones are harder to maneuver, anyway."

"Not for a skilled captain."

"No?"

She shook her head. "Not one that knows his vessel. They welcome the challenge."

"Ah," said Simon. "It's boats we're talking about."

"What did you think—" The woman broke off midsentence. She put her hands on her hips and gave Simon an appropriate scowl. "You are quite the devil."

"I had a long day."

"I had a longer day, believe me. And English is my fourth language. It wasn't fair."

"In that case, I apologize."

"Accepted." They came to the top of the incline. A broad plaza offered pedestrians a promontory for looking over the port and across to the palace. "Well, it is nice to end the day with a laugh, isn't it, Mr. Riske?"

"You remembered."

"I did," she said.

A soft breeze was blowing off the sea, feathering the woman's hair, scattering strands across her face.

"Shall we start over?" said Simon.

The woman stepped closer, close enough that he could see the flecks of amber in her eyes and the white-blond hairs in her eyebrows and linger in the delicate wash of her perfume. "Why not?"

"Simon Riske."

"Victoria Brandt." She offered a hand and gave a firm shake. "My friends call me Vika."

"Vika," said Simon. *Vee-ka.* "That's unique."

"I hope so."

"Time for a nightcap?"

"I don't drink."

"Coffee?"

"No, thank you."

"Herbal tea?"

"Do I look like a woman who drinks herbal tea?"

The answer was final, but she did not seem in a hurry to go.

"Shall we go back, then?" he suggested.

Victoria Brandt—Vika to her friends—nodded. They walked side by side without speaking. Once inside the hotel, Simon summoned the elevator, and when it arrived he allowed her to take it alone. "Good night, Ms. Brandt."

"Good night, Mr. Riske."

CHAPTER 17

Simon rose at dawn. He threw on his athletic gear and took a run down the hill past the port, the array of giant yachts distracting him from his exertions until he reached the far side. From there it was an uphill slog to the Palais des Princes. He made a circuit of the grand square and then called it quits. Five kilometers was enough for any reasonable human being. He rewarded his discipline with a warm chocolate croissant and an espresso at a café overlooking Port Hercule. The weather was holding nicely, the sea air crisp and invigorating. According to his weather app, the first chance of rain wasn't until Saturday, the day of the rally. It figured.

He walked back to the hotel, wandering onto the docks, not to admire the boats but to size up security measures. A tall white mesh fence ran the length of the port. He counted five entrances, each manned by guards. If there were real police in the vicinity, Simon didn't see them. The gates were left open, the atmosphere one of relaxed, convivial authority. Everyone was among friends here. The flow of men and women in and out of the docks was constant. Crew, technicians, repairmen, press, and of course the owners of the yachts, their family and friends.

He wondered which boat belonged to the unremarkable bland man with the remarkable run of luck. One thing was for certain: the boats were neither bland nor unremarkable. Something about this observation rankled him, no matter how random it might be. The man didn't go with the boats—any of them.

The bells of the cathedral tolled eight o'clock. He had an hour before the rally briefing was set to begin. The location was the Sporting Club at the eastern end of the principality. He'd have to hurry to make it on time. Still, he made no move to return to the hotel.

Simon jogged across the street and entered a storefront selling nautical supplies. He purchased a cap with the name of a prominent shipbuilder on it and a flashy navy and white windbreaker. On his way back to the dock, he stopped at a kiosk to buy a coffee.

"Large."

He poured out half and replaced it with milk. He had no intention of burning anyone.

Cup in hand, wearing his new purchases, Simon moved to the nearest entrance. Several young men dressed in pressed khaki shorts and white short-sleeved shirts—ship's crew—were passing through the gate. All wore their entry badges on lanyards around their necks. Simon aimed for the shortest in the group. Head down, he collided with the man's shoulder, spilling his coffee onto the man's shorts.

"*Pardon*," exclaimed Simon, playing up his Gallic roots, arms waving. "*Désolé*."

"Crap," said the sailor, retreating while brushing the liquid off his shorts.

Simon remained uncomfortably close to him, making ineffectual gestures to help clean up the mess.

The sailor's friends erupted into laughter. They were Australian and immediately set about ribbing their unlucky shipmate, calling him a "bloody blind donkey" and making other comments about him wetting his pants, or worse, while assuring Simon that it was their friend's fault, not his.

After a minute, Simon parted company with the group. The first rule of pickpocketing was to put as much distance as possible between you and the mark with the shortest possible delay.

Tucking the sailor's badge into his pocket, he headed to the opposite end of the port, skirting the public swimming pool before stopping to check that the Aussie crew wasn't following him. Satisfied that he'd pulled off the theft, he put the badge around his neck, picture facing his chest. He continued to the security checkpoint at the western end of the port, flashing his badge and giving a thumbs-up, not for a moment slowing. The guards waved him past without a second look.

Inside the fence, he made a sharp left and essentially retraced his steps. There was the usual dockside traffic. Crew members on errands to get hold of one part or another. Mechanics driving ATVs loaded with pumps, valves, driveshafts, and propellers. The air smelled strongly of diesel fuel cut with salt and bacon. Representatives from firms maintaining booths at the show hurried to their appointments and stood in tight knots, conversing with ship captains. Simon fit right in.

He reached the eastern end of the port and turned right at the first dock extending into the harbor. It was his aim to follow the path taken by the balding man the night before. The yachts were moored cheek by jowl, fantail facing the dock. The megayachts—three hundred feet and up— were moored farthest out, hugging the contours of the port. Those a class smaller had spots in the center of the harbor. Simon came to a dock extending to his left and slowed. It was here he'd last seen the balding man. He put his phone to his ear, feigning conversation as he studied the boats moored nearby. Five yachts shared this section of the dock. Pulling his cap a shade lower, Simon walked past them. The *Alexis* out of Hamburg, the *Magnum Opus* out of Porto Cervo, the *Golden Crown* out of Piraeus, the *Czarina* out of Nassau. Not a modest name among them. Then again, there was nothing modest about a three-deck motor yacht measuring the length of a football field. The *Magnum Opus* boasted a landing pad with a black Bell Jet Ranger tied down and ready for service. The *Golden Crown* carried four Jet Skis on its rear deck. Simon preferred the *Czarina*'s vintage Riva motorboat with its lacquered wooden hull, shiny as the day it was made, hanging from davits on the afterdeck. But nowhere did he see anyone resembling his friend from the casino.

Simon came to the end of the dock. The last boat was named the *Lady S,* out of Biarritz, the only one with a navy-blue hull. A gangway was lowered from the aft sundeck to the dock. He saw no one on deck or inside the cabin. He zipped up his jacket, put down his coffee. Sitting on the dock across from him was a coil of rope with a small pump, most likely broken, set atop it. He picked up the pump, examining it to see if there were any visible flaws. He saw none.

With confidence, he walked up the gangway onto the boat. The glass doors to the salon stood open. It was a large room, leather couches running along each side, a polished wooden table in its center, plush white carpeting. An enormous flat-screen television took up the far wall. Closer, a young woman clad in a T-shirt and shorts, hair a mess, face puffy, lay on a chaise longue, engrossed in the mysteries of her phone. She glanced up at Simon, then returned her attention to the phone.

"Where's the captain?" he asked first in French, then in English. The woman shrugged, not giving him another look.

So much for security.

Simon advanced to the back of the salon. Stairs led down to the guest quarters and the engine room. Belowdecks was off-limits for a ship's chandler delivering a pump. Another set of stairs led up to the second level. He climbed them to the dining room. The table wasn't set for breakfast. Sales brochures, a photograph of the *Lady S* on the cover, were strewn over the surface. He picked one up and turned it over to see the name of the broker and the price. Eighty million euros, knocked down from one hundred twenty.

"Can I help you?" The ship's captain addressed Simon from a sliding door leading to the deck. He was tall and bronzed and wore his uniform well.

Simon held up the pump. "From the chandlery. Your replacement bilge pump."

"Wrong boat."

"This is the *Lady S*."

"We didn't order a new pump. Our bilge pump is ten times that size. That's for a sailboat."

Simon held his ground. "You're certain? I was told the *Lady S*."

"Boat show," said the captain, shaking his head. He was Italian, though his French was near perfect. "Everything is a mess. Can't wait till it's over. Good luck with that."

"Thank you. Nice boat. Who's the owner?"

"It's on the account. But if you're looking for work, you're on the wrong vessel. We haven't put to sea in a month. Owner can't afford the fuel. I hope he's paying your bills, because he isn't paying my salary."

Simon left the boat, dropping the pump where he'd found it. He might not know the owner's name, but he'd learned plenty more. Under his arm, he held one of the sales brochures. Amazing the things people will tell you if only you keep your mouth closed.

CHAPTER 18

A group of thirty men milled around the auditorium on the second floor of the Sporting Club. Most were over forty and there wasn't a woman in sight. A slim formal gentleman in a blazer and gray trousers moved to the lectern and introduced himself as André Solier, president of the Monaco Rally Club. He spent fifteen minutes giving a history of the club before reading off the names of the drivers participating in Saturday's race and the automobiles they would be competing in. Each man in turn raised a hand and offered a hello. Simon recognized two of the drivers as clients whose vehicles he'd restored, though neither was driving a Ferrari on this occasion.

"And a last-minute entrant, Simon Riske, of London, England, racing in a nineteen seventy-two Ferrari Daytona."

Simon kept his gaze straight ahead as all eyes turned to him. So much for keeping a low profile.

"This is Mr. Riske's first time racing with us. Let's be sure to offer him our warmest welcome."

The president of the Rally Club went on to discuss the details of the event: arrival time, prerace judging, and the order of start. Simon drew place fifteen, squarely in the middle. The rally was a time trial. The cars were far too valuable to race head-to-head.

The lights dimmed and a map of the course appeared on the screen. Solier spent an hour going over the circuit. He pointed out three areas of concern. The first was a hairpin turn just past the town of La Turbie that fed immediately into another sharp turn—"a real dipsy doo," according to Solier. "Slow down. This is not the place to gain time." The second was a steep descent at the fifteen-kilometer mark that ended with a ninety-degree right-hand turn. "Do not test your brakes," Solier warned. The last area of concern was a section he called the "camel's back," a series of subtle dips and rises where excessive speed would cause the vehicle to catch air. "And if you do, perhaps our new friend, Mr. Riske, will have the pleasure of repairing your vehicle."

The course measured thirty kilometers, or eighteen miles. Drivers made three circuits. Prizes were awarded for the fastest time overall, the fastest single circuit, and the fastest short course, a section of the circuit where drivers could let it all hang out. Each winner received a gold cup and an invitation to a private cocktail party with Prince Albert of Monaco, the club's patron.

"I look forward to seeing you all at the Dîner de Gala on Thursday night," said Solier in closing.

There was a smattering of applause as the lights came up. Simon gathered the folder he'd been given and headed for the exit.

"Riske, isn't it?" A slim, rugged man intercepted him at the door.

"Hello."

"Dov Dragan. I chair the racing committee. Have a moment?"

"Of course."

"Rather a last-minute entry. You kept us on our toes."

"Like Monsieur Solier said, I usually fix cars."

"Yes, I know. I looked you up. Not often we have mechanics racing. Or are you the owner of the car, too?"

When registering for the Concours, it was obligatory to indicate the name of the car's owner. As chair of the racing committee, and thus someone privy to the entry forms, Dragan knew full well that the Daytona did not belong to Simon. "I hope it didn't cause a problem."

Dragan waved off the suggestion. "Same group's been racing for the last ten years. It will be nice to have someone new to beat."

He was around sixty, of indeterminate nationality, with steely blue eyes and silver hair cut very short. Despite the insouciant tone, he was not a nice man. Simon knew this at once.

"Sounds like you're afraid that I might win," he said.

"That's not possible," Dragan replied. "My Bugatti Veyron does zero to sixty in three seconds. Yours manages eight at best. It's a dinosaur. Beautiful, mind you, but as for racing? I think not."

Simon thought it best not to respond. He had his own opinions. The Bugatti Veyron was a two-million-dollar piece of high-tech junk, a publicity stunt trading on the Bugatti name—not an automobile of distinction.

"Still, it is a scenic course," continued Dragan. "Very touristic. At your pace you'll have plenty of time to enjoy the views."

Simon made a note to get Harry Mason down there to see what he could do about putting a little more vim into the Daytona's engine. "I know the course. I have that going for me."

Concern tightened Dragan's already tight face. "Have you driven professionally?"

"In a manner of speaking." Simon didn't elaborate and he could see Dragan forcing himself not to inquire further. "I grew up here."

"No one grows up in Monaco."

"I meant in the area. Marseille. And you, Mr. Dragan: where are you from?"

"Cap Ferrat. At least for now."

Simon looked rudely at his watch. "Excuse me. I have to run. I have a car to repair."

Dragan didn't smile at the gibe. He watched Simon leave without another word.

Outside, the wind had freshened. The ocean was a flurry of whitecaps. Gusts forced women to grab their skirts and men to hold on to their hats.

As Simon walked, he tried to place Dragan's accent. Central European? Russian? Further east, maybe? He wasn't sure. He decided that Dragan reminded him of a senator from ancient Rome. The one who'd stabbed Caesar.

CHAPTER 19

Vika arrived at the headquarters of the police *judiciaire* at 9 Rue Suffren Reymond at exactly ten o'clock. It was a four-story concrete slab sandwiched between other like buildings a block up from the port. She gazed up at its angular, undistinguished facade, thinking that surely it deserved an award for being proudly ugly and entirely forgettable at the same time. The word POLICE stood above the entry in large red block letters that she could tell lit up at night.

At the reception, she gave her name and asked for the *commissaire*.

"He is expecting you," said a secretary without meeting her gaze. "Please sit."

Vika looked at the row of plastic chairs and decided to remain standing. From the start it had been a difficult day. A day for confronting the past, for taking a long hard look at herself, and for coming to terms with the present.

It had begun at five, when daybreak was two hours away and the bed was suddenly her worst enemy. Unable to sleep, she'd risen and visited the hotel's fitness room, where she'd spent an hour on the elliptical. After a breakfast of coffee and toast, she'd put on her sensible shoes and made her way to Princess Grace Hospital to claim her mother's body. It wasn't her first visit to a morgue. All of her family had predeceased her, excepting her son. She was expecting the institutional lights, the odor of tart disinfectant that made her eyes water and set her instantly on edge, the alien environment that screamed *"This is not a place where the living belong."* Nonetheless, the sight of the corpse, partially burned, the face disfigured, the neck swollen grotesquely, had upset her. She hadn't expected to cry.

A daughter should not have to look upon her mother's lifeless body when they hadn't seen each other in years, not when the last time they'd spoken her mother had been blind drunk, and mostly not when there wasn't a detail about her death that made a whit of sense.

A visit to the *mairie,* or town hall, followed. There she'd signed a raft of papers, necessary to officially proclaim her mother deceased. She'd lost count of the number of times she'd signed her name. The paperwork had calmed her, if only by blunting her emotions.

And now the police.

A door slammed farther back in the building. Footsteps advanced down the hall. A brisk, officious man dressed in his formal uniform, silver epaulets, a braided cordon hanging from his shoulder, approached her. "Hello, Madame la…"

"Ms. Brandt."

The man bowed his head. "I wasn't sure how to address you. I am Rémy Le Juste, *commissaire* of the Police Urbaine. Follow me."

Le Juste was fit and bald and walked as if on parade, which Vika imagined he thought he was. Three officers, also in formal uniforms, lined the corridor, backs to the wall, heads bowed. She wished them good morning and followed Commissaire Le Juste into his office. He showed her to a chair facing his desk and waited until she sat before taking his own seat.

"So," he began. "You have been to the hospital and to the town hall."

"Yes. Very efficient," said Vika, with a nod of the head. "I appreciate all you've done."

"Only our duty. It is a tragedy."

"Thankfully no one else was hurt."

"This is true." Le Juste inquired about her trip and her lodging, showing surprise that she was staying in the hotel when she had other options.

Vika scooted to the edge of her chair.

"Please, Commissaire, can you walk me through the incident again?" she asked. "I was distraught when we spoke the other night. The surprise…you can imagine."

She was lying, at least a little. The news, sudden though it was, had not been entirely unexpected. It wasn't her mother's passing so much as the details surrounding the accident that caused her agitation.

Three nights earlier, Le Juste began, Vika's mother, Stefanie, age seventy-two, had left her apartment alone and driven her Rolls-Royce convertible to the Grande Corniche, where she guided the car west, in the direction of Villefranche and Nice.

(Vika knew the route well. The Grande Corniche was a narrow, curvy, constantly hazardous road running along the crest of the mountains from Monaco to Nice. It had hardly been improved since Napoleon had built it two hundred years earlier.)

A few kilometers past the turnoff for the N4 autoroute, she'd missed a curve, crashed through a guardrail, and driven straight off the cliff. From the trajectory of the car's flight, it was estimated that she was driving well over the speed limit, probably faster than one hundred kilometers per hour. There were no skid marks. The automobile fell one hundred meters before landing on its roof and tumbling a further distance down the mountainside. There had been a fire. At some point, Vika's mother had broken her neck. Death was instantaneous, the doctor had assured him.

All this Commissaire Le Juste explained with his deepest sympathy.

"And this occurred at what time?" Vika asked.

"Just after midnight."

"How can you be sure?"

"The clock."

"Pardon?"

"The car had an analog clock in the dashboard that stopped at the time of the accident."

Meaning, Vika understood, that it had stopped when the car smashed onto the rocks below.

"And there was no one else in the car?"

"No, madame."

"Just my mother?"

Le Juste shifted in his chair. It was apparent that he resented her questions. "*Ah, oui.* She was intoxicated."

"Intoxicated people often drive with others."

"I have the report for your inspection…"

"She was always intoxicated," said Vika. "That's why she never drove."

She clasped her hands in her lap and sat up straight, a teacher speaking to a difficult student. "*Monsieur le commissaire,* my mother had a detached retina in her right eye. It was difficult for her to drive under any circumstance. At night, it was impossible due to the refraction of light from oncoming headlights."

"Is that so?" asked Le Juste.

"It is. She rarely left her apartment. When she did, she had a helper who drove. A woman who did her shopping and took her to doctor's appointments."

Le Juste considered this as long as politeness demanded. "And yet, that evening she did," he said.

"That's my point. It doesn't make sense."

"Madame Brandt, I am a policeman. My opinions are not my own. They are dictated by the evidence. In this matter, the facts are unequivocal."

"Then you don't have all the facts."

Le Juste sat forward, eager to parry her retort. "Is there something you are not telling us? If so, please. I'm waiting. I welcome any evidence you wish to add to the record."

Vika did not answer. There was something else, something that in her view was sufficient to launch an investigation. She doubted, however, that the police would find a voice mail left by a woman in a blackout drunk reliable grounds to do so.

"*Vika, are you there? Can you hear me?*" her mother had begun on the voice mail that constituted their last communication. Her words were clear, her diction impeccable. "*I'm in trouble. You've got to come down and help me. There's a man. He wants to know about the family. I didn't tell him anything. Of course, you know I'd never. But he keeps asking. I'm worried for you. For Fritz. I didn't say a word. Please, darling. I thought he was my friend, but now I'm worried. He scares me."*

At that point, the conversation took a sharp turn. The diction lost its precision. The voice grew clotted. Vika had realized that her mother was drunk. Very drunk.

"You were always your father's favorite. Far more than I was. The bastard. He was a sick man. You know that, don't you? He got what he deserved." A crazed laugh, then a lengthy pause, a rattling of glass in the background, and her mother started over in her clear aristocratic voice, as if the phone had just picked up and she was leaving her message all over again.

"Vika, are you there? Can you hear me? I'm in trouble. You've got to come down and help me. There's a man."

"No," said Vika. "I don't have any additional evidence. I was hoping that enlightening you about my mother's condition would lead you to reexamine the accident."

"And open a criminal case? Are you suggesting she was murdered?"

"No," said Vika, and she meant it. "I'm suggesting she may not have been alone that night. All I know is that she could not...*she would not*...have driven her car up to the Grande Corniche—then, or at any other time—all by herself. It's out of the question."

"Do you have an idea who she might have driven with? A name, perhaps? If so, we would be more than happy to speak with this person."

"If I had, I certainly would have told you. I mean, just where in the hell was she supposed to be going?" Vika said in frustration, at once angry with herself for losing her calm.

"I don't think you should be considering murder, but perhaps something else."

Vika flinched. At least he was polite enough not to say it. Suicide. The thought had crossed her mind and vanished immediately thereafter. Her mother was a devout Catholic. Besides that, she was happy, living in her own little world, manufacturing all her byzantine plots and rumors, having her vodkas, dressing for lunch and dinner, and ordering her helper, poor Elena, hither and yon. Le Juste was wrong, but Vika couldn't fault his logic.

"Madame?" Le Juste pushed a box of tissues she didn't need across the desk. Vika pushed them back. After a moment, she said, "What about the tapes from her apartment?"

"Tapes?"

"Security cameras. Something showing her driving out of the garage that night. Or one from the lobby or elevator. The building has cameras everywhere. Have you looked at them?"

"No."

"Why not?"

Le Juste considered this. "We would need to open a criminal investigation in order to gain access to the building's security apparatus. If, that is, there are tapes and they are still intact."

"What do you mean?"

"Security systems are all the same. After a few days the tapes or discs record over themselves. It is a question of storage space."

"Is that so?" Vika's smile was exquisite torture. "Then we had better check today."

Le Juste squirmed in his chair, already shaking his head.

"We won't know until we look," Vika continued. "Given everything I've just told you, I would think you would be as interested as I am to see what's on those cameras."

"It is not so simple," said Rémy Le Juste, with offense. A line had been crossed. A diplomatic incident risked. "Only a *juge d'instruction* can issue a subpoena for such tapes. It is not a question of just 'checking.' A formal case must be opened and for that we must have grounds."

"Perhaps the tape will provide the grounds."

"The facts are clear, madame. Your mother's Rolls-Royce drove off the Grande Corniche a little after midnight with a sole occupant. It was an accident. Nothing more."

"I thought the job of police was to investigate. What are you afraid of finding?" Vika stood. "I've taken up too much of your time already. You've been very helpful."

Le Juste rose and made to come around the desk. Vika stopped him with an icy glance. "Thank you again."

Le Juste sank back into his chair. "My assistant will give you your mother's affairs."

Vika left the station, a tight smile on her face, lips pursed to keep her from shouting exactly what she thought of Le Juste and his "grounds." The meeting had not gone as expected. She'd arrived certain that when told about her mother's condition, Le Juste would be quick to adopt her point of view and zealously launch an investigation into her mother's death. That was not the case.

Gazing with disdain at the building's unwelcoming facade, she crossed the street and walked into the first café she saw. Inside, she set the plastic bag containing her mother's effects on the table and ordered an espresso. She drank it slowly, pondering her next steps. Over the years, she'd developed what some called a "contrary nature." The word "no" had stopped having its intended effect. Instead, it acted as an accelerant, urging her to follow her own inevitably more logical and well-reasoned course of action. In this case, however, she didn't know where to begin.

First things first.

One last inventory.

Vika finished her espresso and opened the plastic bag holding her mother's affairs.

One watch, Papa's old Breitling Navitimer, which had hung like a millstone on Mama's wrist.

One diamond ring. Eight carats, pear-shaped, so white it threatened to blind you, as near flawless as such a large stone can be, set on a platinum band.

Vika couldn't imagine wearing such a thing. It was an affront, a million-dollar middle finger raised at the rest of the world. The rest of the world being not only the less moneyed but the untitled. Those poor lambs not mentioned in the pages of the *Almanach de Gotha*.

One wedding band.

Not from husband two—Bismarck, they had called him because he claimed to be German, but he wasn't. Not really. It was the wedding ring Papa had given her. A simple gold band. A tear came to Vika's eye as she rolled the ring between her fingers. Her mother and father had truly loved each other, if in their own strange way.

Vika decided that she'd wear it when she remarried. Or rather, *if.* Any man who opted to marry into the family would have to be crazy, and thus, by definition, unsuitable.

She swiped angrily at her cheek and proceeded through her mother's effects.

One Cartier tennis bracelet.

One Bulgari *serpenti* wristlet.

One wallet. A single credit card. The stupid black one for snobs only. No driver's license. No other identification. No money. It was a point of pride that Mama never carried paper currency. And tucked inside a fold, photos of Vika and Fritz. *It's just the two of us now,* Vika thought, looking at her son. *The rest are all gone.*

One pair of sunglasses. Black aviators. Odd for someone to take with them on a midnight drive. But odd enough to constitute grounds for an investigation?

She set them down.

The bag was empty.

It took Vika a moment to realize that something was missing. Not just something, but the most important thing.

She ran her fingers through the bag, though she could see perfectly well that nothing more was inside.

Vika clasped her hands and put them on the table. When she was angry or upset, which was far too often, she made herself sit still and take a deep breath. The ring bearing the family crest was missing. A chunk of fourteen-karat gold with their ancient coat of arms expertly carved into a square face. Two hundred years old, and itself a replica of those that came before it. In all her life, Vika had never seen her mother without it. And before her, Papa the same.

"He wants to know about the family . . . I didn't say a word."

A chill gripped Vika. She hadn't given those particular words much thought. It was her mother's fear of being harmed that had roused Vika's concern. But now, with the ring missing, she knew she'd discounted them too soon. Maybe he wasn't just asking but digging for information about the family's most private affairs.

Vika turned her head in the direction of the police station. Was the ring enough to rouse Le Juste's concern, too?

Of course it wasn't. She had the feeling that Le Juste's mind had been made up.

Vika left a twenty-euro note on the table and fled the café. She knew what must be done. She'd spent the last ten years saving the family, defending it against all comers, prevailing over indomitable odds. This was different, however. Her foe was not the law, not some obscure codicil from a dusty legal tome or a technicality in the tax codes. It was a person.

"Please, darling. I thought he was my friend, but now I'm worried. He scares me."

One last crusade, then. Le Juste could go to hell. It would be up to Vika to find out exactly what had happened to her mother and how it came to be that she was driving on the Grande Corniche at midnight.

First things first.

Where was the ring?

Chapter 20

Vika left the café and headed toward Boulevard Albert 1er and the hotel. It was just after ten. An offshore breeze made the sun more bearable. Everyone was dressed in shorts and colorful attire. Music playing from loudspeakers along the port drifted through the narrow streets. For all intents and purposes, summer was still in full swing.

She hadn't expected it to be so warm, not ten days into October. Fall was well advanced at home. The forest around her estate burned fiery shades of persimmon and rust. The next storm would dash the last stubborn leaves from the trees. Vika wiped a bead of sweat from her forehead and looked up the incline toward the opera house. Her mother had lived on the other side of the hill, halfway down the Plage du Larvotto. Vika dug in her purse for the keys, only to drop them back inside. The apartment couldn't answer her questions. She knew one person who could.

Vika found a piece of shade beneath the awning of a small *gelateria*. A stream of cold air escaped the door, along with the enticing scents of chocolate and *fragolini*. She consulted her phone and noted that Elena had still not returned her calls. Elena Mancini, her mother's helper, was sixty-something, a squat, earthy Sicilian, more peasant than not, though Vika knew that was a horrible thing to say.

For the past ten years, Elena had spent nearly every day with Vika's mother. She was not just her helper, but her companion, maid, and, most important, her confidante. As such, she was forbidden from being anything more than polite to Vika. Battle lines between mother and daughter had been drawn long ago. Like her Sicilian ancestors, Elena was loyal to a fault.

Vika phoned her again. Again, the call rolled to voice mail. She frowned. Apparently, omertà was not reserved for the mafia alone. Vika brought up her list of contacts. She had two addresses for Elena. One for her apartment in the city, the second for her home in the hills above Ventimiglia, an hour's drive across the Italian border. Vika mapped the apartment's location and saw that it was on the outskirts of the city, a twenty-five-minute walk uphill. Everything in Monaco was either up the hill or down the hill. So be it, then. Pulling the strap of her purse over her shoulder, she set off up the hill.

She left the commercial district, mostly office buildings housing notaries, attorneys, and accountants, with the occasional pharmacy or hair salon. After a quarter of an hour, she could see the botanical garden to her left—even further up the hill. Elena's apartment was to the right. Vika needed a moment before continuing. The short trek made clear that she was not in the shape she'd thought. Vika was a great planner of exercise and a terrible practitioner. Every week, she'd map out a vigorous schedule of Pilates and spin and cardio classes and reserve two mornings for a brisk hour's walk through the forest. Rarely did she honor even one of those commitments.

Gathering her breath, she observed a man walking up the sidewalk a half block behind her. He was slim and dark-haired and pale. It was his legs Vika noticed. He was wearing shorts and his knees and calves were as white as ivory. She'd seen him earlier, across the street from the *gelateria*. He stared right back and his cold gaze sent a shiver up her spine.

Dismissing him, Vika continued to her destination. Elena's apartment was a six-story slab of concrete with shaded terraces and window boxes brimming with colorful flowers. The lobby door stood open. She found Elena's name on the directory—MANCINI 6F—and pushed her buzzer. Vika lowered her ear closer to the intercom. No one responded.

The elevator brought her to the sixth floor. In a measure to keep the building cool, the lights were kept off. A corridor extended to her left, tapering into darkness. She slowed at each doorway to read the name below the doorbell. Of course there were no numbers on the doors. Vika found Elena's apartment at the end of the hall, needing her phone's flashlight to read the nameplate.

She thumbed the doorbell. A buzzer sounded. When no one answered, she knocked and put her ear to the door. Silence. Then a faint meow. She tried the handle. Locked. "Elena," she said. "It's me. Victoria."

"She's not there."

Vika spun, gasping. An older, portly man stood directly behind her. He was dressed in work pants and a stained white T-shirt stretched tightly over an enormous belly. A heavy set of keys hung from his belt. The building superintendent.

"Have you seen her?" Vika asked after a moment.

"Who are you?"

"A friend. Elena worked for my mother."

The man considered this. He had terrible bags under his eyes and a two-day stubble. "Go," he said.

"I only want to know if you've seen Elena."

"I told you. She's not there. Tell your friends."

"Excuse me?"

"I only open the door for family. They weren't family. Neither are you."

"Someone else was here looking for Elena?"

"Go," he said again.

"It's important that I—"

"Now," the man said forcefully, his voice echoing down the hall.

Vika slid around his large form. "Of course," she said.

Outside the building, she saw the pale, dark-haired man still standing at the corner. Hands in his pockets, he leaned against the bus shelter. He made no disguise of the fact that he was watching her.

Vika hugged her bag to her side and hurried down the hill.

CHAPTER 21

Simon sped east along the Grande Corniche, approaching the ancient Roman town of La Turbie. A map spread on the passenger seat showed the time trial route. He glanced at it, then returned his attention to the road, its curves and straightaways, where it widened and where it narrowed, calculating where he might gain time and where he must avoid losing it. He thought of Dov Dragan, his towering arrogance and false sincerity. He decided it would feel good to beat him. Very good.

High on the mountain, Simon enjoyed a view far down the Ligurian coast toward Menton and Ventimiglia and, with the air this clear, across the Bay of Roquebrune to San Remo. To his right, below a vertical precipice diving hundreds of feet, his gaze fell upon the Rock, the elevated peninsula of golden granite jutting from the western border of Monaco that was home to the royal palace and a small army of government buildings.

In a world of elastic borders, warring monarchs, and oft-changing governments, Monaco had been ruled by one family for seven hundred years, the Grimaldis of Genoa. Over that time, the principality's allegiances had shifted from Italy to Sardinia to France (which currently guaranteed the territory's sovereignty, in exchange for a lemminglike adherence to its foreign policy). The territory's size had something to do with its independence. It was a postage stamp with no natural resources, no strategic values, not much of anything to entice an invader to expend precious blood or treasure. Monaco was neither thorn nor rose.

Everything changed with the building of the casino in 1863. It was the era of the grand tour, the Baedeker guide, and the world's first travel agent, Thomas Cook. A stop in Monaco, situated on a scenic spit of coastline between Nice and Capri, two perennial destinations, became de rigueur. Overnight, the principality had a personality where before it had none.

Since then, Monaco had known only growth and prosperity, its coronation as capital of the jet set occurring when the American actress Grace Kelly married Prince Rainier in 1956. Not long afterward, in 1969, the prince abolished income taxes. Monaco's status as a favored home for movie stars, professional athletes, and the obscenely wealthy was forever cemented into place.

Ahead, the road narrowed and curved sharply to the left. Simon downshifted into second gear, using the engine to slow. He did not see the blue station wagon until he was nearly upon it, and he didn't decide to stop and check if it was the same station wagon that had parked behind him the night before at the Hôtel de Paris until he'd gone a good way past.

Simon yanked the car to the dirt berm on his side of the road and killed the engine. He got out and approached the car. German plates. KO for Cologne. It was the same car, all right, but he saw no sign of Vika Brandt.

The front door was ajar. He looked in all directions, but she was nowhere to be found. He noted that a section of the guardrail had recently been replaced and walked over to inspect it. He saw her standing ten meters down the hillside. There was no path. It was a treacherous descent over exposed rock and loose terrain. A few steps below her, the escarpment fell away altogether. Should she slip, she would fall to her death.

A large tourist coach rumbled past behind Simon, distracting him. When he looked back down the hillside, he saw that Vika was bent at the waist examining an object, much as an archaeologist studies an artifact. He called her name but his voice was drowned out by the noise of passing traffic.

Simon climbed over the rail and made his way down the slope. He used his hands to aid his stability; even so, his feet slipped and he loosened a spray of rocks. The woman didn't seem to notice. He sideslipped the last distance, pleased to have reached a narrow plateau of sorts.

"Stay away!" Without warning, the woman spun. She held a pistol in her hand, a compact semiautomatic.

Simon raised his hands, palms outward. "You're pointing a gun at me."

"Keep away, I said."

Simon backed up a step, checking over his shoulder to make sure he had one more, just in case.

"What are you doing here?" she asked.

"I was driving the course for the time trial," he said, gesturing toward the road. "I recognized your station wagon. I thought you might need help."

"I don't."

"I can see that."

"Were you following me last night, too?"

"'Too'? I was out walking. I'm happy we ran into each other. Then, I mean. Now, I'm not so sure."

Vika lowered the pistol, shoulders relaxing. "They make me carry this. It's not even loaded."

"In which case, I feel safer," said Simon. "And you can put it away."

The pistol disappeared into a purse at her side. She brushed past him, her eyes on the incline. Simon offered her a hand. She ignored it and scrambled up the slope. He followed, slipping only once. She was nimbler, and at least he had a nice view. By the time he regained the road, he had plenty of questions, starting with what she was doing risking her life on a steep mountainside. He knew better than to ask.

"You weren't frightened," she said, brushing the dust off her hands.

"Excuse me?"

She continued to the car and tossed her purse and whatever else besides the pistol she'd put inside it onto the front seat. She was dressed in light-colored pants and a blue linen shirt, her tan moccasins unsuitable for exploring anything more treacherous than a department store escalator. Turning back toward Simon, she removed her sunglasses. "I pointed a gun at you and you didn't bat an eye."

"What did you expect me to do?"

"I don't know. Just something more. Show a little surprise. Fear, even. Weren't you?"

"Scared or surprised?"

"Mr. Riske."

"I was certainly surprised."

"That's all you have to say?"

Simon looked at her and nodded. She considered this. Up close, her gaze was so direct it was unsettling. "What do you do, Mr. Riske, for a living?"

He seemed to be getting asked the same question a lot these days. "I own an automobile restoration business in London. On the side, I solve problems."

"Are you sure it isn't the other way around?"

If there was a right answer, Simon didn't know it. "Did you find what you were looking for?" he asked.

"That's my business."

"If you'd like to keep looking, I'm happy to help."

"That won't be necessary."

A sparkle in the sky caught Simon's eye. He walked a few feet from the car, shielding his eyes as he looked upward. There it was again. Only then did he hear the high-pitched whir of an engine. Then he saw it. A drone—a small one, white, four propellers, nearly invisible against the blue sky—hovering a hundred feet above their heads.

"What is it?" she asked.

Simon pointed in the direction of the drone. "There."

Vika looked to the sky, squinting. "I don't see anything."

"Look."

Vika raised her hands to her eyes to block out the sun.

Behind them, a car rounded the curve, its engine screaming. Too loud. Louder than any other car that had passed. At once, Simon spun. A sedan. Silver. Traveling at high speed. The car crossed the center line, going far too wide, seemingly out of control. The sun reflected off the windscreen so that Simon could not see the driver. Instead of correcting, the car continued straight at them. At Vika. The tires howled as the driver veered onto the hardscrabble berm. Simon ran at Vika, grabbing her in his arms and throwing them both onto the ground. A shower of gravel and dirt. The deafening growl of the engine. A terrific screech as the tires regained the asphalt, and the car was gone.

Simon lay still, aware that he was lying on top of the woman, too stunned to do anything about it. "You okay?"

Vika nodded. "Was that an accident?" she asked.

Simon looked over his shoulder and gazed into the sky. The drone was gone. "Possibly."

"Only possibly?"

He rolled off the woman. Getting to his feet, he offered her a hand. This time she accepted it. She stood and brushed herself off. Her shirt was torn. Through the flap of fabric, he could see a trace of blood, an abrasion on her shoulder.

"It's nothing," said Vika, eyeing the wound.

"You're sure?"

"Considering the alternative." She angled her head. "Only possibly? Really?"

Simon's silence was the best answer he could give. The real answer was, "No. Not possibly. Certainly." He had no doubt that the driver had been aiming for Vika. He thought it wiser not to sound the alarm until he knew more about her.

They stood for a moment, not speaking, each's eyes on the other. Something had changed between them. A bond existed where none was before.

"Mr. Riske," she said, "exactly what kind of problems do you solve?"

"Difficult ones."

Vika Brandt drew a breath and spent a moment arranging her hair. The color had returned to her face. She drew her shoulders back and a sense of purpose took hold of her.

An army of one, Simon thought.

"Shall we have lunch?" she said. "I know a place in Èze."

"Would you like me to drive?"

Her hands were rock steady as she took the keys from her purse. "Follow me."

CHAPTER 22

The restaurant was in an old stone home with a shaded garden. They sat at a table beneath a centuries-old oak whose leaves showed the first hint of gold. Their feet brushed a carpet of white gravel. Tête de Chien, the enormous outcropping of stone that kept vigil over Monaco, loomed in the distance. They'd both ordered the salade Niçoise. Neither had managed a bite. No wine for either of them. Just mineral water. Between sips, Vika related the reason for her visit, beginning with details of her mother's accident and her suspicions about it, moving on to her visit to the police that morning ("Damn the *juge d'instruction!*"), and finally, and with reluctance, concluding with the voice mail her mother had left before her death.

"The thing is I didn't believe her," explained Vika Brandt. "It wasn't the first time she'd called in one of her states."

"'States'?"

"Drunk. Wildly drunk. Blackout drunk. It didn't matter. She said the same things sober. She thought people were always looking at her strangely, talking behind her back. Men ogled her. Women said nasty things about her. The help made obscene remarks. She was very imaginative."

"She was ill, then."

"Who knows? Alcoholism, paranoia, delusions of grandeur—it all runs in the family. They used to call people like her 'quirky.' She refused to go to the doctor. For anything. A few years ago, she fell and broke her arm. A hairline fracture. She wouldn't allow Elena to take her to the emergency room until it swelled up like a balloon three days later."

"Elena?"

"Her helper. Elena Mancini. She's been with my mother for years."

"How often did she stop in?"

"Almost every day. She took my mother to church and to lunch, did her shopping, and helped around the place." Vika leaned forward. "Is it true what Le Juste said about not being able to check the security cameras without a warrant?"

"Officially, yes," said Simon. "In reality, no. No way. Apartment managers like to keep on good terms with the police. Given the circumstances, I can't see how they'd refuse a request. Not when it had to do with one of their tenants."

"Then why was Le Juste being so difficult?"

"It seems he had his mind made up. I can't see it." Simon enumerated what he considered the critical facts. Medical evidence of a detached retina, a witness to testify that her mother hadn't driven for years, and finally a message in which her mother expressed concern for her safety.

"There's no witness. Not yet. I haven't spoken to Elena. She hasn't replied to my calls."

"Is that normal?"

"I don't know. I went by her place in town this morning. She wasn't there." Vika shrugged. "She's from the old country. She sees things differently."

"Is there something else?"

Vika averted her eyes. "I didn't tell Le Juste about the call from my mother."

"Oh?"

"It wouldn't have changed his mind."

"It would have changed mine," said Simon, without judgment.

"It's beside the point, anyway," retorted Vika. "Mama did not drive. She couldn't have been alone in the car, call or not. I don't care how frightened she may or may not have been."

Simon took his time before speaking. He could see that she was distraught, that she needed to get something off her chest. "Why didn't you tell Le Juste about the voice mail?" he asked gently.

"The prying. The attention. It's been hard enough keeping her death quiet."

"You think others would be interested?"

Vika shook her head with exasperation. "Only the press of every country in Europe."

"Now there's something you're not telling me."

Vika twisted her napkin, staring past him. "It just doesn't make sense. None of it. Why would anyone want to hurt Mama? She was harmless."

"They wanted to hurt you, too."

"You said possibly."

"I was being diplomatic."

"I didn't tell Commissaire Le Juste about the call because… because…" Vika exhaled loudly and smiled briefly, fixing Simon with a forthcoming gaze. "I owe you an apology, Mr. Riske. I lied to you."

"Oh?"

"My name isn't Brandt. It is Victoria Elizabeth Margaretha Brandenburg von Tiefen und Tassis. And you might as well throw a 'princess' in before all of that. If I'd told Le Juste about the call, it would have been on the front page of every tabloid in Germany tomorrow, and everywhere else the day after. 'Dowager Princess Stefanie Feared for Life Before Fatal Accident.'"

"For once the headline would have been accurate."

Simon's smile was met with a frown. "You're American. You don't know anything about the family."

"True. I don't."

"We're German. From Hesse. Right in the center of the country. The title goes back a thousand years. Silly, I know, but that counts for something. The von Tiefen und Tassis family is the largest private landowner in Germany. Mama is a Schoenberg—nobility to be sure, but penniless. She married my father when she was young and he was middle-aged. She was twenty and wild. She kept her hair dyed pink and practically lived in discotheques. He was nearly sixty and a confirmed bachelor, which, of course, meant he was homosexual. He married Mama because she didn't care who he slept with and because he wanted to further the line. I believe they loved each other dearly.

"For a while they were in the press every day. They called Mama 'Princess TNT.' She loved it. She fulfilled her part of the bargain and gave my father three children. Over the years, we did our best to maintain the family reputation as crazed, tragic aristocrats. Papa had a heart attack in his lover's bed. My two older brothers died at a young age. Freddy was killed in a racing accident—now you know why I feel the way I do about cars—and Michael took drugs. My own husband, Christof, died shortly after we were married. Cancer."

"I'm sorry."

"We've provided enough fodder for the press all these years. I've labored to my wit's end to erase our family legacy. Perhaps now you'll understand why I chose to edit the information I provided to the police."

"I think I do. I appreciate you trusting me."

"I don't trust you, Mr. Riske, at least not yet. I need your help. That is all."

The server arrived to clear their plates, not masking his offense that they had not eaten their salads. "It was not good?" he asked repeatedly. Vika promised him it was delicious and ordered coffee. Simon asked for tea. They commented on the flowers and the unseasonably warm weather. The tea and coffee arrived. She drank hers black. Simon added cream and sugar. He allowed a few minutes to pass in companionable silence.

He finished his tea and moved the saucer to the side of the table.

"May I ask you a few questions?" he began.

"Of course."

He smiled knowingly. "I'd prefer truthful answers."

Vika responded in kind. "I'll do my best."

"How much is your family worth?"

"Is that really important?"

"I'll know after you answer."

Vika made a show of blowing out her breath, all puffed cheeks and pursed lips. She listed her assets as if dogged by a poor memory. There were castles and artworks and bonds and shares, she explained in fits and starts, and a yacht and apartments here and villas there, but in the end, what Vika's family had most was land, owning over three million acres, primarily wild, uninhabited old-growth forests in the central state of Hesse. When pressed to put a dollar value on it all, Vika grew even more cagey. All the numbers were just pie-in-the-sky estimations. Her accountants couldn't be trusted. No one really knew what any of it was worth.

"Approximately," said Simon.

"Ten billion dollars." Vika threw out the number as if it were a guess.

Simon simply nodded. He understood now why she carried a pistol. If it were him, he would have carried a much larger one with dumdum bullets and a spare magazine.

"Actually, closer to twelve," she added, as if disappointed she hadn't gotten the response she'd wanted.

"Twelve," said Simon.

"But it's primarily tied up in fixed assets, mind you, not to mention an irrevocable trust. It's not like there is a pile of money lying around."

"I imagine you have at least two percent liquid." The rule was five percent up to a hundred million, then a declining scale above that.

"Please," said Vika, taken aback. "Never less than six."

"Six hundred million."

She nodded, indicating that it was a prudent figure.

"Six hundred million is a lot of cash."

"I see that look in your eye. Don't say anything. You're right. It is a large sum."

"Vast," said Simon.

"Vast."

"Enormous."

"Yes, it is enormous."

"Incomprehensible."

A narrowing of the eyes. "Not even close."

Simon laughed.

"May I continue?" asked Vika, unamused.

"Please."

"After my father died, I was sent away to boarding school in Switzerland. I was ten. It was just then that the scale of his mismanagement of the family estate was coming to light. We learned in short order that we had no cash. And I mean zero, *nul, nichts*. Nothing. Our accounts were empty or overdrawn. Our properties had been mortgaged and mortgaged again. It's quite amazing the stupid things that smart people can do."

Simon merely nodded, aware that this was not a story that Vika revealed to many others.

"So, anyway," she said, drawing a breath, "there I was at boarding school. At first, I was happy to be away from Mother and her antics. I longed for stability. For a chance to be someone other than the daughter of Princess TNT. I thought being on my own was a godsend. I was wrong. The day I arrived I realized something was different. All the other girls were boarding buses to go on a field trip to Milan to see an opera at La Scala. I wasn't permitted to go. I was informed then, and for the first time, that I was a scholarship student. My tuition would be paid for by public relations work done on behalf of the school…You know, the pretty blond German princess holding her books under one arm…"

"Not so bad," said Simon.

"And," she added, "by working in the school kitchen. I was to report to the cafeteria thirty minutes before each meal and stay one hour after to help clear and wash the dishes. Weekends, my hours were six a.m. to twelve noon. Saturday *and* Sunday."

"I worked in a kitchen," said Simon. "Hard duty."

"When you were ten?"

"Twenty-six," he conceded.

Vika exhaled and averted her gaze, looking off into the distance. "Cherries," she said.

"Pardon?"

"Cherries," she repeated, her gaze coming back to him. "My first Saturday, I arrived to find five garbage pails filled with cherries at my station in the kitchen. The school fund-raiser was to take place that evening. Cherry tarts were on the menu for dessert. There were three hundred guests. Each was to receive two tarts. Four cherries on each. My job was to pit the cherries. Do you know how to pit a cherry, Mr. Riske?"

Simon said he did not.

"You take hold of one like so." Vika picked up an imaginary cherry with her thumb and forefinger. "Then you insert the pitting knife at the bottom, thrust upward, turn, and voilà, the pit comes out with the knife. It's quite easy once you get the hang of it."

Simon could see that it wasn't easy at all, certainly not for a ten-year-old girl who'd probably never sliced an apple for herself.

"Seven hours," she said. "That's how long it took. No break. There wasn't time. When I finished, the pastry chef told me I'd gone through three thousand cherries to get the twenty-four-hundred intact ones needed for the tarts." Vika held out her hand across the table. Simon took it. It was a beautiful hand—long tapered fingers, no rings, nail polish a rich shade of caramel. "My fingers were dyed crimson for a month. Sometimes I still think I can see a bit deep under the skin. Did I mention it was an all-girls school? They had very imaginative nicknames for me." She made a fist and angled it to one side. "See there…that knot?"

Simon looked closely. "A knot?"

"I didn't like some of the nicknames. I let the others know."

"With your fist?"

"Both of them." She nodded solemnly, then pulled her hand back. "So you see, Mr. Riske, after four years of serving as a kitchen maid, and many more years of work after that, until I was able to sort out the family's affairs myself, I learned the value of having money in the bank."

Simon met her eyes but said nothing. The server arrived once again and noted with pleasure that they'd enjoyed their coffee and tea. He asked if they desired something to enliven their palates before they left. A Calvados, perhaps? Or a Williams? Vika thanked him, but no. The server cleared away their dishes and promised to return with the bill.

Simon wiped his mouth and set the napkin in his lap. "I have one more question," he said.

"I've talked far too much about the family for one day."

"It isn't about the family."

"I'm waiting."

"What did you find on the hillside?"

109

Vika sat back, surprised. "I suppose I should be pleased you're so observant." She removed a trinket from her clutch and set it on the table. It was a cuff link, though half of the face was chipped off.

"I'd say you're the observant one. How did you spot this?"

"Good eyes."

"I take it this isn't your mother's."

"Not unless she began wearing men's cuff links in the past year. Oh, and she was wearing a dress when she died."

Simon picked it up. An oval face, or half of one, a white enamel background with a sword or a star and symbols that looked like ancient runes. It was difficult to tell anything further.

"My mother did not drive off the cliff, Mr. Riske. Someone killed her. Someone abominable."

"I believe you," said Simon. "The question is, why?"

CHAPTER 23

Ratka was watching soccer.

He sat on the recliner in the main salon of the *Lady S,* eyes trained on the wall-mounted screen. It was the 2006 Serbian Cup final. Belgrade in black was playing Novi Sad in red. Regulation time had ended with the score tied one to one. It had come to a penalty shoot-out. The score was tied three to three. Each team had one try remaining.

Ratka had viewed the match over a hundred times, the very first time as the owner of FK Novi Sad and standing on the sidelines inside the stadium. He'd purchased the team in 2005, when it was a third-division club whose roster consisted of hard-playing amateurs, most of whom held down blue-collar jobs forty hours a week. He'd known from the start that it was hopeless to expect them to compete with teams in the higher divisions, in which all the players were professionals.

And so Ratka had proposed his own unique solution to the problem. If his players couldn't win on their own, he would give them a hand. People often referred to the fans as the twelfth player. The fans in Novi Sad didn't count for spit, so he introduced a twelfth player, and a thirteenth and a fourteenth. Their names were blackmail, extortion, bribery, and, if necessary, outright assault. That was fifteen players, but so what? The only math he'd ever learned was how to count stolen money.

Ratka, born Zoltan Alexander Mikhailovic, was chief of the Silver Tigers crime syndicate, originally formed in Belgrade, the capital of the former Yugoslavia, in the 1980s. The Silver Tigers had made their name carrying out bank robberies, jewelry thefts, and kidnappings. With the fall of the Iron Curtain, the gang expanded its zone of activity across all of Europe. Good times. At least for a while. After a few setbacks, including his stint in prison, Ratka brought the gang to the South of France, a newly rich hunting ground after the resurgence of Russia. Antibes, Cannes, Saint-Tropez, and Monaco were favored haunts of the megarich oligarch class.

That was almost ten years ago. It felt like one hundred since he'd been on that sideline.

Ratka sat up, driving away his laments. Now he had a chance to get back to where he'd been. Not just as the owner of a soccer club. That was small potatoes. He had his eye on something bigger. Far bigger.

On the screen, his team's best player set the ball on the spot, made his approach, and fired. The goalie jumped right. The ball went right. Too far right and missed the goal entirely.

"Govno!" Ratka shouted, jumping toward the television, fist balled. It was Serbian for "shit."

If Belgrade made the next penalty, they would win the championship.

Ratka stifled a bitter smile. Having foreseen this very possibility all those years ago, he'd kidnapped number 23's mother and sister and let the player know that they would be released only if Belgrade lost. Otherwise, they would be killed. He'd made the call to the player himself.

Number 23 placed the ball on the spot. The crowd, already deafening, grew louder still. One hundred thousand crazed Serbs—seventy thousand for Belgrade, thirty thousand for Novi Sad—shouted at the top of their lungs.

Ratka watched himself on the screen, standing there on the sidelines with his arms crossed, his future hanging in the balance. In contrast to the opposing team's owner, Ratka was the picture of calm. Handsome, composed, confident that his side would prevail.

The referee blew the whistle.

Number 23 lined up his shot. He began his approach. As was his habit, he stutter-stepped, nearly halting his advance before accelerating and striking the ball with his left foot.

The goalie dove to one side. The ball went to the other, a rocket that disappeared into the corner of the net.

Belgrade four, Novi Sad three.

Game over.

Ratka covered his eyes, the pain of defeat as excruciating as on that day long ago. He rewound the tape and stopped it as number 23 prepared his approach. Using the remote, Ratka zoomed in on the player's face, laboring to see if he could spot the pending betrayal.

He saw only determination, the will to win.

Number 23 had not considered missing for one second.

A month after the game, Ratka was arrested for the kidnapping. For his crimes, he served five years and forfeited ownership of the team. Belgrade wasn't the same afterward. A new boss had taken his place. The police refused to be bought. He was a target and a target couldn't do business. All that was about to change.

Taking a beer from the refrigerator, Ratka left the lounge and passed through the sliding door onto the afterdeck. Two women sunbathed on the chaise longues. Seeing him, they sat up and greeted him. The boat was for sale and they were meant to lure buyers. Ratka ignored them. If he wasn't going to screw them, he couldn't be bothered. He put a hand on the railing, appraising the yacht in the adjacent slip. The *Czarina,* a 226-foot Feadship superyacht that looked like his hard-on if he'd made it into a boat. It was for sale, too. Priced at a hundred and forty-five million dollars. He just might be able to afford it after all was said and done.

But he had no interest in yachts. He was tired of Monaco. Tired of the Côte d'Azur. He wanted to go home. To Belgrade.

Two figures turned the corner of the dock and approached the boat. Ratka's temper flared at the sight of them. He retreated to the salon. A few moments later, two sets of feet pounded up the gangway. Tommy and Pavel entered the salon. Tommy was tall and lean, maybe twenty-five, his black hair combed back over his forehead with greasy kid stuff. Pavel was short and stocky, forty, hair shorn to the scalp, as hard and unfeeling as a rod of pig iron.

Ratka regarded them, then stepped toward Tommy. Tommy, who had been driving the car. "Well?" Ratka said.

Tommy stared at the floor hard enough to drill a hole in it.

"Well?" Ratka repeated, delivering an openhanded blow to the side of his head. "What do you think you were doing?"

Tommy winced, then cast a sidelong glance at Pavel, who was smart enough to keep his eyes on Ratka. "I was—"

"Don't talk," said Ratka. "That wasn't a question. Did you think I wasn't going to see it? Did you forget that the picture goes to the television? You nearly killed her."

"No, it was an—"

Ratka placed a finger an inch from Tommy's nose.

Tommy shut up.

"I said to follow her and to scare her if you had a chance. You tried to run her over. I saw it. What could you have been thinking?" Ratka balled his fists. "And then what? What would we do if she were dead? Did you think about what would happen next?"

"I thought she found something. Pavel told me…"

"Pavel was not driving the car. Pavel was piloting the drone."

Ratka had watched it all from the salon, the drone transmitting the picture wirelessly. He'd seen the woman stop at the site of her mother's accident, then make her way down the hill, though he could not tell if she'd found anything. What could she find, anyway? He'd watched the Ferrari arrive, the man join her on the hillside, then throw her out of the path of Tommy's car. He didn't recognize the man, but whoever he was, Ratka wanted to kiss him on both cheeks. Without the princess, nothing could go forward.

"Did you follow them?"

"The drone ran out of batteries," said Pavel. "Only a twenty-seven-minute charge. My fault."

Ratka patted Pavel on the shoulder. "Not your fault, unless you know how to engineer a better battery."

"No, sir."

"That makes two of us." Ratka returned his attention to Tommy. "You're a good boy. You made a mistake. Not again."

"Yes, Ratka."

"Good. That is what I want to hear." He walked to the bar and opened the freezer, from which he took out a handful of ice cubes that he wrapped in a dishcloth. "Hold this," he said to Tommy.

Ratka next took out a bottle of vodka, Stolichnaya, sheathed in an ice collar. He unscrewed the top but did not pour any into a glass. He left the bottle standing on the bar.

Then, to Pavel: "Give it to me. You know what."

Pavel slid his switchblade from his jacket and handed it to Ratka. It was a long slim instrument, black pearl handle polished to a sheen. Ratka hit the release and the blade swung into place, too quick for the eye to see. He ran his thumb along one edge, then looked back at Tommy. "You didn't think we were finished? Someone has to teach you to obey instructions. It's for your own good, believe me. Otherwise, who knows what trouble you will get into?"

Ratka took Tommy's hand into his own and squeezed it, massaging the palm. Gently, he led Tommy to the bar. There was a cutting board on the surface, a lemon and a lime on top of it. He dumped them into the sink and placed Tommy's hand on the flat surface.

Tommy said nothing. Sweat beaded on his forehead, despite the arctic blast of air-conditioning. His complexion had gone paler than a ghost's.

Ratka used the tip of the blade to separate the fingers, each the same distance from the next. "I was just like you once. As a boy, I refused to listen to anyone. I thought I knew best. My behavior didn't please my father. He was not a subtle man. He was a laborer. A field hand. One day I beat up a boy at school. Not just any boy. The son of the man who owned the land my father worked on. This upset my father. He had no time for lectures. Do you know how he taught me? He hit me. Just once. His hard laborer's fist in my face. It was enough. I had a black eye for a week. Worse, everyone knew he'd done it. I never disobeyed him again. But we don't have that kind of time, Tommy, do we?"

The tip of the blade had come to rest between Tommy's pinkie and ring finger.

"You will obey me from now on, yes?"

Tommy nodded, perspiration dripping from his forehead.

"Now, you may speak."

"Yes, Ratka. I will obey you."

"Always?"

"Always."

"I know you will." Ratka smiled and patted Tommy's cheek with affection. "You're a good boy."

Tommy sighed, sensing he had escaped his punishment.

At that moment, Ratka grasped Tommy's wrist. The smile had left his face. The blade fell across the center of Tommy's pinkie. Metal carved bone and ligament. Tommy cried out, his eyes appraising the gore with horror.

Ratka lifted the hand and poured the vodka over the wound. Tommy rammed what was left of his finger into the cold dishcloth.

Ratka left the men in the salon. He felt as though he'd done something positive with his day. A good deed, even.

Pavel really did keep his knife nice and sharp.

Chapter 24

Dov Dragan stared at the name on the screen and walked with the phone onto the terrace overlooking the Golfe de Saint-Hospice. He could not think of anything worse than receiving an unsolicited phone call from his lawyer. "Hello, Michael."

"Did you know about this?" barked Michael Bach.

Dragan was taken aback. It was not his lawyer's combative tone. Michael's prickly manner was the reason he earned fifteen hundred dollars an hour. It was the pronoun—"this." At that moment, there were a dozen things he might be referring to. None of them good.

There was the status of his home, the Villa Leopolda, two million euros in property tax arrears and subject to repossession by the state. Or the failure of the medical trials conducted by the start-up pharmaceutical company in which he'd invested his last twenty million dollars. Or the repo notice for the Bugatti.

When Dragan failed to answer, his attorney continued. "The legislation."

"What legislation?" It was Dragan's turn to be irritated. He was not aware of any legislation, either in France or Israel, or for that matter anywhere in Europe, that might trigger such a fevered call. "The question isn't if I knew about it!" he shouted back. "It's, why didn't you?"

"It was attached as a rider onto an immigration bill," explained Bach. "A last-minute idea to help fund the relief programs."

"Jesus," said Dragan, already imagining the worst. "Don't be shy. Tell me what the hell this is about."

Bach lowered his voice. "It concerns the matters you'd asked me to check on a few months ago."

"Go on."

"The *lex mortis*. A decision to increase the transfer tax on estates skipping generations. It passed the upper and lower houses with an overwhelming majority in both. There's talk of a legal challenge, but that's far down the road. For now, it's the law."

"What kind of increase are we talking about?"

"An additional one-half percent, the entire amount to be paid upon transfer of title."

"Bringing the total to two and one-half percent." A one-half percent increase sounded insignificant, but given the size of the estate in question, it constituted a monumental sum. A sum they had not foreseen.

"The law is to be retroactively applied to all estates settled during the past six months. Even I can't find a way around it."

"Stop with the good news."

"I wanted to let you know right away," Bach continued. "In case you need to make adjustments in your planning."

"Thank you, Michael."

"Dov, you can still reconsider."

Reconsider? Dragan didn't know the meaning of the word. "Shalom."

Dragan ended the call. His hand dropped to his side. He'd seen stronger men collapse under such a blow. He walked to the edge of the esplanade and looked out over the water toward Beaulieu-sur-Mer. The Villa Leopolda sat at the very top of Cap Ferrat on three acres of the most beautiful land on earth. Built by the king of Belgium at the turn of the twentieth century, the fifty-thousand-square-foot Beaux Arts mansion included two tennis courts (clay and hard), an Olympic-sized swimming pool, a glass greenhouse the length of a football pitch, a topiary, and, of course, the famed grand ballroom. There was a rumor that the great violinist Paganini's bones were buried in a grotto at sea's edge. In the ten years that he'd owned the property, Dragan had formed an attachment to it like no other. The prospect of losing it roused an anger in him that was feral in its intensity.

An increase of one-half percent. A rider to an immigration bill.

Dragan was an immigrant himself and no one had ever given his family a shekel. In the aftermath of the Second World War, the Dragans had fled Yugoslavia for the safer and warmer confines of Israel. He had grown up on a kibbutz in the driest corner of the Negev Desert. After his national service and time at university, he'd joined the Mossad, the Israeli foreign intelligence service. It was there that he'd spent the next twenty-five years of his life, moving up through the ranks, seeing every dark corner of the Israeli spy apparatus, performing every dirty job, until eventually he became its deputy director for covert operations. Nearing fifty, tired and disillusioned, he'd left his country's employ, taking with him a top-secret surveillance software program he'd spent years developing. With that software, he'd started Audiax Technologies. Two years later, he'd sold the company for just over one billion dollars.

And the money was gone now. A string of bad investments, a propensity for gambling, two divorces. Not a penny left. The Villa Leopolda was the first purchase made with his winnings, and now it was the last remaining. He vowed not to let it go without a fight.

Dragan returned inside. Already his spy's mind was planning, scheming, strategizing. The change in tax law was a challenge, nothing more. A last hurdle to overcome.

Another phone call, this one from Dragan.

"Double the teams on duty this evening."

"Why?"

"And double the betting limits."

"I thought we decided twelve per shift was pushing it. The black boy isn't the only one who noticed."

"And we'll take care of anyone else who does, too."

"Dov, what's going on?"

"We're short."

"How…? Why? You said we were on track."

"We were," said Dragan. "Now we are not. Double the teams."

"How much? How much are we short?"

"Fifty million."

Chapter 25

At the hotel, Simon accompanied Vika to her room.

"You'd be doing me a favor if you'd stay inside for the rest of the day."

"It's four p.m."

"Read a book," he suggested. "Have a coffee. Order room service."

"I refuse to be a prisoner."

A smile to sweeten the medicine. "It's not too bad as far as jails go."

At her door, Vika slipped the key from her purse and spoke almost under her breath. "I need to get to Mama's apartment. There will be so many things to go through. I can't imagine—"

"No," said Simon, without the smile.

Vika spun to face him, her eyes wide. "Pardon me?"

"No," he repeated. "You need to stay inside your room."

"I appreciate your concern, but really, I think I can take care of myself."

"It's not concern. It's common sense."

"Whatever it is, I'll make my own decisions, thank you."

"Please," said Simon. "Think this through. We have no idea what is going on out there...but believe me, something is."

"I didn't say I was going out. You're missing my point."

"Which is?"

"I will not be told what to do. By you or anyone else."

Simon held his tongue. It was the first time he'd caught the princess in her. The woman born to a title. All afternoon she'd done her best to downplay her blue-blooded ancestry. It was clear that her unstable upbringing had weaned her of arrogance and entitlement. Nearly. She was surprisingly unmannered and down-to-earth. But there was no getting around the von Tiefen und Tassis fortune. Twelve billion dollars placed hers among the richest families in Europe. Financial gain was the primary motive behind most criminal acts. It was always about the money.

"We can go to your mother's apartment in the morning," he said, the beacon of reason. "Together."

"I don't need you to keep me safe."

Simon let her think about that for a moment. "I'd feel better," he said.

"And you?" asked Vika, archly. "What are you going to do? Hide out, as well?"

"I have plans."

"What's her name?"

"There is no 'her.'" Simon leaned in closer. "For your information, I didn't come for the time trial or the Concours," he said. "I'm here on a job."

"Really?" said Vika, still playing coy.

"Really." Simon stared into her eyes, wondering if he was making any impression whatsoever. A few hundred years ago she would have made a formidable ruler. Today...*this afternoon*...she was merely an uncooperative client, even if their arrangement was informal, and she was ticking him off. "Don't forget what happened earlier. It wasn't an accident. Stay in your room. That's an order."

With a full head of steam, he walked down the hall to the elevator. "And lock the goddamned door!" he shouted.

Returning to his room, Simon tossed his jacket on the bed, then undressed and lay down in his undershorts and a Sex Pistols T-shirt. If Princess Victoria couldn't appreciate the shirt, Simon was certain her late mother, Princess TNT, could. It was his habit to nap for an hour if he knew he was going to be out late. He intended to stay at the casino as long as it took to find something. He closed his eyes and relaxed his limbs. He turned off his inner voice and listened to the sounds around him. A door closing in the hall. Footsteps receding into the distance. The *tick tick tick* of the hotel's plumbing. Sleep eluded him. He was still angry, exasperated, and concerned, though not sure in which order.

He'd taken on too much. That was the problem. He was here on paid assignment on behalf of the Société des Bains de Mer and Lord Toby Stonewood. He had no business trying to help Vika. Her mother's death, accidental or otherwise, was a matter for the police. He was no homicide investigator. As he'd said earlier, he was a problem solver. If an employee was embezzling money from your firm, he was your man. If your daughter ran away with a bad element, he was more than happy to find her. Purloined industrial secrets? Stolen jewelry? A missing letter? Sign him up.

But murder?

Murder was a bridge too far.

The first thing to do was call Commissaire Le Juste. The French police were well trained, efficient, and thorough. Incorruptible, however, was a trait he was not willing to ascribe to them. Simon knew a thing or two about how things worked on the Côte d'Azur. It was a clubby place where friendships, family, and long-established ties counted more than rote obeyance of the law. The fact was, he didn't know Rémy Le Juste and so he couldn't trust him. Or, to put a finer point on it, he couldn't entrust Vika to him.

Going to the police was out.

So was a nap.

After twenty minutes, Simon rose and made himself an espresso. Between sips, he opened his laptop, logged on to the net, and read up on the von Tiefen und Tassis family. The headlines said it all. PRINCE LUDWIG TO MARRY WOMAN THIRTY YEARS HIS JUNIOR. WEDDING OF THE CENTURY AT SCHLOSS BRANDENBURG. FROM PINUP TO PRINCESS: STEFANIE'S RISE FROM PAGE 3 TO THE PALACE. There was a picture of a saucy blond woman wearing a bikini, or rather a bikini bottom, and nothing else. Her hair was in pigtails and her smile said she was up for anything. The prince had gotten himself a handful.

Simon continued reading.

PRINCESS TNT GIVES BIRTH TO HEIR. FINALLY, A PRINCESS!…A GIRL, VICTORIA ELIZABETH, BORN…And then plenty of articles about the

mother and her brood, pictures of blond boys and their sister in traditional German garb: lederhosen, dirndls. All rosy cheeks and Teutonic
goodwill, such as it is. The myth of the Aryan superman had never entirely left the German consciousness. Then: PRINCE LUDWIG DEAD AT 64:
HEART ATTACK IN MALE LOVER'S BED. THE FIGHT OVER DEATH DUTIES:
THE CURIOUS CASE OF VON TIEFEN UND TASSIS. PRINCESS STEFANIE MAKES
A NEW LIFE IN MONACO. STEFANIE TO REMARRY INTO DYNASTY.

Fast-forward ten years. More headlines, but with a decidedly more serious tone.

PRINCESS VICTORIA STRUGGLES TO SAVE FAMILY FORTUNE. TNT LOSES
MILLIONS IN STOCK SCANDAL. PRINCESS MBA GRADUATES INSEAD WITH
HONORS. And most recently: A NEW BEGINNING: THE RESURGENCE OF
THE HOUSE OF VON TIEFEN UND TASSIS.

As Simon read excerpts from each article, he recalled the colorful stories Vika had told him about growing up in such a chaotic atmosphere,
believing herself rich one day and destitute the next. She hadn't mentioned earning an MBA at INSEAD, Europe's finest business school, or
her efforts to restructure the family assets to lessen inheritance taxes and
preserve the estate for future generations. He'd known right off the bat
that she was smart. He found her exceptionally attractive. He would have
to add "accomplished" and "tenacious."

Simon showered and dressed in a dark suit with an open-collar shirt,
plain white. Feeling hungry, he consulted the room service menu. There
was tournedos Rossini, Dover sole, veal steak with *morilles*. Prisoners
should have it so good. He decided on a burger and fries, and a side salad
with Roquefort dressing (millionaire's blue cheese).

"How would monsieur like that cooked?" asked the room service operator.

Simon cleared his throat. "Medium well."

Somewhere Auguste Escoffier was turning over in his grave.

Simon retrieved the stainless steel case and freed his surveillance
tools. He set the lighter-shaped camera hunter and its earpiece on the
desk. Still inside the case was a plastic bag with a number of button-
shaped objects inside. Opening the bag, he shook a few into the palm of

his hand. Each was a miniature tracking device. Smooth, matte-textured, and difficult to detect on one side. On the other, equipped with itsy-bitsy claws designed to grasp fabrics and not let go.

It was Simon who'd come up with the solution, the idea stemming from his own criminal past. Sooner or later, the team had to regroup, if only to hand over the money earned at the casino, in the form of either checks or cash. Every thief knew that you kept the loot in a safe location. Therefore, it was a matter of determining who was cheating, then mapping their movements. All he had to do was follow their tracks.

There was a knock at the door. Room service. Simon covered his electronic toys with a towel before allowing the server to enter and set up a dining spot. The hamburger was perfectly cooked, and he added ketchup and mustard, though he refrained from raw onion to spare any casino guests who might be seated beside him. Sitting at the beautifully laid table, he placed a napkin in the neck of his shirt and another on his lap. He wasn't a messy eater, but this was his last shirt. He couldn't hit the casino dressed like a fan of the Sex Pistols.

After dinner, he put on a necktie and a splash of cologne. Taking care, he gathered his electronic weapons of war, slid them into his jacket pockets, and headed to the door, ready for battle. He was interrupted by a phone call.

"Simon, it's Toby."

"Toby?" The familiarity caught him off guard.

"Toby Stonewood. Remember me?"

"Of course—Toby. Please excuse me."

"How was the journey?"

"Eventful."

"Oh?"

"But nothing to keep me from getting started."

"Everything to your liking?"

Simon took a look around the room. At the elegant black lacquer table, the exquisitely comfortable sofa, the seventy-inch flat-screen television, the spray of yellow gladiolas that lent the space an invigorating scent. "Just about."

"We tend to overdo things down there," said Toby Stonewood. "I know it's too soon to ask if you've made any progress, but we lost another six hundred thousand euros last night. They're still working the place."

"I spent the evening there. I need time to get a better feel for things, but I noticed a thing or two that wasn't quite right."

"Can you elaborate?"

"Not yet. I'm headed back now. I hope to have something for you in a day or two."

"I'd encourage you to take your time, but we haven't much left."

"I'll do my best."

"One more thing."

Simon noted the marked change in tone. "Yes?"

"One of our dealers was found dead this afternoon," Toby went on. "In fact, I'm just off the phone with the Monégasque police. The man was Vincent Morehead. He's Ronnie Morehead's brother."

The news shook Simon. "Ronnie…from Les Ambassadeurs?"

"Yes."

"What happened?"

"They found the body in a quarry on the Italian border. He'd been beaten to death."

The natural question for Toby was whether he thought it had anything to do with the problems at the casino. Simon already knew the answer.

"The police suspect he may have been in debt to an organized crime syndicate," said Toby. "The inspector hinted that they'd seen this kind of thing before."

Something fired inside Simon and he only just managed to keep his temper. It wasn't about debts. Vincent Morehead had seen something and now he was dead. "Nonsense. He was killed because he noticed something."

"I suspect you're right. But Simon, you need to be careful. Morehead died with every bone in his body broken and his skull rent in by a blunt instrument. These people—whoever they may be—are vicious."

"Count on it." Simon ended the call.

On the way to the elevator, he phoned Vika. There was no answer. He rode down to the lobby and, using a hotel phone, asked to be connected to her room.

"Ms. Brandt has asked that she not be disturbed," said the operator.

"It's an emergency." Simon gave his name and stated that he, too, was a hotel guest.

"I'm sorry, sir, but our policy is to respect the guest's wishes."

Simon hung up. In a minute's time, he was standing at Vika's door. When no one answered, he put an ear to the panel. He heard nothing. No television. No music. No voices.

He banged again, three times in succession, very hard.

A chambermaid eyed him from the end of the hall. "May I help you?" she asked.

"I'm worried about Ms. Brandt," said Simon. "Can you open her room?"

"Ms. Brandt? She is not there."

"Oh?"

"She left a few minutes ago."

"Alone?"

The chambermaid nodded. "I saw her enter the elevator."

"Great," said Simon. "Just great."

"Pardon me?"

"Never mind," he said. "Some people just don't listen."

Chapter 26

It was the worst day of his entire life.

Robby pulled his jumper over his head, smoothed his hair, then closed his locker. He was the last one in the gym and the noise echoed off the shower tiles and the old, high ceilings, making him feel lonelier than he already was. It was nearly six. Practice had ended an hour ago. Dinner was already being served at the *culi*—which was short for *culinarium,* some dumb Swiss name for the cafeteria. Wednesdays meant schnitzel and *pommes frites*. His favorite. Tonight he could care less. Throwing his book bag over his shoulder, he made his way outside.

Robby pushed open the gymnasium door and put his hand out. Though the sky had turned dark as coal, not a drop dampened his palm. He gazed past the field and into the mountains. The rest of the team had left directly after practice, heading into the forest with Karl Marshal for a secret bonfire. Robby spotted a wisp of smoke drifting skyward from the pine canopy.

"You have to be a starter," he'd said to Robby. "Or at least have played in a game. Sorry, pal."

Robby started up the hill toward his dorm. All afternoon, clouds had been rolling in and he hoped it would rain. He hoped it would come down like cats and dogs and that there was thunder and lightning, a proper electrical show, and that the team would come running back to school drenched and freezing and scared out of their wits and find him safe and warm and dry in the dorm. That would teach Karl Marshal a lesson.

He imagined he heard laughter drifting down from the forest. Paulie Jackson was probably telling dirty jokes. He knew a ton of them. Robby wondered if Karl Marshal really had gotten beer. He doubted it.

"Elisabeth is coming with us, too," he'd said. "Not that she'd notice you're missing."

Robby knew he was lying. She would never hang out with a bunch of high school kids, even first formers. He pictured Karl Marshal and his big head and his broad shoulders and his confident manner. Was there any way in the world she might actually like him?

Robby shook his head angrily. Never. Not in a million years. Furious for even considering it, he crossed the track and started up the field, occasionally taking a sidelong glance at the forest to see if the smoke was still there.

The bonfire wasn't the only thing bothering him. On Thursday afternoons, sixth formers at Zuoz were allowed to "hit town," or go on their own into the village. It was a short walk, no more than five minutes, and students could spend time strolling along the main street. The first stop was always Café Simmens, where they could choose from hot chocolate and pastries—mille-feuille and strawberry tarts were favorites—or, of course, a Coupe Dänemark: vanilla ice cream and chocolate sauce with a generous topping of fresh whipped cream. Across the street was a dime store called Vario that sold pretty much everything: magazines, comics, coloring books, stuffed animals, and even toys. There was a jewelry store, a pharmacy, and of course a grocery, a butcher, and a bakery. Robby's mother kept him on a strict allowance. He had fifteen francs to spend and took care before making his purchases.

One-quarter of Robby's classmates were day students. The privilege meant little to them. Often, they invited friends to their homes, typically chalets in St. Moritz or Pontresina. Robby's family also had a chalet above Pontresina. The family used it only for ski holidays. The rest of the year it sat boarded up and deserted. But to Robby, "hitting town" was a big deal, an occasion that merited much strategizing and discussion.

He'd asked two of his schoolmates to accompany him. Both had turned him down. It was Robby's first year at Zuoz and classes had started barely six weeks earlier. He didn't think it odd that he had yet to make any friends. The fact was that he had never been exceptionally good at palling around. While some kids were naturally popular—take Karl Marshal, for example, who was never seen without two or three friends in tow, even a girl sometimes—Robby could claim no such luck. He was friendly enough in his way. He said hello when addressed. He loved jokes, even if he was terrible at telling them. He was polite and respectful and, most important, never talked badly about anyone.

And yet despite trying all week, Robby had no one to hit town with and no invitation to visit a friend's home. Maybe he'd just stay at school and get a head start on his homework. He stopped in his tracks. No one stayed at school and did their homework. What was wrong with him?

At that moment, Robby decided he was done trying to do the right thing. He was done never complaining, never teasing the other boys, never making fun of the ugly girls. From now on, he'd do the same as the others. He'd carp about the food at the *culi*. He'd rib Franz Maeder for being so fat. He'd call his mother and pout about how the others were treating him.

He laughed out loud—not even a laugh, but a cackle. Robby never cackled. He was already on the right track and enjoying himself immensely.

"Robert!"

At the sound of a woman's voice he froze. He turned his head. It was her. It was Elisabeth taking her afternoon walk, though an hour later than usual. She waved. "Where is everyone?"

"In the forest," he said. "Having a bonfire." Only then did he realize he'd said too much. He looked like a loser for having been left behind.

"Without you?"

Robby struggled to make up a reasonable explanation for not having been invited. He couldn't. "It's a secret party, but I wasn't invited because I've never played in a game."

Elisabeth stared at him, considering this. She didn't say "Oh well" or "They're the ones missing out" or "I wouldn't worry." Instead, she left the walking path and crossed the field to where he stood. "That's not very nice of them."

"I have to get better before I can play," said Robby.

"Yes," she said. "You do. I've watched you play."

"You have? *Me? Why?*"

"My brother was a very good rugby player. He played on the German team."

"The German national team?"

Elisabeth nodded and a lock of her blond hair fell across her face. "But he wasn't always good. How old are you, Robert?"

Robby needed a second. He was in a state of paralysis. She'd remembered his name. "Twelve," he said. "Actually, twelve and a half."

"He was much smaller than you at twelve. A real shrimp."

"He was?"

Elisabeth nodded again. "Know how big he is now?"

Robby shook his head.

"Six feet four inches tall, and he weighs two hundred twenty pounds."

"That's big."

"I'll bet your father is tall."

"He was. He's dead."

"So there." A smile to light the darkest winter night. "Just a matter of time."

"Think so?"

"Know it."

Robby stood up straighter, already feeling two inches taller.

"Tell you what," said Elisabeth, placing her hand on his shoulder, leaning close enough to make Robby's heart nearly explode. "No school on Thursday afternoons, right? Meet me in town for a coffee. Would you like that?"

Robby didn't answer at first. The sight of her so close, the smell of her, the touch of her hand on his shoulder, had locked him in some kind of wonderful trance. Finally, he said, "Yes. Yes, I would."

"Don't bring your friends. It will be just you and me."

"Sure," said Robby. "Just you and me."

"How about two o'clock at Café Simmens? Meet me on the corner. Deal?"

"Deal."

"Okay, then. *Tschuss.*"

"Tschuss."

Elisabeth kissed him on the cheek and continued on her walk. Robby watched her go, his feet glued to the ground. If he took one step, if he moved a muscle, he was sure he'd wake up and find that the entire encounter had been nothing but a dream.

CHAPTER 27

*I*t was all set forth in the trust. The ring was to be held by the most senior male of full-blood lineage in the family succession. If there was no male, then by the most senior female, until a male attained the age of majority.

Upon Papa's death, the ring had gone to Mama, and upon Mama's death, it was to go to Vika, who would hold it until her son, and only living progeny, Fritz, attained his majority at age twenty-one. On that date, in a ceremony performed since the twelfth century, she would give the ring to him and the von Tiefen und Tassis estate would be his. All of it.

The ring was of paramount importance.

Vika hadn't intended to go to her mother's apartment. She hadn't been thinking about the ring at all until she saw him later that evening, after she'd had her dinner downstairs.

Her first thought after she'd returned to her room was about Fritz. She had no idea what was going on, but as Mr. Riske had said, something was. She might be a tad flippant regarding her own safety, but her attitude toward her son couldn't be more different.

She placed a call to the headmaster's office at the Lyceum Zuoz. When informed that Dr. Brunner was gone for the day, she called him on his private number. It was not a courtesy to be abused.

"Frau Brandenburg, how may I be of help?" said Dr. Andreas Brunner, sixty years old, climber, philatelist, and former member of the Swiss Guard. (Alas, the vow of lifelong chastity had proved too onerous. Brunner had fallen in love with a Roman beauty—a Protestant, no less. Thirty years later they were still married.)

"Something has come up," Vika began, appreciating Brunner's no-nonsense manner. In vague terms, she sketched out the events of the past days, suggesting that there might be an unholy interest in the family by people unfriendly to the cause.

"Shall we send Robert to you?"

"I don't want him disturbed. There's no reason to believe he's in any kind of jeopardy. Please have our mutual friend keep a close eye on him. You might want to hire on an extra teacher for the next few weeks. If possible, he could even stay in Fritz's hall."

"I'll see to all matters myself and of course help as much as I can personally."

"That would be nice."

"Is there anything else?"

"Keep my boy safe, Dr. Brunner."

Vika ended the call and a weight lifted from her. Prior to her son's arrival at the school, arrangements had been made to provide him with a minder—not a bodyguard so much as an attentive uncle able to react in a decisive manner if called upon. He was a member of the faculty with past military experience, time in combat. She'd met the man and had every confidence in him.

Unburdened of one responsibility, she took a shower, put on a robe, and watched television. The news in France was as unsettling as in Germany, or anywhere else these days. Six o'clock rolled around. Feeling cooped up and in need of fresh air, she decided that a trip downstairs and a jaunt around the lobby would lift her spirits. She didn't consider calling Riske. She was a big girl. She resented his autocratic display, no matter his experience or the events that had transpired earlier in the day. Besides, how dangerous could it be? This was the Hôtel de Paris.

When she reached the lobby and saw it bustling with elegant, well-dressed men and women, numerous hotel staff in plain sight, even two police officers standing at the front door, she dismissed her concerns altogether. She was in her element. Surely she was as safe here as anyplace.

She found a table at the Bar Américain and ordered her favorite drink, a *dulap*: grape juice, Sprite, and a healthy chunk of lime. For the first time all day, she relaxed. A dinner of veal scaloppine and brussels sprouts heightened her sense of security. Minute by minute, the memory of the car careening around the corner and heading straight for her grew dimmer, and Riske's order that she stay in her room and "lock the goddamned door" seemed increasingly alarmist.

It was then that she began thinking about the ring. It came to her that maybe Mama had taken it off and that Vika would find it in her jewelry chest, and if not there, in the safe or by the sink where she set all her cosmetics. Over and over she heard her mother's voice telling her, *"He wants to know about the family . . . He scares me."* Vika's determination to act . . . *to do something* . . . grew. She couldn't just sit still.

And then she saw him and her mind was made up.

It was after eight when Simon Riske walked across the lobby and left the hotel. He wore a dark suit cut impeccably and looked very sharp; to any observer, he was a man out for a night on the town. Work indeed. Vika's eyes followed him out the door and across the street to the casino. Up the stairs he went with a spring in his step, clapping the doorman on the arm as he entered. What type of job involved visiting a casino dressed to the nines?

Vika's cheeks flushed. She clasped her hands together, then tore them apart. The man was a liar. She had the entirely irrational thought that if he could do as he pleased, then so could she.

Hesitation left her.

Vika paid her bill and left the hotel, as intent on getting to Mama's as Simon Riske had been to enter the casino. She only hoped she had as much brio in her manner as he did.

Vika took no notice of the sturdy, dark-haired man with the pronounced widow's peak and crooked nose watching her from a table at the Café de Paris. After she passed by, the man said a word to his colleagues, both of whom resembled him to an unnerving degree, and set off after her.

Ratka had a good idea where she was heading and kept a safe distance between them. She was a beautiful woman and he enjoyed the sway of her hips. She had changed her clothes from this afternoon. She wore a maroon dress that hugged her shapely ass to perfection. He enjoyed even more the scoop cut that showed off her breasts. He noted how she kept her head raised as she walked, her jaw held high. Like a real princess. This angered him. He despised haughty women. At the same time, he felt a surge in his groin.

He watched as she turned her head, checking for traffic, before crossing the street. He noted the crisp line of her jaw. So damned perfect. She lifted her hand as she crossed, as if commanding the cars to stop. He walked more quickly, his anger growing with every step. He had his own opinion about princesses, real or otherwise, and how they should be treated. The same way all women were to be treated.

A thought came to him. His blood began to race in his veins. He decided that Tommy had not properly scared her. Look at her promenading alone on the streets as if nothing had happened. Her arrogance was brazen, offensive. Ratka did not want her feeling so safe, so free to pursue her every inclination. The princess needed to be taught her place. He knew how. He'd done it many times before.

He would teach her respect.

And fear.

Chapter 28

Simon entered the Casino de Monte-Carlo a few minutes past eight. He crossed the gallery, his shoes echoing off the marble floors, the main *salle de jeux* in sight. He had a mental picture of what to look for. The criminals would be working in teams. One to film the cards as he or she cut them, several at a table, all of them receiving instructions on how to wager. They would do their best to blend in. Nothing flashy. If anything, the opposite, like the bland man at his table last night...the wallflower who'd ended the evening on a two-hundred-million-dollar yacht. If they had cocktails, they would not be drinking them.

They were professionals. And they were killers. Vincent Morehead had spotted them and Vincent Morehead was dead. Simon would do well not to forget it.

Once upstairs, he took the first open seat he found. The minimum bet was five hundred euros. He unbuttoned his jacket and cleared his throat noisily, waving an arm to signal a server. With ceremony, he opened his wallet and counted out five thousand euros, slapping them on the baize tabletop. The dealer gave him his chips and Simon spent time arranging them. He ordered a Campari and soda and began his play.

Two men were dead. It was imperative that Simon be sharp-eyed and observant while at the same time appearing to be indiscriminate and in his cups. Law enforcement came in many shapes and forms, but drunk was not one of them.

A woman to his right had the shoe. She was sixty, corpulent, and as red as a lobster, with gold jewelry around her neck and wrists and fingers, and probably her toes, if Simon dared to look. Every player ponied up the minimum bet. Four other players sat at the table, all men. The woman dealt the cards. Two hands. Two cards each, all faceup. A six and seven for the house—*banco*—or three. A king and a two for the player—*punto*—or two.

At this point, everyone was permitted to increase their bet, either on the *punto* or the *banco*. The odds were more or less even between the two hands. Simon bet two hundred euros on *banco*, the woman holding the shoe. The other four players all bet on *punto*. The first two men bet two hundred euros, the second two a thousand euros.

The woman dealt the cards. One more to each hand.

Punto drew a six, giving them an eight.

Banco drew a four, giving it a seven.

Punto won.

As the woman had lost, rules called for her to pass the shoe. The next player declined and the shoe returned to the house. A new hand was dealt.

A pattern quickly developed. Two of the four players (not the woman, who was German and informed Simon that her name was Brünnhilde and that she was unmarried) always bet the same amount on one hand. The winning hand.

Simon made sure not to mimic their bets or to pay undue attention to anyone except his new object of desire, Brünnhilde from Hamburg. He played a dozen hands, winning and losing equally. Time came to reshuffle the shoe. A new stack of 416 cards—eight decks pre-shuffled—was loaded into the shoe.

This was the moment Eightball Eddie had told Simon to watch for.

The dealer offered the shoe to the player who had won the most money on the last hand and gave him a yellow cutting card. The player—middle-aged, dark hair, casual but elegant attire, eyeglasses—pulled the shoe closer and ran the edge of the cutting card over it in an upward direction. It was a quick motion—*zip* and it was done. Then the man slipped the card into the center of the shoe. The dealer took the shoe and cut the cards accordingly. Next he burned the first ten cards, dealing them into a pile and consigning the pile to a slot in the table, never to be seen again. After this, the dealer played two dummy hands to conclusion and consigned these cards to oblivion as well.

All this Simon watched with passing interest, pretending to be concerned with Brünnhilde's tall tales and making sure that they both had a fresh cocktail before play restarted. In fact, his eye never left the man who had cut the cards. Vikram Singh had been correct. Simon had not been able to observe any behavior that might tip him off that the man was cheating. No sign of a camera. No artfully concealed earpieces. Most important, there was no pinging in his own earpiece to signal the presence of a camera. In fact, he realized belatedly, there was no sound at all. He rose too quickly, nearly spilling a drink, then asked to be dealt out of the next hand.

Inside the restroom, he locked himself in a stall and examined the Zippo-shaped camera hunter. The operating light was not on. He depressed the switch. The green light burned brightly. A low-level hum filled his ear. Cursing his ineptitude, he replaced the device in his pocket—carefully this time.

Ready to get down to business, he headed back to the table. Something strange happened on the way. The steady hum was replaced by a pinging noise not dissimilar to sonar. The pinging grew more rapid, faster still, until it reached a steady pitch. The strange part was that this happened as he walked past the table in the gaming room next to his.

Simon continued walking and the pulse slowed, only to increase again as he neared his table, turning once again to a steady tone as he passed the dark-haired man who had cut the cards a few minutes earlier.

Not one camera, but two.

"I'm back," Simon said to the players in a jocular tone as he retook his seat. "We can all start again. I, for one, now intend to win!"

There were smiles all around. Brünnhilde welcomed him back with a bibulous hug.

Play resumed.

Simon gambled for another half hour. He recognized the cheaters' methods and bet with the winners each time. He left the table with ten thousand euros, double his stake. He calculated that the cheaters, if it really was them, had won over one hundred thousand.

He continued to the next room and assumed a position by a back wall, watching the man he'd identified as holding the camera. After a while, the man left the table and visited the restroom. Simon kept his distance. When the man emerged, Simon was right there on his way in, jostling him only slightly as he passed.

Inside the bathroom, he washed his hands, counting to twenty before leaving. He made a beeline for the main staircase and was outside in the fresh night air a minute later. He had placed tracking devices on four persons, two of whom he knew for certain were part of the team robbing Lord Toby Stonewood and the Société des Bains de Mer of millions, and two others he suspected of being their associates.

On top of that he had one new wallet to shore up his research.

He didn't dare look at it until he was back in the confines of his hotel room.

For now, he had another pressing matter.

Chapter 29

It was a thirty-minute walk from the hotel, and Vika was careful to stay on the populated track, following the sidewalk down the hill, then losing herself in the procession of pedestrians taking an evening stroll along the promenade. It was only when she left the seafront and traversed the three blocks uphill to the Boulevard du Larvotto that she found herself alone and the narrow streets quiet and desolate. She covered the distance as briskly as she could, without jogging or in any way betraying her anxieties. She checked over her shoulder and looked at reflections in storefront windows to see if anyone was following. She was a longtime fan of John le Carré's novels and could match George Smiley's tradecraft, if not Toby Esterhase's. To her relief, she saw no one, and as she entered the lobby of the Château Perigord, stopping to look behind her a final time, she felt rather foolish, like the victim of a practical joke.

The Château Perigord was a twenty-story apartment building on the Boulevard d'Italie, overlooking the sea. In Monaco, people didn't rent apartments; they owned them. Twenty-five years earlier, Vika's mother had purchased a three-bedroom flat on the top floor. Papa had recently died, and like many wealthy Europeans facing onerous taxes, Mama had fled to Monaco. Her mother claimed that she needed a fresh start, a chance to build a new life with new friends in a new place where the press didn't follow her from morning to night and it didn't rain every day but Sunday. Things had not gone well since.

Vika rode the old elevator to the top floor. The hall carpets were the same color, the little tables and decorations unchanged since her last visit a decade before. The building had smelled tart and antiseptic then—like a hospital, she'd always remarked—and it still did.

She stopped in front of the door and removed a set of keys, each with a colored fob. Red was for Marbella, green for Pontresina, blue for Barbados. There were ten of them. And black for Mama's place in Monaco. Vika needed several tries to get the key into the lock. Her hand was trembling, not out of fear but another emotion she disliked every bit as much.

Vika stepped inside, leaving the door open behind her. If anything happened, she wanted someone to hear her scream. The apartment was dark as a crypt. She flipped on the lights and observed that the curtains were drawn. They were blackout curtains, velvet, the color of blood. Daylight was the drinker's enemy.

Then she took in the living room.

Vika covered her mouth as her eyes jumped from the messy coffee table to the upended chair to the shattered brandy glass. There was an empty bottle of Wyborowa, the Polish vodka her mother drank like Perrier, lying underneath the dining room table. Advancing carefully, as if she were barefoot and avoiding the broken glass, she grabbed the neck of the bottle and set it on the table. Her first reaction was that she needed to call Commissaire Le Juste. There had been a fight. A battle royale, from the looks of things. Any rational person would come to the same conclusion. Here at last was the evidence Vika needed.

But when she put her hand on her mother's telephone, she paused.

A fight or the normal state of affairs for a raging alcoholic?

Vika woke in her bed and sat up.

Music from Mama's party carried through the rafters below and into her room. She put her feet on the floor and felt the pounding rhythmic beat in her stomach. It was too loud. Frightened, she padded down the broad staircase of the grand chalet, eyes blinking back the bright light, trying to make sense of the confusion of bodies, the colorful sweaters and blouses dancing and mingling and she wasn't sure what else.

There was a tall man wearing a silver fur jacket standing on the onyx coffee table, making circles and swinging a hand in the air. It took Vika a moment to realize that Mama was on the table, too, dancing with him.

Vika made her way through the merrymakers and tugged at her mother's skirt. "You'll wake the boys."

Her mother betrayed no surprise at seeing her ten-year-old daughter at three in the morning standing in her flannel Lanz nightgown, rubbing the sleep from her eyes. "Come, Victoria!" she shouted over the music. "Come dance with us."

"Mama, it's late."

"Quatsch," her mother laughed. Nonsense. "The party is only getting started. Your mama is forty years old. Can you believe it?" Her mother turned her head away and addressed her friends, arms spread wide. "Ich bin vierzig!" she half sang, half yelled, then dissolved in a fit of laughter. I'm forty.

Vika tugged her skirt again and her mother came down off the table. Instead of taking her back to her room and tucking her in, she led her daughter around the spacious den, with its floor-to-ceiling windows and large fireplace and arolla pine walls decorated with dozens of bleached ram horns, and introduced her to her friends.

"This is Rolf. This is Michael. This is Katya."

Vika shook their hands as she'd been taught, making a little curtsy each time, sure to lift the hem of her nightgown off the floor.

Finally, her mother led her to the man in the fur coat. "And this is Gunther. He's going to be your father one day."

"Good evening, Princess Victoria," Gunther had said, bowing. "It is an honor to meet you."

He was tall and tanned brown, with long silver hair. He was a famous man in Germany. They called him a playboy. Once he had been married to a famous French movie star.

"I don't want another father," Vika had said, upset.

"Don't listen to your mother," Gunther had said. "I can never take your father's place." He leaned closer. "Your mama is a bit drunk. It is her birthday, so we must forgive her."

"She's forty," said Vika.

"I'm fifty," said Gunther. "A dinosaur."

Vika smiled.

"Do you know what I do when I'm not dancing?"

"You do the bobsleigh." She saw that he was wearing a sweater with the badge of the St. Moritz Bobsleigh Club.

"Besides that."

Vika shook her head.

"I take photographs. I'm going to take one of you."

"But I'm not pretty."

"But you are. And very serious."

"Not tonight."

"Another time."

From across the room there was a shriek and a glass shattered. Then laughter, much too wild for Vika's liking. Her mother had tripped over a chair and cut herself. She was crying.

"Back to bed with you," said Gunther, putting one enormous hand on the small of her back. "Don't worry. I'll look after your mother."

As Vika climbed up the stairs to her room, she made out the words of the song.

"Let's dance, the last dance. So let's dance, the last dance . . . tonight."

A fight or a party?

Vika examined the room in a more skeptical light. A record album spun round and round on the turntable, Papa's treasured Bang and Olufsen. She turned it off and when the album stopped spinning she read the name of the artist. It was Donna Summer's greatest hits.

A party, then?

If so, why hadn't Elena cleaned up? Vika felt a surge of anger at the Sicilian woman. She poked her head into the bathroom and winced. Someone had urinated in the toilet and failed to flush it. The kitchen was a mess. There was an empty wine bottle on the counter, dirty plates in the sink, and a serving dish with the remnants of prosciutto and melon. Grandmama's crystal salt and pepper shakers lay on the floor like bowling pins, along with a soiled dish towel and several pieces of cutlery.

Vika stood very still and took another look at things. She recalled the voice mail. *"He wants to know about the family . . . He scares me."*

Or was it a fight?

She was confused, unable to make sense of what had happened here. It came to her that she couldn't answer.

"Damn you, Mama!" she shouted, overcome with emotion.

Ratka followed at a safe distance, amused at the woman's clumsy countersurveillance methods. Again, he grew angry at Tommy for his rash actions. Maybe taking half a finger wasn't enough. Still, at least he knew that she carried a pistol.

The woman left the beachfront and walked up the hill toward the apartment. Ratka turned up a block earlier and was in position to see her emerge onto the Boulevard d'Italie and enter her mother's building. Through the windows, he could see that the lobby was an ornate two-story affair with mirrors everywhere and shiny stone floors. He saw her standing at the elevator bank. With mounting excitement, he studied her figure, enjoying the fit of her dress, her trim waist, her long, slender legs. He imagined her naked. Crying. Begging for him to be gentle. It had been too long since he'd taken a woman by force. The memory stirred his loins and awakened his darker instincts. The animal lurking within every man demanded release.

He hurried around the corner and down the steep alley off which residents entered the subterranean parking garage. He had a key for the maintenance door. Inside he navigated several corridors to the freight elevator. He had a smaller key for this. His heart raced as he rode to the top floor.

In his feverish mind, he saw his hands ripping off her shirt, tearing off her brassiere, kneading her breasts. He hoped she screamed. He would slap her. He hoped she struggled. He would subdue her. He would control her absolutely.

The elevator slowed. The doors opened.

It had been too long.

Days of fire.

Civil war had been raging for over a year across the country previously known as Yugoslavia. Now it was every man for himself. Ratka viewed the conflict as the chance to assert the Serbian's God-given ethnic supe-riority. An opportunity to cleanse the land of its Muslim neighbors. Islam was a race, not a religion, a filthy subhuman race that tainted their com-mon flag and weakened their nation.

Ratka headed the Serbian Volunteer Force, known as the Silver Tigers, and though neither he nor the two hundred men who served un-der him were members of the military, they had been given uniforms, automatic weapons, jeeps, and even a half-dozen armored personnel car-riers.

They had arrived in Srebrenica at dawn, after devastating the meager forces defending the city. The streets were deserted. White flags hung from windows. Ratka went building by building, home by home, ferreting out the men hiding in cellars and closets and beneath beds—cowards all—and corralling them into a pen in the town square. It was a mael-strom of emotion, the women screaming, children bawling, life and death played in operatic crescendos over and over again. He gave his men free rein to plunder, pillage, and rape. This was what it was like to conquer, to subjugate, to rule absolutely.

He chose the most beautiful woman for himself. She was the mayor's wife, tall, statuesque, and, best, proud. The mayor was dead, dispatched by a bullet to the head from Ratka's rifle. Her strength in the face of it all, her resolution, was like a last redoubt to be stormed. He ordered her into the bedroom, and when she refused, chin held high, defiance in her eyes, he hit her across the face with the muzzle of his pistol and dragged her inside by the collar. She fought him and her every shout and strug-gle aroused him further. He took her twice, and when he was done, all resistance had been bled from her. She lay on the floor as defiant as a used dishrag, whimpering, begging him to kill her. He refused. It gave him pleasure to know she would suffer to the end of her days.

And now, as he let himself into the princess's home through the ser-vants' entrance, he would know those feelings again.

Vika had her cry.

She wasn't sure how long she sat there, head in hand, asking why things had turned out as they had and why she hadn't tried harder to change it all. She'd asked herself the same questions many times before. The answer was that she had tried to change things, over and over again, but her mother hadn't wanted to listen, let alone act. More difficult to accept was that too often one's best efforts counted for nothing. Things just turned out the way they did.

A creak from the foyer cut short her silent tirade.

"Hello?" Vika called.

No one responded.

She crossed the living room to the front door and peered down the corridor. "Hello?" she tried again.

The corridor was dark, the lights activated by motion sensors.

Reassured, she closed the door and locked it. No one could hear her scream anyway and she preferred not to have someone sneak up on her.

She walked down the hall toward Mama's bedroom, tucking her head into the guest rooms along the way. Both were made up and appeared untouched since Vika's last visit.

The door to the master was ajar, which frightened her more than the shattered brandy glass, the empty vodka bottle, or the pee in the toilet. Doors in a home were either open or closed. Never ajar. With her fingertips, she gave it a shove. The door swung inward.

Vika took a step, steeling herself.

The room was immaculate. The king-sized bed neatly made, the sable bedspread placed just so, the silver lamé throws arranged as Mama liked them. There was a stack of books on her night table, and Vika was reassured to note that they were the same books as ten years earlier: Donna Leon's biggest hits of the aughts. Next to them, arranged as neatly as soldiers on a parade ground, were Mama's pills. A rogues' gallery of vitamins, nutrients, and supplements that would have done Severus Snape proud. (She was the mother of a twelve-year-old boy. Of course she'd read Harry Potter.) If Vika saw eye of newt she wouldn't have been surprised. Herbs, yes. Doctors, no. Nothing better illustrated her mother's mental state.

She picked up a bottle to read the label and noted a sudden change in the light. Bright to dim to bright again. Startled, she spun, expecting to confront an intruder. A moth fluttered below the ceiling lamp.

Vika expelled her breath. A look down the hallway calmed her. Of course there was no one there.

Seized with the urge to find what she'd come for, she entered the master bathroom. The sinks and countertops were as spic-and-span as the bedroom, toothpaste, toothbrush, eye cream, and a variety of cosmetic nostrums all in their rightful places. There was no glint of metal to be seen, no chunk of gold hiding anywhere on the white stone surface. Vika dismissed the sink with an unprincess-like snort. It had been foolish to think Mama would leave it there. If the ring was anywhere, surely it was in the safe.

Vika marched into the closet. Dropping to her knees, she swept aside row upon row of shoes like a scythe through wheat. Decorum be damned. She needed to find the ring.

A corner of the carpet was dog-eared. She took hold of it and yanked ferociously, peeling it back to reveal the floor safe. The combination was Papa's birthday, of course. The door sprang upward.

A spray of diamonds winked at her. Vika had seen the tiara a thousand times but it dazzled her nonetheless. One hundred carats of diamonds, half again as many of rubies and sapphires. It was named the Brandenburg tiara, created in 1815 for another Princess von Tiefen und Tassis's appearance at the very first opera ball celebrating the Congress of Vienna.

Why wasn't it in its proper case?

Vika propped herself up on an elbow and removed the tiara. Looking closer, she noted that there were a few diamonds missing and that one arm was slightly bent. *Oh Mama,* she thought, imagining her mother parading around in one of her drunken states while wearing the tiara and probably a formal gown as well.

With care, she set the tiara aside.

She lay on her belly and sorted through the safe's contents. There were legal documents and bundles of cash in different currencies, some long since out of use. (French francs, anyone? Dutch guilders?) There at the bottom was Mama's jewelry box, black velvet with her initials embossed in gold. *Finally,* thought Vika. She stretched a hand into the safe to retrieve it.

"Zat's a fuck lot of diamonds."

Vika screamed as a giant's hand took her by the neck and dragged her to her feet. Out of the corner of her eye, she glimpsed a hooded figure, a large man in dark clothing, a balaclava pulled over his face. He yanked her head back and she cried out.

"Jebena kučka," he growled in a Slavic language she did not understand. "Now we have some fun. You and me."

The fingers dug into the muscles of her neck, paralyzing her. He guided her out of the closet to the bedroom, slamming her against the wall, shoving her onto the fur bedspread, never lessening his grip on her neck. Stunned, panicked, too confused to make sense of what was happening, Vika lay facedown, motionless, fighting for breath. Then he was on her, his weight smothering her, his loins shoved against her. She smelled his breath. Liver and onions and coffee. She gagged. She felt him, insistent and hostile. A hand slipped into her pants. She threw an elbow and hit something hard. The man grunted. His weight shifted, and she slid off the bed, tried to stand, desperately wanting to reach the door, only to be slammed onto the floor, her cheek landing first, a tooth coming loose. She tasted blood.

The man ripped her pants to her knees. She was hurt, frightened, in shock. She writhed. She fought. A fist slugged the side of her face. She stopped struggling. Rough hands pulled at her panties. Fabric ripped. She felt him against her, ugly and probing.

"Stop it!" she screamed.

Another fist landed on her skull.

She saw stars.

"Help me," she whimpered.

Suddenly, the weight lifted. He was no longer on top of her. Someone else was in the room…Another man…It was Simon Riske. He was yelling… something French— *"Espèce de salaud"*—and he grabbed the attacker by his shoulders, hauled him to his feet, and tossed him against the dresser.

*   *   *

Simon glanced at Vika, saw her head move, blood on the carpet. She was alive, thank God. He looked back as the attacker regained his balance, pulling up his pants. The man grabbed a glass vase and backhanded it at Simon, the vase glancing off his head, stunning him. The attacker charged, leading with a shoulder, slamming him against the wall, pinning him with his body weight. Thick hands found Simon's neck, thumbs digging into his throat, collapsing his windpipe. Simon forced an open palm under the man's jaw, pressing up with all his might. His left hand dropped to his side and he thrust it into the man's unzipped trousers, took hold of his testicles, and crushed them.

An unholy scream filled the room.

The grip on Simon's neck loosened. The hands fell away and Simon head-butted the man, forcing him back a step. Simon curled his knuckles and launched a jab at his larynx, sending him stumbling. In desperation, the man grabbed a drawer and pulled it clear of the dresser, the contents falling onto the floor as he swung wildly.

Simon turned, taking the blow with his shoulder, the force splintering the wood. The attacker dropped the drawer and snapped up something on the floor. A letter opener, long and sharp as a dagger. He lunged at Simon, just missing. Simon grabbed a book off the nightstand and, clutching it with both hands, used it to deflect the next blow, and the next. He allowed the third blow closer, too close, feeling the blade slice into his belly, and brought the book down on the man's wrist, swinging his shoulders in an arc, driving the book into the attacker's throat. In the same motion, he aimed a kick at the man's knee.

The attacker was agile for his size and dodged the kick, retreating several steps.

It was a standoff. The men faced each other, panting. The attacker's eyes were black and hooded and Simon promised never to forget them. He felt light-headed, his throat swelling, his gut aching terribly.

The attacker flipped the letter opener in his hand so that he held it by the tip. In a lightning motion, he threw it at Vika, as deftly as a knife thrower at a circus. The blade embedded itself below her shoulder blade. She cried out. In that instant, the man fled.

Simon pursued him down the hall and into the kitchen, the man dashing through the maid's entrance and down a flight of stairs. It was the same entrance that Simon had used minutes before. The stairwell was dark and promised danger.

He pulled up. "I will find you!" he shouted, consumed with rage. "You are dead. Do you hear me? Dead!"

Simon hurried back to Vika, who was still on the floor. With care he freed the blade, noting that it had not gone in too deeply. He told her to remain still and returned with a warm washcloth. He knelt down next to her and held it in place as she sat up.

"I'm sorry," she said.

Simon placed an arm around her. She laid her head on his shoulder. She sobbed once, then was quiet. They sat that way for a while. Simon suggested that it was time they go to the hospital. She would need stitches. It was important that a doctor see her. He noted that there was blood on his shirt and the fabric was torn. He was certainly doing a number on his wardrobe.

"He didn't," said Vika, answering a question Simon would not ask.

"I'll find him."

"How?"

Simon could only shake his head, for he had no answer.

CHAPTER 30

A distant church tolled the midnight hour as Ratka climbed the gangway to the *Lady S.* He headed fore, where lights burned in the salon. He descended two flights of stairs, past the living quarters and the pantry. He entered the office without knocking.

"Well?" asked the man behind the desk.

"Four million." Ratka tossed an envelope containing the checks onto the table. "So far. Two hours left."

The man swept it into the top drawer, locking it afterward. Honor among thieves was overrated. He looked more closely at Ratka. "What happened to you?" he asked, then raised a finger. "And don't even think of lying to me."

Ratka poured himself a glass of raki, the Turkish firewater the Jew was fond of, and slipped into a chair. "Bitch," he murmured.

"What have you been up to?"

"She went to the apartment. I wanted to have a little fun."

"Fun? You and I have different conceptions of the word."

Ratka ran a hand over his throat, wincing at the spot where he'd been slugged. Reluctantly, he related the details of what had transpired. He hated the Jew as he hated all Jews, but he respected him. They were partners, and without him, Ratka knew none of their plans would have been possible. When he'd finished, the man simply stared at him. It was the look a man gave an animal, a beast of burden, not another man. Ratka threw back the rest of the raki. Maybe he was an animal. God knew that he had done things other men could not.

"Why?" asked the Jew, more mystified than angered, a hand appraising his shorn silver hair.

Ratka met the blue eyes and looked past them, to a time twenty-five years earlier, when he'd met the gaze of a man who'd looked very much like him. Not a Jew, but a Bosnian Muslim, a Bosniak. Ratka had not been looking at him across a sleek teak table aboard a luxury vessel, but through the crosshatched wire of a fence at a makeshift concentration camp Ratka and his men had built in a secluded valley ten kilometers outside the town of Srebrenica.

Ratka had ordered the men in the camp to dig a slit trench deep in the forest. It was to be used as a latrine, he'd told them. He'd taken the prisoners there in groups of twenty and executed them. Three thousand over the course of a day. Including one Bosniak who'd looked as if he could be the Jew's twin.

"Why?" Ratka shrugged, the memory of his requited power fresh after all these years. "Because I could."

"Do you know who saved her?"

"The same as before."

"The one with the Ferrari?"

Ratka nodded without shame. "I will find him."

"That won't be necessary," said Dov Dragan. "I know where he is."

Chapter 31

They crossed the lobby like survivors of a catastrophe, their path uncertain, leaning on each other, the only important thing to keep moving. It was three in the morning. A skeleton staff presided over the hotel. A clerk left her position behind reception and floated ahead to summon the elevator.

Simon took Vika to his room. She entered without protest. He gave her a T-shirt and a pair of boxers. She entered the bathroom with a tired smile, saying she wanted to clean up. Simon kicked off his shoes and collapsed into an armchair. He wore a doctor's smock under his jacket. A strip of gauze covered his wound. Four stitches and a staple deeper down. The doctor had warned him that the blade had nearly penetrated the peritoneum. All Simon knew was that it hurt like hell. Vika's stitch tally was lower and she escaped without a staple, but her injury was the worse, psychological and long-lasting.

The bathroom door opened and Vika came out looking very much younger and vulnerable, the T-shirt much too large and falling midthigh.

"I hate the Sex Pistols," she said.

"It's more about the statement," said Simon.

"I'll take Brahms any day."

"A lover of the classics."

"Of course," she said, with flair. "I'm a princess, after all."

She was suddenly wide awake, her eyes bright, her motions lively. "Want something?" she asked from the bar. "Tea? Shall I make you a drink?" She turned to look at him, hands on her hips. "You're a whiskey man, but definitely not scotch."

"Amen to that."

"Bourbon?"

"Why not? Neat."

She found a bottle of bourbon among the others and poured a healthy measure in a short glass. For herself, she decided on mineral water in a champagne glass. His eyes didn't leave her as she crossed the room. She handed him the drink, then joined him where he sat, nimbly placing one knee to either side of him and settling on his lap.

They touched glasses. "Cheers," she said.

Simon sipped the bourbon and set down the glass. Vika lowered her face to his and kissed him twice.

"One for each time you saved my life."

For once, Simon was at a loss for words. He looked into her eyes and felt a part of himself slipping away, slipping into her. It was not a feeling he was familiar with and it made him at once giddy and uncomfortable. He was in dangerous waters.

"Why did you come?" she asked.

"I was worried when you weren't in your room."

"You checked?"

"Of course."

"How did you find me?"

"I have my ways."

"No, really…"

"The telephone directory. Crafty of me."

"I saw you leaving the hotel and go to the casino. It made me angry."

"Work."

"You looked so excited."

"That's part of it. I was engaged to look into a spate of cheating. Actually, more than a spate. It's important that I appear to be just another gambler."

"Did you find them?"

"Maybe. It's not just a question of finding them, but of proving how they do it." There was a last thing that Simon failed to mention. He intended to track down the stolen money and return it to Lord Toby Stonewood. Every last penny.

"Actually, I was jealous," Vika said shyly, as if admitting it to herself only now. "I wanted you to be with me."

She brushed her lips against his. Simon ran a hand across the small of her back. Her skin was warm to the touch. They kissed. Softly, at first, slowly, an exploration. He touched her breast. Her nipple hardened. She gasped, and kissed him harder, passionately giving herself to him.

"Are you sure?" he whispered.

Vika nodded.

Simon placed a hand beneath her buttocks and stood, carrying her to the bed. He lowered her to the sheets and, with care, pulled her shirt over her head. She lifted her hips wantonly, and he slipped off the boxer shorts, thinking they looked better on her than they ever would on him. He undressed and lay beside her.

"Carefully," he said as he took her in his arms.

He knew that they were both riding out the adrenaline, his born of savagery, hers of fear. He also knew that this was the start of something.

He kissed her neck and her breasts, running his fingers across her shoulders, her arms. His hand found hers and their fingers interlocked. She was as hungry as he, and they used each other's bodies without shame, climaxing together, and afterward shared a good-natured, loving smile.

She closed her eyes and was asleep instantly. Simon lay beside her, studying her features, the tip of her nose, the ridges of her lips, the rise and fall of her chest. He was bewitched.

Dangerous waters.

Sleep wouldn't come.

Simon rose and left the bedroom, drawing the pocket doors so as not to disturb her. He made himself an espresso and sat at the desk, laptop open. He accessed a software program called Apache. It was Vikram Singh's name, chosen because of the Apache Indians' famed ability to track an adversary over any surface. The screen showed a map of Monte Carlo. Simon pulled down the menu. Four objects were listed: SR1, SR2, SR3, and SR4, each a designation assigned to one of the miniature tracking devices he'd deployed in the casino.

He double-clicked on the first—SR1—and a track in the form of a solid line appeared on the map, with dots along the path indicating five-minute intervals. The track started at the casino, passed by the Café de Paris, then carved a winding route through the city. In turn, Simon selected the next three objects. One line was black, one blue, one red, and one green. Finished, he studied the map and smiled.

Bingo.

Had he placed the trackers on four random individuals, he could expect their paths to lead in different directions. Two might intertwine, or even end up at locations near each other, but not all four. The odds were a billion to one that four people with no association with one another would follow the same path, even for a short distance.

And yet that was precisely what Simon saw when he studied the map. It appeared, prima facie, that the men he'd tagged had shared a common path, at least part of the way. All four colored lines left the casino and went directly to the Café de Paris next door, just twenty meters away. There the lines blended into one as they entered the restaurant and—here was the first giveaway that they were not only associated with one another and thus part of a larger team but professionals—continued out the rear.

Curious as to their activities inside the café, Simon drilled down by shading a section of the track corresponding with the interior of the café and requesting the corresponding time stamp. Again, he was rewarded. None of the four had spent longer than two minutes inside the café. All stopped at the same location for just under sixty seconds. Either they had all decided to take a nice long leak at exactly the same bathroom at exactly the same restaurant or they were making a drop.

From the Café de Paris, the men went their separate ways. Two, however, ended up at the same address, where Simon deduced they were sleeping at this moment. The other paths ended abruptly after the men had traveled more than ten kilometers and their transmitters had dropped out of range.

Simon wrote down the address on the Avenue Georges Guynemer where the two men boarded. He decided it might be interesting to follow them in order to learn more about their daily activities. If, by a stroke of luck, the men wore the same clothing tomorrow, the tracker would do his job for him.

It was a start.

Simon closed the laptop. A yawn caught him by surprise and he returned to the bedroom. He dropped into an overstuffed chair beside the bed and watched Vika sleep. She looked peaceful and without worry.

Yet Simon sensed that she was hiding something from him. Before they left her mother's apartment, he'd put away the tiara and jewelry and locked the safe. Vika had said she had come to sort through her mother's things, but it was apparent there was another reason, a reason she had yet to divulge. He'd seen it in the tightness of her mouth when they'd left, the rigidity of her shoulders. Something was compelling her to remain even after all that had happened.

Gazing at her in repose, Simon knew that when he found the man who'd attacked her and learned the reason behind her mother's death, she would have to tell him. And it would have to be on her own.

CHAPTER 32

Robby woke at seven sharp, excited about the day to come. Stretching, he sat up and pushed back the covers. The air was frigid. He shivered. He touched his toes to the floor and lifted them right back up again. The wooden floorboards were cold as ice. He turned his head to listen for the groaning of the heating pipes coming to life. Old buildings were like old people. They made all kinds of strange, unexpected noises. The dorm was silent. It was too early in the season to turn on the central heating, though he didn't know it. He steeled himself to the cold and walked to his sink to brush his teeth. There was a strange stillness in the air, a quiet more than quiet. He put his toothbrush back in its glass and opened the curtains.

White.

Everywhere white.

"It's snowing!" he shouted.

The snow fell in fat, feathery billows past his window. A layer two fingers thick covered the rooftops. The courtyard was white as an ice rink. Clouds hovered low over the mountains, the pine forest a pale canopy. He opened the window and thrust out his hand. A pile grew quickly on his palm and he licked it off, tasting nothing, only prickly cold.

Robby closed the window and made a beeline for his armoire. Yesterday he'd spent ten minutes picking out his clothes for this morning. He had to start all over again. He sorted through his shirts and trousers. There wasn't much to choose from. Students at Zuoz had to wear a uniform. He had two extra pairs of trousers, a few colorful sweaters, and his father's Moncler parka, which was far too big for him.

He grabbed the parka and put it on over his pajamas, trying to disregard how long the sleeves were and the fact that he looked like a Q-tip wrapped up in a purple comforter. A terrifying thought came to him. The storm would worsen. The school would cancel leave. He wouldn't be allowed to hit town. He'd miss his date with Elisabeth.

Robby dashed to the nightstand and scooped up his phone. The weather app said the snow would continue until Monday. He left his room and ran down the hall, banging on doors until he discovered someone awake, and demanded to know if he thought leave would be canceled.

"No," said Edmond Fang.

"No," said Mattias Gross.

"No," said Pranay Gupta.

Robby returned to his room, only partially mollified. One set of nerves replaced another. He was going to see her. It was really going to happen.

His hands digging into the pockets of the enormous purple parka, he tapped his feet on the ground impatiently. He could think only of her. Of her blond hair and broad smile, of her warm, singsongy voice and the curve of her figure beneath her sweater.

His heart beat faster.

He had a half day of school to get through before his life would change forever.

CHAPTER 33

Simon had been working for an hour when he heard the pocket doors open and Vika came out of the bedroom.

"Guten Morgen," he said, sliding the chair from the desk, offering a smile.

Vika walked past him, eyes cast down, a wan, dissatisfied smile on her face, and disappeared into the bathroom. The door closed. The sound of the lock slamming home felt like a slap in the face. His German wasn't that bad.

Simon went back to work. The laptop was open. The Apache software showed no change in the trackers' location from last night. Two of the transmitters remained at the address on the Avenue Georges Guynemer. A check of the street view on Google Maps showed the home to be a run-down salmon-colored villa located in a hilly part of the city, a stone's throw from the Italian border.

Simon's attention, however, was not on the laptop. It was on the leather wallet he'd lifted the previous evening from the man he'd identified as using a hidden camera to film the shoe. The wallet contained no means of identification, no bank or credit cards, no photographs, no love notes, or any of the other doodads one tends to collect in the course of daily life. The wallet held two thousand euros. That was all.

Simon opened the fold and ran a finger inside it. Out of habit, he searched every nook and cranny. In his old life, he did it to find drugs—a spindle of coke or something better—not information. His reward was a wrinkled piece of paper—some kind of ticket, at first look. Printed on one side were several groupings of letters and a time stamp: "19:17 16.6.18" (7:17 p.m., June 16, 2018). The other side was blank except for a watermark of an eagle's head and a stylized abbreviation: "BTA."

Simon put down the slip of paper and opened a new window on the laptop. In the search bar he typed the letter groupings as well as the abbreviation: "ZTW RSR BTA."

He hit SEND and the gods of the Internet delivered unto him an answer. The slip of paper was indeed a ticket. A twenty-four-hour urban transit pass purchased at the Žarkovo station in New Belgrade and issued by the Belgrade Transit Authority.

Simon picked up the paper again. By rights, it should mean nothing. Yet his heart was beating more quickly than it had been a minute before, and there was no mistaking the surge of adrenaline that had him rising from his chair. During his drive from London, he'd been pursued by men whose driver's licenses had identified them as residents of Croatia, part of the former Yugoslavia. They'd followed him to get revenge for the breaking up of their scam at Les Ambassadeurs.

Belgrade was the capital of Serbia, also part of the former Yugoslavia.

Simon drew the only natural conclusion.

There was a gang of Slavic criminals hitting casinos all across Europe.

Before he could give his thesis further consideration, Vika emerged from the bathroom. She was dressed in her clothing from the night before. Her face was scrubbed and she gave him an officious smile as she passed by.

"How are you feeling?" Simon followed her into the bedroom.

"Better."

She picked up the phone and called room service, her back to him as she ordered breakfast for one. Simon put his hands around her waist and she peeled them off, holding them limply. "About last night."

"Yes?"

"I owe you an apology," she said. "I took advantage of you."

"Of me?" Already Simon did not like the direction in which the conversation was headed.

"I needed to feel whole. Clean. I needed to erase the memory. Please, let's not make anything more out of it."

Simon flinched. "Oh?"

Vika gave his hands a squeeze and released them. "Again, I'm sorry."

"Of course," he said. "I mean, yes, you're right. It was the moment. We got carried away."

"Exactly. I'm glad you agree." She smiled too kindly. "Of course, it was very nice. You were wonderful. I just don't want you to get any ideas."

"Ideas?"

"About us. About, well, you know. We're two adults. These things happen."

Simon nodded. Vika was speaking as if she were describing a lively game of charades. Infuriated, fighting to keep his anger and embarrassment in check, he excused himself, saying it was time for a shower.

He closed the bathroom door and turned the lock every bit as forcefully as she had. His head was spinning. How had his emotions betrayed him? Was he so desperate for connection that he mistook sex for love? He knew too much about the first and very little about the second. Despair fell over him like a cloud blocking the sun. His world had suddenly grown colder, darker.

He faced himself in the mirror and stood up straighter, trying to find the old Simon, "old" meaning prior to meeting Victoria Brandenburg. She of the direct gaze and patronizing tone. He tried the well-worn admonition "Snap out of it, man!," but the words carried no heft.

Instead, he fell back on logic. An objective review of the facts. He reminded himself that he'd met her thirty-six hours ago. He barely knew her. She was a princess. A *real* princess. And a billionaire to boot. Not to mention an MBA who'd graduated with high honors from Europe's top business school.

Simon was a hood working to make amends for a past as black as ever there was. He was a car thief, a bank robber, and a convicted felon who'd spent four years in a French prison where he'd murdered a man, a fellow inmate he'd killed with malice, forethought, and premeditation. Yes, he'd graduated from the London School of Economics and earned a graduate degree at the Sorbonne, but it was window dressing. He looked at the tattoo inked on his forearm, the symbol for the gang of Corsican criminals who'd made him one of their own. That was the real Simon Riske and it always would be.

The fact was that he had no business assuming she had feelings for him.

He had no parents, no relatives, and had never bothered to trace his heritage past his grandparents. She traced her lineage back a thousand years.

No business at all.

He met his eyes in the mirror. Was there anything more ridiculous than a fool?

He took a shower, then dressed quickly, throwing on tan chinos and a navy polo shirt. He left the bathroom, barely in control of himself. "We need to go to your mother's apartment."

"But why?"

Simon brushed past her, stuffing his wallet and phone into his pockets, popping a Fisherman's Friend into his mouth. Damn the memories. "Bring your mother's pistol. And this time load it."

"What for?"

"You want to find out what happened to your mother? The answer's there."

Chapter 34

It was nicer to enter through the lobby, thought Simon as he held the door to the Château Perigord for Vika. There was no doorman, but a desk manned by a real estate agent eager to sell them an apartment in the developer's new building on Portier Cove, the man-made spit of land being dredged up from the seafloor, enlarging the city's beach. Studios started at nine million. It was pleasing to learn that there was a place more expensive than London. Simon made a note to come back in the next life as a developer.

The elevator was slow but had what was once called character. They rode without speaking, an invisible wall between them, no doubt of his making. Vika's marching rhythm lost its vigor as they approached her mother's apartment. Simon offered no bluff words of encouragement. Some things a person needed to reckon for themselves.

At the door, Vika took the pistol from her purse and gave it to Simon. He checked that a bullet was chambered and thumbed off the safety. He stood by as she searched for the proper key. He counted ten or more on her key chain, each coded with a different colored fob. She caught him observing her. "A master key for each house," she stated.

"How many do you own?"

"Own or visit?"

This was a twist Simon hadn't heard before. "Visit."

"Five regularly. Marbella, Como, Manhattan…" She shrugged. "Paris and Pontresina."

"Where's home?"

"Schloss Brandenburg."

"Sounds cozy."

"Actually, it is rather—" She looked at him. "You're poking fun at me."

Her hand steadied and she slid the key home. Simon opened the door and stepped inside. The foyer was pitch-dark. He listened and knew the place was deserted.

"Come in," he said. "No one's here."

Vika crossed the room to draw the curtains. Daylight robbed the place of its violent history. It was no longer the scene of a crime but a large, beautifully decorated flat that looked as though a gang of teenagers had thrown a rager in it the night before.

She gave the room a look, hands on her hips, like a general inspecting her troops. "What are we looking for?"

"Something that shouldn't be here," said Simon.

Vika led the way to the kitchen. She opened the refrigerator and handed Simon an ice-cold bottle of spirits. "We can start with this. Mama did not drink grappa."

Grappa di Brancaia. The price tag was still affixed to the base: 249 euros. The good stuff. Someone else, then, had polished off half the bottle.

"Boyfriend?" Simon reasoned that a woman wouldn't bring a bottle of grappa as a present, not if she knew her host hated the stuff. That was a man, all right. Ditto forgetting to take off the price tag.

"It must be the person she mentioned on the voice mail."

"The one she thought was trying to hurt her."

"Yes."

"I think it's time you played me the message."

Vika hesitated, looking as if he'd suggested she have a root canal. The fact that she did not trust him twisted the knife a little further.

"Now," he said, and she drew the phone from her purse and accessed the voice mail message left by her mother.

"Vika, are you there? Can you hear me? I'm in trouble. You've got to come down and help me. There's a man. He wants to know about the family. I didn't tell him anything. Of course, you know I'd never. But he keeps asking. I'm wor-

ried for you. For Fritz. I didn't say a word. Please, darling. I thought he was my friend, but now I'm worried. He scares me."

Vika stopped the message. "That's all you need to hear. She goes a little crazy. It's personal."

Simon took the phone and replayed the message several times, listening for nuances, memorizing it verbatim. He zeroed in on the fact that Vika had forgotten to mention. "Who is Fritz?"

"My son."

"Is he here?"

"God, no. He's away at boarding school."

"Where?"

"Switzerland. In the mountains. There's a teacher who looks after him. A man who used to be in the military. Fritz doesn't know, of course."

"Any other children?" Simon demanded.

"No."

"So why would your mother be worried about him?"

"I told you yesterday. She was paranoid. Everyone was out to get her. The shopgirl selling her gloves gave her dirty looks. The waiter was eyeing her purse. She even claimed that people broke into the apartment and searched her closet while she was out."

"Maybe they did."

Vika's expression darkened. She was not a woman who encountered much resistance in her daily life.

"Let's assume she had her friend over," Simon went on. "You said she didn't get out much. Where might she have met him?"

"She ate lunch three or four days a week at an Italian place down the street."

"By herself?"

"With Elena."

"Still no word?"

Vika shook her head, indicating that she hadn't had any luck.

"Call her. Please."

Vika placed the call. No one answered. Instead of rolling to voice mail, a disembodied voice stated that the mailbox was full.

"Is that like her?"

Vika shook her head.

"When we're done here, we'll see about checking the security cameras downstairs."

"Commissaire Le Juste said that we needed a—"

"I know what he said."

"But—"

Simon raised a hand. "This is the kind of problem I solve."

Vika nodded, and he was pleased to see that she was getting used to the fact that he would be the one calling the shots.

Back in the living room, he asked, "Was it like this when you visited before?"

"Elena picked up after her, but Mama could let things slide. Growing up, things could get rather sordid."

Simon picked up the stem of a broken glass. "This kind of sordid?"

Vika said yes and Simon continued his tour of the room, kneeling to look under the furniture, lifting sofa cushions and pillows, peering behind armoires and dressers. Vika followed at his shoulder and he sensed that she was nervous, overly protective. Instead of wanting him to discover a clue as to what had gone on there, she was afraid. Afraid of him finding *the wrong thing*.

She needn't have worried. Besides a pack of cigarettes, a few coins, and a TV remote control, he turned up nothing of interest. When he'd finished looking, the two were standing at the end of the hallway. The door to the bedroom was open. "Do you want to come with me?"

"Of course," she said, with false conviction. She led the way, stopping at the entry. The room was as they'd left it. The only sign of the altercation was the splintered dresser drawer lying on the bedspread. In contrast to the rest of the apartment, the bedroom was neat and tidy, a triangular vacuum pattern still partially visible on the carpet.

"Did Elena stick to cleaning bedrooms?"

"What are you suggesting?"

"I think your mother was harmed here."

*   *   *

Vika stood in the doorway, one hand on the frame. She wasn't accustomed to others doing her work for her, or for that matter to answering pointed questions and taking instruction from others.

Her eyes took in the room. She felt no fear of entering, no post-traumatic anything. It might come later, but she doubted it. Her entire life had been rife with drama. She'd learned at an early age to build walls, inside and out. It was another woman who'd been attacked. A woman she knew well, but had little feeling for.

She watched Simon move around the room, his concentration absolute. She wasn't sure why the prospect of his finding the ring frightened her. Maybe it was the fact that she thought of him as "Simon" a day after meeting him, or that he already knew much too much about her. She reminded herself that this man had saved her life and that hours earlier she had made love to him and given herself to him as she rarely had anyone, including her husband. Maybe that was why she harbored a growing antipathy toward him. He was an outsider. A stranger. At best an interloper. At worst a palace thief. It wasn't the ring he was after. It was something else. Something that Vika had never let anyone have entirely. Her heart.

It was jarring how memory can paint over a place, thought Simon. The bedroom was bright and sunny and smelled of pine-scented floor cleaner. Yet he couldn't take a step without a shadow darkening the room, without hearing Vika's desperate whimpering and reliving the shock of coming upon her.

"If they cleaned up, it's because they left behind a mess," he said. "Not just something broken, but something on the carpet or the floor."

"Blood?"

"For example."

He lowered himself to all fours, running his hands through the carpet. Something pricked his finger. It was a sliver of glass, hardly thicker than a hair. He came across a spot still damp at its base. He brushed the fibers back and forth. Was it darker than the rest? He peeked beneath the chairs, the dressers, the bed. He found nothing. Not even a dust ball.

Simon rose, looked at Vika, then entered the bathroom. It was the size of a locker room, with travertine floors and Wenge wood cabinets and brushed-stone counters with polished silver fixtures. He walked the perimeter, acutely sensitive to the pine-scented cleaner. Whatever had happened, it had happened here. A dozen white towels were rolled up like scrolls and stacked in an open-faced cabinet. He sorted through them and found red specks on one that he surmised had been placed at the bottom on purpose.

The contents of the drawers were neatly arranged. Too neatly, he thought, as if readied for a photo shoot for *OCD Monthly*. They'd been looking for something. That explained the living room, as well.

"Is anything missing?" he asked.

"Excuse me?"

"Isn't that why you opened the safe?"

"I was checking on Mama's things. When I saw the living room, I thought there might have been a robbery."

"And?"

"No," she said. "Not that I noticed."

In the top drawer beneath the sink, he found several rings laid out in a row. He picked up a diamond solitaire. Three carats at least. Brilliant clarity. D or E, and he was ready to wager nearly flawless. VVS or VVS1. Value: two hundred thousand dollars at a minimum. Simon knew his precious stones. "It wasn't a robbery."

Vika said nothing.

Simon replaced the ring and shut the drawer. He opened the shower stall, glass on two sides, a rugged stone basin with a tile mosaic inlaid. A medieval shield with three roses in a yellow stripe running diagonally across it, and a knight's helmet resting atop it. Across the bottom were the numbers "1016."

"The family crest," Vika said.

"A thousand years old," said Simon.

"Just."

His eye went to the ceiling and he saw it. There in the corner, next to a can light, was a skein of blood, long and unruly. He sniffed the pine cleaner, the ammonia hidden within making his eyes water. There had been more blood. Oh yes. Much more. They had killed her here, then taken her to the garage through the servants' entrance. The car accident was an improvisation—the only way to hide her true cause of death.

Simon was forming a mental picture of what had happened. There was no forced entry. Stefanie Brandenburg had let her killer in or accompanied him from another location. They'd met at the Italian restaurant. He brought her the grappa because she liked Italian food. Drinks were poured. The grappa for him, Polish vodka for her. It wasn't his first time here. Maybe he'd seen the Bang and Olufsen turntable and had promised to bring his favorite "oldies." Hence the record album. They were the same age, or close.

He'd come for a reason. The same reason he'd gone to the restaurant to meet her. The same reason he'd been asking questions about the family—questions that had frightened Vika's mother.

He wanted something. Something more valuable than a diamond ring worth a few hundred thousand dollars.

Vika knew what it was.

"You're sure everything was in the safe?" Simon asked.

"Yes."

"And no one has tampered with it?"

She shook her head. "I'd know."

He stared at her from beneath his furrowed brow. There was nothing subtle about it. He doubted her veracity. She added nothing. After a moment, he nodded, not pressing her, but far from certain she was telling the truth. He left the bathroom without mentioning the blood on the ceiling.

The sun was reaching its high point, flashing atop the bay. Simon opened the door to the balcony and stepped outside to be met by a breeze. Yachts of all shapes and sizes cut through the water. Farther out, a French warship was moored, gray and hulking, a cruiser or destroyer, looking out of place among the festive boaters.

Vika joined him, gazing at the sea. The wind played with her hair and Simon liked that she didn't bother trying to keep it in place. "I know it's a bit awkward," he said.

"Pardon?"

"Between us."

"Is it?" said Vika. "I'm sorry if I seem distant. It's better that we concentrate on why we're here."

"You're probably right."

"I don't mean to hurt your feelings," she said, knowing she was doing exactly that. "You were wonderful. *It* was wonderful, but…"

"Don't read too much into this, Vika. We're both adults. I think we have more important matters in front of us."

She nodded, too enthusiastically, in Simon's opinion. The smile that accompanied it screamed relief and salvation. One more suitor disposed of. At least things were settled between them.

"Did we learn anything?" she asked.

"I think so."

"Would you care to tell me?"

Simon turned to her. If he wanted to, he could put his hands on her waist and draw her to him. He could tell her how he felt. He could say he was in love with her, already, right now. He saw nothing in her eyes that indicated she might reciprocate the feeling.

"I'd like to go to the garage," he said.

"What for?"

Simon left the balcony, closing the door after she'd followed. On the way to the foyer, he spotted a framed photograph on the top shelf of a glass and chrome armoire. A boy. Thin and pale, wearing a rugby jersey, with Vika's straight nose, a thatch of curly blond hair, and blue eyes that looked right through you. "Fritz?"

Vika smiled adoringly and picked up the photograph. "Well, that's what we call him. His full name is Robert Frederick Maximillian. He's away at school in Switzerland." She returned the photograph to its place. "His friends call him Robby."

*   *   *

Only half of the spaces in the garage were taken. Stefanie Brandenburg's parking spot was ten paces from the elevator, befitting her age, title, and pocketbook, though probably not in that order. There was an oil stain from a leaky carburetor. And another stain a few feet away that was nearly as dark, but not oil.

The overhead lights were weak and fluttered as if they might go out at any moment. Simon activated his phone's flashlight and moved it in an arc. Something sparkled, there against the wall. Gold. He picked it up.

"Look familiar?" he said, handing the cuff link to Vika. White enamel with a sword and shield and strange runes. This one was in perfect condition. "Now we know for certain," he said. "Whoever it was that visited your mother the other night, he killed her."

CHAPTER 35

There was no need for Commissaire Le Juste's warrant or Simon's expertise with a lockpick. A princess's request sufficed.

With alacrity, the apartment manager led Vika and Simon to his office and into an adjacent room filled floor to ceiling with television monitors displaying live feeds from the building's thirty-one security cameras.

It was almost too easy, thought Simon.

"Please understand," the apartment manager explained, and the other shoe dropped. "If I could fulfill your request, I would. Alas, our system was subjected to some kind of attack just three days ago. Somehow our recordings…our entire hard drive…were destroyed. 'Wiped clean' are the words our security expert used. We are at a loss. One day all was working properly. The next, we were unable to record a thing. Kaput!"

"You're certain?" Vika shared Simon's disappointment. "You have nothing from Sunday night?"

"Nothing. *Rien.* But rest assured, Madame la Princesse, the system is once again functioning perfectly. It was a one-time problem. Never again."

Vika thanked the multilingual manager graciously and he responded with something between a bow, a curtsy, and the Hitler *gruss.* A man to satisfy every client. Simon gave him a hard look to let him know he wasn't entirely satisfied with his explanation, but there was nothing to be done.

"Bad luck," said Vika when they were on the street.

"Luck had nothing to do with it." The destruction of the hard disc added a level of sophistication to the crime that he would be wise to respect. It wasn't difficult to wipe a drive. All you needed was an industrial magnet and access to the machines. It was the fact that they'd thought ahead. Stefanie Brandenburg's murder was premeditated.

"How could they do such a thing?" asked Vika.

By now Simon was only half listening. "Come on," he said, standing on the curb, scanning traffic. When she hesitated, he took her hand and crossed the street with her in tow. He opened the door to the Pharmacie Mougins directly facing the Château Perigord. She entered, confused, looking to Simon for an explanation. At the counter, he asked the pharmacist if he could speak to the manager. An attractive middle-aged woman wearing a crisp white coat, glasses tucked into her hair, emerged from the storage area. "How may I be of assistance?"

Simon walked to the far side of the counter and slipped a folded thousand-euro note across the surface. The woman's brown eyes took in the bill and jumped angrily to Simon, who explained that he had not come for a "special" prescription. He offered a story about a stolen car and a wayward son and inquired if by any chance the pharmacy kept a camera trained on the front door. He knew the answer. He'd spotted it from across the street and believed there was a good chance it captured traffic moving in both directions along the Boulevard d'Italie. "I must find my boy," he said, with emotion.

The banknote disappeared into the woman's coat pocket.

She lifted the barrier, and a minute later, Simon and Vika found themselves wedged in a supply closet working the controls of a four-camera multiplex and recording system. The top right screen broadcast the sidewalk and front door in full-color high-def. Cars driving past in both directions were visible and Simon noted that he could make out their license plates.

It was a new setup, no more than a year old. Simon plugged in a date and time (up to ninety-six hours earlier). He started the recorded images at eleven p.m. the night Vika's mother was murdered. In low light, the picture quality was fuzzed and shallow. They were looking for a Rolls-Royce Phantom IV and they found it at 11:46:15 as it left the driveway of the Château Perigord, turned left onto the Boulevard d'Italie, and drove past the pharmacy.

"That's her car," Vika said.

Simon froze the picture when the car was closest to the camera. Two men occupied the front seats. It was too dark to see their faces clearly, though he could make out the driver's profile, his dark hairline forming the point of a widow's peak. His passenger wore a driving cap and sunglasses. *The boss,* thought Simon. His sleeves were rolled up to the elbow. It was hard work lifting a body. Easy to lose a cuff link.

Simon used his phone to take a picture of the screen. There was a chance his friends at Interpol could clean it up, run it through their facial-recognition software, and get a read. He wasn't optimistic.

He let the recording continue and his eyes went to a car following the Rolls-Royce. It was moving slowly, as if it had just pulled away from the curb. It was easier to see the men inside—pale, dark hair—but what interested him more was the car itself, a late-model Mercedes-Benz sedan, and, more precisely, its license plates. They were not Monaco plates, or plates from France, Italy, Germany, or any country belonging to the European Union. Plates issued by the EU sported a navy stripe emblazoned with a wreath of stars running down the left-hand side. These plates had no stars and no stripe, just numbers and letters. Simon froze the picture. All markings were plain to read.

656 SR 877

A tinge of unease ran down Simon's spine. He was right that the license plate had not been issued by the European Union. It came from a country he was beginning to get to know all too well and dislike even more.

SR stood for Serbia.

Chapter 36

Patience was a luxury Simon Riske could no longer afford. Driving Vika's station wagon east along the A8 into Italy, he kept his speed twenty kilometers above the limit and his eyes on the rearview mirror. He saw no unwelcome company, with Serbian plates or without. It was not often that events left him confused. Rarer still, utterly at a loss. Yet despite his most strenuous efforts, he could identify no ties between his discovery that a gang of Serbian criminals was robbing the Casino de Monte-Carlo of hundreds of millions of euros and probable Serbian involvement in the death of Princess Stefanie von Tiefen und Tassis. The only link between the two was Simon himself. It was maddening.

Rule number one: There is no such thing as coincidence.

Simon looked at Vika, more curious than ever to know what it was she was hiding from him. She was not a thief. He'd wager his life on that. She certainly wasn't Serbian. Yet more and more, he sensed an aura of distrust coming from her, a desire to distance herself from him.

Wait, he told himself. *Concentrate on one matter at a time.* If there was something there, it would make itself known.

Simon gripped the steering wheel harder.

Patience was a luxury he could no longer afford.

The city of Ventimiglia hugged the slopes of the Bay of Genoa, twenty kilometers east of the French border. Originally the site of a Roman garrison, it couldn't be more different from Monaco. There were no fancy apartment buildings, no five-star hotels, no casinos, and no port

176

packed to the gills with luxury motor yachts three times the size of a Roman trireme. To look at, Ventimiglia hadn't changed from the turn of the century—the nineteenth century. It was a stalwart bastion of earth tones climbing the hillside, sand and olive and rust, nothing taller than three stories, all faded from decades beneath the Mediterranean sun, and crowned by the spire of Santa Maria del Popolo.

Simon steered the car off the highway and along an ever-narrowing series of roads snaking through the hills behind the city. He had his own private history with Ventimiglia, one he'd never share with a princess. It was here that he'd lost his virginity to a buxom, raven-haired beauty named Giulietta. He was sixteen, though it was not a case of teen romance. He was not her Romeo, or anything like her first love. Giulietta was a thirtysomething-year-old prostitute who worked at Mama Lina's, the most notorious house of ill repute on the Ligurian coast. A gift from Simon's criminal brethren on the occasion of his stealing his first car.

"Been here before?" Vika asked.

"Once," he said, looking at her. "School trip."

"Those were fun."

"Some more than others."

"I know so very little about you," she said. "Are you American or French or something else entirely?"

"My father was American. My parents divorced when I was small. I lived with him in England until he died. I was still a kid and went to live with my mother in Marseille."

"That explains your French."

Simon nodded and Vika asked, "Is that where you received your tattoo? I saw that it has an anchor."

It also had a skeleton and a half-naked woman, but he was happy she'd noted the artwork's nautical motif. "I ran with a wild crew," he said. "Took me a while to get serious."

He told her about his studies at the LSE and the Sorbonne, followed by his years at the bank in London until he found his new calling. She had no reason to ask about the gap between the ages of nineteen and twenty-three or to suspect he'd spent those years in prison, two of them in solitary confinement. And he had no reason to tell her. If she could keep secrets, so could he.

He no longer felt like chitchatting.

"Where is this place?" he asked.

"Just follow the map."

"*Jawohl,* Frau Brandt."

His tone jarred Vika back to their agreed-upon roles: employer and employee, or perhaps she'd prefer master and servant. He was rapidly considering charging for his services.

The car made a sharp turn onto a single-lane road. Bushes encroached from both sides. He rolled down the windows, and the scent of rosemary and coastal scrub filled the car. A salmon-colored villa with turquoise shutters sat atop a rise.

"That's it," said Vika.

Simon stopped the car a hundred meters shy of the villa. He asked Vika to give Elena another call. The voice mailbox was still full. "Let's walk from here," he said.

"But…"

Simon opened his door and she followed suit. He felt the butt of her gun digging into his waist. Rather than comforting him, it added to his unease. He had no business being anywhere near a firearm, and no business he engaged in should break that rule.

They walked to the house, each on their own side of the road. Though it was a warm day, all the shutters covering Elena's windows were closed tight. A wind chime hanging from a pepper tree swayed with the breeze, tinkling mournfully.

"Elena," Vika called as she approached the front door. "Are you home? Hello!"

So much for the element of surprise, thought Simon.

They banged on the door, and when there was no answer, Vika removed her set of magic keys.

"Is this number eleven?" asked Simon, wondering acidly if whoever bought someone a house was entitled to keep a key.

"That's enough out of you, Mr. Riske."

"Back to Mr. and Ms.?"

"It's better that way."

"Very well, Ms. Brandt. Or is it Brandenburg? Or maybe Madame la Princesse is easiest."

"Shut up," said Vika, jaw clenched, gaze fixed straight ahead. Maybe, thought Simon, there was a heart beneath all that ermine.

She knocked once more and Simon put his ear to the door. He signaled that he heard nothing, then walked to the garage and peered through the peeling slats. "There's a car. A Fiat."

Vika said she had no idea what kind of car Elena drove, but that she had relatives in Sicily and might very well be there. Vika found the correct key and unlocked the door. Simon entered first. The foyer was cool and crisp, and smelled pleasantly of rosemary and garlic. A meal had been prepared recently.

"Elena," Vika called. "It's Madame Brandenburg."

There was no answer.

Simon felt the hairs on his neck bristle. If Elena wasn't here, who was? He told Vika to stay where she was and started up the stairs. It was a three-story house, and the stairway wound up and along the walls. He stopped on the second-floor landing, looking, listening. All was quiet, unnaturally so. *Who had made lunch?* he asked himself again, fighting the urge to draw the pistol. Why wasn't anyone answering?

"Elena," he called out.

Vika remained on the ground floor, gazing up. When there was no answer, she shrugged, lifting her hands.

Simon craned his neck and searched the third-floor landing. No one. He felt the floor behind him depress. The parquet creaked. He only just saw the flash of color out of the corner of his eye before the man hit him, crashing into him and toppling him to the ground. A blow glanced off Simon's cheek before he could react. He threw up a hand in time to stop a fist from breaking his nose. His assailant's shaggy black hair covered a red, agitated face. Simon turned the fist and the man howled. He couldn't weigh more than 150 pounds and Simon saw that he was a teenager, sixteen or seventeen at most. He was wiry and strong and squirmed like a snake.

Before Simon knew what was happening, the kid had his hand on the gun and yanked it clear, pointing the barrel at Simon's face. Simon rolled to his right, driving his arm between them, forcing the pistol away as it fired. So close to his ear, the blast deafened him. Simon grabbed the boy's shooting hand by the wrist and held it tightly. The pistol dropped to the floor.

"Stop it," he shouted in his peasant's Italian. "I'm a friend."

The boy thrashed and struggled. Simon thrust his knee out, knocking the boy off-balance, then followed it with a fist to the gut.

Winded, the kid rolled off Simon and onto the floor, grasping his mid-section.

"Dammit." Simon got to his feet, touching his cheek gingerly, then peered over the railing. "You didn't tell me she had a son."

"Rico?" called Vika. "Are you all right? What happened?"

"He's fine," said Simon. "Me too, by the way."

The young man managed to sit up and Simon helped him to his feet. He was taller by an inch, skinny as a string of pasta. At some point, Simon must have hit him in the face because his lip was cut and there was a streak of blood on his chin.

"*Vaffanculo,*" spat the kid, every bit as stupid and full of piss and vinegar as Simon had been at that age.

Simon shoved him against the wall to teach him manners, and, well, because he felt like it.

"Where's your mother?"

Simon had seen plenty of badly beaten men in his life. In truth, he'd inflicted the punishment himself more times than he cared to remember. Sometimes he'd liked it. But he'd never seen a human being so savagely attacked as Elena Mancini, and it made his heart cry out.

She lay in a single bed in a small whitewashed room on the top floor of the villa. A cross hung on the wall above her head. A sheet covered her body. Vika had said she was sixty years old, but her face was so swollen, her eyes hardly visible inside great mounds of purple and blue, that it was impossible to have any idea how old she was—eighteen or eighty.

"They came Monday morning," Rico explained. "I found her when I came home from school. She wouldn't let me take her to the hospital. She was too afraid. I called the doctor and he came to us. He pleaded with her to seek treatment. When she said no, he did what he could. Her cheekbone is fractured. Her nose, too. She lost three of her teeth. Her eardrum is ruptured." Rico turned and stared at Simon. "Who did this to my mother?"

Simon shook his head. If he didn't know their names, he knew their type. He was all too familiar with intimidation tactics. The beating was administered to instill fear, the injuries calculated to ensure that she didn't forget it anytime soon.

Rico nodded coldly. "Whoever it is, sir, please do the same to them. Tell them it is from her son. And please, repay with interest."

Simon didn't think it his place to answer. He was not Vika's hired muscle, nor did he want anyone to think he was. He remained at the doorway and motioned for her to join him. "Ask her what the men wanted and if she can describe them. I'll wait downstairs. I don't imagine she's happy to have a strange man in the house."

Simon walked downstairs, passing through the kitchen and into the garden. He found a place in the shade and accessed the Apache software. One of the markers had moved to a spot above the port. One of the men he'd tagged must have donned the jacket worn the night before. Simon zoomed in on the map until the name of a restaurant blossomed. The Brigantine. He doubted the man was eating alone, and suddenly Simon very much wanted to return to Monaco and get back to the job he'd come for.

Simon glanced up at Elena's bedroom window. Vika had been with her for a quarter of an hour. It was easy to imagine the threats they'd made against her. Rico's life was in play, whether he knew it or not. People capable of such savagery did not make empty promises, nor did they stop with one victim.

"*Jebena kučka.*"

Simon said the words aloud, recognizing them. He remembered the rapist's black eyes. He would be lying if he said that he'd seen into them and found them soulless and desolate, or cruel and debauched. Only now could he state that they were without regard for life or decency.

Simon walked up a dirt path and sat down on a stone bench. He now knew who these people were, if not their names. Slavs. Serbians, to be exact. He knew from firsthand experience that there was no one more brutal. Slav criminals killed blindly. They maimed without reason. They inflicted pain for pain's sake. Everyone else could stand in line for second place. Chechens. Sicilians. Corsicans. They were all pikers compared to the Slavs.

No matter how he turned things around, it came back to the same question: What were the Serbs doing interfering with the royal family of von Tiefen und Tassis?

CHAPTER 37

Well?" asked Simon as they walked down the drive.

"She was too afraid to talk," said Vika.

"Nothing? Not what they looked like, what they wanted to know, who was with your mother the night she died?"

"They threatened to kill Rico."

"So she knows who did it?"

Vika nodded and he shook his head, visibly upset that he'd let her speak with Elena alone. He stopped suddenly, fixing her with a resolute stare, then gazed back at the villa. His intent was evident.

"You can't," she said. "I won't allow it."

"She knows," said Simon.

"And she's been through enough."

"She can save your life."

"I'm sorry."

Simon walked to the driver's side without offering to open her door and started the car before she could fasten her safety belt. He drove very fast, frustration pulling at his features. Several times, he looked at her and she could see that he wanted to ask her why she hadn't tried harder, that he took her inability to force Elena to talk as his own fault. There was nothing she could say to change his opinion. Still, Elena had told her something, even if Vika couldn't tell it to Simon Riske.

This was a problem she needed to solve herself.

*   *   *

"Dear Elena, I'm so sorry," Vika had begun after entering the room. She pulled a chair closer to the bed and waited for Rico to leave before continuing. "Are you certain you shouldn't be in a hospital?"

Elena shook her head.

"We'll take you to Monaco," Vika continued cheerfully. "I'll call the Grimaldis. They loved Mama. I promise you'll be safe there. No one would dare touch you."

"No." Elena's voice was like a nail drawn against a chalkboard. She tried to sit up, hands pushing weakly against the mattress.

Vika laid a hand on her shoulder. "All right, then. We'll stay here. Are you comfortable?"

Elena fell back. She nodded, her relief palpable.

"And you have enough to eat?"

"Yes."

Vika moved closer, arranging the sheets on the bed so they were just so, tucking a strand of Elena's hair. "Elena, Mama is dead."

The woman's chin dipped to her chest. Tears overflowed her swollen eyes. She knew already. Rico must have seen it in the papers.

"They say she drove her car off a cliff." Vika tried to sound factual rather than terrified. "Can you imagine such a thing? Mama driving alone at night." A smile to punctuate the horror. "It can't be the truth. Someone did this to her. Someone evil. Then they did this to you."

Elena remained mute, a tremor seizing her face, her shoulders.

"Someone was at the apartment the night she died," Vika continued. "It was a man. We found a cuff link. I saw that there was a plate of prosciutto in the kitchen. You always made it when I came for a visit, with melon from your garden." With care, Vika took Elena's hand in her own. "Who came to visit that evening?"

Elena shook her head, sobbed. "I don't know."

"Mama told me she was frightened. You're frightened, too. Why, Elena? Why was she so afraid? What did the men say to you? Did they tell you not to talk?"

"Yes."

"Not to tell me who was visiting Mama?"

"Yes."

"You know?"

"Yes."

"Tell me, Elena. Please."

A shake of the head, violent in comparison to those before.

"For Mama. For Fritz."

Tears flowed freely from beneath her closed lids. "Rico," she said.

"Does Rico know?" Vika asked.

A hand latched onto Vika's arm. Elena's head lifted off the pillow. "He will kill Rico if I talk."

Vika wiped Elena's cheeks with a handkerchief. "It's all right, dear Elena. The men made you promise not to tell me or they will kill Rico. I understand. Really, I do."

"So sorry. Very. Very."

Vika patted her arm. "Family," she said.

Elena raised her hand and beckoned Vika closer. "I know where."

"Know what?"

"I hide it."

"You did?" Still Vika didn't understand what Elena was hinting at.

"For your mother. She scared."

"You hid it? *The ring?* You hid the ring!"

Elena nodded.

"Where? Oh, Elena, thank God." She kissed the woman's forehead and listened very closely as Elena lifted her head from the pillow and told her.

"Almost there," said Vika, offering a smile of conciliation.

They'd left the Moyenne Corniche and he was driving much too rapidly down the hill, approaching the Avenue Saint-Michel, which served as the invisible border between France and Monaco.

Simon nodded but said nothing.

Her smile evaporated. Vika folded her arms, withdrawing into herself. He hadn't spoken the entire ride back to the hotel, making it all too clear that he knew she was keeping something from him. It was his form of protest. Look at him, so smug, so self-righteous. The idea that he believed he had any right to expect her to tell him anything infuriated her.

She cocked her head and stared at him. If he could suspect her of dissembling, she could do the same with him. She tried on the role of investigator herself. Suppose he wasn't who he said. Start there. Suddenly, she saw things in a new and disturbing light. She thought about his arrival at the hotel and later "running into her" while strolling at night. Was it just luck, or something else? And what about his rescuing her only moments before she was to be violated? He was a strong man, very strong, yet why had he let her assailant escape? And what to make of his reticence to stay in Elena's room? Did he not wish to be recognized? Was there something bothering his conscience that had forced him to leave?

What if Simon Riske was one of them?

Vika scolded herself. She was thinking like her mother. Cruel and paranoid and divorced from reality. But wasn't there a saying about even the paranoid being right some of the time?

It couldn't be. Not Simon. She refused to believe it. Madness.

She recalled his touch in the bedroom, the look in his eyes, the moments of pleasure he'd given her. If she was honest, it was the same look to be found in her eyes. No wonder it was so easy to recognize.

The hostility between them was her fault. Conditioned by a lifetime of betrayal, deceit, and falsehoods, she was simply unable to trust another person.

Just then, Simon laughed. It was such a joyous, good-natured laugh that she couldn't keep from smiling herself. At once, her suspicions disappeared. She was ashamed of herself for harboring such thoughts.

"What is it?" she asked, wanting very much to take his hand and tell him how she really felt.

Simon pointed to a small, stout man in a driving cap and blue windbreaker standing at the entrance to the hotel. "Well, look who it is? I'll be goddamned. He made it."

"Who?"

"Harry."

CHAPTER 38

He should have brought a sled.

Robby meandered along the path leading from school into town, marveling at the snow. It was a ten-minute walk, but with a sled, he'd be there by now. He would have probably even had time to go back up the hill for a second run. He yanked on a fir bough and scurried away to escape the cascade of snow. He'd been silly to worry about the school canceling leave. He rounded a curve and saw the spire of the town church. He was nearly there.

His mind turned to Elisabeth. He'd imagined he was going to be nervous, so he'd prepared a list of subjects they might discuss. He didn't want to just sit there like a bump on a log. So far, his list included soccer, comics, music, and the best games to play on your phone.

"Robby! That you? Hold up!"

At the sound of the loud adult voice, the unmistakable accent, Robby turned. Coach MacAndrews had rounded the bend behind him and was hurrying to catch up. He wore a dark jacket and a knitted cap with a silly ball dangling like a tassel. He was smiling. Coach MacAndrews never smiled.

"Hello," said Robby.

"Where are you off to, then?"

"Town." Wasn't it obvious?

"Me too. I could use a hot chocolate at Simmens. Care to join me?"

Robby cringed inside. "I'm meeting someone."

"Are you, now? Good on you. One of your school buddies. Is he on the team?"

"Just a friend," said Robby. He kept his head bowed and his hands bur-rowed in his pockets, hoping Coach MacAndrews would get the message. But after a few more steps, it was apparent that the man had nowhere else to go. Robby couldn't believe his bad luck.

"So, how are you getting on, then?"

"Fine," said Robby.

"You like your new school?"

"It's fine."

"Better than that glum pile of stones you came from. Don't care for that part of England."

Robby shot him a glance. He wondered how Coach MacAndrews knew that he'd been at school in Newcastle for a term last year to learn English.

They walked for a while without talking, crossing a meadow with an alp on one side. An alp was an old low-slung wooden barn where farmers kept their dairy cows all winter long. The cows were still on the mountain. The storm had come too fast for the farmers to bring them in. Even so, the smell of hay and manure made Robby's eyes water.

They came to a flight of stairs descending the hillside, broad, de-caying flats of wood cut into the earth. Robby waited for Coach to go ahead. Coach had a habit of flinging himself down the stairs two at a time to show off how fit he was. In fact, he was always moving faster than anyone at school. Karl Marshal said he had a rocket permanently inserted up his butt. Maddeningly, Coach waited for Robby to go first.

"Mind your step," he said, as if Robby were a little girl. "So, you're meeting a friend. Maybe we'll all have hot chocolate together. My treat."

At this, Robby moaned. He knew it was rude, but he couldn't help it. And to be honest, he didn't care.

"What's that?" said Coach.

"Nothing." Robby summoned his courage. "It's just that I'd rather meet my friend by myself." And having said the words, he stopped in his tracks and looked Coach in the eye.

"Come now, lad. Nothing wrong with a bit of company."

"You don't understand..." Robby hated him for making him explain.

Why couldn't he just go on his way? It was as if he was forcing him to say yes. "I'm not supposed to bring any friends."

"That so?"

"I'm supposed to come all by myself," said Robby.

Coach came closer. He wasn't smiling any longer. "And who told you that?"

"My friend."

"He got a name?"

"It's a she," Robby admitted.

"A 'she.' Really?"

"I told him," said Elisabeth.

She stood at the base of the stairs. She was wearing blue jeans and a dark parka. There was a dusting of snow on her hair, as if she'd been waiting for him for a while. Robby noticed she wasn't wearing makeup. She looked harder, unfriendly, even. He waved, relieved to see her, giving no thought as to why she was here and not outside Café Simmens.

Elisabeth didn't wave back. Her hands hung by her sides, close to her legs, almost as if she was hiding something.

Coach slid past Robby down the stairs so that he stood between them. "Robert," he said. "Run back to school. Go inside and find matron. Tell her you need to see the head. If she's not there, go to your room and lock the door."

"Don't move," said Elisabeth in a voice that Robby hadn't heard before. It was a throaty, demanding voice and it scared him.

"Do as I say, Robert." Coach MacAndrews's hand came out of his parka. He was holding a gun...a black pistol like the Navy SEALs carried in *Call of Duty*. Robby was frightened and confused. He looked at Elisabeth, but she didn't seem either frightened or confused.

"Go," said Coach. "I won't tell you again."

There was a pop, like a firecracker, and Coach MacAndrews toppled forward and rolled down the stairs. Robby looked over his shoulder. Two men stood behind him. Tall, fit, dressed in dark clothing and wearing knit caps. One held a pistol, and smoke streamed from its barrel. The other man had silver stripes on his pants and a machine gun slung over his shoulder. A car was parked in the woods behind them. Robby recognized it at once. It was his mother's Range Rover. Racing white with luggage racks on the roof and fog lamps mounted on the front grille. Someone was behind the wheel. It was not his mother.

Robby froze. He was unsure what to do, if he should run or cry out. He turned back toward Elisabeth. She stood over Coach. She had a pistol, too, and it appeared much too large for her hands. Coach turned on his side and reached an arm toward her. For a moment Robby could see his pale face, his eyes opened wide. She fired the gun and Coach dropped to the snow. The gunshot was louder than before, shockingly loud, and Robby jumped in his skin.

And then one of the men was upon him—the one with the machine gun—ripping one of the stripes off his pants and slapping it across Robby's mouth. It was duct tape. He picked Robby up in both hands and bundled him to the car, tossing him into the back seat and climbing in next to him. Someone opened the rear and Robby was aware of the other man rolling Coach's body into the back and covering it with a woolen blanket. The hatch closed. The second man climbed in next to Robby. Elisabeth got into the front seat. The car began to drive over the uneven road.

"We're taking you to your house," said Elisabeth, turning to face him, her elbow thrown over the back of her seat. She was smiling, just as she'd smiled at him on the athletic field. As if she hadn't just fired a bullet into a man's back. "To Chesa Madrun. I'm sorry about your coach. We couldn't have him talking to anyone. I could see that he recognized me. You don't have to worry about anything. Soon your mother will be here, too. Then we can tell what this is all about. Are you going to cooperate?"

Robby nodded. He wasn't scared anymore. The last gunshot had done something to him. He felt as if he no longer had any emotions. He was like one of the zombies he saw on television, all cold inside but possessed of a single, all-important purpose.

They drove in silence. Robby watched the familiar sights pass. Ten kilometers outside Pontresina, they turned onto a private road that climbed into the forest, making a series of sweeping curves until finally reaching a plateau offering a view down into the valley. Robby had seen it a hundred times, yet for some reason it looked different. Maybe it was him.

He caught sight of the tower and then they were at the Chesa Madrun.

They parked in the garage. Elisabeth had a key for the elevator. This bothered him tremendously. How did she get it? Who gave it to her? They took him to the third floor. She walked with him to his bedroom, holding his hand as if he were a toddler.

"Viktor is going to stay with you," she said, her voice full of forced kindness. "He's going to be your friend. If you need anything, ask him. I want you to be a good boy. Do as you're told and everything will work out fine. You're smart. You know what this is about. Do as we say and you'll be back at school Monday." She kissed him on the cheek. "You're my good boy. *Tschuss.*"

"*Tschuss,*" Robby whispered as she left the room.

Viktor used a church key to lock the door. He had hair white as snow and blue eyes. A pink scar pulled at the side of his mouth, making him look as if he'd just eaten something that tasted bad. He pulled out a chair from Robby's desk and sat, placing his pistol on the desktop.

Robby climbed onto his bed, crossing his legs Indian style. It wasn't a big room and it was hard not to stare at Viktor. There were three shelves above the desk and on them were Robby's toy soldiers, hundreds of them. They'd belonged to his father and his father before him. They were fashioned from iron and expertly painted. One shelf was for Napoleon and his men. The next was for Wellington and the British. The top shelf was for Blücher, who was German and without whose cavalry Wellington would never have defeated Napoleon at Waterloo. Waterloo was in Belgium. All this his father had taught Robby as they'd played with the soldiers hour after hour on snowy winter afternoons.

Viktor picked up one of the soldiers and examined it.

"That's a hussar," said Robby. "Do you speak English?"

"Little," said Viktor.

"You can have him."

"Thank you, but…" Viktor replaced the soldier on the shelf.

Robby smiled. The thought came to him again that he had changed. Over and over, he saw Coach's hand drop to the snow, as effortlessly as if he were some kind of toy that had been unplugged. Was that all dying was—being unplugged? It didn't sound so scary. The only thoughts he'd ever had about death concerned his mother. He loved her more than anything. He didn't want her to die.

He told himself he was like those zombies. He had no feelings. Nothing could hurt him. He was driven by one motivation and one motivation only.

He had to get free.

He had to save his mother.

Chapter 39

I came for the football tickets," said Harry Mason.

"Get my car in shape and I'll buy you a season pass."

"Box seats?"

"In the trainer's lap."

"I'd set him straight, that's for sure."

Simon introduced Harry Mason to Vika, calling her Ms. Brandt, as she preferred to be known to strangers. Harry was a lifelong Labourite, but he had a traditional love of queen and country, and all things royal. There was no telling the extent of the fawning if he learned she was a blue blood.

"What are you doing with him?" Harry demanded of her.

"Mr. Riske is helping me sort some matters out," Vika explained diplomatically.

"Good luck with that," said Harry with a roll of the eyes, and they all had a laugh.

"I think I like Mr. Mason," said Vika.

"No better man," said Simon, giving his shoulder a hug, and Harry blushed three shades of red.

The Daytona was brought up from the garage. Harry spotted the damage from Simon's collision with the hay cart. He gave his employer a nasty look. "Not again."

"Couldn't be avoided," said Simon. "There's a decent garage in Cap d'Ail, ten minutes down the road, that handles most of the high-end trade in these parts. They're waiting for you. Anything you need is yours. But

Harry, it's not the cosmetics I'm concerned about as much as the performance. I need to soup this baby up. Give me everything you can find."

"You have my word. Dare I ask why?"

"You daren't," said Simon. "You have until tomorrow morning. Do whatever it takes."

"What kind of car exactly are you wanting to beat?"

"Bugatti Veyron."

Harry's face soured as if Simon had just recommended a brand of blended scotch.

"My feelings exactly," said Simon.

"One thousand horsepower, sixteen cylinders…It's not a car, it's a rocket ship. There's no beauty in that beast."

"He can't use anywhere close to all that horsepower without flying straight through a curve. Give me a car that will keep me close. I'll outdrive the man."

"I'll see what I can do." Harry climbed into the Daytona, pulled his cap low on his forehead, and put the car in gear. He made the loop around the Place du Casino, gunning the engine as he went up the hill.

"That was for you," Simon said to Vika.

"I find the Irish so colorful. Don't you?"

"That's one way to describe them."

They entered the hotel. Glancing to his right, Simon observed a familiar face in the shadows of the Bar Américain. A tanned gargoyle with cropped silver hair in search of his senator's toga. Simon freshened his pace and accompanied Vika to her room.

"I'm arranging for our doctor to visit Elena," she said as they stood at her door.

"She should be in the hospital, but I understand her wishes. I'd be scared, too."

Vika turned to face him, hands clasped at her waist. "I'm sorry if I was hard on you earlier."

"Don't be. You weren't." Simon didn't need any woman feeling sorry for him for any reason. "Stay in your room. It might look safe out there, but it's not. Whoever killed your mother knows you're here. They followed you to the crash site yesterday. They followed you to the apartment last night. You've learned that, right?"

Vika nodded.

"Just in case," Simon went on, "I'm putting a valet at the end of the hall. If he sees you, he's to call me."

"I've had enough of going out. Promise."

Simon almost believed her. "I'll be down in a bit to check on you. I've got some research to do. You can join me tonight at the casino."

"That would be nice."

"I have work to do and I don't want to be distracted thinking about what kind of monkey business you're getting up to." He stepped closer to her. "We both know you're not telling me everything."

Vika said nothing, her eyes afire with indignation. The princess had been called out.

"Are you?" he continued.

"I've told you everything you need to know. Some things are, and always will be, private."

"Not if it puts my life in jeopardy, too."

Simon said goodbye. On the way to his room, he checked the status of the Apache app. The map of Monaco lit up the phone's screen. He noted the position of the trackers and stopped cold. At last! After leaving the restaurant Brigantine, one of the men he'd tagged had proceeded to an address on the Rue Chaussée. What made that remarkable, though, was that one of the trackers who had moved out of range had reappeared and was presently at the same address. Simon zoomed in on the map, committing the street name and number to memory. Rue Chaussée 476. For once he had a real lead.

It was in a spirit of heightened enthusiasm that he regained his room. His phone buzzed before he could take off his jacket. It was Thierry Vallance, deputy director of Interpol.

"Allo, mon ami," answered Simon, cautiously hopeful that Vallance had some useful information about the men who'd followed him from London.

"Winning anything?" said Vallance.

"Yeah, but not honestly."

"Oh?"

"There's a ring of cheats down here. Serbs, I think. You'll know more when I do."

"Nasty types. Be careful."

"Good news?"

"I don't know if it's good news, but it is interesting. The men following you, Goran Zisnic and Ivan Boskovic, they are Croats, not Serbs. Either way, we know them well. They are in the drug trade. Part of the Solntsevo Brotherhood. Big-time traffickers and distributors. Heroin. Cocaine. Methamphetamine. The bad stuff. Large quantities only. They are active all over Europe and the Middle East, but they are based in London."

Simon had been mistaken about them being part of an international gambling ring. The new information, however, did little to explain why they had been following him. "Drugs? Why would they be after me?"

"I cannot answer that question. Are you working on anything related?"

"Hold on. Where in the Middle East?"

"Dubai, of course. Beirut. Tripoli. Does that help?"

"Not sure."

Since Simon had Vallance on the line, he read off the number of the Serbian license plate belonging to the car that had followed Stefanie Brandenburg's Rolls the night she was killed.

"Don't hold your breath," said Vallance. "Serbia isn't tied into our European Commission vehicle database. Normally, I'd need to go through their department of justice."

"It's a priority," said Simon. "I'm certain they had a hand in murdering a woman."

"Since when do you investigate murders? Isn't that strictly police work?"

"Since yesterday," said Simon, and Vallance knew better than to go any further.

"Understood. I'll see if I can pull some strings."

"Pull a lot of them. I owe you."

Simon put down the phone. He poured himself a mineral water, finally took off his jacket, then sat down at the desk. He opened his laptop and pulled up the address for the house on Rue Chaussée on Google Maps, clicking on STREET VIEW. Located above the hill from the botanical garden, it was an older villa in good repair set back from the street, with a steep driveway leading to a single-car garage. It appeared to be a house like any other, a residence of a moderately successful man or woman. The paint was fresh, the windows clean. Simon studied the house from as many angles as possible. At some point, he was going to have to break in to gather the evidence he needed for Lord Toby Stonewood.

Finished with that task, Simon dug in his pocket for the cuff link he'd found in Princess Stefanie's parking space and dropped it on the desktop. It rolled around in a tight circle and he picked it back up, studying it closely. Painted on an oval white enamel background was the tip of a broadsword, its base enveloped in flames, a five-pointed golden star where the handle should have been. To either side of the blade was a palm frond, and across the bottom, following the curve of the link, were two squiggly lines that looked like runes or some sort of Elven language that Simon might have found in the Tolkien books he'd once loved.

The design was an insignia of some kind, either from the military or a government organization. He was put in mind of his own cuff links from MI5, the ones that had failed him miserably at Les Ambassadeurs. He took a picture of the link with his phone and emailed it to Roger Jenkins, his contact at Box, the term insiders used to refer to the British security service, and asked for help.

Simon finished his water, then called Jenkins, to make sure the matter received the attention it deserved.

"What are you doing in Monaco?" asked Jenkins upon answering. "English lasses not good enough for you?"

"Aren't you giving away trade secrets?" Simon asked, hiding his pique that MI5 possessed the technology to allow someone to locate him on a whim.

"We know a lot more than that. Nice room you have there, by the way."

"You have not hacked my phone," said Simon.

Jenkins laughed. "Not yet we haven't. Better be a good chap or else."

Simon informed Jenkins of the purpose of his call and all levity fled their discussion. Jenkins pulled up the email with the photo attachment. "Can't say I recognize the insignia, but you're right about one thing. Definitely military. With the sword and the star, I'm tempted to say Russia— rather totalitarian, don't you think?—but the fronds throw me."

"And the lines at the bottom? It's a foreign alphabet. I'm sure."

"I was just looking at those. Sumerian? Babylonian? Could be window dressing—you know, artistic flair."

"Doubtful."

"You check the back for an inscription?"

"A what? Damn it all! Hold on a sec." Simon scrambled to examine the underside of the cuff link. Jenkins had been smart to ask him to look. There was something. Again the runes. Four markings, two of which repeated. Simon took a picture using his flash and emailed it posthaste.

"Let me take this round. Someone's sure to pick it out."

"Could it be Serbian Cyrillic?"

"Serbian? The plot thickens." Jenkins hemmed and hawed. "Don't think so. It isn't Cyrillic at all. Anything else we can help with?"

Simon thanked him and asked him to do his best to obtain a speedy reply. He'd barely hung up when the phone buzzed again. He didn't recognize the number. French country code. Nice city code. "Yes?"

"Mr. Riske. My favorite mechanic. Time for a drink? I've got some news about the time trial that might interest you."

It was the gargoyle from the Bar Américain. Dov Dragan.

Simon needed a moment before giving his answer.

Chapter 40

King of the world!" shouted Martin Harriri after he'd snorted a quarter gram of cocaine off the hooker's cleanly shaved mons veneris. He rolled off the king-sized bed and stumbled naked to the window. A steady rain fell on Hyde Park. Mist hung low over the green canopy. "What do they call that again?" he asked, pointing to the blue finger of water barely visible in the center of the park.

"The Serpentine," said the hooker, who was raven-haired, busty, and gorgeous. "Give me another, darling."

"On the table. Have all you want."

She rubbed his back and kissed him. She was from Latvia or Estonia or someplace that escaped Martin. He freed a magnum of Cristal Rosé from the ice bucket, guzzling what remained from the bottle. His heart was beating madly and he was having trouble keeping everything straight. The problem with coke was that the more you did, the more you wanted to do, and the more you wanted to do, the more you needed to do just to get back to where you were a few minutes before. Supply wasn't a problem. He'd come to the hotel equipped to hide out for as long as necessary. There was an ounce in the desk and another kilo back at his apartment. The apartment was out of bounds for the moment. He couldn't go anywhere until he knew that matters were settled with the Solntsevo Brotherhood.

"Eric!" he yelled into the next room. "Call room service and get us another bloody mags." "Mags" for magnum, which the Dorchester on Park Lane was offering for one thousand pounds a bottle.

There was no response. Martin staggered into the drawing room. The place was a shambles. Clothing strewn over the furniture. Dirty dishes littering the tables. Half-empty glasses smeared with lipstick.

"Eric?"

His friend's head peeked out from the corner of the sofa. A girl lay on top of him. They were both passed out. Martin vaguely remembered giving them a Xanny to chill. Had they eaten the entire plank? He'd been going for fifty-odd hours himself and considered seriously whether it was time for him to take a Xanax, too, and let the party come to its ceremonious conclusion.

Martin glanced back into the bedroom, where Bella was chopping a line for herself. He stared at her naked body. Those tits! There was no point in stopping while there were still ample party supplies. He called room service and ordered another magnum of champagne, a tin of caviar, and, for the hell of it, an order of eggs Benedict, though the thought of eating made him want to retch.

There was a knock at the door and he thought that was damned swift, even for the Dorchester. He wrapped a towel around his waist and opened the door.

Two men stood there. Both wore dark suits and white shirts. One had a cast on his left wrist. The other's face was bruised, one eye swollen. They could have been brothers. Simon Riske would have recognized them as the men who'd followed him into the mountains two days earlier, Goran Zisnic and Ivan Boskovic, and whom he'd just learned were two of London's most notorious drug lords.

"You won't ask us in?" said Goran.

"Come in. Come in, my friends," said Martin, throwing open the door, thinking only vaguely that there was no reason for them to be here…and *how the hell did they know where he was, anyway?*

Ivan followed Goran into Martin's terrace penthouse. "How much they charge? For this?"

"Per day? Ten thousand. But if you book it for a week, they cut you a break."

"Ten thousand," said Goran, walking through the rooms as if he owned the place. "And still you can't pay us."

"You have the car," said Martin. "That settles our business until I make things right. It's only a few hundred thousand pounds. The car's worth a few million. Relax."

"No car," said Ivan.

Martin only half heard him. He was headed into the bedroom and straight to the mound of cocaine on the desk, lowering his head and snorting it without the aid of a straw or rolled-up banknote. Had Ivan said "No car"? What did he mean by that? Martin had told them where to find the Daytona as well as about Simon Riske's plan to drive it to Monaco for the Concours d'Élégance. All they had to do was take it back. Had they miffed that up somehow?

Determined to find out, Martin raised his head from the desk in time to meet Goran's fist straight on. He felt his nose break and saw stars, falling to his knees as blood rushed from his nostrils and warmed the back of his throat. He dropped his head and spat a fat red gob onto the carpet.

Rough hands lifted him to his feet. Goran handed him a washcloth. Dazed, Martin pressed it against his ruined nose. Behind him, Ivan was talking to Bella in a common language. She was from Croatia… *That was it.* She kissed him twice, once on each cheek, then gathered her clothing and fled the room.

"What do you mean 'No car'?" Martin demanded, trying to regain some measure of respect.

"You tell him we were coming?" asked Goran.

"Riske? What do you mean? Tell him about you? Of course not."

"He sees us. He does this to Ivan. I wrecked my Audi. Nice car. I think you told him we are coming."

"Slow down," said Martin in an effort to make sense of it all. "Where is the Daytona?"

"Who the fuck knows?" said Ivan.

"You didn't steal it from him?"

"We don't *steal* nothing," said Goran heatedly. "We take what is ours… what you owe us." He approached Martin with a smile. "We are here today in spirit of friendship. You got ten thousand a day for this place, you got the two hundred thousand you owe us."

"Three hundred thousand," said Ivan from the drawing room. "Don't forget the car."

"Not insured," said Goran, with a shrug of irritation. "Three hundred thousand."

Martin looked around the spacious suite. "This? This is credit. My father's account. He stays here all the time."

"Get cash from hotel."

"I can't. Maybe a thousand pounds from the front desk. Come on, Goran. Do a line. Make yourself a drink. Calm down. Life is good. Let's settle this like gentlemen."

Martin saw Bella and her friend finish dressing and leave. Ivan stood near the couch, facing Eric. Suddenly, Eric's hands shot in the air. There came a muffled cry of distress. Ivan was holding a pillow over Eric's face, leaning on him with considerable effort. Before Martin could protest, Goran slugged him in the stomach. He bent double.

"Last chance."

"Five thousand in my jacket," said Martin after he'd gotten his breath. "Eric has a few thousand, too. That's all."

Martin watched as Ivan moved away from the couch. He was holding the pillow and coming toward him.

"Eric?" he said. "Are you okay? Eric?"

"No," said Ivan. "He not okay. Not ever again."

Martin began to cry. Panic overtook him. Until now, a voice had been telling him that he had nothing to worry about. He was the son of a billionaire. He was rich. If he'd bought too much cocaine without paying, it was a matter they could rectify. After all, they were gentlemen.

He'd been wrong. Goran and Ivan were going to kill him. Even in his stupor, he knew enough to be deathly frightened.

Martin dashed toward the drawing room. Goran stopped him without difficulty, pinning his arms behind him. Goran said something to Ivan, who dropped the pillow and went to the desk, opening the top drawer and taking out the baggie of cocaine.

"Take it," said Martin between sobs. "That and the cash. The car is in

Monaco. Get it there. He's doing a time trial this weekend. Steal it from the garage. Piece of cake."

"Maybe. Maybe not."

"Please."

Ivan opened the baggie and peered inside. "We don't do drugs. Drugs for weak people. Idiots. People like you." He dug his fingers into the powder and removed a handful.

"Eat it," said Goran. "You like it so much."

"It's too much," said Martin. "I can't."

Goran held him tighter as Ivan forced his mouth open and rammed his fingers inside it, depositing a fistful of the white powder. Martin fought and fought, but finally he swallowed, gagging. He felt his heart jump. His vision cleared. For a moment, he felt better, even that he might come out of this okay. Then Ivan put another handful into his mouth. He swallowed quickly this time, thinking it might not be so bad after all. As soon as they left, he'd drink a gallon of water and call the hotel doctor. Then he'd make himself throw up.

Ivan dumped all that was left of the baggie into his hand and pushed it into Martin's mouth. Martin's cheeks flushed and he felt himself growing hot. In less than a minute, he'd consumed more than an ounce of high-quality cocaine. A toxic amount. His head began to pound and there was a terrible pressure behind his eyes.

Ivan dropped the empty baggie onto the ground. Goran released Martin. He fell onto the bed, onto the cool sheets. His heart was beating like a jackhammer, the rush of blood in his veins deafening. He was hot. Too hot. His forehead felt as if it were afire. Cheeks, too. He tried to sit up and the muscles in his back spasmed. There was something warm filling his mouth. He turned his head and frothy white liquid poured onto the sheets, gushing out of him like water from a broken hydrant.

The pounding in his chest grew faster still. The roar in his ears louder. It was hard to draw a breath.

And louder still.

Oh Lord, he was dying.

And then the pounding stopped.

Martin looked at Goran and exhaled.

It was all better.

Eyes wide open, he fell onto the sheet. Dead.

Goran looked at Ivan. "You ever been to Monaco?"

Ivan shook his head. "Fuck no."

"What do you think? That car really worth two million?"

"More."

Goran put his hand on Ivan's shoulder as they walked to the door. "This time that son of a bitch won't know we're coming."

CHAPTER 41

The family was under attack.

Someone had killed Mama.

Someone had tried to kill her.

Elena Mancini had been beaten within an inch of her life.

Vika acknowledged these facts as she would any others affecting her welfare and the welfare of those she loved. Not with fear, trepidation, and panic. But calmly, rationally, and with a desire bordering on the pathological to find whoever was responsible and make them pay. If anyone expected her to fall to pieces and let someone else do all the work, they had the wrong woman.

Thankful to be back in her room, she kicked off her shoes and collapsed into one of the club chairs. Her first order of business was to place a call to Fritz's school. She was pleased to find Dr. Brunner in his office. She asked after her son and the headmaster informed her that Robert had gone into town as all the boys did on Thursdays after school. As per her wishes, he had dispatched Coach MacAndrews to tag along and see if he might join Robert. Dr. Brunner had heard nothing back, so he assumed all was fine. Vika thanked him and hung up. She considered calling her son but didn't want to embarrass him if he was with friends. It had taken long enough for him to be comfortable on his own. She didn't want to jeopardize his independence. She had interviewed MacAndrews herself. He was a capable man with a solid record. Fritz was in good hands.

Vika put down the phone. If only she could curl up on the bed and sleep. If only she could cry out, "Please help me. It's too much." Capitulation, sweet and fragrant as a poisonous flower, beckoned. Yield. Yield. Yield.

And then what?

She'd learned long ago that to rely on another was as dangerous as doing nothing. It didn't matter that she was frightened and fragile and altogether out of her depths. She could not bend. She could not break. She could not yield.

Vika stood suddenly, surprising herself. Shelter could be found in her own history. This was not the first time they had been threatened. The family's thousand-year history was strewn with battles and treachery and attempts to wrest its birthright, and its fortune, from its members. Her home, Schloss Brandenburg, had been built in the sixteenth century on a mountain redoubt overlooking the valley in all directions. The castle boasted thirty-foot walls, sentry towers, and even a portcullis. If there was a family motto it might be "Take No Chances." Deep in the cellar, there once had been a room for boiling oil, with a medieval delivery system to transport great cauldrons of the stuff to the parapets, from where it could be poured down onto the heads of the enemy. As a child, she'd run her hand along the sections of stone burned smooth by the boiling liquid. Her family knew about marauders.

"He wants to know about the family . . . He scares me."

And now her mother's fear had proved justified. If they wanted the ring, it meant they knew about the codicil. Either mother had divulged it, accidentally or otherwise, or someone outside the family had done so. Vika could count on one hand the individuals who knew about it. There was Herr Bruderer, their eighty-year-old family attorney. Out of the question. It was easier to get blood from a stone. And Herr Notnagel, the family accountant, the fourth generation of Notnagels to hold the post. Never. Of course, there was "Bismarck," Mama's ex-husband, but he was as rich as they. The Holzenstein dynasty went back as far as their own. None of the above had motive to reveal the codicil to an outside party.

Even so, Vika called them all and apprised them of what had happened. She asked if there had been any undue attention, any questions asked, any change in the law or their family circumstance that she should know about. The answer was an unambiguous no, apart from a law that had passed only a few days earlier, a rider to an immigration bill raising the death duty on the transfer of estates by one-half percent. That was of no concern.

Vika herself had instigated the tax planning that had saved the von Tiefen und Tassis fortune. The estate would pass from Papa to Fritz upon his twenty-first birthday. No one would be allowed to touch it until then. By skipping one generation, the family would benefit from a tax holiday implemented to prevent the breakup of great estates. There were additional restrictions on the sale of family assets, but Vika couldn't see how anyone outside the family could benefit from trying to sell them off.

Which brought her back to the ring.

Vika went to the window overlooking the Place du Casino. Elena had told her where it was hidden. It was safe, that much Vika knew. And close. Close enough to retrieve on foot and be back in her hotel room in an hour. She scanned the busy sidewalks, the throngs of men and women. It was hard to believe that out there somewhere was someone who wished her harm.

Vika crossed the room and opened the door to the hall. Peeking out, she gazed in the direction of the elevator. She was willing to wager Riske had been lying about stationing a valet to keep an eye on her. Surely he had believed her this time when she'd said she would stay put. She opened the door further and stepped into the hall. A head poked out from the elevator vestibule. A man was staring at her. A hotel valet.

Vika jumped back into her room and slammed the door.

Damn Simon Riske for keeping his word.

CHAPTER 42

Simon threw on a blazer and headed downstairs. The last thing he felt like doing after such an emotionally taxing day was make chitchat with Dov Dragan. But Dragan was a race steward and Simon had come to Monaco to take part in the time trial. Cover was something you lived. He considered asking Vika to join him, then decided against it. It wouldn't be fair to her, and more important, he needed to wean himself off his feelings for her. It was a dead end. The sooner he got that through his head the better.

Simon found Dragan seated at a table in the rear of the bar. He was wearing a canary-yellow blazer over a black T-shirt with navy slacks that desperately needed ironing. He was a remarkably bad dresser. And that was before Simon caught sight of the espadrilles.

"So nice of you to join me," said Dragan, pulling himself from his chair and extending a hand in greeting. "And at such short notice."

"You said you had some news about the time trial. It sounded urgent."

The handshake was weak and noncommittal. A dead fish. Nothing told Simon more about a person.

Dragan sat and motioned for Simon to do the same. "We've decided to move up the time trial by one day. A severe storm system is headed our way and the forecasters promise torrential rain. There's no chance the race can take place. What do you say?"

"Good idea."

"You'll be ready?"

"I'm having the car serviced now. You had me so worried I flew down my best mechanic from London."

"You don't really think there's anything you can do to that engine to make it compete with my Bugatti?"

"We'll see, won't we?"

Dragan had a laugh to himself. "How did a man like you get from Marseille to London?"

"What do you mean?"

"I noticed your artwork the other day. We don't see that often at the club. Just trying to put two and two together."

"I was young. I grew up. Nothing more to it than that. And you, Mr. Dragan: where did you come from before Cap Ferrat?"

"Here and there... Tel Aviv, mostly."

Dragan was Israeli. That was the accent, though it was apparent Dragan worked hard to lessen its bite. He was a tough Jew in a part of the world that didn't particularly welcome the type. "That Dragan," said Simon. "Pardon my lapse. I may have purchased shares in the company you founded. Remind me."

"Audiax. We had a patent on sensitive listening devices. Surveillance, that kind of thing. Very popular with the defense industry. The IPO was after I'd left. I fear I sold too early. It's hard to turn down a billion dollars."

"I wouldn't know."

"You were a broker?"

"Private banking, actually."

"My bankers are Swiss. Pictet in Geneva."

"Banque Pictet is a good firm."

"Finest in the world," said Dragan. "I have friends in London. Where did you work? Perhaps they know you."

"It's been a while," said Simon. "Unless they have a Ferrari that needs fixing up, I probably wouldn't know them."

The waiter arrived and Dragan ordered Negronis for both of them. Simon wasn't a fan of the drink, which was Campari, gin, and vermouth. He found it bitter and cloying, and vermouth had never done anything for him to begin with. But Dragan wouldn't stop praising it, or the bartender's skill in preparing it, and Simon went along. He knew Dragan's type: always lauding his every accomplishment, acquisition, and association as the best. Audiax had earned him a billion dollars. Banque Pictet was the finest in the world. And the Negroni was a cocktail nonpareil. Maybe they should both unzip their pants, yank them out, and see whose was bigger then and there.

Simon asked how long he'd been living in the South of France, and Dragan said, "Not long enough." He'd purchased the Villa Leopolda ("the most beautiful property on the coast") ten years earlier and had his eye on an adjoining property to enlarge his estate.

The drinks came and Dragan raised his glass with relish. One would have thought it was going to add fifty years to his life, or at least make him a little better looking. "Chin-chin."

"Cheers," said Simon, and after he took a sip, "Delicious."

"Told you." Dragan smiled, delighted with himself. "The best!" He put down the drink and leaned across the table, a hand motioning Simon closer. "I saw you arrive earlier with a lovely woman. Your wife?"

If Dragan had noticed his tattoo when he was wearing a blazer, surely he would have remarked on the absence of a wedding ring. "A friend," said Simon.

"Some friend." Dragan raised his eyebrows suggestively. "Though she looked rather tense."

"She's had a difficult day."

"Too bad you couldn't find a way to *ease* her worries."

"I did what I could."

"For a friend."

Simon's temperature rose a notch. "Yes."

But Dragan wasn't done with the subject. "She's someone," he said, screwing up his face as he searched his memory. "Now I know. Princess Victoria of Germany. Of course. I read that her mother died recently. Pulled a Princess Grace and drove straight off a cliff. My, my, Mr. Riske, you move in fancy circles."

"And I'm not even a billionaire."

"If you're not helping her with her car, what are you helping her with?"

Simon finished his Negroni. It was worse than he remembered. "It's getting late, Mr. Dragan. If you'll excuse me."

"Give the princess my regards. Let's hope she's every bit as wild as that mother of hers. She certainly shares the same figure."

As Simon rose, his fingers locked around the armrest of his chair. If he let go they'd be around Dragan's neck, even if the man was twenty years older and weighed fifty pounds less. Simon decided he was going to beat Dragan at the time trial if it was the last thing he did.

He left the Bar Américain in a foul mood.

Being an investigator was about contacts, thought Simon as he rode the elevator back to his floor. Who you knew, who you trusted, and who you could count on in a pinch. You never lied. You never misled. You never turned down a request when it might benefit a colleague. And you expected the same in return. It was the professional's code.

Most important, you left yourself out of the equation. It wasn't about you. It was about the client.

And so, it was in brazen defiance of this last rule that Simon called one of his oldest and most trusted sources. Her name was Isabelle Guyot. She was Swiss and worked for Banque Pictet in Geneva.

"*Salut,* Isabelle," he began.

"You. It's been a while."

"I need your help."

"Uh-oh."

"You guys have a client I'm interested in. A real piece of work."

"Don't go there."

"Just personal curiosity. I'm not building a dossier on him."

"Aren't you forgetting something? Bank secrecy."

"The name is Dov Dragan. D-o-v-d-r-a-g-a-n."

"Simon, please…It's the law."

"Founder of Audiax Technologies. Israeli citizen. Resident of Cap Ferrat. Chairman of the racing committee of the Monaco Rally Club. And client of Banque Pictet and Cie. *The finest private bank in the world.* See? I'm practically a family member."

"You sound funny. What has this guy done to you?"

"He's got me riled up, but I've got a feeling about him. Something doesn't quite match."

"And you're asking me to break the law because…well, just because? Simon, this isn't like you."

The elevator arrived at the fourth floor and Simon walked down the corridor to his room. "Indulge me. I'll take you to dinner next time you're in London. Bibendum. That's your favorite place, right?"

There was a long sigh. Simon imagined Isabelle in Pictet's lavish offices on the Route des Acacias in Geneva. She was a year or two younger but a decade more mature, with straight black hair and eyes the color of topaz. No one looked better in a navy two-piece. As for Pictet, it might not be the finest private bank in the world, but it was one of the oldest and enjoyed a sterling reputation. It was the private banker's private bank.

"I couldn't if I wanted to," said Isabelle. "These days it is impossible to access a client's account without leaving a record. I'd have to have a reason why. I'm not his PM or his AR."

"PM" for portfolio manager. "AR" for account representative.

"Didn't I hear through the grapevine that you were promoted? *Directeur adjoint, n'est-ce pas?*"

"That's correct."

"Air's pretty thin up there."

"And the view's a lot better."

They laughed and Simon wondered if she was remembering the same things he was.

"So, it wouldn't be out of place for someone in your lofty position to check Mr. Dragan's account to make sure he's being well taken care of…You know, to be sure that Pictet didn't miss a chance to sell him something."

"I always forget you used to do this, too," said Isabelle.

"I just wasn't as good as you."

"Ha! If you'd taken the job we offered, you'd be running the place by now."

"I'd be working for you."

"Even better."

There was a pause, a lengthy silence replete with expectations dashed and unspoken hurt.

"Still no Mrs. Riske?"

"The position remains vacant."

"And always shall…"

He didn't need to ask if she'd married.

"Goodbye, Simon."

CHAPTER 43

"Charge it to Mr. Riske's room," called Dragan to the bartender as he left the Bar Américain.

He jogged across the street and hurried down the incline to the port. He'd poured it on a little thick, but he'd gotten the result he needed. There could be no doubt that Riske was attached to Princess Victoria Brandenburg von Tiefen und Tassis. The nature of the attachment was unclear, as was Riske's reason for being in Monaco. The time trial was a pretext. For the moment, though, neither mattered. Riske fancied himself the princess's knight in shining armor. It was up to Dragan to tarnish his shield or knock him off his horse altogether.

At the port, he flashed his badge and passed through the security gate, hardly slowing.

Ratka was sprawled on a couch in the main salon watching a football match when Dragan arrived. "Six million," muttered the Serb, sitting up. "Last night's take. Not bad, eh?"

Dragan snapped up the remote and turned off the television. "Haven't you seen that match enough times? You lost. Remember?" With disgust, he tossed the remote onto the table. "Six million isn't enough."

"The hell you say." Ratka jumped to his feet, instantly defiant. "Our biggest single night's haul. My boys did damned good."

"It's my software that did damned good. Your boys did as they were told."

"Always you, always you. Jesus, you got some problem."

"Send in every team tonight. Casino and Sporting Club. I want twelve tables in play."

"Twelve? You are out of your mind. We can just send up flares telling everyone what we're doing."

Dragan was in no mood for dissent. Ratka was a thug who thought his gold Rolex bought him the class he'd never have. Worse, he was a stupid thug. He needed to be told what to do and how to do it. "And double the betting limits. No, triple them. I don't care who's looking. It's all over after tonight."

"We'll need a controller at each spot," said Ratka, frowning.

"And I'll make sure one is there."

"How much do we need?"

Dragan told him the exact amount.

"Fuck me."

"Get your men suited up. Let me worry about the fallout. I'll talk to him and give him a heads-up."

"You better."

Calmer, Dragan walked to the large dining table, where sales brochures for the *Lady S* were arrayed in a fan shape. "Anyone interested in this bucket of bolts?"

"Not for the price he's asking. Everyone wants the latest and greatest. The *Lady S* was built twenty-five years ago. She might as well have oars, benches, and a drum."

"He won't have to sell when we're done."

"He's already bought a slot in Italy to build something bigger," said Ratka. "I'm glad he's confident."

"Aren't you?"

"Confidence got me eleven years behind bars."

Dragan ran his hand over his scalp. "We have another issue that requires our attention first."

"First when? Before I send twelve teams in tonight?"

"This can't wait. It's Riske."

"Who?"

"The man with the black Daytona. Your friend from last night."

"What about him?"

"He's gotten too close to our princess. He's certain to complicate things."

"We take care of him when we take care of her."

"How did that turn out last time?" asked Dragan, not needing an answer before going on. "He's got to go now."

"He's here to race his car. Don't worry."

"I'm not so sure."

"You holding something back from Ratka? Who is this guy?"

"I don't know. I can tell you one thing. He's not a mechanic who fixes fancy cars. He was one of you once."

"Lucky him," said Ratka.

"I spent my life around people with hidden motives, professional liars, killers. He's all three. I want him gone."

"You're the boss."

"There's a cocktail party for the race starting in a few hours at the Salle des Étoiles in the Sporting Club. I'll see to it he has a reason to go out to the portico. When he does, take him. I'll arrange for his things to be moved out of his room. It will look as though he left town and disappeared. I don't want his body washing up in a fishing net."

"It was a weighted net," protested Ratka.

"Never to be seen again."

Ratka glowered at him.

"Twelve teams. Triple bets. Twenty million. Any questions?"

CHAPTER 44

Roger Jenkins left his office on the fourth floor of Thames House, headquarters of MI5, the British security service, with a tight grin on his face. It wasn't often he got a chance to put one over on Riske. He'd greatly enjoyed hearing the normally unflappable American rebel at the news that Jenkins knew his present location on planet Earth to the last millimeter.

Jenkins took the elevator to six—counterintelligence—and walked to the far north side of the building. Something was up. The hall was teeming with officers, looking even grimmer than usual. Sadly, that was the norm rather than the exception these days. It was MI5's job to protect Britain against any and all terrorist threats, as well as to conduct policing on a national level. The last years had witnessed a slew of attacks, and a far greater number thwarted. Jenkins didn't dare ask the cause of the kerfuffle. It was all very much "need to know."

Jenkins's work with Box was of an entirely different nature. There was more than one way to stop a crime.

A set of double doors blocked the way. Jenkins slid his badge into the reader, then pressed his right eye to the retinal scanner. He waited for two beeps, then withdrew the badge and opened the door. A guard sitting in a glassed-in office asked to see his ID, though they'd known each other for years.

"Afternoon, sir."

"Afternoon, Alwyn."

"Mr. Sethna is expecting you. Not happy about it. Warn you right now."

Jenkins passed through the second set of doors and continued down the hall. He had to admit to a bit of resentment that his position didn't demand such stringent security measures. It was whispered that a nuclear bomb could land square on the roof of Thames House, and the counter-terrorism offices on the sixth floor would survive intact and unscathed.

"Bully for them," whispered Jenkins through pressed lips. He was a round, jolly man, pleasant enough to look at, if entirely unmemorable. With thinning hair, watery blue eyes, and an air of perpetual distraction, he gave the impression of being lost and in desperate need of assistance wherever he went.

Roger Jenkins's title was assistant deputy director of investments. Prior to joining the security service, he'd worked as an equities analyst at Barclays at the same time that Simon Riske was earning his stripes in the City. For Jenkins as for Riske, a life of chasing a bigger office and fatter salary quickly lost its luster. When he saw an advert in the *Financial Times* looking for experts in finance and venture capital, he jumped.

It was not generally known that the security service allocated a significant percentage of its budget for investing in technologies designed to make the world, and Britain in particular, safer. It was Jenkins's job to comb the world for those technologies.

Recently, he'd been the one to discover a German company, Wolf Systems, that had patented a means (via an SS7 exploit) to pinpoint a mobile phone's location anywhere in the world. It was a tool MI5 and its sister agency across the river, MI6, the Secret Intelligence Service, coveted. After a short negotiation, Wolf Systems was acquired by a secretive British investment fund, Trafalgar Holdings. The nation's combined security and law enforcement agencies had been using Wolf's technology since.

The sad fact was that once an individual elected to own a smartphone, he or she was as easy to find as the nose on your face…whether the person was using the phone or not. Word on the street was that the Yanks had a more robust version of the same technology and were tracking, recording, and storing away the location of their citizens…*every one of them*…just in case.

So much for privacy.

"Knock knock," said Jenkins as he rapped on Zaab Sethna's door.

"Enter." A wiry, dark-skinned man looked up from his desk. "It's you."

"You were expecting…?"

"*Hoping*…you wouldn't make it."

Zaab Sethna, assistant director for counterintelligence, Middle East, pushed his chair back from his desk and motioned for Jenkins to take a seat. Sethna was Iraqi by birth but had lived his entire life in the UK. He had a Saudi king's nose and beady black eyes he kept hidden behind tinted Gandhi glasses. As usual, he was dressed impeccably, far better than his government salary would allow.

"Take a look at these." Jenkins handed Sethna his phone, the photos Riske had sent ready for viewing.

"So?" Sethna betrayed minimal interest.

"Figured you might be able to tell me who they belong to."

"I'm busy…Don't you know what's going on?" Sethna realized his error. "Of course you don't."

"Apparently whoever these cuffs belong to may have murdered someone."

"Apparently?"

"Just have a look, Zaab," said Jenkins. "Have a pint at the club on me."

"And a second if I give you the answer?"

"As you wish."

Sethna took off his glasses and examined the photographs of the cuff links. "A sword enveloped in flames resting on a five-pointed star and surrounded by palm fronds."

"And check the runes at the bottom."

Sethna shot Jenkins an evil look. "Honestly, couldn't you figure this out? Didn't you read your Bible at that fancy public school you went to?"

"Too busy being buggered by my classmates, I guess. Now shut up and spill."

"Judges seven. The sword of God. Gideon used it to slay the Midianites. I could be wrong, but it's along those lines."

"And the runes…the script at the bottom."

Sethna squinted. "Ancient Hebrew."

"Is that so?"

"'Hear all, see all, know all.'"

"Mean anything to you?" asked Jenkins.

"Not offhand."

"Go to the next photo. There's an inscription on the back."

"Dammit, man. I don't have time for this."

"Another minute. That's all. I promise."

Sethna swiped right. "Eight two zero zero. There's your answer. Should have showed me those first." He handed the phone back to Jenkins. "Now get out of here."

"You mean you know the answer?"

"Out!"

"'Sword of God.' 'Hear all, see all, know all.' 'Eight two zero zero,'" recited Jenkins. "What does it mean? I feel like Indiana Jones."

The phone on Sethna's desk rang. It was a special jingle that Jenkins knew meant trouble. Sethna lunged for it as if it might explode after another ring. "Yes," he said, and his face dropped. "Yes, I understand. I'll be right down. And Evan, keep it together. It will be all right."

"What is it?" asked Jenkins. "Another bomb? A truck on the sidewalk? What?"

But Sethna was already rising from his chair and yanking his jacket off the hanger on the back of his door. He bolted from the room, Jenkins trailing him down the corridor.

"Zaab, you were saying: eight two zero zero. The sword of God."

Sethna stopped on a dime. "Not now, Roger," he said icily.

His sudden calm was more unsettling than his ire.

"Tomorrow. If we're still here."

Chapter 45

"She still in her room?"

The valet stationed by the third-floor elevator indicated that she was, and Simon continued to Vika's door, knocking twice.

"Surprised?" Vika opened the door a few inches, making no motion to invite him in.

"I forgot to mention that there's a cocktail party this evening at seven at the Sporting Club. Part of the events for the Concours. Would you care to join me?"

"No, thank you. I'm sure I don't have anything to wear."

Simon was sure that she did. Her flippant manner was the cherry on top of his unpleasant afternoon. "So, now you're happy staying in?"

"Not happy, but I will be remaining in my room, as per your instructions."

"My orders," said Simon, leaning gently against the door. "Let's keep things straight."

"Very funny."

"Do I really have to remind you that it's for your own safety?"

"When will this end, Mr. Riske?"

"I'm hoping tonight."

"Does that mean you've made progress identifying the owner of the cuff links?"

"I've put out feelers."

"If you're getting close, don't you think you ought to contact the police?"

"I'm not there yet. With luck, you and I can pay them a visit in the morning."

"I'm not feeling particularly lucky, are you?" Vika flashed a mean smile and closed the door in his face.

Simon showered and shaved. His shirts had come back from the laundry and were hanging in his closet. The bill was attached. Four shirts, eighty euros. He winced before remembering it was on Lord Toby's account. He picked out a pale blue shirt and a dark suit, then toyed with the idea of a pocket square, ultimately deciding against it. A sliver of white was acceptable for business; anything else was ornamental. He wasn't a peacock.

The stainless steel case went onto the bed. He unlocked it and took out his tools. Once more into the breech. He knew how they were stealing; it was a question of gathering the evidence. He wanted the camera, the earpiece, and, most important, the smoking gun, in the form of the software that analyzed the card order and instructed the players when and how much to bet.

He wanted more. He wanted the money back. But first things first.

Simon slid the surveillance instruments into his pockets. To save precious battery life, he'd wait until in position to activate the tracker. Getting his hands on the scoundrels' hidden camera and earpiece wouldn't be a problem. The question was how to find the laptop…or whatever device held the software. He needed something able to locate the Bluetooth signal, an electronic divining rod of sorts. He was sure that such a device existed, but not so sure it was available to the general public on a weekday evening in the principality of Monaco.

What now?

He sat down on the bed with a thud. If one were to place a caption above his head, it wouldn't say "Eureka!" but "You should have thought of this earlier!" Mohammed didn't need to go to the mountain. He would make the mountain come to him.

Simon jumped to his feet and snatched his phone from the charger, embarking on a frantic search for all the computer stores in Monaco. Unsurprisingly, there were only two. At six o'clock, both were closed. He found a store in Nice, thirty kilometers away, but it didn't have what he required. The mountain wasn't getting any closer.

And so? The next step came to him in an instant. No caption required. The nephew of an old friend was a big shot in the tech business, a PhD and ranking executive at a French telecom firm. Simon was certain he'd know where to lay his hands on what he needed. There were two problems. The first was that Simon hadn't seen the man in years. The second was that the man's uncle wasn't really a friend at all. He was a capo in La Brise de Mer, the gang Simon had run with twenty years earlier. The uncle's name was Jojo Matta. He and Simon had a history, and not the romantic kind. In principle, Jojo didn't traffic with people on the other side of the law…Simon's side.

On a wing and a prayer, Simon called him.

The phone picked up on the first ring. *"Allo."*

"Jojo, it's Simon Ledoux. Don't hang up." Ledoux was his mother's married name. He'd taken it when he moved to Marseille to live with her following his father's death.

"You again?"

"I need a favor."

"A favor?" said Jojo. "Can't bother with a 'Hello, how are you?'? You've lost your manners since you started working with the cops."

"It happens. I'm in a hurry."

"I guess I better listen if I don't want to end up doing twenty years alongside Tino."

Tino Coluzzi had once been a mutual friend. Things changed. Now he was in prison as a result of Simon's actions.

Simon asked Jojo if his nephew was still at the telecom company and if he lived in the area. He was and he did, said Jojo. Simon told Jojo what he needed, insisting that he write it down. Jojo told him to wait ten minutes while he contacted his nephew, adding at the last moment that there was a chance he was in Paris or Rome, or for that matter the Far East.

Twelve excruciating minutes later, Jojo called back. "Price is five grand," said the gangster.

Simon hid his relief. "I can get it tomorrow for five hundred in any store on the coast."

"Go ahead."

Sometimes you had the cards, sometimes you didn't. "Two grand," said Simon, "and you should be happy. Found money."

"Three and you've got a deal."

Simon agreed, knowing he'd gotten a bargain and that he would have paid ten. They made plans to meet later that night, and Simon ended the call, not quite as elated as he might have been. There was always something shifty with Jojo, an angle you didn't see coming. It came to Simon that Jojo had agreed on the price too quickly. Jojo was a haggler. He'd nickel-and-dime a guy for an hour over twenty euros.

As Simon left the hotel and headed to the cocktail reception, he wasn't sure if he'd be met with a shiv or the portable Wi-Fi signal jammer he'd requested.

CHAPTER 46

They had set out the toy soldiers on the large play table in three groups facing one another: the French, the British, and the Prussians. Robby had placed the soldiers as his father had taught him: several lines of infantry up front, cavalry in the back. There were even a dozen cannons.

It was Napoleon versus Wellington and Blücher, though after so long Robby couldn't remember the details except that it was Blücher and his cavalry that had swept in and saved the day, defeating Napoleon and sending him into exile on Saint Helena, an island that his father had said was "precisely in the middle of nowhere."

"This one is a grenadier," said Robby, plucking a kneeling soldier, rifle at his shoulder and awaiting his commander's order to fire, and handing it to Viktor. "They were Blücher's crack troops. They could climb mountains, ford rivers, and sneak up on the enemy for a surprise attack."

Viktor examined the soldier. "Me grenadier, too."

"You were a soldier?"

Viktor nodded.

"For who?"

"Serbia."

"Where's that?"

"Yugoslavia."

"You were a grenadier?" Robby knew it was smart to make friends with your captors. The more they liked you, the better they treated you. And the more difficult it would be for them to harm you when the time came. He'd seen that in plenty of films.

"Can I see your gun?" asked Robby.

"No," said Viktor harshly, giving him back the grenadier, and Robby knew better than to ask again. Instead, he picked up a man riding a large brown charger, sword raised high. "This is Blücher," he said. "He's a field marshal. You can tell by his funny hat. Prussians are like Germans."

Viktor looked at the soldier closely. "The big boss."

"Yes," said Robby. "The big boss. Like you?"

"Not me."

"Who?"

Viktor handed Blücher back to him. "Not me."

"I'm hungry," said Robby. "We've been here for hours. There's ice cream in the freezer downstairs. Can I go get some?"

"Elisabeth will bring dinner."

"I'm hungry now. I'll stay here. I promise. I'd like a scoop of chocolate, please. Get whatever you'd like. You must be hungry, too."

Viktor considered this. He stood and slipped his pistol into his waistband. "Stay," he said. "Yes?"

Robby nodded. "Promise."

Viktor unlocked the door and left. Robby listened as the church key slid home and the door was locked from the outside.

He jumped to his feet and went to the window. The *rollladen,* a metal shade that went up and down, covered the window. It was old and noisy and had been there for as long as Robby could remember. To raise and lower it, you took a long metal wand and turned one end of it. He began spinning the handle, slowly, slowly. The *rollladen* groaned as if it was rusted into place. It didn't move. Robby gave the handle a stiff push. The *rollladen* shuddered and began to rise. No matter how slowly he raised it, it whined and squeaked. When he'd gotten it up a foot or so, he stopped. He opened the window and looked down. It was a long drop, two stories, but wind had banked the snow against the wall. It was nearly dark. The breeze nipped at his cheeks and he felt a chill run the length of his spine. He put on his parka and slid out the window, lowering one leg, then the next.

He heard the key enter the lock and saw the door open as he lowered himself by his hands and hung on the windowsill.

"You!" shouted Viktor. He held a tray with two bowls of ice cream and two cans of cola. "Stop!"

Robby looked down and released his grip. He landed in the snow and toppled backward, his head striking the ground. Dazed, he stood up.

"Stop! Come back!" Viktor's head poked out the window. Their eyes met. He aimed the pistol at Robby, then lowered it.

Robby took off.

He had a good head start. He had been clever not to open the *rollladen* any higher. It was too narrow for Viktor to fit through and it would have taken him a minute to open it all the way. He was probably scared of heights. Now he'd have to run downstairs and out the back door to follow him.

Robby headed up the hill, away from the house, away from the road, and into the forest. The snow was ankle-deep but didn't slow him down. He had on his boots and his parka. He told himself he could go all night. He ran straight up the hill, dodging the pine trees. Somewhere there was a trail that led to the top of the mountain, but he had only a vague idea where.

Among the trees, it was darker. He slowed, already losing his breath. It was colder than he'd expected. Two days ago, they'd had practice in shorts and jerseys

He'd been running for five minutes when he heard them. At first, their voices were faint, like shouts you hear at night in the city. Soon they grew clearer, though he didn't understand the language they spoke—Serbian, he supposed. He stopped and concealed himself behind a tree. It was getting more difficult to see. He caught a fleeting shadow far down the slope. And another to his left. He didn't know how many of them there were. Two or three. They were still a good distance off, but he felt certain that they'd seen him.

From here, the hillside grew steeper. The trees were fewer and there were wide-open spaces where no trees grew at all. Suddenly, he felt hungry—starving, even. He'd been too nervous to eat lunch. He didn't have the energy he needed. He thought about his mother, lowered his head, and kept going. His pace slowed to a steady march. Viktor hadn't shot him. That meant he needed him to be alive.

Robby stumbled on an exposed stone and looked up. Before him rose a tall rockfall where there had been an avalanche. The stones at the bottom were as big as boulders, but they grew smaller toward the top. The scree stretched as far as Robby could see to his left and right. If he ran around it, they would catch him.

Without another thought, Robby began climbing. Above the avalanche there was a broad meadow and a hut where hikers could rest and take shelter. When he was little, his mother and father would take him on long treks through the mountains. Often they stopped at the hut. There was a table inside and chairs and blankets. Maybe, thought Robby, there was a place to hide, too.

He scrambled from rock to rock, wedging his feet into gaps, finding handholds, pulling himself up when his feet couldn't push him higher. The going was easy at first, but quickly grew challenging as the rocks became smaller and less sturdy. Time and again, he kicked a rock loose and felt his stomach shudder as he momentarily lost his balance. It was snowing harder now. His fingers had grown numb long ago and felt hard as wood. The wind came and went, the gusts as frightening as the thought of the men he could not see.

Robby tried not to look down. He kept his face close to the rocks, always seeking the next spot to place his hands and feet. He was moving slower, painstakingly slow, stopping every few feet to gather his breath.

Without warning, a shard of rock exploded above his head. The gunshot came a split second later. He looked down between his feet and saw Viktor below, the gun aimed at him.

"Come down!" the Serb shouted.

Robby gripped the rock harder. There was no chance he was going down—he couldn't if he wanted to. He glimpsed a man at the far side of the avalanche moving up the hillside. It was the one who'd shot Coach MacAndrews. If Robby didn't hurry, the man would be waiting for him at the top.

Robby kicked at the rocks below him until one came free and plummeted down the face. Then he kicked another and another. He didn't look to see what happened. He found a spot for his right foot, then his left. He began moving more quickly up the nearly vertical face. And then the incline grew less severe. Rock turned to scree. He could walk, albeit cautiously. Reaching the top, he came to the meadow, the snow-covered field gray in the twilight. He saw the hut, not fifty steps away. He ran.

There was a combination lock on the door. Windows on every side of the hut were boarded up. Robby circled to the rear and found a pile of cut wood stacked to the eaves of the overhanging roof. An ax rested against the wall. He picked it up and found it heavy and ungainly.

He could think of only one thing to do.

Mustering all his remaining energy, he hefted the ax over his shoulder and hacked at the boarded window. Again and again, he threw the sharpened head against it until the wood splintered, then the glass, too. It was dark inside, but that didn't matter. Robby threw the ax on the ground and peeked around the corner of the hut.

He saw one man at the far end of the meadow, headed his way. There was no sign of Viktor, and Robby wondered guiltily if he'd killed him.

He discarded the thought in an instant.

Robby had only a minute or two.

It wasn't enough time.

Chapter 47

The Sporting Club sat on a secluded rise at the eastern end of Larvotto Beach, encircled by pepper trees and reached by a private two-lane road. It was at once an open-air theater, a restaurant, and a casino, and it had built its reputation as a last bastion of the glamour that had once made the Côte d'Azur the glittering playground of the world's rich and famous. Jackets were required for gentlemen, cocktail dresses for ladies. Its elegant, tastefully wicked atmosphere harked back to the era when words like "jet set" and "playboy" and "heiress" filled the society pages alongside names like Agnelli, Rubirosa, and the Aga Khan.

During the summer, acts of a certain niveau performed beneath the stars. The finer pop stars, jazz musicians, and big bands. Entertainers whose reputations preceded them the world over. This evening, the music was delivered by a discreet jazz quintet playing beneath an eave of poplars. Stars of a different variety held center stage. A perfectly restored 1939 Mercedes 770K, an exquisitely polished black and chrome dream screaming for Marlene Dietrich to extend one sublime leg from its door, sat on one side of the stage. The other was occupied by a gleaming yellow 1948 Citroën Traction Avant, reeking of danger and calling out to be driven by Bob le Flambeur.

The main floor had been cleared of dining tables. White-jacketed servers passed amongst the guests, offering champagne and canapés, and screens on either side of the stage showcased photographs of the automobiles that would be participating in the Concours d'Élégance and time trial.

Simon Riske plucked a glass of champagne from a passing tray and exchanged pleasantries with his fellow drivers. He was the only man without a woman on his arm and, on the job or not, it bothered him. Sooner or later, it was no longer amusing, exciting, or interesting to be playing the field. A woman was the measure of a man. Her character spoke to his. What did it say that nearing forty he was alone and without prospects?

To be sure, he'd had his share of companions, most often choosing partners for their looks, availability, and willingness not to demand too much of him. As well as for other, more private skills. His longest relationship had lasted six months and ended badly. Since then, he'd justified his behavior as requisite for his profession, or, to be perfectly honest, he hadn't justified it at all. It suited him. That was enough.

No longer.

Simon finished his champagne. Defying his better judgment, he took another glass, enjoying much too big of a sip. His manners were slipping. He wished he could say it was a delightful Perrier-Jouët brut, just dry enough, with a hint of oak, but his palate was untrained. It was cold, bubbly, and not too sweet. Ninety five points on the Riske scale.

He spotted a magician plying his trade from group to group, entertaining guests with his sleight of hand. From a distance, Simon judged the man's tricks outstanding and his aplomb such that the magician could have easily made a handsome living on Jojo Matta's side of the law. The man picked a pocket. He lifted a watch. He discovered a king of hearts inside a woman's pocketbook. (Yes, it was *her card*.) Naturally, he returned his spoils. His reward, besides a round of applause, was three hundred euros in tips. Not bad, but he could put his skills to better use.

Simon felt a familiar tingling in his fingertips. He shouldn't…really.

He approached the magician, hoping to appear wide-eyed, ignorant, and desperate to be fooled. In short, the perfect mark.

"Pick a card," said the magician, a slim, dark-haired man with Satan's neatly trimmed goatee and arched eyebrows to match. Make no mistake: he was a professional.

Simon chose a card.

"Give it to a friend," said the magician. "And please, do not let me see it."

Simon handed the card to a Middle Eastern gentleman. Ace of clubs.

"And another," said the magician.

Simon picked a second card. Ten of diamonds. The magician asked him to show the card to the others. Simon turned toward several men and women gathered nearby and showed them the card. Afterward, the magician asked Simon to put the card back in the deck. He did so. The magician then asked the Middle Eastern man to do the same.

So now both Simon and the Middle Eastern man had replaced the cards at different spots in the deck.

The magician fanned the deck, faces up, so the audience could see them. He asked if everyone saw the cards that had been chosen, but to be sure not to tell him which cards. The ten of diamonds and the ace of clubs were at seemingly random spots in the deck.

Then came the trick.

As the magician straightened the cards, he "flew" the top card in a boomerang, meaning he launched the top card with his thumb and then caught it as it returned faceup between two halves of the deck. In itself, it was a formidable display of legerdemain.

The magician then split the deck to reveal that the two cards that had been chosen—the ten of diamonds and the ace of clubs—were on either side of the card he'd "flown" and recaptured.

The audience gasped, then broke into applause. It was a nice trick requiring thousands of hours of practice. But Simon had caught it all. The Herrmann pass. The Charlier cut. The pinkie jog.

Simon handed the magician a one-hundred-euro note. The others followed suit.

"One thing," said Simon as the magician pocketed his tips. "I think you dropped something."

"Oh?" the magician said, immediately on edge.

Simon bent over and let the magician's watch slip into his palm so that it appeared he'd picked it up from the ground. "Omega," he said, studying the face. "Wouldn't want to lose that."

The magician took back his watch.

"And this," said Simon. "Not sure how you lost it." He handed the magician back his wallet. "Money's still in it."

"How?" one of the onlookers asked.

"Don't ask me," said Simon. "It's magic."

The sleight of hand artist was no longer smiling. Simon whispered an apology in his ear. "Road not taken," he said. "Wanted to remember what it felt like."

André Solier, president of the Rally Club, mounted the stage to give information about the time trial. Where and when they were to meet. Number of assistants allowed to prepare the car. The medals to be given in each class. Last, he gave the order of start. Simon was to go immediately after Dov Dragan.

"There you are," said Vika. "I've been looking all over for you."

Simon opened his mouth to speak, but the words caught in his throat. Dressed like this, she was definitely Victoria, and as she'd told him the day before, he might as well add "princess." Her dress was black and sheer and simple, cut low to reveal her décolletage and falling to her knees. She wore freshwater pearls, knotted at just the right spot, daring the eye to dive lower. Her hair was up, at once elegant and playful. He'd never seen her made up to go out, and now he knew why. She turned every head in the place. He wasn't the only one choking on his roasted brussels sprout.

"Quite the affair," she went on. "You should have told me. This is far more than just a cocktail party."

"I didn't…I mean, I wasn't sure what…"

"Are you all right?" She angled her head, a concerned party, but the effect was to only make her more beautiful.

"You found something," he managed, finally. "To wear, that is."

"Amazing what a girl can do in an emergency."

"This is an emergen—" he began to ask.

"Shh." She put a finger to his lips, then kissed him. "Do you forgive me?"

The kiss brought him back to his senses. Surprise gave way to anger. She had no business leaving the hotel. "How did you get here?"

"I borrowed a friend from Albert."

"Albert who?"

She whispered in his ear. "Prince Albert. We blue bloods stick together. One of his bodyguards escorted me. His name is Philippe. He's standing ten paces behind me."

Simon's eyes darted over her shoulder. A tall man with broad shoulders and a crew cut was looking directly at him. "You should have asked me first."

"Then you wouldn't have been surprised. I couldn't have that. I actually had an entire speech prepared."

Simon crossed his arms. "I'm listening."

It was Vika's turn to be angry. Or pretend to be. "You don't really want to hear it."

"The moon is out. It's a lovely evening. I may even hear a violin playing somewhere."

"Well, then…" Vika swallowed and drew herself up, equal to the challenge. "I was going to say that I behaved terribly today and that I should never have said the things I did. They were awful and untrue. You frightened me…I think you know how I mean. Maybe I frightened you, too. Anyway, I feel quite the—"

"Shh." Simon kissed her softly. He felt her body push against his. "Words," he said, "are overrated."

They stood close enough that their waists brushed against each other. His hand rested on the swell of her back, a finger feeling the rise of her buttocks. She smelled of roses and desire, and when he looked into her eyes, she looked back. Something happened. Something that he couldn't put into words.

At that instant, a poisoned premonition sullied his joy. If he were to lose her, he'd never recover.

"Simon?"

The thought vanished as if it had never come to him.

"I'm sorry," he said, not entirely composed. "I wasn't expecting this."

"Do you mind?"

"Mind? You've made me very happy."

She took his hand and squeezed it. The band had launched into a bossa nova rendition of "Summertime." "Is this work or pleasure?" she asked.

"Very much work."

"Don't let me interrupt."

"I was headed into the gaming room. Join me."

"I don't gamble."

"Bring me luck, then." Hand in hand, they crossed the floor. There at the bar in front of them stood Dov Dragan, dressed in a tan suit and black shirt and bloodred tie. He was staring at them, caught unawares, and the expression on his face was one of simmering fury.

Simon looked away, disconcerted, and continued into the building.

"What shall we play?" asked Vika.

"I only play baccarat."

"Really? I would have thought poker more your style. Baccarat is a game of luck... Oh." She caught herself. "I see. Work."

"Quick learner."

"Can you talk about it?"

"Some bad people have been cheating the casino out of a lot of money. I'm here to find out who they are."

Simon held the door for Vika and they passed into a large, high-ceilinged gaming room, very much in the Vegas style: tables to the right, tables to the left, slots on their own in an adjoining room. The lights were dim, but not too dim, oxygen pumped in to keep everyone awake and tossing away their savings. It was 8:30. The tables were exceptionally crowded. Simon hadn't expected this level of activity. He found his earpiece and, in a deft motion, tucked it into his ear canal. A flick of the thumb activated the scanner. A humming tone filled his ear. No pings.

"Sure you can leave the party?" Vika asked, her arm threaded through his.

"I put in an appearance. That should suffice."

"The Concours is your excuse to be in Monaco."

"In a manner of speaking. It's window dressing—in case someone suspects why I'm really here."

"What would happen if they did?"

Simon didn't think it was the right time to tell her about Vincent Morehead or the inspector who'd ended his days with a sea bass in his mouth. "Look," he said. "Let's sit here."

They took two places at a baccarat table and he asked for five thousand in chips. They played several hands, betting the minimum.

"See anything?" she asked after finishing her second *dulap*.

"No," said Simon.

"How do you spot them?"

"I have some help."

"You mean assistants? Are there others here"—she brought her head close to his— *"undercover?"*

Simon didn't answer. He was listening to a pinging in his ear that hadn't been there a second before. "Stay here," he said.

He left the table and, nodding to Philippe, walked across the room. The pinging grew more rapid. Simon stopped a few feet from a table ringed with spectators. By now the pinging was faster than his pulse and his pulse had just jumped a few beats. A man seated at the table looked familiar. He was balding, bland to look at, dressed in a plaid shirt, with spectacles and a mustache. Simon looked over his shoulder and noted that Vika had placed a mountain of chips on the betting ring. *While the cat's away . . .*

He shouldered his way closer to the table. It was him, the same man whom Simon had sat with two nights earlier. Not only was he wearing the same shirt, but he had the same air of fevered concentration. The pinging reached the speed of a sweeping second hand. Simon circled the table, getting a look at the other players, doing his best to pinpoint which of them had the camera and how many of the five men and three women playing were professional criminals. He stayed to watch two hands played, noting who won and who lost and the size of their bets.

Three of the players, all men, placed large bets, ten thousand euros each, then at the last moment doubled them. All three bet on *punto*, the player. The cards were dealt. *Punto* received a five and a four. A perfect nine. The bets paid off at seven to one. Each player had won one hundred forty thousand euros. And then they did something that no professional would do. All three let the full amount ride and bet again on *punto*.

A pit boss stood at the dealer's side, one hand to his earpiece, unable to hide his consternation. Simon had found himself in the right place at the right time. This was happening now. Where the hell was Jojo?

The dealer slid the cards across the baize surface.

Eight for *punto*.

Seven for *banco*.

Punto wins.

In the space of two minutes, the casino had lost nearly one million euros.

Simon felt his phone buzz. He checked the caller and was disappointed. Not Jojo, but someone as important, if for different reasons. "Hello, Toby."

"They're at it again," said Lord Toby Stonewood. "It's a bloody tsunami tonight."

"I'm at the Sporting Club," said Simon.

"So am I. Came for the cocktail party and the big event tomorrow. Didn't see you round. Can you free yourself up and meet me outside?"

Simon watched the crooks place their bets. He disliked reporting to a client midway through a job. Anything shy of completion came off as an excuse. Toby couldn't have called at a worse time. "Sure," Simon said. "But quickly."

"You sound vexed. Are you onto something? Goddammit, I hope so. Listen, I won't keep you. Front entrance. Far right side. Valet's stand."

Simon slipped the phone into his pocket and hurried back to Vika, explaining that he had to step outside to speak to someone.

"Who are you meeting?" she asked, barely looking up from her chips.

"My employer."

"Who's that?"

Client information was sacrosanct. "One of you. A blue blood. I'll be right back."

Simon left the building the way he'd come, crossing the open-air Salle des Étoiles. Dov Dragan was deep in conversation with André Solier, the

Rally Club president, but Simon felt his acid gaze as he passed by. He continued out of the Salle des Étoiles and into the forecourt, stopping when he reached the Sporting Club's main entrance.

He didn't see Toby's gray hair or square jaw and walked to the valet booth. He looked this way and that. By now the cheats had probably won another hand or two. He checked his phone in case he'd missed Jojo's call. Nothing. A screech of tires called his attention to a Mercedes driving recklessly into the forecourt. He stepped away from the curb as the car drew to a halt. Two men stepped out. Dark hair. Suits. Possessed of urgent purpose.

"You Riske?"

At the mention of his name, Simon turned to face a pale, stocky man, taller by an inch, with dark hooded eyes and a pronounced widow's peak. Simon had seen the face before, and maybe the car, too, on Pharmacie Mougins's surveillance video. He quickly checked the Mercedes. Serbian plates.

"My name is Ratka," said the man. "You come with me."

Before Simon could answer, before he could give a thought to escape, Ratka pressed a stun gun against Simon's chest. Fifty thousand volts flooded his body. His every muscle seized. He collapsed. The two men caught him and threw him into the back seat.

Simon's last image before losing consciousness was of the indigo sky and the palm fronds hanging over the drive. A cloud had blocked the moon.

The storm was arriving ahead of schedule.

CHAPTER 48

Robby stood in the center of the hut. One room. Benches along two walls. A plank floor. He blinked, willing his eyes to adjust to the fading light. A table. A chair. A coil of climbing rope. Walking sticks. A folded Swiss Army blanket. He made a circuit of the room, not knowing what he should be looking for, near sick with fear and desperation. He found a first aid kit in a cupboard, scissors, moleskin, and a bottle of spirits with twigs and leaves floating inside it and a label that read GÉNÉPI— IL FAIT DU BIEN POUR LA MADAME QUAND LE MONSIEUR LE BOIT. Translated: GÉNÉPI—IT MAKES A WIFE HAPPY WHEN THE HUSBAND DRINKS IT. Robby didn't understand what that meant, but he knew what was inside. His father used to drink something like it. He called it "eau-de-vie." Robby yanked the cork and put his nose to the bottle. His eyes watered. He took a drink all the same, wincing as the viscous liquid burned a path to his stomach. He exhaled, half expecting to breathe fire. Almost instantly, he felt better, warmer, and strangely hopeful. He continued his frantic search. Also in the cupboard were a clear bottle marked KEROSENE, a hurricane lamp, and a box of safety matches.

For a moment, he stopped what he was doing and stood as if frozen. He wasn't listening for the man he'd seen far across the meadow, Coach MacAndrews's killer. He was thinking, imagining, plotting.

The pieces of a plan fell into place on their own.

He grabbed the bottle of kerosene, the hurricane lamp, and the box of safety matches from the cupboard and set them on the table. He laid the musty army blanket on the floor, dumping the contents of a small trash

239

bin onto it—candy wrappers, an empty packet of cigarettes, paper napkins, tissues—and then dousing all of it with the kerosene. What was left of the flammable liquid he poured all over the hurricane lamp.

Done.

Lamp and matches in hand, he crawled out the window and stood unsteadily atop the woodpile. He put the items on the roof, then pulled himself up. Lying flat, he had a clear view across the meadow. He stifled a gasp. The man he'd seen at the far end of the meadow was barely ten steps away. Robby had gotten out just in time. He heard the man try the door without success, his steps trudging through the snow as he circled the hut. It was then that Robby saw he'd cut himself. A shard of glass extended from the parka halfway up his forearm. Blood flowed out of the sleeve and across the top of his hand, dripping onto the rooftop. He felt nothing, only the cold and the wild beating of his heart.

The man had reached the smashed window. Robby knew he could not see inside the hut, not all of it. The window was too high. Robby imagined him searching for footprints in the snow, determining if there was anywhere else Robby might have gotten to. There were no footsteps, no trail to follow. Robby could only be hiding in one place.

"Boy," the man called out. "You there? Boy?"

Robby held his breath. There came an exasperated sigh. A grunt. The rustling of wood as the man climbed the woodpile to see through the window. More scratching as he slid through the window and into the hut. Robby felt him land on the plank floor. He turned himself around and slid toward the edge of the roof, then farther, his head poised above the window. He saw the man's figure inside. He lit a match and held it to the hurricane lamp, which caught fire immediately. With a swing of the wrist, he tossed the burning lamp into the hut. The lamp shattered. Flames burst from the doused blanket, shooting up toward the ceiling. A cry of alarm.

Robby had brought one last item with him. He took hold of a knotted piece of wood the length of his arm and twice its width. The man's head popped out of the window, a hand extended to pull himself clear. Robby swung the log harder than he'd swung anything in his life. The blow landed squarely on the man's forehead and cheekbone. He faltered. Robby swung again, the force of the blow traveling the length of his arm, aching in the bone. The man toppled out of the window and lay still.

Robby lowered himself to the ground. He looked at the immobile figure. There was a gash across his forehead that was bleeding profusely. Robby's first instinct was to help him. Then he remembered what the man had done to Coach and the thought vanished. He hoped the man would bleed to death. He remembered his own wound and glanced down to see his left hand covered in blood.

A voice inside his head shouted for him to run. Instead, he lowered himself to a knee and freed the man's pistol from his waistband. The gun was heavier than Robby had expected, the cold steel against his palm filling him with dread and possibility in equal measures. He noticed that the air was still. The snow had stopped He gazed up and saw a small patch in the clouds. A single star was visible. A moment later, it disappeared. Suddenly, the air filled with snowflakes, smaller and wetter than before.

He started across the meadow. He picked out headlights below in the valley, driving along the highway. He didn't know how far it was—an hour's walk, at least—only that he was shivering, bleeding, and couldn't think of anywhere else to go. He certainly wasn't going to continue up the hill. He'd freeze to death or die of exhaustion.

He set off down the mountain, soon entering the stand of pines that belted the lower slope. He could feel the temperature falling. It was windier, too, the branches bending and groaning under the force of gusts. Whatever hope or courage the alcohol had provided had fled. He wanted someone to look after him, to lead him down the hill and take him inside a warm home and feed him. He wanted his mother. His eyes grew warm and wet.

She's not here. She can't help you. You're a big boy. It was the voice that had told him to run. He'd never heard it before. It was confident and fearless, and a little frightening. He knew that he must listen to it for his own good. *The reason you ran away from those bad people was to help her, remember? You have to warn her. Now go!*

Robby wiped his nose and stood taller. He pressed the palm of his hand against his wound to stop the bleeding. After a moment, the tears ceased altogether. He redoubled his efforts. His pace grew steadier. His only thought was of reaching the road and signaling for help.

Time passed. He forgot his fatigue and hunger. He was aware of his feet rising and falling and the snow wet against his cheeks. Something shone in his eye. He glanced up, annoyed. Not a hundred yards away, a car zoomed past on the highway. He began to run, leaving the cover of the trees. Another set of lights approached. Robby shouted and jumped up and down, waving his arms madly. The car flashed its brights, then turned off the highway onto a feeder road. The car had seen him. He was safe.

Robby bent at the waist, hands on his thighs, gathering his breath. He tried to think of what to say, how to explain everything that had happened.

The car drew nearer. He could hear the engine downshift, the tires crunching the snow and ice. The fog lamps on the car's grille came to life, blinding him. They were yellow lamps like those on his mother's car. Robby squinted, raising a hand to deflect the high beams. He noted the luggage rack on the car's roof. He took a step, and another. The car drew closer still. It was a Range Rover. Racing white. The engine quit and the door opened. Elisabeth got out.

"Hello, Robby," she said. "Or would you like me to call you Fritz?"

Robby held the pistol with both hands, pointing it at her chest. He placed his finger on the trigger. The metal was smooth and inviting. "Go away!" he shouted. "Now. I mean it."

"I can't do that," said Elisabeth. "Is that George's gun? Look...Viktor is in the car. You hurt him badly. He's quite upset, but he'll be all right."

Robby looked past Elisabeth. He made out a vague silhouette in the passenger seat. A flash of white hair. A bandage over one eye.

"He was chasing me. He wanted to hurt me."

"No one wants to hurt you, Robby."

"He shot at me."

"To scare you. If he wanted to hurt you, he could have. Believe me."

"Go away," Robby repeated, less forcefully.

"I'm going to take you home. You're going to have a nice warm meal and a bath." She was walking toward him, closing the gap between them.

"Stop."

She smiled her warm smile. "No one wants to hurt you. I'll tell you all about what we had planned once we get home. Come, *schatzi.*"

Shoot her, said the voice in his head. *She's going to kill you. Then she's going to kill Mama.*

Robby pulled the trigger. Nothing happened. He tried again, then turned the gun on its side, searching for the safety.

Elisabeth snatched the gun from his hand.

Robby stared at her.

She slapped him across the face. "Get in the car."

Chapter 49

It was ten o'clock in the evening when Isabelle Guyot finished preparing her reports for her meeting the next morning. The client was an English film director who kept nearly two hundred million euros on deposit with Banque Pictet and thought it gave him the right to pinch her bottom and call her "honey." She'd disabused him of both notions.

She finished her coffee and straightened her papers. There on top of the rest was the note she'd taken while speaking to Simon Riske.

Dov Dr—

At that point, she'd stopped writing.

Without considering what she was doing, she typed the letters into her computer, completing the family name. He was not her client, but she knew who Simon had been talking about. Banque Pictet was not a large organization. Dov Dragan had visited often enough to be a personality. Secrecy began outside the front door.

Isabelle stared at the letters, then positioned her finger above the SEND button. Her gaze lifted to the window and the lights of Geneva burning with verve and promise. A spotlight illuminated the *jet d'eau,* the magnificent plume of water sent skyward hundreds of feet. She'd always viewed it as a symbol of hope, of a future that would grant her her every wish and lift her fortunes every bit as high. Not any longer.

Isabelle was well on the downslope to forty, with a fat bank account, a fancy title, and a fabulous wardrobe. All that was meaningful when she was inside these four walls. When she left for the day, she confronted a different reality. She was unmarried and unconnected and, with each passing year, increasingly unmoored. She had suitors, plenty of them, from her trainer at the gym to the director of a rival bank. None had captured her heart. She was beginning to fear that no one would.

There are rules, she'd told Simon. *Le secret bancaire* was only one of them.

They'd met ten years earlier at a financial conference in Paris when she'd sat next to him during a presentation on portfolio diversification. Upon its conclusion, he'd looked at her and touched her hand. He might as well have hypnotized her. Without a word, he'd led her out of the room and out of the hotel. She missed the last scheduled talk. It was a contravention of her duties and the first rule she'd break that weekend.

The next thing she knew it was Sunday evening and she was in a taxi heading to Charles de Gaulle for her flight back to Geneva. In between, they'd had dinner at Le Drugstore, danced half the night at Castel, visited the flea market in Clichy, ran through Cimetière du Père-Lachaise, and eaten ice cream while contemplating Rodin's *The Thinker*. There wasn't a place where Simon didn't know someone, and always someone who mattered. Nice places and not so nice places.

And of course there was the sex. He knew her body as if it were his own. Nice places and not so nice places.

A weekend in London followed a month later. Another whirlwind tour with the best guide she'd ever known.

Then the real world raised its head above the sheets.

First, she turned down a trip to Amsterdam because of a corporate retreat she absolutely had to attend. Then she missed a weekend closer to home in Gstaad for a reason she couldn't remember but that she had sworn was all-important at the time. The last straw was a planned weekend in London to celebrate his birthday.

Simon had reserved a table at the restaurant Bibendum in Michelin House. It was their favorite place, mostly because it was there that over a dinner of linguini and white truffles they'd realized they were in love. For an encore, he'd procured tickets to a show in the West End.

At the last minute, she'd called to cancel. A client had arrived without warning and demanded to see her. He was a big client, a billion-dollar client, and when the boss told her she had to stay, she didn't hesitate. Not for a second.

Rules were rules.

Simon never made a show of being disappointed. He told her he understood and that she was only doing what her job demanded. They both valued their careers. It took her a while to realize what had happened. The calls when they came were polite and professional. No more whispered nothings about sexual transgressions past and to come. No more intimations of how she brightened his life. And no more invitations.

Then the calls stopped coming altogether.

Isabelle caught her reflection in the mirror. She was still attractive. Beautiful, maybe. But the circles under her eyes were darker than in the past. She noted a line at the corner of her mouth that hadn't been there the day before. The Botox didn't eliminate those pesky frown lines for as long as it used to.

Rules.

Isabelle hit the SEND button hard enough to break it.

The screen filled with the particulars of Mr. Dov M. Dragan's account at Banque Pictet. She continued on to the second page, then the third.

She read all the pages, confused. Then read them again. Nothing made sense. How could any of this have happened without raising a flag?

She made a note to call Simon Riske first thing in the morning.

He'd been right to worry.

CHAPTER 50

A kick in the gut opened Simon's eyes.

Everything was blurry. A collage of colors dangled above him. Reds and blues and oranges. He lay on a marble floor beneath a chandelier made from hundreds of cut glass pendants. His head throbbed. His body felt sore and jittery, as if the current from the stun gun hadn't fully dissipated.

Strong hands lifted him to his feet. The two men from the Sporting Club let him go. He bent double and retched. Someone slapped him across the face.

"Control yourself." Ratka stood facing Simon. Ratka who'd politely introduced himself before throttling Simon with enough juice to light up Frankenstein's monster and his bride. Ratka who'd murdered Vika's mother and, Simon was reasonably sure, had tried to rape Vika. Ratka who'd beaten a defenseless woman to within an inch of her life to guarantee her silence.

Simon spat a gob of blood and phlegm onto the toe of Ratka's shoe, then looked up. "Sorry. Won't happen again."

Ratka buried a fist in Simon's stomach. Simon felt his stitches tear. Time passed and he could breathe again.

"Why are you here?" asked Ratka. "Why are you helping the princess?"

Simon took his time answering. He'd just landed in the last act of a play and he wasn't in a hurry to get to the end. "I just met her," he said. "I'm here for the Concours, for the time trial. I'm not helping her at all."

"Bullshit."

The two men who'd thrown him into the car held lengths of lead pipe in their hands, and each tapped one end threateningly in his palm.

"What do you want with her?" asked Ratka.

"Nothing," said Simon. "She's a friend. That's all."

"And so you follow her around all over the place, to the top of the mountain, to her apartment at night, to her apartment in the morning, to see her friends. Who are you really?"

"I was worried about her. I don't want anything from her. I barely know her."

Ratka took this in, his mouth curled skeptically. "Where did you learn to fight?"

"What do you mean?"

Ratka came closer, face-to-face, tilting his head to make sure Simon was looking at him, looking into his eyes. "You know who I am. I know who you are. You think I'd forget a guy who had his hand on my balls? I'll kill you for that alone." He paused to examine Simon and didn't like what he saw. "My friend says you were like me once. Me, I'm not sure."

"How like you?"

"Businessman. You know: tough guy." The words were said with pride.

"What friend?"

Ratka sighed, looking to the other two and throwing up his hands. "I'm going to give you one more chance, Mr. Simon. Maybe you tell me something, I'll let you go. I don't want to hurt a nice guy. Ratka isn't like that."

It was a sham, a charade. Simon knew it. Ratka knew it. What surprised Simon, however, was the Serb's disinterest in the proceedings. He didn't care if Simon was helping the princess or what his motivations might be. Nor did he have any idea about Simon's true reason for coming to Monaco. It wasn't just that Simon's fate was already decided. Ratka was going to kill him. That part was clear. It was that he didn't view Simon as a threat. There was nothing Simon might know that could strengthen Ratka's hand. Everything had already been decided and it had been decided in Ratka's favor.

"Okay, listen," said Simon, addressing him tough guy to tough guy.

"Whatever happened happened. I don't want any trouble. I don't care about the princess. She's pretty. I was trying to help."

"Talk, talk, talk."

"A man like you can understand what I was really after," Simon went on. "There's nothing more to it than that. I just want to drive my car, then go home. You and me, we'll never see each other again. I swear—"

Ratka shot a jab into Simon's throat, knuckles curled. Simon hit the floor, and Ratka kicked him repeatedly with everything he had. "You think I got nothing else to do? You think I like you wasting my time? Ratka has plans. When he asks you a question, you answer. You don't give him any bullshit. Why aren't you answering me now? Where's all your talk?"

Ratka knelt next to Simon. He held a pistol in one hand, and with the other he forced Simon's mouth open and rammed the muzzle into it. "You're lying to me. I don't know what you want with her…maybe the tiara, I'm thinking. You're some kind of thief, maybe something else…but listen to me, we're gonna get it. We're gonna get all of it. We've been working a long time and we're not going to let some Mr. Slick like you come from England or wherever the fuck and mess things up. Not going to happen. Ratka has plans."

He dragged Simon to a sitting position, the gun, tasting of smoke and iron, rattling against his teeth. Simon looked at him, eye to eye, daring him.

"See you later, Mr. Slick."

Ratka pulled the trigger.

Metal struck metal.

The chamber was empty.

Ratka pulled the gun from Simon's mouth and stood. "You think I'm going to make a mess in my house? Marble's hard to clean. Carrara marble. From Italy. Just like in the old lady's bathroom." A last kick, arms flailing like a drunk sailing a beer can down the road. "It doesn't matter anyway. My friends here will take care of you. Outside. It's cleaner that way. Bye-bye."

Simon collapsed to the floor, his heart pounding. He gasped, blinking, trying to make sense of what had happened, why he was still alive. Pain directed his thoughts to his person. He knew that at least one rib was cracked. His throat felt like a crushed soda straw. He was having difficulty breathing, or even swallowing, for that matter. He heard Ratka fire off instructions to his men in Serbian. He caught the words *Benzin, pozni,* and *nista, nista, nista.* Gasoline, fire, and nothing, nothing, nothing. He didn't like the sound of any of it.

Ratka stopped at the front door. "Mr. Simon, I'm gonna tell my friend he was wrong. You're not like me at all. Not a tough guy. You're a pussy."

The door closed. Simon eyed the two men. His perspective on his situation changed. He was alive. He had a chance. Maybe it wasn't the last act.

"Up, up," said one of the men. "Hurry."

Simon struggled to his feet. He looked at the men with the pipes in their hands.

He thought of Vincent Morehead. He thought of Elena Mancini. *"We're gonna get it. We're gonna get all of it."* Mostly he thought of Ratka, and what Simon was going to do when he caught him.

"Give me a second." He raised a hand to signal that he was complying and stood up more unsteadily than he felt. "Belgrade," he said, remembering the transit ticket he'd found in the cheat's wallet. "Žarkovo. I knew a girl who lived there. A beauty. You're Serbian, right?"

The men shared a look. "Žarkovo… You been?" asked the slimmer one.

"Beautiful city. Great beer."

Booze and broads. The common denominator among males under eighty.

"You like Jelen?" asked the stockier one, naming a brand of beer.

"The lager," said Simon. "Liv… Lev…"

"Lav?" suggested the slimmer one, with the slicked-back black hair, Elvis.

"That's it," said Simon. "Lav."

"Lav no good," said Elvis. "Like water." He pointed to Simon. "Americans don't know shit about beer."

"You're making me scared standing there with those pipes."

Elvis shot the bully a look and muttered something.

"That's right," said Simon. "This is a mistake. Like I told Ratka. Let's figure this out. I'm one of the good guys."

"Maybe," said Elvis.

More words were exchanged. The stockier man's jaw hardened and Simon realized he'd lost the argument. The bully came at him with lethal intent and swung the bar at his head. Simon shook off his false stupor, his hand rising with blinding speed to catch the man by his wrist. "I told you," he said, matching the man's strength with his own. "Wrong guy."

The bully fought to free himself, unable to gain the leverage necessary to strike Simon with his free hand. After a moment, Elvis came to life, circling to find the best position to belt Simon.

"No, wait!" Simon swung a foot to knock the feet out from under the bully. The bully jumped back. Distracted, Simon didn't see the pipe cut through the air behind him and strike his back. The blow wasn't delivered with full force, but it was enough to leave him stunned and winded. He released the bully, who shouted at once, *"Tommy, Ubij ga!"*

Simon knew what "Kill him!" sounded like in any language. He flicked open the switchblade he'd lifted from the bully's pocket. It was a big knife with a big blade.

They circled him, the bully smiling, ashamed to have been bested, eager to finish him off, or just plain rabid. Seeing the knife, Elvis, or Tommy, or whatever his name was, dropped his pipe and dug into his jacket for something more efficient.

The bully charged Simon, waving the pipe like a madman. Simon dodged the first blow, then slid to the floor as if taking home plate, thrusting the knife upward. The blade entered the underside of the bully's thigh, burying itself to the hilt. Simon spun his grip around so that he clutched the knife overhand and ripped it downward, carving through flesh and muscle. The blade severed the femoral artery. Blood sprayed across the room, a garish plume of gore. The bully collapsed to the floor, writhing. The accompanying scream made the hair on the back of Simon's neck stand up.

One down.

Simon snapped up the pipe as Elvis cleared his pistol and fired, not bothering to aim. Ten feet separated them. He was not a trained gunman and the shots went high, the muzzle blast close enough to burn Simon's cheek. In desperation, he chucked the pipe at the man. Elvis ducked, loosing a bullet into the ceiling. An arm of the chandelier crashed to the floor, dozens of pendants scattering across the marble, shards of glass ricocheting everywhere.

Simon bolted for a large, well-furnished room to his left. At the far side was a sliding glass door leading to a terrace. It was his only chance. He jumped over the mortally wounded man. By now blood covered half the floor. Landing, he slipped and lost his balance. A hand reached up and took hold of his ankle.

Not mortal yet.

Simon kicked to get free, but the grip only tightened. Elvis straightened his arm, sighting down the barrel.

Simon struggled harder.

And then several things happened at the same instant. A black dot appeared on the gunman's cheek. The window behind Simon shattered. Somewhere behind him a pistol fired.

Simon freed himself from the bully's grip, only to slip again, his hands catching his fall. When he looked up, Elvis was dead. He lay on his stomach, eyes open, a bit of brain peeking out from behind his ear.

Simon clambered to his feet as a familiar figure stepped through the broken window.

"Still got it." The man was wiry and sixty, and very, very tan, dressed in chef's whites. "First time I've fired a gun in a year. What do you say to that?"

"Hello, Jojo."

CHAPTER 51

After five minutes, Vika was curious. After ten, she was nervous. Twenty-two minutes after Simon left the table she was nearing a Category 4 meltdown.

She stood and abandoned the baccarat table, leaving her chips where they were. "Did you see where he went?" she asked Philippe, her body-guard.

"Toward the Salle des Étoiles, ma'am." He pointed at the table. "Your chips?"

"Who cares?" Vika made a beeline for the double doors leading outside. More than anything, she was angry. Simon had to realize that she'd worry if he was gone too long. It was inexcusable not to text or even put his precious employer on hold for a moment to call and let her know that he'd be a while. A gentleman didn't leave a lady seated alone at a gambling establishment.

Vika stopped abruptly, her breath leaving her. One thing she knew about Simon: he was a gentleman. If he hadn't returned, if he hadn't taken a moment to let her know he'd been delayed, it was because something had happened. Something unfortunate.

She threw open the glass doors and embarked on a hectic search of the outdoor area. Half the guests had left. Those remaining milled in islands of four or five. Nowhere did she see a dark-haired man dressed in a navy suit and possessed of an unstoppable momentum. She arrived at the far side of the floor, looking around desperately for where to continue her search.

"May I be of service?"

Vika looked over to the bar, where an older, weathered man with steel-gray hair sat alone, nursing a glass of brandy. "Excuse me?" she said.

"I saw you earlier today with my friend, Mr. Riske."

"You did?"

"At the hotel."

"Have you seen him recently?"

"Have you lost him, or is it vice versa?" The man chuckled. "My name is Dov Dragan. I'm a steward with the Rally Club."

"Simon…Mr. Riske…stepped outside a few minutes ago and now I can't find him."

"I can't imagine he'd leave without saying goodbye. He said you were close friends."

"He did? When?"

"We shared a drink this afternoon at the hotel. After you'd returned from Italy."

"He told you about Italy?"

"He said he was ready to go back to London. Something about finishing his real job and letting other people solve their own problems."

"Really?" Vika put a hand on the bar, suddenly unsteady. "He said that?"

"And more, my dearest princess. You look peaked. May I offer you a cocktail? I believe your mother quite enjoyed martinis."

"How do you know my mother?"

"I thought everyone did. Didn't she throw a martini ball all those years ago at the Adlon in Berlin? She made her entrance swimming in a giant martini glass."

Vika blushed. It was true. It was one of the stories from her childhood that she'd done her best to repress. The party had made news across Europe (as intended) and had landed her mother on the cover of all the gossip glossies: *Hello!*, *Gala*, and even *Paris Match*.

"So you haven't seen him in the last few minutes?" asked Vika, determined to be pleasant.

The man waved a hand toward an empty stool. "Have a seat. I'm sure he mentioned me. He's convinced he's going to beat my Bugatti tomorrow. I told him it was impossible, but he's a stubborn one." Dragan leaned in, his blue eyes pouchy and bloodshot with drink. "Does he really just restore cars? Surely there's something he's not telling us?"

Vika had a strong urge to slap this impudent and ill-bred troll. "I wouldn't know," she managed. "You must excuse me."

"But no, please stay." He placed a hand on her arm.

"Good night." The hand lifted, but only after she glared at him.

Vika left the grand floor and hurried along the leafy entry corridor to the forecourt. A line of guests waited for their cars to be brought up. She saw no sign of Simon. She dug her phone out of her purse and called him. After eight rings the call went to his voice mail. "Simon, would you please—"

A hand landed on her shoulder. "Victoria, is that you?"

She spun to face a tall, handsome gray-haired man dressed in his trademark double-breasted navy blazer, the gold buttons shiny as ever. "Tobias…Hello."

"I'm so sorry about your mother."

"So sorry you couldn't phone?"

"My apologies," he said graciously. "It's been a difficult time. The Société des Bains de Mer is having a hard go of it."

They spoke in German, as was their custom. "Too bad," she said, looking over his shoulder, combing the sea of faces.

"Have you set a date for the service?" he asked.

"Not yet. But it will be at Schloss Brandenburg. I'll be sure to let you know."

"Stefanie had many friends in the principality. It might be nice to have a small get-together here. A 'celebration of life.' Maybe at that Italian place she loved so much."

"You are her ex-husband and you do live here, at least some of the time. May I impose on you to arrange it?"

"It's been ten years. I wouldn't know where to start."

"The divorce was never finalized. Technically, you are still married."

"Your mother refused to sign."

"She said it was you who refused."

"Let's not start this. Are we really going to rely on her word?"

Vika put on her most polite smile. She'd been unprepared to see Lord Toby Stonewood, born Tobias Holzenstein, a.k.a. "Bismarck." Like the Battenbergs before them, who'd inverted their name when they'd fled Germany to become the Mountbattens, Toby's great-grandparents had made a change in order to better fit in. "Holzenstein" became "Steinholz," which in turn was translated to "Stonewood." Ever so English.

After all this time, she'd never come to terms with how to view him. Certainly not as family, despite the fact that he'd been married to her mother for many years and had, Vika was the first to admit, given her much happiness, if only in the form of the status his English title bestowed. (Mama had never gotten over being born poor, even with a title of her own.) And yet, Vika realized, besides Robby, Toby was the only family she had left, like it or not.

"You all right?" he asked. "You look distracted."

"I've lost someone. He must have gone back to the hotel."

"A new beau? It's about time someone helped you run things."

"I'm more than capable," said Vika, "as you well know."

"Of course you are, my dear," said Lord Toby, smooth as ever.

It would take more than a mention of their past disputes to upset him. All that English reserve and cool. Stay calm and have a gin and tonic. Or, in Toby's case, a dozen. He hid his alcoholism better than anyone she'd known. It was one of the things Mama had loved best about him. He could match her drink for drink and somehow maintain a semblance of sobriety. Vika imagined that his liver looked like a withered grape.

She studied the ruddy cheeks, the legion of burst blood vessels hiding below the surface. The only time she'd seen him lose his temper was one day a few months before he'd married her mother. The subject was money. He didn't want to sign prenups, either for him or her, arguing that it was beneath them. Everyone knew that the Holzenstein dynasty was one of the richest in Europe. His English holdings alone were worth more than the Brandenburgs'. On her mother's behalf (and her own), Vika had insisted on the prenups. She'd seen how fortunes waxed and waned.

Toby smiled decorously. "I'm heading out. Busy day tomorrow. Give you a lift?"

An idea popped into Vika's head. Then and there, she decided that she'd never have a better opportunity. God knew she was anxious to show Simon that she was capable, too. She drew Philippe aside and told him that she would return to the hotel with her stepfather and that she couldn't be in safer hands. The bodyguard exchanged words with Toby. The men shook hands.

A minute later, the valet arrived with Toby's Bentley. As they left the main drive and turned toward the hotel, she placed a hand on Toby's arm. "Let's go to church," she said.

"Church?" said Toby, the devout Anglican who regarded Catholicism as one step removed from voodoo. "Whatever for?"

"Église Saint-Marc. It's just around the corner. I believe there's an evening Mass."

CHAPTER 52

I know these two. Tommy and Pavel."

Jojo Matta circled the floor, looking at the men with interest, careful not to poke the toe of his white loafer into the lake of blood.

"You missed their boss," said Simon. "Ratka."

"You mean he missed me. I had to hide as he came out of the house."

"You took your sweet time."

"Thought you deserved to get to know them better, with all you done. I saw you at the Sporting Club. Followed you. Hey, what are you doing?"

Simon had taken off his belt and was applying a tourniquet to the bully Pavel's leg. "He's alive. Maybe he can tell me something."

"Why's everyone trying to kill you?"

"They have their reasons."

"What are you doing down here, anyway?"

"Ratka has a crew stealing from the casino. Sophisticated, organized. I was brought in to find out what's what, get rid of them." One minute with Jojo and Simon was talking like the old days.

"Sophisticated? Ratka? Not a chance. He's a strong-arm man. Fucking war criminal."

"He's gotten smarter. They've taken the casino for millions over the last six months."

Simon realized he was saying too much, but Jojo had been family once, and Simon needed to talk. He was rattled. Too much had happened in too short a time. At some point, he was going to have to have a long sit-down and think everything through, make sure his head was still screwed on straight. This wasn't the time.

He notched the belt just below the man's groin, though he wasn't sure what good it would do. Simon tapped his cheek. The Serb's eyes fluttered and he grunted.

"Pavel, listen to me. Why did Ratka kill Princess Stefanie? I saw you in the car following him."

Pavel's eyes opened wide. "Fuck off."

"Who was with Ratka?"

Pavel shook his head.

"Please," Simon continued. "Who do you have inside the casino? Someone's helping you. I know it. Give me the name."

Pavel tried to push Simon away, and when he failed, he made an effort to undo the tourniquet. Simon restrained his hands. "Pavel, talk to me. Why did Ratka kill Stefanie? Who else was with you?"

"I never say shit to you." Pavel glared at Jojo. "Fuck you, too."

Before Simon could stop him, Jojo came closer, put the gun to Pavel's forehead, and shot him. Simon jumped back, splatter all over his face. "What the hell? Jesus—"

"Fucking Serbs," said Jojo. "Piss me off. Don't look at me like that. Get water from a stone sooner than these guys snitch."

Simon half walked, half stumbled into the living room. Only when he'd sat down on the couch did he see the trail of bloody tracks he'd left. He didn't care about the carpet. The shoe prints were evidence.

"This Ratka's place?" asked Jojo.

"That's what he said. You have it, right? The jammer?"

"Think I followed you here to save your ass? Come all this way, I want my money."

"You'll get it."

"What does the thing do, anyway?"

"Blocks phones and computers from talking to each other. Stops their signals."

Jojo wasn't interested. "Three thousand," he said.

Simon handed over the money and Jojo peered greedily into his wallet. "How much you got there?"

"I don't know. Ten grand."

Jojo's gaze shifted from the wad of bills to Simon. "I could shoot you like that and take it. What's stopping me?" He stepped back and pointed the pistol at Simon. "Not like anyone would know. How 'bout it, Ledoux? Give me the money."

Fast as lightning, Simon snatched the pistol out of Jojo's hand and pointed it right back at him. In the same motion he was up off the couch, clutching a fistful of Jojo's tunic. "You were saying?"

"It was a joke. You know that. We're family. La Brise forever."

Simon jammed the muzzle into the skin hanging from Jojo's jaw. He'd had enough of tough guys for one night.

"Ledoux, please. I'm sorry."

"Save it." Simon gave him a good tug before releasing him. Jojo brushed off his tunic, the color taking a while to return to his face.

"I'm talking about real money," said Simon. "Couple hundred thousand at least."

"You serious?"

"What do you think?" said Simon. "I need someone to help me sort things out. Go in heavy. You remember what that means. It's the drop house. It might get messy."

"We talking about Ratka?"

Simon nodded.

"And you're serious about the hundred thousand?"

"More than that."

"I'd about pay you to take that asshole out," said Jojo. "Fucking Serbs. Come down here. Make like they own the place. Russians are one thing. I mean, Russia's a real country. But Serbia...it's smaller than Corsica. Someone's got to send them home. When are you thinking?"

"Tonight."

"Tonight? It's already eleven. It'll take me some time."

"I have some work to do first."

"At the casino?"

"Yes."

"With that gizmo?"

"Yes, Jojo. With that gizmo."

Jojo considered the proposition, then nodded his agreement. He returned to the front door, tiptoeing around the perimeter of the foyer, which was now entirely covered in blood. There was red marble, too, thought Simon. Carrara *rosso*. He didn't think it was quarried in Serbia.

"Let's go," called Jojo, standing at the door. "Too many dead people in here."

"I'm not done."

Jojo appeared confused. "There someone else here you want to kill?"

"Wait here." Simon went upstairs. He was more or less certain there was no one else in the house, and he wasn't interested in killing such a person should he find him or her. It was Ratka's words that prompted him to search the place, his vow not to let Simon mess up his "big plan" or allow Simon to stop him from "getting it all." Big plans left a trail, and if Simon wasn't sure which of Vika's things Ratka wanted, he understood his intent loud and clear.

It was evident that Ratka was not planning on staying in the house. Packing boxes, taped shut, lined the upstairs corridors. Rooms were empty or nearly so. Almost all the furniture had been removed. Only large pieces remained—oak armoires that dated from the nineteenth century, squat chests that would have looked at home in a Spanish galleon, and a white grand piano with an elaborate candelabra on top. Who knew Liberace was big in Belgrade? Each box was marked with Ratka's real name, Zoltan Mikhailovic. An hour of phoning freight companies would yield the forwarding address.

Simon came to the end of the hall. The door was locked. He kicked at the fixture, once, twice; the second time, his shoe rendered a hole in the wood laminate. Easy does it, he told himself, yanking his foot clear. Drawing a breath, he entered Ratka's study.

A heavy wooden desk facing a stone fireplace held pride of place. The bookshelves were empty. The only decoration was a tall flag draped from a stand, the kind of thing Simon had seen in diplomats' offices. Out of curiosity, he lifted the corners. The colors were scarlet, black, and white. He didn't know what country it represented, but he recognized the angular geometric symbol at its center. The design was an adaptation of the *hakenkreuz,* the ancient Aryan symbol that the National Socialist German Workers' Party had made into the swastika, and that of late had been adopted by other equally vile nationalist groups across Europe. A scroll running across the bottom of the flag read SERBIA USTAJ.

A hefty binder sat on the desk. Simon noted the image of the flag on its cover and picked it up. Inside were photographs of different men. Close-ups, long shots, alone and with others. It was clear to Simon that they were all criminals. He knew the look. Each man had his own see-through sleeve, his name typed on a label affixed to the lower right-hand corner. On the back of each sleeve a page listed the men's activities and associates and the region of the city from which they operated. Simon was right. All the men were criminals. It was his guess that Ratka was going to kill them. Ratka hoped to return to Belgrade in style.

Big plans.

Before heading downstairs, Simon stopped in Ratka's bedroom. Simon's clothing was crusted with blood, sleeves stiff as cardboard. He tore off his clothes and washed up as quickly as possible. From Ratka's closet he picked out the suit he considered the least awful. It was two sizes too large, but it would have to do. Finished changing, Simon washed his face, then rolled up his soiled clothing and brought it with him.

Simon found Jojo in the garden out back. He pointed to a dented jerry can. "They were going to burn you up, Ledoux," he said. "You owe me."

A second jerry can was at his feet, as was a black body bag. Nearby, a spade stood in the dirt next to a neatly dug pit.

Benzin, pozni, nista, nista, nista.

Simon turned to look at the house, and the rage he'd been working so hard to stifle bubbled right back up. The gun in his mouth, Elena's battered face, Vika fighting for her life. He was at the edge. Maybe a step beyond it.

"What did you say?" asked Jojo.

Simon came out of his trance, unaware that he'd spoken. "Pick up the jerry can and follow me," he said. "You still smoke, right?"

Gasoline. Fire. Nothing. Nothing. Nothing.

Chapter 53

A church's doors are always open.

Vika stepped inside the vestibule of the Église Saint-Marc and pressed her back to the door. The nave was dark, a dimmed spotlight illuminating the altar and chancel. The air was cool and dry, smelling pleasantly of plaster and beeswax. Her eyes lifted to the dome and the painting of Saint Paul on the road to Damascus decorated with gold leaf.

There was no liturgy on a Thursday night. She'd lied. While Catholicism was the state religion of Monaco, most of the principality's residents were a few "Hail Mary"s and "Our Father"s short of devout. The Église Saint-Marc satisfied its parishioners with a daily morning Mass, a late afternoon service on Saturday, and two high Masses on Sunday.

A moment passed and Vika advanced down the aisle. She stopped at the third pew. Following Elena's instructions, she slid to the far right-hand side. Her hand fell to the kneeler and she lowered it into place before clasping her hands. By long habit, she recited the Lord's Prayer and made the sign of the cross upon herself. Having completed her proper hello to God, she ran her fingers below the hymnal rack, leaning forward as she sought a touch of velvet. She prayed again, this time asking that she find what she'd come for, and that Elena had not only hidden the family ring but hidden it well.

"Victoria, everything all right?"

Vika looked over her shoulder to see Toby Stonewood standing at the back of the church. "Fine," she said awkwardly. "I'll just be a minute."

She groped beneath the rack, fingers probing every which way, discovering a wad of gum hard as rock, and another, not so hard. *Come now, Elena, I'm right where you said I should be. What have you done with Mama's*

263

ring? She looked back again. Toby hadn't moved. He stood with hands clasped and head bowed like a proper English schoolboy. Vika lowered her shoulder, stretching her arm as far as it would go. She touched something soft and smooth. Her fingertips danced across its surface. Velveteen. Hallelujah! A moment later, she'd pried the jewelry bag free and held it in her hand. She couldn't help but open it to make sure the ring was inside. A round piece of gold fell into her palm. She took it between her thumb and forefinger, eyes embracing the family crest.

Footsteps approached. "Finished?" asked Toby. "I always say my prayers beside my bed."

Vika fumbled with the strings to the jewelry bag. The ring fell to the ground, the tinkle of metal sounding to her ears like a tray of cutlery crashing onto the kitchen floor. She bent and scooped up the ring.

"What have you got there?" Toby eyed her questioningly. She'd been caught red-handed.

"Mama's ring."

"The diamond solitaire? Goodness me. Let me help."

Vika shook her head. She saw Toby's expression of concern and felt ashamed for her subterfuge. "The family crest."

"Did Stefanie lose it?" he asked. "Here…in church?" For all his wealth and experience, he was always a step behind.

"She hid it. Or rather, Elena did."

"Now I am confused."

Vika rose and made her way to the aisle. "We need to talk."

"What about?"

"About Mama."

"Seems as good a place as any to talk about the dead."

Vika turned and put her hands on his arms, looking into those handsome blue eyes. "Mama didn't drive herself off the road."

"What do you mean? Of course she did."

Vika shook her head. "It wasn't an accident."

Toby took a step back, as if frightened of what might be coming. "What was it, then?"

"She was murdered."

CHAPTER 54

A tired Harry Mason wiped off his wrench and dropped it into the tool-box. The first rule of garage etiquette demanded that you leave your tools as clean as you found them. He'd learned it fifty years earlier and hadn't disobeyed it since. Taking the hand spot off its hook, he shone the light over the engine, making one last visual inspection.

It was something to look at. A quad cam Colombo-designed 4.4-liter V12 topped with a bank of six twin choke carburetors, six gleaming valves set in a straight row that sparkled more brightly than the Queen's silver. Back in its day, the Daytona was the fastest production car in the world, with top speeds of 175 miles per hour and a monstrous 352 horse-power, with enough torque to make you feel like a fighter pilot pulling ten gs in a negative roll.

Of course, Simon wanted more. More speed, more horsepower, more torque. He'd come to the right man. If anyone could find an additional hundred horsepower, it was Harry Mason. The older the car, the more difficult the task, but he'd managed. He'd had to recalibrate the carbu-retor and modify the headers, and Simon would need to gas up with hundred-octane fuel, but he'd have his extra horsepower, goddammit… for all the good it would do him.

Harry closed the bonnet with care, then went to the washroom to get cleaned up. His love affair with automobiles had begun a half century ago. He'd grown up in the slums of Limerick (more or less the whole damned city), the fifth of six boys, the shortest, the plumpest, and the one with the reddest hair. In truth, he was a fine little scholar and enjoyed school until the bigger lads had taken it upon themselves to beat up the "wee tomato" day in and day out. He was as tough as any and took what they dished out, certain it would all sort itself out when he stopped being so "wee." The problem was, he never grew. He was the wee-est in kindergarten and the wee-est in sixth form. When he turned fourteen and remained the shortest in his class, he'd had enough. Tough was tough, but only a mental deficient put himself through that kind of punishment. He wanted to have a few teeth left when he turned eighteen. School was out for Harry Mason.

Every day, he left home with his book bag and gave his ma a kiss on the cheek, but instead of turning left to walk down Island Road to St. Mary's National School, he turned right and spent the day wandering the streets. For some reason, he found himself coming again and again to a new car dealership. He'd spend hours staring through the window at the shiny Austins, imagining himself behind the wheel. It was a pipe dream. No Mason had ever owned a car, and a man without a proper education didn't stand a chance of earning enough to buy one. Harry didn't know it, but someone had noticed his loitering.

One day, a sturdy red-haired man not much taller than he asked if he'd like to have a look around. Harry Mason started work in the dealership's service bay the next day. Years passed. He moved from working on Austins to Rovers to Jaguars, then made the leap overseas (figuratively speaking) to Mercedes, and finally, one hallowed day, to Ferraris. His textbooks were written in grease and sweat. His final exams drove out of the garage and fulfilled other people's dreams. The work must have agreed with him because over the years he grew. Not much. But five foot seven was a hell of a lot bigger than five foot two.

Harry checked that the garage was spic-and-span, then made his way to the back door. Another car occupied the slot adjacent to the black Daytona. It was a shiny silver contraption with a bulbous nose and great big tires. More of a rocket ship than a sports car. It was a Bugatti Veyron and it had rolled in sometime after five for a tune-up. The car was rare enough that Harry knew it must belong to one of Simon's fellow competitors.

Harry loved Simon like the son he'd never had, but fact was fact, truth was truth, and horsepower was horsepower. There was no way on God's green earth that a Ferrari Daytona could beat a Bugatti Veyron in a flat-out race. The great Eddie Irvine on his best day couldn't bring it off. And Simon Riske, bless his soul, wasn't even an Irishman.

Leaving the garage, Harry jumped into a waiting taxi. He had a few more things to look at in the morning. A mechanic's work was never done.

"Hôtel de Paris," he told the driver with a pat on the shoulder. *"Et vite . . . très vite!"*

CHAPTER 55

Simon sat in the passenger seat of Jojo's old Peugeot, phone pressed to his ear as they rattled down the mountainside.

"Vika? Are you okay?"

"I'm fine. You're the one who went missing."

"The call went longer than expected."

"What happened? I looked everywhere for you." Her voice jumped from relief to anger to worry in the course of a sentence.

"I had a little run-in. That's all."

"You sound funny. Are you sure everything is all right?"

The car hit a pothole and Simon's head knocked against the ceiling. *Hoods,* he thought to himself. They spent all their time figuring out how to make a score, and when they did, they couldn't even afford a decent set of wheels. He looked behind him. Flames shot above the trees, turning the sky a warm, smoky orange. He covered the phone. "Faster," he said to Jojo. Then to Vika: "I'm fine. Where are you?"

"Didn't you get my message? I'm back at the hotel."

"At the hotel?"

"Yes. In my room, safe and sound."

Simon hadn't had time to listen to his messages. Besides the one from Vika, there were six from Toby Stonewood, all of which, he imagined, had to do with just where the hell Simon was. "I'm glad you're okay," he said. "Stay there."

"When will you be back?"

"Not for a while. I'm trying to finish up my job tonight."

"And get back to London?" she asked sharply.

"Eventually," he said, struck by her tone. "Why are you asking?"

"A man at the Sporting Club told me. Dov Dragan. He said he was your friend."

"Dov Dragan is not a friend. He's a…a…"

"I couldn't agree more," said Vika. "He introduced himself as I was looking for you. I don't know when I've met a more unsavory individual."

Simon hadn't thought it possible to dislike the man more than he already did. "I'll tell you everything when I get back to the hotel. You have my word."

"Stop by my room when you return. I don't care the time. There's something I need to tell you, too."

"It might be late."

"Simon…"

"Yes?"

"I don't want to lie to you anymore. I found what they were looking for at my mother's house. You don't have to worry about me any longer. It's all going to be all right."

She ended the call.

A moment later, there was a large explosion behind them. Then a second, even larger, that shook the car's windows. A shock wave rattled the car. Simon looked over his shoulder as a fireball rose in the sky.

"What the hell was in that house?" asked Jojo.

Simon didn't answer. Ratka had done more than compile a binder of his hometown enemies. He'd already begun stocking up on the tools he'd need to take them out. From the sound of the explosions, it was going to be a big job. "Shut up and drive."

Jojo dropped Simon back at the Sporting Club. It might not be as busy as the Casino de Monte-Carlo, but Simon knew who to look for and where to look. A hunter couldn't ask for anything more. It was a question of flushing the pheasants from the tall grass. Instead of hounds, he had his portable Wi-Fi signal jammer. Slim enough to fit in his coat pocket, the device looked identical to a handheld recorder, only with three blunt (foldable) antennas extending from its top. Turn it on, and all communications on the Bluetooth bandwidth within fifty meters would be interrupted. The birds would fly. All he wanted was a clear shot.

Inside the casino, he quickly located the team of cheats. They had switched tables, but by the looks of the chips in front of them their fortunes hadn't suffered as a result. Every seat was taken. The crowd watching had thinned, however. Even winning gets boring after a while.

Simon stopped at the bar. "Vodka," he said. "Triple."

"Sir?"

"Need something to kill the pain." Simon winced. His pain was real, not a by-product of bad luck at the tables. A smarter man would have been in bed with enough ice wrapped around his ribs to flash-freeze a steer.

He drank the vodka in a single go, then ordered a champagne to show that he belonged in the place despite Ratka's baggy suit and permanent-press shirt. He shoved off and headed to the table. He had set the jammer to block a 2.5-gigahertz signal, nothing higher, thus not interfering with cell phone traffic. He stopped a fair distance from the cheats and observed as two hands were played. From the pattern of betting, he confirmed that they were still at it. He suspected the dealer of being in on it, too.

Dropping a hand into his pocket, Simon activated the jammer.

The dealer called for bets. Two players ponied up immediately, dropping their chips on *banco*. A South Asian woman followed suit, sliding a thousand euros onto *punto*. A fourth player was more judicious, betting the minimum, also on *punto*. All eyes fell on the three men who had yet to place their bets.

"Gentlemen?" said the dealer.

Until now, none of the men had said a word to one another. It wasn't uncommon to strike up momentary friendships with tablemates, just as one often speaks to a seatmate on a plane. Gambling, like air travel, has a shared sense of urgency that breaks down social barriers and encourages honest, often intimate conversation. Who cares what you say to someone you will never see again? But even now, none of the men said a word. Not a peep.

"Bets?" said the dealer, too patiently.

One of the men shook his head, then the second, and the third.

"Very well," said the dealer.

Cards were dealt; the hands played out. Two for *punto*. Six for *banco*. *Banco* won.

All this time, Simon studied the cheats. None betrayed the slightest indication that their equipment had failed. They were slick, all right. Simon imagined that there must be confusion on the other end of the operation, too. But it was apparent something wasn't right. None had yet to place a bet.

The next hand began.

To speed up matters, Simon leaned closer to the table and said, "If you're not going to play, give up your seats. Some of us would like to take them."

The dealer shot him a dark look. "Place your bets," he said.

The cheats all placed minimum bets on *banco*. The hand was played. *Punto* won.

One of the cheats left the table and headed toward the main entry. Simon held his ground, and a moment later, a second man left, following his partner. Only then did Simon give pursuit.

He followed the men out of the room and took up position near a bank of slot machines as the two, deep in conversation, left the building and hurried down the long driveway. One of them had a hand to his ear. He was out of the jammer's range and Simon was certain he was speaking to his controller.

He allowed them a few more steps, then left the casino. A median with palm trees planted every ten steps divided the road into two lanes— coming and going. Simon ducked onto the opposite side, staying in the trees' shadows. A car idled at the foot of the driveway. The men climbed into the back seat. The car zoomed away, and there was a moment when Simon thought he'd blown it, and that they were taking off for good. Twenty meters farther, the car pulled to a halt so as not to block the exit.

A few minutes passed. The doors opened. The men left the car. Simon observed both men placing what were surely new receivers into their ear canals, checking that they worked, then heading back to the casino to resume their assignment.

Crouched in the shadows, Simon watched them pass, then ran to the car. He didn't know how many people were inside. He didn't care. Pistol leading the way, he threw open the door. There were two men: a driver behind the wheel and the controller in the back, laptop open, images of cards about to be dealt visible in one of several open windows. Simon spun the pistol in his hand, held it by the muzzle, and clubbed the driver with its butt. One blow to the temple was enough. The man slumped to one side, unconscious, head resting against the window.

Simon dropped into the back seat and pulled the door closed. All throughout his career as an investigator, he'd forsworn the use of guns. Not tonight. The pistol was a nine-millimeter SIG Sauer, courtesy of Elvis. There were six bullets remaining in the clip. Simon had one chambered and thumbed the hammer as he placed the barrel against the second man's cheek.

"Don't say a word."

An earpiece with an attached microphone was plugged into the laptop. Simon yanked it free and inserted the earpiece.

"Who are you?" the controller asked, his accented English depressingly familiar. He was thirty, pale as soapstone, with two days' stubble and shaggy black hair that fell into his eyes.

"Police," said Simon. "You're parked in a red zone."

"Bullshit," said the man.

Simon slammed his head against the glass. "We take traffic violations seriously."

The man shrunk back, properly warned. "How much do you want?" he asked.

"All of it."

The man shook his head. "Fuck off."

Simon was beginning to understand why Jojo hated these guys so much. "How much are you up tonight?"

"Up? What you mean? What you talk about?"

"Where's Ratka?"

"Who?"

"Your boss. I'm wearing his suit. Recognize it? I was just up at his place with Tommy and Pavel. Nice chandelier. By the way, they're dead."

"You're crazy."

Simon dug out his phone and showed him a picture of the two men. It had sickened him to take the photo, but he'd reasoned that it could have some persuasive value. At the sight of the blood and the bodies, the controller turned an unpleasant shade of green.

"What's your name?" Simon kept the gun to his cheek.

"Radek."

"Okay, Radek. Now that we know who's who and what's what, I'm going to ask you a few questions. Rue Chaussée four seventy-six. Is that the drop house?"

Radek stared straight ahead. He was loyal and he was brave. Simon gave him that much. "I'll count to three, then I'll blow your friend's brains all over the front window. One."

"No! He's my brother."

"All right, then. I'll kill you first, then him. Two."

"Yes," said Radek, spitting out the word. "Rue Chaussée is the drop house. Tonight is last night. Everyone stops at two a.m. Deliver money."

"And Ratka?"

"He'll be there. He's in charge."

"Who else is with him?"

"Usually Tommy and Pavel. We go, give him money, then get out."

"When does he pay you?"

"No one paid till it all over."

"When what's all over?" Radek's words didn't ring true. Crooks didn't wait to get paid.

"Ratka keeping the money for now."

"All of it?"

Radek nodded.

"He hasn't paid you in all this time you've been robbing the casino?"

"Little bit. We split it later. There's more then."

"More than you steal from the casino?"

"Lots more."

"Tell me."

"One million," said Radek.

"For all of you?" asked Simon, purposely misunderstanding him.

"Each," said Radek, pridefully. The male ego was an amazingly simple instrument to manipulate.

"Why is tonight the last night?"

"We got enough."

"How much is enough?"

"I don't know. Lots."

"Who's the one who decides how much is enough?"

"Ratka. Who you think?"

"And he's paying you a million?"

Radek nodded.

Simon thought of Jojo's crapped-out Peugeot. Yes, he decided, for a million euros Jojo would wait, too. Everyone wanted a shot at the big money, a spin of the wheel of fortune. A million went a long way back home in Serbia. All of which begged the question: If a soldier like Radek stood to earn a million, how much was the man in charge looking to take down? Ten times that amount? A hundred? Big plans cost big money.

If Ratka and his gang had already stolen over two hundred million euros, how much more were they looking to earn?

The answer came to him courtesy of a striking German blonde with more brains than he'd ever have, and, he was beginning to suspect, more backbone.

The family is worth twelve billion dollars, Vika had said over lunch in Èze.

And Ratka wanted to get all of it. Taking control of all organized crime in a big city was expensive.

"And what about the princess?" asked Simon.

"What princess?" demanded Radek, evidently concerned that Simon might know more than him. Honesty stuck out like a neon sign in the dead of night. Simon was pretty sure Radek didn't know anything about Ratka's big plans.

So, thought Simon, there were two operations, and they were connected. The first involved stealing from the casino, the second from Princess Victoria Brandenburg von Tiefen und Tassis, and it had required killing her mother. *Going to get all of it.* Ratka might not have been sophisticated, but he was ambitious and without morals. If Vika had found what Ratka wanted, she was in more danger, not less.

Looking at the laptop's screen, Simon noted that the two cheats had returned to the table in time for a new shoe. The laptop was his front row seat to watching how the bad guys played their game.

A window in the corner broadcast a live feed from a camera planted in one of the cheats' sleeves—the man who had not left the table. The dealer offered him the shoe to cut the cards. The cheat ran the yellow plastic cutting card across the entire shoe from bottom to top before pulling the card away and sliding it into the center of the deck. All this the hidden camera filmed and transmitted to the controller.

The dealer took the shoe back and cut the cards accordingly, then followed his defined practice of burning the top five cards and playing two mock hands. Now official play could begin.

"What exactly do you have to do?" Simon asked Radek.

"First, I input where our players sit at the table, give them betting limits. The software give a probability to every hand. It never always right, who wins, who loses—*punto* or *banco*. I tell players how to bet. Bet heavy if this number high"—he pointed to a figure indicating the ratio of success—"bet less if smaller. Sometime we have to lose, so it looks okay. Like I say, software not right all the time."

"Who wrote the program?"

"A friend of Ratka, I think. I don't know. Whoever it is, he's a mathematical genius."

Simon studied the screen, putting it all together. Custom software, trained controllers, disciplined teams to hit the casinos. Something didn't jibe. Jojo had been right when he said that Ratka wasn't sophisticated. So, if he wasn't running the show, who was?

"From now on, you work for me," said Simon. "Do what I say and I'll let you and your brother go. Do not fuck with me."

Radek nodded eagerly. Simon didn't believe his sincerity for a minute.

On the screen, a new hand was dealt. Immediately figures showing the probabilities for *punto* and *banco* appeared in separate windows.

"Go ahead," said Simon. "But this time make them lose."

"Lose?"

"Lose big."

"Ratka won't like it."

"He can see?"

"Sure. Everything goes to a central unit, so he can see who's winning and how much."

Of course Ratka could see, thought Simon. If a genius had designed the software, he'd certainly make sure to keep track of their winnings on a real-time basis. Simon wanted that computer. Evidence from day one.

Ten minutes later, the three cheats had forfeited two hundred thousand euros of their winnings. One of them could be heard muttering through the receiver.

"Tell him to keep playing," said Simon.

Another hand was dealt. Another loss for Team Serbia. Fifty thousand back to the Société des Bains de Mer. Simon looked forward to giving Toby Stonewood the good news.

"He's coming," said Radek.

"Who?"

"Team leader."

"Good. I'd like to meet him."

The driver stirred, moaning as he came to. Simon glanced in his direction, immediately on guard, ready to give him another lump if necessary. Radek saw his chance. He threw himself at Simon, knocking the pistol away, forcing him against the door. Simon grunted, the pain from his ribs making his eyes water. He tried to push Radek off him, but the man had him pinned. Radek fought for the gun, hands battling to pry it from Simon. The Sig had a hair trigger. The gun fired, blowing a hole in the car's roof. Simon drove his fist into Radek's jaw, but the blow had no effect. If anything, Radek fought harder. The noise had roused the driver. Seeing what was going on, he clambered over his seat, arms extended, hands grabbing Simon's arms. Simon kicked him in the jaw and kicked him again. The driver's head caromed off the roof. His eyes rolled back in his head and he slid, limp, back into his seat.

Radek closed his fingers around Simon's fist. He was very strong and Simon felt himself losing his grip on the weapon. His left hand closed around Radek's windpipe, fingers digging into his flesh. Blood dribbled over his fingertips. The Serb's face grew red, his eyes unnaturally large in their sockets. Another shot exploded in the confined space, shattering the window. Simon dropped the weapon onto the street and took hold of the door frame, drawing his knees to his chest and thrusting Radek off him. Radek lunged at him like a rabid beast. Simon wrapped his legs around the Serb's head, locking his ankles, and turned his torso viciously to his right. Radek's neck cracked like a twig but did not break. He continued to struggle, but Simon was too strong. Leaning forward, he grabbed a handful of Radek's hair, yanked his head back, and hit him with a closed fist, shattering his nose. He hit him again. Moaning, Radek covered his face and slumped against the door.

Simon fell back against the seat, physically and emotionally spent. His hand throbbed and his knuckles were scraped bloody. He sat up, recalling Radek's words that his colleague was coming, no doubt to inquire about what was going on. Looking out the rear window, Simon spotted a man hurrying down the drive. It had to be the team leader.

With no time to spare, Simon hauled the driver out of his seat and messily folded him into the passenger seat. Simon slid behind the wheel, started the car, and drove away from the Sporting Club, careful to keep his speed reasonable—nothing to cause alarm.

Behind him, the team leader started running, then gave up, throwing his hands in the air.

Simon rolled down the window and waved.

CHAPTER 56

A firm hand knocked three times. "Victoria, it's me."

Vika hurried to the door, looking through the peephole to make sure it was Toby Stonewood. "There you are."

"Sorry, dear. Business. Had to take a call. Several, actually. Didn't mean to keep you waiting, especially when we have so much to discuss."

"I'm sorry to drop this on you out of the blue," said Vika. "I can understand it's a shock."

"Nonsense. If there's been foul play we need to get to the bottom of it. I hope you won't mistake my surprise for disbelief. As you said, it's a shock." Toby dropped into a club chair and exhaled. "Mind making me a drink? You're scaring the hell out of this old man. A double, if you don't mind."

Vika mixed Toby a stiff gin and tonic and handed it to him. He thanked her and proceeded to drink half of it. "That's better," he said. "Now I can think. Murder? That's a serious word."

Vika sat down in a chair beside him. "It is."

"You've gone to the police?"

"I brought it up with Commissaire Le Juste when I arrived."

"Good man. Head of the criminal department."

"I told him that something wasn't right," Vika began. "Mama hadn't driven at night in years. She couldn't see out of her right eye. In fact, she barely drove at all. Elena took her everywhere." She gazed at Toby inquisitively. "Didn't you ask yourself what she was doing on the Grande Corniche at midnight all by herself? And in the Rolls? She hadn't taken it out in a year."

"I may have," said Toby, "if I'm entirely honest with myself. But you know…I wrote it off to drink. I'd seen her around town a few times over the past year and she wasn't looking herself."

"I'm not blaming you," Vika was quick to add.

"Of course you're not. It's just that it's your mother we're talking about. Murder? Hard to wrap my mind around the idea."

"Think of her as a princess with a fortune and what I have to say will make more sense."

"I'll try. Go on, then."

"Le Juste felt the same as you. He said there was no reason to think it was anything other than an accident. He asked if I had any evidence that might give weight to my suspicions."

"Did you?"

"Not then."

"You do now?" Toby leaned forward, cupping the drink in both hands. Vika looked at his firm jaw, the inquiring eyes. His easy manner was gone. He looked ten years younger, formidable, and more than a little intimidating.

"After meeting with Commissaire Le Juste, I drove up to the site of the accident. I had to see for myself. Of course, they'd picked the perfect spot."

"'They'?"

"At a sharp bend, no streetlights," continued Vika. "Easy to see how a car driven by an older person, supposedly drunk, could go off the road. If I were Le Juste I'd think it was an accident, too. I had a look around, and I found something, something that to my eye didn't belong there." She noted the skeptical glint in Toby's eye. "I'll come back to that," she said. "And that was the first time they tried to harm me."

"Harm you? What happened?"

"A car tried to run me over."

"Good God!"

"I was standing by the side of the road when out of nowhere a car appeared around the curve and came straight at me. The driver didn't look frightened or out of control. He stared right at me and kept on coming. If it wasn't for Simon, I'd be dead."

"Simon?"

"An American," said Vika by way of explanation. "We'd met the night before as I was checking into the hotel. He's here for the Concours. He's driving in the time trial, or that's what he said then. As luck would have it, he was previewing the course when he saw my car. He stopped to see if I was all right."

"And saved you?"

"He pushed me out of the way." Vika noted a change in Toby's manner, his eyes keener than before. "What is it?" she asked.

Toby waved away her comment. "Continue."

"That night I went over to Mama's place at the Château Perigord. I wanted to have a look around." Vika drew herself up, hands clasped. "Actually, that's not entirely true. There's something I forgot to tell you. When I was given Mama's personal affairs at the police station—her watch, wallet, jewelry—something was missing. Her ring with the family coat of arms."

"You thought the police might have taken it…Le Juste?"

"No. Her diamond solitaire was there. It's worth a thousand times more. I was puzzled. She'd never taken off the ring in her life. You know that. I wanted to have a look around her place to see if it was there. The apartment was in shambles. At first, I thought she'd gone on a bender. God knows some of the parties she's thrown. But then I realized it wasn't a party or a drunken fest. Someone had searched her apartment. Ransacked it."

"For the ring?"

"At the time I wasn't sure. Now I am."

"But why? Who could know its value to the family?"

"That's what I don't know," said Vika. "There's more, and please, promise me you won't get upset." Toby nodded sternly and she continued. "While I was there, a man broke in and attacked me."

"Victoria!" Toby raised his hands, beside himself. "We should be at the police station this minute."

"I'm all right, Toby, but thank you. Maybe later. He tried to…well, he tried to rape me. I'm sure he planned on killing me, too. But he didn't…rape me, I mean."

"Thank God you fought him off."

"I didn't. I tried, but he was far too big. An animal. He was Eastern European. A Slav, I think."

"He spoke to you?"

"A few words."

"You said you didn't fight him off. What happened?"

"My friend saved me."

"The same one?"

"His name is Simon Riske."

"The American here for the time trial."

"He's actually here on a job. He's been hired to look into a gang who's been cheating the casino out of millions."

"And he just happened to come along?"

"He was concerned about me after what happened earlier."

"The car trying to run you over…"

Vika nodded. "He'd called my room to see if I was all right, and when I didn't answer he came looking for me."

A quizzical expression crossed Toby's face and she could see he was wrestling with the same questions she'd had: How had he found her mother's apartment? How had he gotten in? Instead of asking, Toby finished his drink and walked to the bar for another. "Simon Riske," he said, half laughing. "I'd say I owe the man a bonus. A bloody big one."

Vika turned in her chair. "Pardon?"

"Riske. Ought to double his salary. Least I can do seeing as how he's doing two jobs."

"You know him?"

Toby nodded. "Of course I know him. I hired him. I'm chairman of the Société des Bains de Mer. I took over the post last year. Who do you think brought him down here? I take it he didn't tell you."

Vika shook her head. "And he didn't tell you about me? About what happened?"

"Why would he? Not part of the job." Toby took a long pull of gin, no tonic. "I was supposed to meet him tonight, but he didn't show." He raised a finger in the air. "That's who you were looking for at the Sporting Club earlier."

Vika nodded.

"You have feelings for him?"

"Please, Toby. I just met the man."

"He has a checkered past. Not quite up to your usual standards. That's all I'll say."

"You hired him," she retorted, betraying her feelings.

"He's meant to be good at what he does, though I'm beginning to wonder. He's up and vanished. Between you and me, I'm damned angry. Last thing I need is for another of our investigators to get himself killed. The board will be all over me. I didn't want to hire another in the first place. Told 'em we could solve the problem in-house."

"'Another'?"

Toby brushed past her, distracted. "It's not your business, Victoria. You have enough to concern yourself with already."

"He's alive," she said. "You don't have to worry about that."

"He is?" said Toby from across the room. After a moment, he raised his glass and drank an extraordinary slug of gin. "Well, thank goodness for that, at least."

"I spoke to him just a little while ago," Vika explained. "He phoned while you were downstairs."

"I don't suppose he told you if he'd found out who's stealing our money."

Vika said that he hadn't and that he'd called to apologize for leaving the Sporting Club without telling her. "He did mention that he hoped to have his business concluded by later tonight."

Toby brightened. "I'll take that as good news."

Vika went on to explain what they'd found when they returned to the Château Perigord the next day.

"A cuff link," said Toby. "That's your proof?"

"It matched one I found at the crash site. Simon's trying to determine to whom it belonged."

"But how is that evidence of murder?"

"It's not. But it is a clue to who may have done it. Mama certainly didn't wear cuff links." Vika crossed her arms. "There's also a video."

Toby took a pull of his drink and waited for her to go on.

"We checked the security cameras at the pharmacy across the street," she said. "They show Mama's Rolls leaving her building late that night not long before the accident. She wasn't driving. There were two men in the front. We can't really identify either one, but it's enough to prove that Mama didn't drive herself off the cliff."

Toby crossed the room, eyes narrowed. "Do you have this tape?"

"It's at the pharmacy."

"And the cuff links?"

"Simon has them. There were strange markings on them. He's asking a friend of his if he can figure out what they are."

"You're certainly keeping him busy," said Toby, shooting her a look of displeasure. "I'm beginning to understand why he hasn't found our gang of thieves."

"He saved my life, Toby. Twice."

"Of course he did. And I'm grateful. Don't misunderstand me, dear. It's just that I have two hats to wear. I'm not paying Riske to look into your mother's death."

"Mama's murder is a far bigger matter than the casino losing a few dollars."

"Two hundred million isn't a few dollars, Victoria."

"It's nothing compared to Mama's life."

Toby finished his drink and set his glass back on the bar. "You're right, of course. You must excuse me. At least now we can go to the police and let them take things over. I don't want you in the middle of this. You're a mother and a businesswoman. You've got Robert to worry about, not to mention your investments and the trust." He fixed her with a no-nonsense stare. "I take it that's the real reason you came down. Make sure there are no difficulties in transferring the estate to your son."

She met his gaze, held it, then nodded.

"Where's the ring now, anyway?"

"Why?"

"Someone's got to keep it safe. I'm going to march it downstairs straightaway and put it in the hotel vault. And you, young lady: you are getting on the first flight out of here in the morning. I won't hear a word otherwise."

"I drove."

"Then you'll drive back. And with a bodyguard. That man, Philippe, or another. I don't care. I'll pay Riske to go with you if he's really finished his business."

Toby buttoned his blazer. "Well," he said. "I'm waiting. Give me the damned ring."

CHAPTER 57

Jojo's beat-up Peugeot sat parked on an incline on the Rue Gauthier, one block over from the drop house. Battered stone villas lined the road. Centuries-old trees hung over their rooftops. It was after midnight. Few lights burned in windows.

Simon flashed his brights, then killed his headlamps as he pulled up behind Jojo. Two men stood with Jojo. One was young, lean, and dark. The other was middle-aged at best, bald, and very fat. Seeing the two, Simon knew he had made a mistake.

"Where did you get the wheels?" asked Jojo as Simon climbed out of the car.

"Borrowed them." Radek and his brother were in the trunk with instructions to keep quiet or else. Simon hoped they'd suffered enough to mind his warning. He had no choice but to keep them hostage. He couldn't allow Ratka to know he was alive.

"Over here." Simon collared Jojo and walked ten steps away from the others. "Who are your friends?"

"You didn't think you and me were going to hit the Serbians alone? You said you wanted to go in heavy."

"Firepower. Not people."

"I got both. So what?"

"The kid is still in diapers. The other one can't make it up a flight of stairs."

"You were a punk once, too. A pretty tough one, if I recall." Jojo returned to the car and opened the trunk. "Besides, give anybody one of these and he's Superman."

Simon looked at the pile of Kalashnikov machine guns strewn one over another and at the stack of magazines. He picked up one of the rifles and put it to his shoulder. He rubbed his finger on the trigger guard and lowered his cheek to check the sights—not that anyone had ever sighted a Kalashnikov. With twenty-five bullets spraying a target in three seconds, accuracy was overrated.

"Fair enough." Simon marched up to the two men and introduced himself. The young one was Salvatore, the fat one Toto. Their accents gave them away as Corsicans and not long off the boat.

"How much?" asked Salvatore, bouncing on his toes. "Jojo said there's a treasure chest in there. Millions, maybe."

"Maybe," said Simon, not sure if the kid's eyes were dilated or if he was imagining it. It was hard to tell in the dark.

Toto rammed a magazine into the machine gun and chambered a round. "I'll go in first," he said. "Clear the place out, let you do your work."

Simon put his hand on the barrel, forcing it toward the ground. He could smell the booze on Toto's breath from five steps away. "Slow down. Before we do anything, I need to scout the place."

"Why?" asked Salvatore. "It's a house. We bust in the front door. Take care of business. Get the take and leave."

"That's the ticket," said Toto. "Hit 'em hard and fast."

Simon had forgotten how they'd done things in the old days, when they'd take down a Brink's truck with ten guys blasting it with their AKs, the police too scared to come within a block. Things hadn't changed.

"Steal money from a thief and no one goes to the police," he said with as much calm as he could muster. "Kill a thief and the police will get involved. Ideally, we surprise them, get the money, and get out."

"Right," said Toto, clearly not buying it.

"They're not just going to give us the money," said Salvatore. "Why take chances? You think they have guns like ours?"

Simon was in a bad place. A cokehead and a drunk. The hits were coming fast and furious. "Get in the car," he said, holding the door open. "I'll be back in ten. Jojo: no one moves a muscle. Clear?"

"Sure thing," said Jojo, offering a smile by way of consent, his white teeth gleaming against his too tan face. "You're the boss."

Simon walked down the hill, slowing every few steps to allow the pain in his back to dissipate. The street view on his phone's map showed the house on Rue Chaussée to be two stories with a tile roof and a steep brick driveway leading to an attached garage. Some steps led to the front door. Google Earth offered a bird's-eye view and revealed a tight backyard with a pool and a shed set against the house. The city's sprawling botanical garden abutted the property to the rear, and its exotic species had broken out of their boundaries and encroached on the yard. Simon saw the shed as a means of helping him break into an upstairs window…assuming the pictures were still accurate.

As he walked, his mind returned to his confrontation with Radek. Seeing the mechanics of the operation from the inside had given him a clearer perspective on the overall plan. Again, he saw it as two operations. One involving theft from the casino, the other taking control of the von Tiefen und Tassis fortune. It wasn't a stretch to understand how an organized criminal like Ratka might come up with a plan to cheat at baccarat on a large scale. But how did he come to the idea that he could steal a German aristocrat's family wealth? A man like Ratka didn't mix with the likes of Vika. The two were oil and water. Someone had to have told him about her and her family. But telling wasn't enough. That someone had given Ratka explicit instructions not to pay off his soldiers so that they could put the winnings to better use. Not only that, but he'd convinced Ratka to trust him with the money. No small feat.

And then?

Confounded by his inability to connect the dots, Simon did his best to deconstruct all he knew about Ratka's activities. He saw three distinct events. First came the cheating operation at the casino. Radek had blurted that after tonight the game was over. Ratka had all he needed. Toby Stonewood had stated that the casino had already lost two hundred million euros, and he'd said they were down even more in the last few days.

The second event involved gaining access to Vika's family fortune. Here Simon came to a roadblock. Should someone kill Vika and her entire family, the money would pass to the next relative...a cousin, a nephew, whoever. When twelve billion dollars was in play, you could count on plenty of people popping out of the woodwork.

Which left extortion of some kind...a plan to force Vika to sign over her assets. That didn't jibe either. Wouldn't it have been easier to put pressure on the old woman? Why had they killed Stefanie, and what had they been looking for in the apartment?

Simon kept coming back to the same issue: Why did Ratka need two hundred million euros and change to get his hands on Vika's fortune?

One person knew the answer...and he or she was the one calling the shots.

It always came back to Vika. It had to be someone close to her. Simon felt the answer floating just beyond his fingertips. He was close...oh so close.

Simon put away the problem as he reached the corner and looked up the Rue Chaussée. There were no cars in any direction. The only noise was the gentle rush of the wind and the swaying of the trees. Living in London, he had forgotten that elsewhere most people were safely tucked into bed by midnight.

Not seeing any approaching headlamps, Simon jogged up the hill. He stopped twenty meters from the house, ducking into the driveway of a neighboring villa. Alone among its neighbors, the drop house appeared lived-in and awake. Lights glowed from windows on all floors. Two cars were parked in the driveway. A Mercedes and a Renault. As Simon watched, the front door opened. A man left the building and descended the steps. He went to the second car, the Renault, climbed in, and drove away.

Simon used the sound of its departing motor to cover his approach. Instead of taking the steps, he navigated his way up a cut of earth beside the garage, all vines and loose dirt, arriving at the rear of the villa. He imagined the layout of the home to be similar to that of others from its era. A kitchen to the rear of the ground floor, the dining room adjoining, with a door leading to the yard. The storm shutters on the ground floor were closed. He crept closer. Through a crack in the wood, he observed two men seated at a table. One wore a shoulder holster with the butt of his weapon visible. Where there's money, there's muscle. Simon tried the back door. Locked.

He backed up a few steps. A window on the second floor was open and he caught the scent of tobacco. Voices carried on the still air. A heated conversation in a language he did not speak.

Simon checked his watch, thinking about Jojo and his friends waiting for him in the car. Salvatore worried him the most. Simon had been gone just seven minutes, but seven minutes felt like seventy when you were coked up. Simon recalled the reckless ambition fueled by alcohol, drugs, and mostly youth itself. Salvatore wouldn't wait in that car forever. Jojo wouldn't either, despite his promises. Simon guessed it had been a rough summer for the boys in Marseille. Jojo and his friends could smell the feeding trough.

Ten steps took him to the shed. The second-floor window was above and to the left. It made sense that the counting room was upstairs in the most secure room in the house. He extended his arms to the shed's roof and he recoiled in agony. His hands could go no higher than his head. Stubbornly, he tried again. The pain was worse still and he vowed to take revenge on Ratka.

A drainpipe ran up the side of the house. A firm tug established its sturdiness as fair to middling. Tonight those odds sounded good. Simon wedged a foot between the building and the pipe and managed to work his way to the top. An arm's length separated him from the open window. He could hear the conversation as if he were in the room himself.

Two men were engaged in a frank exchange of views. They were speaking Serbian, but Simon would have known one of them if he were speaking Chinese.

Ratka.

Simon listened, trying to catch a word here or there. He was vaguely aware of an engine approaching, tires complaining as brakes were applied too firmly. He was perched too precariously to give it much thought. He held his phone in one hand, arm extended, hoping it would record the conversation.

A door in the house slammed and the men stopped speaking. A chair slid across the floor. The door closed again, this time more quietly.

Simon leaned closer to the open window. He was just able to make out a faint reflection in the glass of two persons facing each other.

"What are you doing here?" said Ratka.

The answer was delivered in a crusty stentorian voice made softer by a plummy English accent.

"You fucked up," said Lord Toby Stonewood. "Simon Riske is alive."

Chapter 58

Riske is dead. We took him to my house. My men killed him. I was there."

"You saw it? With your own eyes?"

Ratka regarded the tall Englishman standing in his house, challenging him, all but accusing him of making the mistake himself. One day, he told himself. But after. Only after. "I left before to go to the casino and pick up the money. Our money. Why are you telling me this?"

"Riske called Victoria at the hotel not long ago. I don't know what happened, but your men failed to carry out my instructions."

"Wait." Ratka turned his back to the Englishman and telephoned first Tommy and then Pavel. Neither answered. He'd suspected something was wrong for the past hour or so. Earlier, he'd received a call from the team at the Sporting Club saying that Radek was acting strange and had disappeared before they'd finished for the evening. Radek hadn't answered his phone either.

"I'll find him," said Ratka. "I'll kill him. And with my own hands."

"It doesn't matter," said Toby. "He can't hurt us. I've found it."

"The ring? She gave it to you?"

"You scared her sufficiently. But tell me this: Why did you go to her apartment? That was bloody stupid of you."

Ratka stared at the Englishman, despising his notions of right and wrong. There was only strong and weak. He offered no reply.

Toby Stonewood moved toward the desk, turning the monitor toward himself. "How much are we up tonight?"

"Sixteen million," said Ratka.

"That's four short. I told you we need twenty."

"Still two hours to go. Relax."

"We can't be a penny shy. The law is the law. You can't cheat the tax-man." Stonewood sat down and unbuttoned his blazer. "Get me a drink, will you? A bloody big one."

"Maybe you've had enough tonight already."

The Englishman fixed him with a liverish gaze. "I'm not asking."

"Yeah, sure." Ratka went downstairs to the kitchen. In a cabinet, he found a bottle left over from the Englishman's last visit. He held it up to the light. It was half full. Short visit. He put a few cubes of ice in a glass and filled it to the top. Then he spit in it.

His phone rang as he climbed the stairs. Le Juste.

"What do you want?" said Ratka.

"Do you know that your house has burned down?"

Ratka stopped, putting a hand to the wall. "Burned down? How? I was there two hours ago. What are you talking about?"

"It appears to be arson. Several gasoline cans were found nearby."

The shock of the news robbed Ratka of words. He thought of Tommy and Pavel, at a loss to imagine how they'd failed so horribly. And what about Radek and his brother? Where had they gotten to? Was that Riske, too? Maybe Stonewood was right about him having been a criminal.

"Two men were found inside," Le Juste continued. "They did not die of burns or smoke inhalation. Both were shot in the head. They have been identified as Pavel Katic and Thomas Pupin. They're your men, aren't they?"

"Yes."

"There's more. A prosecutor has been assigned to your case."

"Already?"

"Already."

A fire . . . the police . . . a prosecutor—it was all moving too fast for him to get his head around.

Ratka ran a hand across the back of his neck, angered at his men's in-competence. "Do something, dammit."

"It's out of my hands."

"How is that possible? You are the chief of the criminal division. You're responsible for arson and homicide."

"No one cares about the fire, or the dead men. They're more interested to know what you had hidden inside your house. The *pompiers* couldn't get close to it because of all the explosives going off. One man was injured by an exploding grenade. Another was hit by shrapnel and may lose a leg. This is now officially a terrorist investigation. The national police have taken over."

"Terrorism?"

"Apparently, there was enough matériel to bring down an entire city. Bullets, grenades, RPGs. Every man on the force is looking for you. I suggest you go back to Serbia at once."

Ratka hung up the phone. He was getting out of the country, all right. But he was not headed to Serbia. Not yet. He drew a breath to gain a measure of calm. He decided it was better not to say anything to the Englishman. The less he knew the better.

Ratka returned to the counting room and delivered the drink.

"Took your bloody time." Stonewood drank down half the glass as if it were water.

"You're welcome." Ratka checked the computer. "Another two million came in. I told you not to worry."

"Get all the cash and checks you have in this place together."

"Now?"

"This minute," said Stonewood. "Have your men bring me the rest later."

Ratka opened the safe and stuffed the evening's take into a leather satchel. The Englishman finished his drink and rose. "You can get her now."

"At the hotel?"

"Here's the key to her room. Go in the back way. I've warned off security. Keep an eye out for Riske. I wouldn't be surprised if he's there. He has a thing for my stepdaughter. If he's fucking her, shoot him in the balls. And Ratka, you can knock her around a little—she deserves it. But try anything else and it's you who'll get the bullet."

Ratka stepped closer to Stonewood. Enough of this arrogant talk. Maybe it was he who needed to be knocked around a little.

"Well?" said Stonewood.

There came a shout from downstairs. A door banged against a wall. Automatic weapons fire exploded inside the house.

"What the hell is that?" Stonewood had gone pale as a ghost.

"It's a machine gun. What do you think?"

Ratka's first thought was *The police: somehow, they'd discovered he was renting the home on Rue Chaussée from an absentee Frenchman.* He shoved Stonewood against the wall and drew his pistol. Then he remembered that his name wasn't on the rental agreement. The barrage continued. So loud that his brain shook inside his skull. A man screamed. Paintings crashed to the floor. Glass shattered. Ratka recognized the sound of the weapons. Not the police at all. No cop had ever fired a Kalashnikov on duty.

"Stay here," he said, rushing into the hall.

Ratka looked over the railing. Two of his men were down. A fat man he'd never seen was reloading his machine gun and having difficulty doing so. Ratka shot him in the chest. He dropped like a pauper on the gallows. Ratka shot him again.

The second shooter was younger, with shiny dark hair. Seeing Ratka, he spun and fired, the weapon on full automatic. The bullets carved an arc in the ceiling above Ratka's head. Kalashnikovs kicked high and to the right. You had to aim at the left knee of the man you wanted to kill. The machine gun ran out of ammunition. The shooter was quick to drop his magazine and replace it with a fresh one. Not quick enough. Descending the staircase, Ratka shot him three times. The man dropped his weapon but stubbornly remained standing.

Once on the ground floor, Ratka approached him with caution. He was young, not even twenty. Ratka looked around the room. There was no sign of Riske.

"Why are you here?" he asked.

"For the money, asshole. Why do you think?"

"And who told you?"

The shooter's lips parted in a defiant smile. Blood ran from the corner of his mouth.

Ratka put the pistol to his eye and fired.

Just then, a man ran out the front door. Ratka spun, caught a flash of white and gray, and took cover against the wall, expecting the man to turn and open fire. When nothing came, Ratka checked the rest of the ground floor. Two of his men were wounded but not dead.

"Come down!" he shouted to Stonewood. "Bring the money and the computer."

"Is it safe?" asked the Englishman.

"Now! I'm not asking."

Ratka knew that they needed to move fast. The gunfire had been loud enough to be heard all the way in Italy. If the police were already on alert, they'd have extra patrols on duty. It would be a matter of minutes before they arrived. Ratka frisked the fat man and found his wallet. His driver's license gave his name as Theodore Randisi of Ajaccio. Ratka rolled up the man's sleeve and saw the anchor and skeleton tattoo, *La Brise de Mer*.

Fucking Corsicans.

Ratka dropped the man's arm to the floor. The dead man grunted. A gob of blood flew out of his mouth and into the air. Ratka jumped to his feet. He fired two shots into the man's chest. He'd had enough surprises for one night.

Toby Stonewood stood at the bottom of the stairs, eyes wide.

"What?" said Ratka. "You've never seen a dead guy before? Get the fuck out of here. Now. I'll find you later."

Stonewood didn't answer. He hurried past Ratka and out the front door.

Ratka returned to his wounded men. He knelt by each and made the sign of the cross over them. There was no question what had to be done. The men knew too much. It was that simple. Serbs gave no quarter and asked for none in return.

He shot each man in the head.

Then he left.

CHAPTER 59

At the sound of automatic weapons fire, Simon slid down the drainpipe to the ground. He'd been right to worry about Jojo and his friends. As his feet touched the lawn, bullets from inside the house tore apart the shutters, spraying him with wood splinters and glass. He dropped and hugged the earth, a hand freeing the pistol from the hem of his pants. His eyes found the back door. There was no way he was going to put himself in front of Salvatore and Toto and who knew how many of Ratka's men. Only a fool ran into a shoot-out.

The harsh rat-a-tat-tat of machine-gun fire ceased. Simon got to a knee only to hear the higher-pitched crack of a pistol. He dared a glance through the ruined shutters, saw no one, then ran around the side of the house. There was no time to think, only to act. He stopped at the front corner. He ventured a look and saw Toby Stonewood, satchel in hand, climbing into a white Bentley parked close behind the Mercedes.

Lord Toby. He was the connection. He'd called Vika his stepdaughter. Simon recalled seeing a headline about Princess Stefanie remarrying, but he hadn't looked further. He'd been more interested in Vika. By then she was making her own impressive headlines. Simon rued his oversight. If only he'd looked closer. It was all right there. The day before, Vika had referred to her stepfather as "Bismarck." Simon hadn't thought anything more of it.

He took aim at the Bentley. If he put a few rounds into the engine block, maybe he could stop Toby from getting away. The sights drifted up a notch. He closed an eye and drew a bead on the man behind the wheel. Or maybe he could stop him altogether? Before he could fire, a bullet struck the wall above his head. A spray of cement stunned him. He saw Ratka emerging from the house's front door, a laptop computer clutched to his side.

The Bentley reversed down the driveway much too quickly, sparks flying as the rear bottomed out onto the road. The car continued in reverse down the Rue Chaussée, demolishing a mailbox and running over a trash can.

Simon poked his head around the corner of the house. Ratka raised his pistol and pulled the trigger, but his pistol was out of ammunition.

"Stop," said Simon, moving into the open, pistol aimed at Ratka's chest. He had every right to shoot. Here was the man who'd killed Vincent Morehead and beaten Elena Mancini, who'd attacked Vika with the intention of raping her, who'd stolen millions from the casino, and who'd, if in fact he was a war criminal, killed untold others. But Simon didn't pull the trigger. He wasn't an executioner.

"Don't move," he said.

"Fuck you." Ratka ran down the steps. Simon slid down the cut of earth and crossed the driveway to the foot of the steps, blocking the Serb's path.

"Stay right there or I'll shoot you."

Ratka backed away. "What do you want, anyway? First you are with the princess, now you are here? Who the fuck are you?"

Simon said nothing. He wanted to ask Ratka a dozen questions. How had he met Toby? Whose idea was it to rob the casino? What was the two hundred million for? And what had Toby meant when he said they couldn't "cheat the taxman"? All that would have to wait. Right now, he needed proof.

"The computer," said Simon. "Give it to me."

Ratka held it closer. "Did you burn down my house, too?"

"Hand me the computer."

"You want the computer? You have to shoot Ratka."

Simon slipped the pistol into the back of his pants and stepped toward him.

Ratka frowned. "You think you can just take it?"

Simon threw a jab. The Serb was slow to react and the blow landed on his jaw. His head snapped back, but the punch had little power. Simon could barely extend his arm. The punch cost him more than Ratka.

Ratka tossed the computer onto the ground and threw Simon against the car, slugging him in the gut, following with an uppercut. Simon parried the blow, just, and Ratka's fist glanced his jaw. He grasped Ratka's wrist, and with his free hand applied an arm bar, locking the Serb's elbow. He spun to his left, forcing the taller, heavier man to bend at the waist, then kneed him in the torso. Ratka fell to the ground. To maintain his hold, Simon had to step forward. With perfect timing, Ratka thrust an open palm upward, squarely catching the underside of Simon's jaw. Teeth gnashed. A molar cracked. Simon saw stars. Dazed, he fell against the car. His pistol clattered to the ground, landing under the chassis.

Ratka leapt to his feet and tossed Simon aside, crouching to pick up the gun. Simon stumbled but didn't fall. Catching himself, he regained his balance as Ratka's fingers closed around the weapon. The Serb stood, bringing the gun to bear. Simon spun and delivered a roundhouse kick, connecting flush with his cheek. Ratka's head caromed off the roof of the car. The pistol flew from his hand. He took a step toward Simon, eyes glazed, and said, "You!" His knees gave out and he fell forward. Simon moved aside to let his face meet the driveway.

Barely had Simon recovered when an approaching automobile drew his attention. Headlights appeared at the bottom of the street. In seconds, the car raced up the driveway. Doors opened. Three men stepped out. Even in the dark, Simon recognized them as the cheats from the Sporting Club. They looked at him. He looked at them. Simon's eyes flitted from the pistol to the computer. The pistol was closer.

He dove for the gun and fired a shot over their head, scuttling to his right in hopes of grabbing the laptop. One of the men fired back and Simon felt the bullet cut the air beside his cheek. The men fanned out, the leader keeping up his fire as Simon ducked behind the car, the garage at his back. He was trapped. He couldn't go down the drive. He couldn't run up the steps into the house. His only hope was to make a run for the hillside and hope the foliage and vegetation would be enough to give him cover.

He gave a last glance at the laptop and swore under his breath. A bullet struck the garage door. He darted into the bushes, staying low, knocking aside branches and danglers blocking his path. After a while, he stopped. He crouched, ear to the wind, listening. No one pursued him. He heard voices and crept back toward the house until he was able to make out the silhouettes of the men.

The three were lifting Ratka to his feet and helping him to their car. A moment later, the car backed up and drove away.

Toby was gone. Ratka was gone. The laptop was gone. And the satchel was gone.

Simon entered the house. Salvatore and Toto lay on the floor of the living room. Two of Ratka's men were nearby. There was no sign of Jojo, and Simon figured he'd been the first one out once things had gone south. It was a messy scene. Simon hoped he never had to look at another dead man in his life. He ran upstairs but found nothing besides some clothing, empty beer bottles, and a power cable for the laptop.

There was a man at the bottom of the driveway when Simon came out of the house. Several others stood behind him, a few holding flashlights. Simon guessed they were neighbors and he noted that lights in windows up and down the street burned brightly. The poor people probably thought World War III had just been fought in front of their homes.

"Bouge pas!" the man shouted. Don't move. Simon saw that he held a rifle in his hand, probably a shotgun.

Simon raised his hand in greeting. *"Allo,"* he said. "I'm a friend."

The man leveled his shotgun at him. So much for the honest approach. At the same time, Simon heard a siren. Check that: sirens, plural. The cavalry was coming.

Unable to see an alternate course of action, he climbed into the one remaining car. It was a Mercedes-Benz, brand-new, meaning it relied on electronic ignition. There was no hope of hot-wiring it. It was Ratka's car, the one with the Serbian plates captured on the pharmacy's surveillance camera as it left the Château Perigord.

Simon put his foot on the brake and hit the starter button. The engine roared to life. He opened the center console. The key fob lay inside. The only person who didn't worry about his car being boosted was a crook.

Simon slipped the car into reverse and backed down the driveway at speed. The crowd scattered and he sent as many sparks flying as Toby had as the chassis scraped the road. Like Toby, Simon reversed all the way to the bottom of the Rue Chaussée, head turned, looking over his shoulder, half out of his seat, doing his best to stay in the center of the road. The neighborhood had sustained enough collateral damage for one night. As he swung onto the Rue Pierre, a broader two-lane street, a dozen blue lights flickered in his rearview. He shifted into drive, only to see another column of police cars barreling toward him.

The lead cop car braked and turned at an angle, blocking the right lane. The car following it cut off the left lane. There was no sidewalk, no median, no shoulder where he might run the gauntlet. Simon slammed the car into reverse. The police blocked his egress in that direction, too.

Simon knew he should stop, step out of the car with his hands held above his head, and turn himself in. He would be taken to the station and thrown into a cell. In due course, he'd be interrogated. He would have a chance to tell his side of the story, to inform the authorities of the reason for his coming to Monaco, and to explain the events of the past few days.

In time, charges would be brought against him. France was governed by the Code Civil, a watered-down descendant of the Napoleonic Code. Habeas corpus, his right to be promptly charged and released, belonged to the other legal system. If luck was on his side, he'd be released in a week. More likely, he'd be looking at the inside of a cell for a month.

Or longer.

There were four dead bodies inside that house. Two more at Ratka's. Simon had fired a pistol. Gunpowder residue was all over his hands. Someone would discover his police record. Twenty years earlier, he'd been convicted of felony armed robbery and attempted murder of a police officer. He'd served four years. An ambitious prosecutor didn't need more than that to see him convicted of murder.

All this he played over in an instant.

"You can get her now," Toby had said to Ratka.

"Her"—meaning Vika.

Giving up was out.

Simon spun the wheel left and drove the Mercedes back up the Rue Chaussée. He tried to remember where the street led, if it might take him to the Moyenne Corniche, where at least he'd have a fighting chance of eluding the police. In his mind's eye, he saw the map and a windy road leading up, up, up, eventually coming to a dead end. There was always the chance that he was mistaken.

He punched the gas. The car shot forward, the torque shoving him into his seat. He neared Ratka's house, horn blaring to warn the neighborhood watch committee. Blue lights sparkled in his rearview mirror. A check of his sideview dampened his hopes. A police cruiser nipped at his tail.

Simon made the sharp left-hand turn, the driveway to the drop house passing to his right. The band of neighbors had failed to heed the horn's warning. Headlamps illuminated a half-dozen persons standing in the road, frozen immobile like rabbits on a midnight moor. The man with the shotgun stood resolutely in the center of the street. Simon hit his brights. There was a flash of orange. He ducked, the car veering left as a rain of pellets struck the hood and peppered the windscreen. When Simon returned his eyes to the road, he saw an old woman and a young child square in his path. He threw both feet onto the brake pedal. Tires howled. The car stopped on a dime. His seat belt locked, the restraint nearly crushing his sternum.

The police car following him had no time to react. It struck the Mercedes with ferocious force. Airbags deployed. The Mercedes spun ninety degrees. When the airbags deflated, Simon saw that he'd come to a halt only feet from the woman and child. He was done driving. A shadow appeared to his left. He turned his head. A pane of glass separated him from the barrel of a shotgun.

Simon didn't have time to close his eyes.

The gun fired.

CHAPTER 60

It was called the Chesa Madrun, and it had been built 130 years earlier as the mountain retreat of the ill-fated Archduke Franz Ferdinand of Austria. Set high in an isolated valley among the towns of Pontresina, Samedan, and Zuoz in the Swiss canton of Engadine, the Chesa Madrun had begun life as a modest hunting lodge comprising four rooms: a great room, a kitchen, a communal sleeping area, and a curing room for air-drying meats.

Since then, the chalet had changed hands numerous times. Upon Franz Ferdinand's assassination in June of 1914, the chalet passed to his brother, who was forced to give it up four years later, when Austria surrendered to the Western alliance and the Hapsburg dynasty fell from power. The next owner was a friend to the Hapsburgs, an Italian, the Count Melzi d'Eril, who kept the lodge until another European conflict robbed his family of its fortune. Melzi sold it in 1946 to a Frenchman, Le Vicomte de Foucault, who, it was discovered, was neither French nor a viscount but a Russian swindler, Serge Stokovsky. The affair ended with Melzi d'Eril dead by suicide and the Russian imprisoned. The Chesa Madrun was put up for auction and purchased in 1948 by a Luxembourg-based lumber concern controlled by a German business-man with a taste for discretion named August Wilhelm Brandenburg von Tiefen und Tassis.

With each new owner, the chalet grew in various and odd ways, so that what had started as a spartan lodge meant to rekindle the values of manliness, modesty, and self-sufficiency ended up a fifteen-thousand-

302

square-foot pleasure palace with ten bedrooms, an Olympic-sized indoor swimming pool, and an authentic German *kegelbahn* alley.

As each renovation, remodel, and addition was designed by a different architect and overseen by a different contractor, it was to be expected that the Chesa Madrun ended up with a few hidden hallways, stairways to nowhere, and bonus rooms that served no purpose other than to give the children who lived there an exquisite territory for playing hide-and-seek.

The last addition was built in 1963, at the height of the Cold War. In keeping with a new federal law, a fallout shelter, or *luftschutzbunker,* was constructed to safeguard the chalet's residents in case of nuclear attack. As the fallout shelter took up too much space to sit empty, and the risk of nuclear annihilation was on the decline, the room had recently been put to different use. It currently housed the chalet's auxiliary water and power plants, a gasoline-powered generator, and an industrial boiler, all necessary in the event that water and power were cut off due to an avalanche, storm, or other unforeseen occurrence.

All this raced through Robby's mind as he lay on his side, trying to keep from falling asleep. He was no longer being held in his bedroom. Elisabeth had taken him to the library instead. It was a cavernous room, his least favorite in the entire house, the ceiling two stories high, shelves and more shelves lining the walls, every inch taken up by books and more books. The only thing he liked at all was the ladder that reached to the very top shelf and ran on a track so that nothing was out of reach. Otherwise, there was a large desk with an old-fashioned reading lamp, several leather chairs, and a giant antique globe set on a spindle. The entire place smelled like a wet blanket.

Most important, though, Robby figured, was what wasn't there: windows. There was no way out except through the door.

At least that's what Elisabeth thought.

Elisabeth was evil. Robby hated her more than any person he'd ever come across. When they'd gotten back to the house, she'd made him take off his jacket and shirt and had whipped him with her fat leather belt. First, she whipped him for Viktor, who'd been hit on the head by the rocks that Robby had kicked loose. After, she whipped him for George, who had had to leave because his nose was broken and he needed stitches for the gash on his forehead. Robby didn't feel bad for either of them. They deserved it. Robby hadn't known that anger could make punishment less painful. Every time Elisabeth had landed the belt on his bare back, he'd sworn that he was going to escape and that he was going to hurt her. He wasn't sure if he could kill her, but he wasn't sure he couldn't either. He only knew that he wished she were dead.

As Robby's eyes closed and he fell asleep, he was thinking of one thing and one thing only. Escaping.

There were other ways to get out of the house. Lots of them.

And Robby knew every last one.

CHAPTER 61

Simon?"

The sound of the door closing woke Vika. She pulled herself upright in the club chair, instantly alert. "Simon, is that you?"

The lights in the hotel room were dimmed and it took her a moment to remember that they'd been fully on earlier...before she'd dozed off.

"Hello?" Someone was in the room. She gazed into the dark, paralyzed by fear. Then she saw it. A figure dressed in black lurked near the entry. "Who's there? Toby?"

Not Toby.

Not Simon either.

He was stockier than either of them. He was watching her. Waiting.

It was him.

Vika lunged for her purse, which held the compact pistol that Simon had made sure was loaded, with one bullet already in the chamber. All she had to do was flick the safety to OFF and pull the trigger. Several times, he said. Keep pulling until there are no more bullets left.

The man started across the room, his intent palpable. Vika dug her hand inside the purse. Her fingers touched steel. The man struck her and the purse fell to the floor. It was the man from the night before. The Serb.

She screamed, and he was on her, his hand covering her mouth.

"Simon can't help you now," he said, his face close to hers. "You're on your own."

305

She saw that he had a widow's peak and she knew he was the man who'd been riding in the passenger seat of Mama's car. She struggled, but he was too strong.

"You belong to Ratka now."

And then the Serb hit her and all was black.

CHAPTER 62

The cell measured ten steps by six. There was a cot and a sink and a john, all the same dull stainless steel. The walls were painted battleship gray. The only other feature worth remarking was a small black dome on the ceiling that hid the security camera.

Simon sat on the cot, knees drawn to his chest. Despite having been fired upon point-blank by a twelve-gauge shotgun, he showed no sign of a gunshot wound. The same could not be said for the self-styled neighborhood vigilante who'd been splattered with ricocheting buckshot. The Mercedes-Benz had been built for the future king of the Belgrade underworld. As such, it had been built to protect its owner against like-minded enemies. The glass was bulletproof. In an odd way, Simon owed Ratka his life.

Upon Simon's arrival at the station, the police had taken his shoes, belt, wallet, watch, and phone. No one had spoken a word to him. Not to ask what he had been doing at the Rue Chaussée, how he had come to have a bloodstained shirt, or whether he required the services of a doctor. Not even to ask his name. He'd been locked up enough times to know that this was not normal procedure. Paperwork came first. They always wanted to know your name. Someone was on Lord Toby's payroll. Someone high up. Simon reasoned that his name was Le Juste.

An hour passed.

Then another.

Pain and isolation focused Simon's thinking. Toby Stonewood had had no business hiring him in the first place. Simon imagined that the board of the Société des Bains de Mer had demanded an investigation into the huge losses being suffered. A top man from a renowned firm was hired. Toby had placed a quick call to Ratka and made sure the man disappeared. When the losses continued, the board had requested another investigator. No doubt Toby had suggested a "fresh set of eyes." Still, Simon should have at least suspected—if not immediately in D'Art's office, then later. All along, the clues had been right in front of him. As an investigator, he'd failed.

Should anything happen to Vika, he was responsible. He and he alone.

As for his present reality, it was apparent that Toby Stonewood wanted him locked up and out of the way, for all intents and purposes dead. Toby would make that wish a reality soon enough, once he could move Simon to an environment more to his liking.

Not going to happen.

Simon unbuttoned his shirt. The sutures hung loose, like the laces of a poorly tied shoe. The puncture wound had reopened and leaked a brownish bloody discharge. It looked bad, it hurt, but it wouldn't kill a man. He stood and walked to the sink. Leaning over the basin (so as to block the security camera), he turned on the water and washed his face. As he did so, he ran one hand beneath the sink and felt for the pivot rod that raised and lowered the stopper. He gave it a jerk, then another. It broke off. He examined the long flat strip of metal. It would do.

Concealing the rod, Simon returned to the cot and lay down on his stomach. He dropped his hand to the floor and rubbed one side of the strip vigorously against the concrete beneath the cot, sharpening the edge into a blade.

Drastic times called for drastic measures.

Simon sat up. The next part he wanted everyone to see.

Gritting his teeth, he slid the strip into the open wound, cutting the sutures. He then angled the blade downward and thrust it into his abdomen, slicing through six layers of the dermis, then a little deeper, into the fascia. He paused and, stifling a cry, yanked the sharpened edge toward his sternum.

Blood flowed down his chest.

He dropped the strip onto the floor.

Then he collapsed.

CHAPTER 63

"A little deeper and you would have done yourself some serious damage."

Simon looked on as the doctor slid the needle into his skin and stitched his self-inflicted wound. He had been in the hospital for an hour. He'd had his blood drawn and his chest x-rayed and received a shot of anesthetic that was beginning to work wonders. Two staples closed up the tear to his muscle. He stopped counting stitches at eighteen and closed his eyes. Sometime later he felt a tug and heard the thread snap.

"Leave them in this time," said the doctor. "They work better that way."

"I'll do my best."

The doctor threw away the needle and gauze. He was fifty and bloated, with shaggy gray hair and a wine lover's nose. "I'm going to get your x-rays. You didn't break your own ribs, too, did you?"

"That was the other guy."

The doctor patted his shoulder and chuckled. "Stay put."

Simon's wrist was cuffed to the table. There was a policeman guarding the door. Where could he go?

The doctor left and closed the door, leaving Simon by himself. Radiology was one floor below. The doctor would take the elevator, walk to the end of the hall, and spend the required time evaluating the x-rays. By the looks of him, a croissant and coffee might be in order on the return trip. He would be gone twenty minutes at least.

Simon waited a few beats, then spat out a small silver object. It was the key to his handcuffs. Policemen always carried two. One they kept attached to their duty belt. The other they slipped into one of their pockets. It had been a simple matter to lift the key from the cop's back pocket during Simon's transport to the hospital. He unlocked himself from the table and took up position behind the door.

"S'il vous plaît!" he shouted. "I'm bleeding. Please help."

The policeman entered the room immediately. He was thirty and fresh-faced and as competent as he needed to be. He'd driven Simon to the hospital after the warders had found him half conscious and thrown him into the back seat of a police car. He had no reason to know that the prisoner was an accomplished pickpocket or to suspect that he'd gutted himself with an eye toward escape.

Simon shut the door. As the policeman turned, Simon threw him into a choke hold, one arm around his neck, the other locking it into position and pressuring the head forward to block circulation to the brain. The cop had no chance to cry out. He struggled briefly, then fell unconscious. Simon maintained the pressure a little longer, not wanting him to wake up too soon. He lowered the policeman to the floor and relieved him of his radio and car keys and a hundred euros.

Simon found a dressing gown in a cupboard. After putting it on, he opened a second cupboard—the one with the drugs—and took out vials of lidocaine and codeine, as well as two syringes and a few isopropyl wipes.

He left the room and walked to the end of the hall, nodding pleasantly at the nurses he passed. Nothing to see here. He entered the stairwell and dashed to the ground floor. He gave himself three minutes, five tops, to get as far away from the hospital as possible.

The police car was parked in a designated space near the emergency room. A column obscured it from viewers. Simon opened the trunk and found a sports bag beneath a fluorescent orange traffic vest. He unzipped the bag and rummaged through a pile of dirty clothing. A wrinkled black Lacoste shirt was the best he could do.

The drive to the hotel took four minutes. Simon parked illegally two blocks away. The time was 8:15. The police radio came to life as he was closing the door. A suspect had escaped custody at Princess Grace

Hospital. A search of the premises was under way. All available patrolmen were to report to Commissaire Le Juste. There was no mention of Simon's name or the fact that he might be heading to the Hôtel de Paris.

He entered through a rear door, ducking into the emergency stairwell and exiting on the third floor. He poked his head into the hallway. Vika's room was halfway down. He saw no one standing guard, though it was impossible to know if Philippe or anyone else was seated on the bank of furniture opposite the elevators. Treading softly, he knocked at Vika's door. When no one answered, he called her name and put an ear to the cool wood. He heard nothing. With mounting unease, he made his way to the elevators. No one was present.

A door opened behind him. He spun to see a maid pushing a trolley emerge from the linen closet. Simon smiled, a fortuitous surprise, and approached.

"Excuse me. I'm in four twenty-one upstairs. I wanted to see Madame Brandenburg in three twenty. She's not answering the door or her phone. I'm worried." He pressed the hundred-euro note into the woman's palm. "Please. Can you come with me so we can both see if she is all right?"

"Madame Brandenburg is no longer here," said the maid, holding out the bill for Simon to take back. He refused. "She left early this morning."

"You're sure?"

The maid brushed past him and marched to Vika's door. "Please," she said, sliding her pass card and allowing Simon to enter.

Vika was gone. The room had been cleaned and made ready for the next guest. Simon contented himself with a rapid look around. Had anything sinister occurred, there was no sign of it. "Of course," he said, breezily. "She's leaving today, not tomorrow. Did you by any chance happen to see if she left with anyone?"

"Ah, non," said the maid. "It was before I came on duty."

"Before seven?"

"I start at five a.m., monsieur."

Simon thanked her, deciding it unwise to ask any further questions. He took the stairs to his floor in a state of panic. Ratka had kidnapped her.

Toby had cleaned things up on the backside. Still, Simon just might have a way of tracking her down.

There was no one in the corridor and he quickly found a maid and had her open his room. One look told him that everything was still in its place. There was no need to clean up after a man stuck in jail.

Simon locked the door, then went directly to the desk and turned on his laptop. He double-clicked on an SOS app that allowed him to control his iPhone remotely. Vika had not called, nor had she texted. He backed up the phone onto the laptop, then issued a kill command, deleting the contents. He wasn't just returning the phone to its original factory settings; he was obliterating the operating system.

Next he opened the Apache app that monitored the trackers he'd placed on the thieves. He was interested in only one: VB 4. He'd placed it in Vika's purse at the Sporting Club the night before so he might know her whereabouts, just in case.

A map of Monaco appeared on the screen. A trail of dots denoted her movements. Clicking anywhere on the line revealed the precise time she'd been at that location.

The trail began at the hotel and made its way to the Sporting Club. After an hour, it curved into the city, stopping at the Église Saint-Marc for seven minutes before continuing back to the hotel, where Vika stayed from 10:12 until 3:50. Simon had no idea why she'd stopped at the church. For the moment, it was of no concern.

At 3:51, the trail left the hotel and led westward across the city to Port de Fontvieille, on the far side of the palace, and farther west still, where it stopped on the border of France and Monaco, at the Héliport de Monaco. The Monaco Heliport.

Vika remained at the heliport for two minutes. Not a second longer.

Simon was looking at a picture of a chopper waiting on the landing pad, rotors turning and Vika being led toward it. Who was with her? Ratka? Or was Toby Stonewood there, too? And where were they taking her?

The final readings, taken thirty seconds apart, showed the helicopter moving on an eastward heading, passing over the Monaco Tennis Club and finally Roquebrune-Cap-Martin. The trail stopped there. The tracker could not transmit its signal any farther.

Simon stared at the screen, running the mouse over Vika's trail.

At 4:02 a.m., Princess Victoria Brandenburg von Tiefen und Tassis had climbed aboard a helicopter and flown east toward Italy.

Chapter 64

It was five minutes past eight a.m. in London when Roger Jenkins tapped on Zaab Sethna's door. "In yet?"

A snort greeted his words. Jenkins poked his head inside the office, where Sethna lay on the floor, his suit jacket folded to make a pillow, his hands clasped over his chest. His dark glasses sat on a book next to him, along with a glass of water. Jenkins stepped inside. Why would Sethna sleep on the floor when there was a perfectly good couch in the break room not ten steps away?

"The break room smells," said Sethna, sitting up. "That's why."

Jenkins jumped out of his socks. "Zaab... Sorry... How did you know?"

"Everyone asks the same thing."

In the morning light, Sethna's eyes were puffy and mole-ish, lending him a shy appearance. He noted Jenkins's intrusive glances and put on his eyeglasses. "It's because of my back, actually. Broke it in a *helo* crash in Ramadi province ages ago. Still gives me a devil of a problem. Worth it. We got him."

"Who?"

"AMZ. Zarkawi. Bad egg."

Jenkins nodded, the name conjuring images of roadside bombs and butchered bodies. "Is the crisis resolved? I didn't catch anything on the news."

"As it should be," said Sethna. "But yes... for now. And please: don't ask."

"Wouldn't dream of it." Jenkins smiled like an altar boy. "The cuff links?"

314

Sethna unfolded his jacket, got up, and hung it behind the door. "Couldn't get there, eh?"

Jenkins shook his head. "'Sword of God.' 'Eight two zero zero.' 'Judges seven.' No, the pieces didn't fit."

Sethna went to his desk. "Mossad," he said, drawing a grand breath. "Israeli intelligence. Unit 8200 is their elite surveillance apparatus. Can hack anything. Listen to anyone. See everywhere. Best in the world by some accounts. Where did you get them, by the way?"

"A friend found them."

"Where?"

"Monaco."

"Figures."

"Why do you say that?"

"All those Israeli boys take their tech and flog it on the open market. Millionaires, the lot of them."

"And the writing?"

"That's what gave it away. It's a name. Dov M. Dragan. Tell your friend that the cuff links belong to the former director of Unit 8200. The post goes to the number two man at the Mossad. If he really is a murderer, this wasn't the first time."

CHAPTER 65

CALL ME read the header on the email from Roger Jenkins at MI5.

"What have you got?" Pen in hand, Simon sat at the desk, praying for news that might help him find Vika. He was operating in crisis mode, moving a heartbeat slower than warp speed. He'd showered, shaved, and put on fresh clothing. A second injection of codeine laced with B12 had him feeling better than a fresh batch of dilithium crystals. He'd phoned Harry Mason and asked him to bring over the Daytona as quickly as possible.

After that, he'd spoken with D'Artagnan Moore, pulling him out of a directors' meeting being held at Claridge's.

"You can't be losing that much money," Moore had bellowed when he'd picked up the phone.

"D'Art. Listen to me. We've been had."

"By whom? How?"

"Toby Stonewood. He's played us from the start."

"Toby? The Duke of Suffolk?"

"One and the same." Simon couldn't stand how the English never wanted to believe the worst of their landed gentry. Even the most casual perusal of English history showed them to be venal, dishonest, and without scruples. And those were the good ones.

"Just listen to me," said Simon. "And button it till I'm done."

He needed ten minutes to explain all that had happened since he'd arrived in Monaco and another five to calm Moore down. When some measure of calm had been restored, Simon played him the recording he'd made while dangling outside the second-floor window of the drop house.

"What is that they're speaking?" Moore asked petulantly.

"Just wait. You'll recognize one of the voices in a minute."

Moore quieted as Lord Toby Stonewood's baritone entered the conversation.

"The bastard," said D'Art when the playback ended. "I'm sorry, Simon."

"You and me both, brother. Just get me the financials I asked for. I want a cavity check of Toby Stonewood's economic livelihood."

"I'll put on the rubber glove myself," said D'Art.

"Be careful. He's not the type to go down without a fight. We don't know who he has in his corner."

"Consider it done. What about you?"

Simon zipped up his bag and set it down next to the stainless steel attaché case. If Vika wasn't welcome in the hotel, neither was he. It was a matter of time before they came looking for him. "Me? I'm going after the girl."

That conversation with D'Art had ended five minutes ago.

"Did you get all that?" asked Jenkins after he'd finished relaying his information.

"Mossad. Unit 8200," said Simon.

"Is it any help?"

"More than you can imagine. I have one more thing to ask."

"Shoot."

"The other day when I called and you knew where I was: Does that software work for all carriers…I mean, for numbers outside the UK?"

"Wouldn't be much good if it didn't."

"A friend has gone missing. She's German. Her mobile has a Frankfurt area code. Don't know her carrier."

"Give me the number."

Simon read off Vika's cell number.

"Nothing," said Jenkins.

"That fast?"

"Speed of light."

"You can get a read on a phone even if it's off. Isn't that right?"

"As long as the phone is in range of a cell tower."

"What if the phone is in the air?"

"No go, I'm afraid."

"Keep trying. And let me know the minute you find out anything. She's important to me."

Simon ended the call, his eyes on the words he'd written in neat block letters. He recalled being seated at his desk in the old office at the bank, reading the prospectus of an offering of shares in a new company called Audiax. "Our CEO holds a PhD in mathematics and worked for the Israeli government for twenty years prior to founding the company."

Of course it hadn't said what Dov Dragan had done for the government. Spy chiefs were wise to keep a low profile after their retirement, especially if they lived where their government couldn't offer year-round protection.

Whoever wrote the program, Radek had boasted to Simon twelve hours earlier, *is a mathematical genius.*

"I fear I sold too early," Dragan had complained in the Bar Américain. *"It's hard to turn down a billion dollars."*

Maybe the billion was gone and he needed to earn another.

The trust is worth twelve billion, Vika had said.

Dov M. Dragan, head of the Monaco Rally Club's racing committee, founder of Audiax Technologies, and former chief of Unit 8200 of the Mossad. If Roger Jenkins couldn't tell Simon where Vika was, Dragan could.

A sharp knock on the door interrupted his violent machinations. Instead of answering it, Simon opened the French doors to the balcony and stepped outside. There was no way down except to jump. He went to the door.

"Open up," said Harry Mason.

Simon showed the mechanic in. "Hello, Harry."

"Why aren't you answering your phone?"

"Misplaced it for the moment."

"Car's out front. Gave you a hundred more horses and enough torque to push your bottom right to the floor. By the way, Lucy called. She can't get ahold of you either. She asked me to tell you that a woman phoned the shop looking for you. She said it was urgent."

"Name?"

Harry Mason scowled. "Knew you'd ask me that. Maybe something French?"

"Isabelle?"

Mason snapped his fingers. "That's it." His eyes fell to the bags set down next to the bed. "Leaving already?"

"I am. And you should, too."

"What about the time trial?"

Simon checked his watch. It was 9:05. The first car had gone off an hour ago. Dragan was set to go at 9:30. There was no reason to think he wouldn't be there. Like everyone else, he thought Simon was in jail. "Thanks for reminding me."

"Reminding you? Isn't that why we came?"

Simon grabbed his bags. "I need a favor," he said, then described how he'd left a laptop computer beneath the front seat of a car he'd parked near the botanical garden the previous night. He told Harry he wanted him to retrieve it. He didn't mention that there were two men in the trunk.

"A laptop under the front seat?"

"It's very important, Harry. After you get it, go directly to the airport and jump on the first plane home. I'm not a popular man in this town."

Simon held the door for Harry and they left the room. "And one more thing," said Simon. "I'm going to need your phone."

CHAPTER 66

The helicopter brushed the treetops, flying so low that Toby Stonewood was sure the uppermost branches would scrape its belly. He didn't know how the pilot could see. The rain had grown steadily worse as they'd crossed the Lombardy plain. The wind had picked up, too, batting the aircraft about like a toy on a string, the engine oscillating wildly, screaming and groaning as the rotors sought purchase. The moisture had turned to sleet and then to snow as they'd passed Como and climbed into the Alps. And now cloud. Dense, unfriendly, dark, restless cloud that played hide-and-seek with them. One moment blinding them, the next vanishing to reveal the valley floor.

Toby sat facing backward; Victoria, his stepdaughter, was opposite him, Ratka beside her. All wore headphones to drown out the engine noise. A microphone allowed them to speak to one another. Ratka was not a "good flyer," as the saying went. His complexion had gone green a while back. He sat, eyes closed, head against the window.

Toby gazed at Victoria, keeping a faint smile on his lips, as calm and relaxed as if they were all sharing a ride to Heathrow. Stonewoods learned at an early age never to betray weakness in any way. He'd kept a check on his emotions for so long that he wondered if he still had any.

Even so, the first few minutes of the trip had been rough. They'd had to tell her they had her boy. Ratka had done the honors, striking her across the cheek and warning her to behave herself after she'd begun threatening them with all manner of ridiculous punishments should the boy be harmed. It was a little embarrassing, actually. Toby nearly felt sorry for the girl.

Even now, Toby could sense the anger brewing beneath the composed surface. Who wouldn't be upset that her son was kidnapped? He had a hard time bringing himself to think about what was to come. There was a word for it. *Familicide.* In the best European tradition, he was guaranteeing his inheritance by the most reliable means known. If it had worked for the Borgias, why not for him?

Toby gazed down at the mountains, the swath of pines covering the slopes. He'd become quite the expert on timber of late. He knew the price that spruce brought at market, and oak and birch. It paid to learn about the commodity that stood to make you rich. On behalf of the family, he'd already conducted exploratory discussions with the chairmen of several of the world's largest logging concerns. The consensus seemed to run to a billion dollars per million acres of old growth forest. It was a start, enough to pay off Ratka and Dragan, have a few crumbs left over to satisfy his creditors, at least partially.

The helicopter dropped abruptly, like a man putting his foot in a puddle and discovering it was a trench. Ratka moaned and shifted in his seat. Poor fellow. He had a hand on the safety straps, his knuckles so white they looked as if they were about to pop through the skin. Toby didn't like turbulence any better, but he'd be damned if he showed it.

It had been a bumpy enough road to get to this spot. He tried to think when it had started going wrong, "it" meaning his life: his loves, his friendships, and mostly his finances. Fifty, he decided. Maybe forty-eight. That was when demon drink began to rule his life and he'd discovered that he was more or less broke. He told himself he should be proud that he'd made it that far.

The family had a motto: *Intra si recta, ne labora.* If right within, trouble not. The problem, Toby thought as he pondered all he'd done and what he was about to do, was that he no longer knew, nor frankly cared, what was right. A better motto might be "Do right for yourself, trouble not."

Toby realized that Victoria was staring at him.

"Why?" she asked.

"Always the same reason," he replied.

"It was you who refused the divorce."

"Thought it was the safe play," said Toby. "Keeping my options open."

"And the Holzenstein fortune?"

"Never quite what it was made out to be. Grandfather sold off most of the land after the Second War. There was some decent art. A few Rembrandts, Turners, a Sargent. Those went, too. I did the rest. If you'd agreed to your mother's prenup, none of this would have been necessary."

"No," said Vika, admonishing him. "You would have gone through that as well."

Toby shrugged. "Probably right."

"And Fritz?"

"You mean Robert. What about him? He's the rightful heir. You know how it goes. Princes in the tower and all that. Whole thing doesn't work if he's around."

She steeled herself, tilted her chin. "And it doesn't bother you?"

He thought about lying, but decided he was past that. "Not in the slightest."

Vika nodded toward Ratka. "And him?"

"Ratka? He's got the manpower. I needed his men to raise the funds to pay the death duties. Your German authorities up and raised the ante last week. Some bill to fund that immigration nonsense. Someone's got to pay for all the darkies coming into the country—oh, excuse me, I mean the 'refugees.' Might as well be the rich."

"You're horrible."

"The truth, Victoria. Only telling the truth. Smart of you to take advantage of that provision to avoid inheritance taxes if you keep the entire estate intact for two generations. You can't touch the assets, but Robert can do whatever he likes. Or the presumptive heir. That would be me. Assuming, that is, I can cover the tax bill."

"So you cheated your own casinos?"

"Riske tell you that?"

"Why did you bring him in, anyway?"

"Didn't have a choice. I'm the chairman of the company. The first man we brought in was an expert. Had it figured out the first night."

"So you killed him."

Toby shot a finger at Ratka. "Not me. Him. That's his line of work. Riske was the perfect alternative, at least at the outset. Good record of working with businesses. Strong recommendations. Honest to a fault. I argued that we needed someone from outside the industry. I wasn't kidding when I said he had a checkered background. He's done serious time. Used to rob banks. Almost killed a few policemen. The board liked that. Takes-one-to-know-one kind of thing. Turned out he was everything he was cracked up to be. Couldn't have that. Problem was that he met you. A little taste of schnitzel got him all fired up."

Vika slapped Toby across the face.

Toby grabbed her wrist. *"Vorsicht, meine Prinzessin,"* he said. "Be careful." He released her and continued. "Anyway, Riske's in jail. He won't be getting out for a long time. Le Juste is making sure he has all the evidence he needs to put him away."

"Le Juste is with you?"

"Everyone is with me, Victoria. Everyone is together on this."

"And what will you do?" she asked. "When you have it all."

"Sell," said Toby. "Sell, sell, sell. The forest. The castles. The art. The furniture. All of it."

"How much are you giving to him?" she asked, looking at Ratka.

"He gets his rightful share. None of your concern. Besides, we're going to be close for a while to come."

A gust rocked the helicopter and it danced sideways, the tail swinging out wide. His stomach went with it.

"What do you mean by that?" asked Vika.

"You'll find out soon enough."

CHAPTER 67

It was nine kilometers up the hill to La Turbie. Simon drove like a madman, not stopping for lights, passing when he could and when he couldn't. He could feel the changes Harry had made to the Daytona. The car had always been fast. Now it was dangerous.

He'd put the phone on the center console. He had Isabelle Guyot on the speaker.

"I shouldn't be doing this," she began. "You know that, don't you? It's against everything I stand for."

"I'm grateful."

"As it turns out, it's me who should be grateful. Or rather the bank. How did you know?"

"I'm not sure I follow."

"You said you were interested in Dragan for personal reasons. But surely it's connected to whatever you're investigating down there. Our side missed it completely."

"Glad I could help," said Simon, though he remained at a loss regarding what Isabelle had discovered. "Dov Dragan gave me a bad feeling. Something didn't mesh."

"As usual, your radar is accurate," replied Isabelle. "Initially, we viewed him as another successful executive and investor. Following the IPO of his company, Audiax, he opened an account with an initial deposit of just over one billion dollars. That was ten years ago. He's always been a player. He bet heavily on currency plays. Placed money with the riskier venture cap funds. Funded a few start-ups himself. If there's the opposite of a Midas touch, Dragan had it. Everything he touched went belly-up. Every month his account lost value. He started taking out large sums of cash over the counter. A million euros at a time. Maybe there was a drug habit or a gambling problem. Over the last two years, the decline became precipitous. He was hemorrhaging money. He started carrying a negative balance."

"You didn't like that." Simon recalled visiting Isabelle at her office. A sense of rectitude was as much a part of the furnishings as the Paul Klee watercolors. There was no word for "overdraft" in the Swiss banking lexicon.

"Finally," she continued, "we sent him a letter informing him that he had to make good or we were going to close his account."

"But you didn't," said Simon, powering a long curve in the road.

"He did as we asked."

"I'm listening." He veered left.

"About nine months ago, just after the beginning of the year, Dragan started making deposits into his account through our rep office in Monaco. I'm not talking twenty thousand here, thirty thousand there. I'm talking real money. Millions."

"Maybe one of his start-ups paid off?"

"Doubtful. Start-ups burn through cash—they don't mint it. Every few days Dragan would show up at the rep office down there and deposit cash and checks issued by the casino to a dozen different people, all signed over to him."

"Sirens didn't start flashing?"

"In Monaco? God, no."

"Monaco isn't Cyprus," said Simon.

Since the rise of the oligarchs and their systematic pillaging of the former Soviet Union, Cyprus had become the black money capital of Europe. Banks there had learned to turn a blind eye.

"A close relation," said Isabelle.

"And in-house? Nothing from compliance?"

"Not a whisper," said Isabelle. "It gets worse. Dragan didn't even keep the money at the bank. A day after depositing the money, two days at most, he'd wire all of it out."

"Not to the same account, I'm guessing."

"To a dozen, maybe more. An account in the Netherlands, one in Liechtenstein, Luxembourg, Panama. The usual suspects."

"Did you get a total of the amounts Dragan wired out to all the accounts?"

"So far around two hundred million euros."

Exactly the amount Toby stated had been stolen from the casino.

"You have a record of the wire instructions?"

"Of course. All holding companies. What else is new?" Isabelle read off a slew of them. "Granite Partners. Oak Ventures. Quartz Millennium Group. Linden Concerns."

The pattern wasn't lost on Simon. Stone. Wood. "No names?"

"That would defeat the purpose."

"Thought I'd give it a shot. I'm rusty."

"Try again."

Simon put on his figurative jacket and tie and sat down at his old desk in the City. "Any of the accounts at Pictet?"

"Maybe you're not so rusty after all. Four of the accounts he regularly wired the money to were opened at our Geneva offices."

"Were you able to take a look?"

Isabelle paused, and Simon knew he was pushing too hard. "Access was denied," she said finally. "The accounts were blocked. The only person allowed to see them was his personal banker."

"But you have the account docs," said Simon, meaning the original paperwork.

"There were no names, but all of them had something interesting in common," explained Isabelle. "All four accounts were opened with a referral from a member of our executive board of directors. The same member."

A bank's executive board usually comprised corporate and social luminaries, retired executives, philanthropists, politicians, aristocrats from inside and outside the region. In this case, none worked directly for Pictet.

"Let me guess," said Simon. "Lord Toby Stonewood."

Isabelle was unable to hide her surprise. "Know him?"

"Not as well as I should."

"Are they his accounts?" she asked.

"I'd say he controls them."

"So you know what this is all about…Dragan's deposits, his transfers—the bunch of it."

"Now I do. If I'd known earlier, I would have told you."

"What are we looking at, Simon?"

"Cash deposits. Wire transfers in and out. Holding companies. A pattern of suspicious activity from a client with no proven means of income who was until recently flat broke. You tell me."

"A criminal endeavor. It should have been caught on day one."

"And it wasn't," said Simon. "For a reason."

"This is bad."

"Isabelle, listen to me. Be careful who you bring this to. This is more serious than you can imagine. These are dangerous people."

"One of our outside attorneys is a friend. I'll ask him to make it look like it was his firm that discovered the problems. Toby Stonewood won't learn about it until he gets a call from the police."

"That's the idea," said Simon. "And move quickly. Freeze the accounts as fast as you can. Today, even."

"That's impossible. You know that it takes a court order to freeze an account."

"Put an internal block on them."

"I can't do that without authority from the top."

"Tell your friend the attorney and set up a meeting with him and the president of the bank. And Isabelle: today."

"I'll do my best."

"I know you will."

Chapter 68

The helicopter put down at an old airstrip near Samedan. A Land Rover waited on the tarmac. Two people got out of the car: a trim, alert man in a leather jacket and a beautiful younger woman with dark blond hair and green eyes. The man put flexicuffs on Vika's wrists and told her not to speak. The woman hugged Ratka and kissed him on both cheeks.

"This is Elisabeth," said Ratka to Vika. "My daughter."

"And my fiancée," said Toby, looping an arm around her waist and kissing her. "Hello, darling. As I said, we're going to be closer. Family, in fact."

"Maybe she'll be a princess one day, too," said Ratka.

"Nice to meet you," said Elisabeth to Vika in flawless German. "Your son is a very polite young man."

Vika threw herself at the woman, but Ratka grabbed her and bundled her into the car.

"Calm yourself," said Toby.

Elisabeth looked on, bemused. She had her father's dead gaze. The apple hadn't fallen far from the tree.

The Land Rover drove rapidly along the highway, making no concession for the snow. Toby rode in front. Vika was sandwiched between Ratka and his daughter.

Until now, Vika had been able to rationalize her fear, to explain away her vulnerability. Somehow, she would get out of this. She would escape from Ratka. She would save Fritz. She'd been taught that confidence wins out, that positive thinking yields the desired result. That was wrong. She wouldn't escape. She could not save Fritz. She was driving to her death.

She looked across the lake at the town of St. Moritz, at the tower of the Palace Hotel and the angular steeple of the Lutheran church. There was a hollow pit where her stomach used to be. Her skin was ice-cold, her heart beating much too fast. She was scared.

Scylla. Charybdis. Stream.

The words arrived on her tongue unbidden. She closed her eyes, recalling the only other moment in her life when she'd been as frightened. She hadn't been in danger, at least not like this. *In imminent peril.* She had been twelve, and if possible she'd been even more scared.

Curzon. Brabazon. Rise.

Vika threw herself back in time. There was a narrow white chute before her, a tall groove of ice so cold as to be blue, and at her feet a sled. To be precise, it was a skeleton, a rectangle of scarred black leather for her to lie down on attached to two long, razor-sharp struts.

Gunther, Mama's silver-haired boyfriend, handed her a helmet and she put it on without hesitation, essentially some kind of automaton. By now she was hyperventilating, out of her mind with terror at what she was being made to do.

For the last three weeks, Gunther had been teaching her how to ride the skeleton. Short runs on hard snow. She'd learned to drag the toe of her right foot and lean left when she wanted to guide the skeleton left and the toe of her left foot and lean right when she wanted to guide it right. She'd learned never to touch the ice with her hands and to keep her head absolutely still. She'd learned to never try and slow down lest she lose control of the skeleton altogether and be rocketed out of the run like a bullet from a gun. But not once had she traveled more than one hundred meters without falling off.

Gunther had drawn her a map of the course and they'd reviewed it turn by turn. Each section had a name. *Curzon. Brabazon. Rise. Scylla. Charybdis. Stream.*

To each name, an instruction.

Turn right. Turn left. Straightaway.

She'd memorized them all, but there was no way to practice the run before attempting the entire course. Once on the ice, you couldn't stop. You could only go faster.

It was called the Cresta run. It was two kilometers long, with a total of sixteen curves. She would reach a speed of 140 kilometers per hour. A week before, a man had lost control of his skeleton and flown out of the run, breaking his back. It had all happened in the blink of an eye. He would be in a wheelchair for the rest of his life. If Vika finished, she would receive a medal.

The starter's tower stood behind her.

A tocsin bell rang once.

A man called her name. All of it, with her title. A crowd of spectators drew near.

Vika stepped to the starting line. Her body quivered like a violin string strung too tight.

"Locker," said Gunther. Relax.

Despite her terror, Vika smiled at him. Even now, thirty years later, she regarded the smile as the single bravest act of her life.

It had been a cloudy day with light flurries, visibility poor, the temperature well below freezing. Vika remembered none of that. Nor did she remember the run itself, or her time of one minute sixteen seconds, a record for a first timer younger than fifteen years of age.

She remembered only the moment when Gunther had said "Go," and she'd started running and thrown herself onto the black leather square. A blink and she was barreling into the orange foam cushions that stopped her flight. It was over. She'd done it.

No one had been there to congratulate her.

She opened her eyes. Ratka was staring at her.

Vika looked at him and grinned.

CHAPTER 69

The town of La Turbie sat atop the mountain like a tile and terra-cotta crown, gazing down from on high upon Monaco and the Côte d'Azur. It was a quiet place, just three thousand inhabitants, famous as much for the Trophée des Alpes, a towering Roman ruin dating from the Emperor Augustus, as for its training grounds, where AS Monaco, the local soccer team, practiced year-round.

Simon guided the Daytona through the narrow streets, slowing to a crawl as he approached the town hall, where participants in the time trial had gathered in the parking lot. There were enough fancy cars and colorful banners and pretty young women with fat older men to look almost like a real Formula One race. A timer straddled the main road. A Jaguar E-type convertible ("roadster," to those in the know) in British racing green, chrome spokes, so pretty that Stirling Moss should have been driving it, took the start flag and roared off. A leaderboard showed the best time as seventeen minutes, sixteen seconds, which counted as either insanely foolhardy or just plain brilliant, given the wildly curving course and the poor condition of the roads.

It was 9:24. Dov Dragan was next to run.

Simon revved the engine as he entered the lot. He wanted Dragan to see him. He wanted Dragan's ass to pucker as he realized that the jig was up. Simon didn't know if it was the smartest move in the book, but it was the only one he could think of. He hadn't slept in a day. He hurt all over. He had no way to locate Vika. He was desperate.

There was a space waiting for him with his name stenciled on the pavement. He killed the engine and climbed out of the car. Many of the drivers were attired in racing gear: jumpsuits decorated with stripes and badges and the makes of their automobiles. Mercedes, Porsche, Lamborghini. Or Bugatti. Wearing sky blue, Dragan was easy to spot, helmet in one hand, a socket wrench in the other.

Simon shouted his name. The Israeli turned. He stared at Simon for a long second. His mouth moved as if he was trying to shout back, but no words materialized.

"Where is she?" asked Simon so everyone would pay attention. "Where did Ratka take her?"

Heads turned. Dragan tried to wave Simon off but couldn't manage it. The knowledge of being a rat caught in a trap robs a man of confidence.

"I have one of your laptops," Simon went on. He could only hope that Harry Mason had found it. "It was Radek's, actually. That's some cheating program. Radek bragged that whoever wrote it was a mathematical genius. Who am I to argue? You and your boys stole over two hundred million from the casino. Hear that, ladies and gentlemen?" Hands held out wide, Simon turned so that all would pay him note. "This man, Dov Dragan, formerly the director of Unit 8200 of the Mossad, a real-life spy in the flesh, wrote a software program that allowed him to cheat at baccarat so efficiently that no one could catch him. Of course, it turns out he had some help on the inside."

A half-dozen people drew nearer, unsure of what was transpiring.

By now Simon was face-to-face with Dragan. "You have one chance to tell me where she is."

"You have nothing," said Dragan. "I don't know how you got out of jail, but that's where you're going back to. Get out of here. You are embarrassing yourself."

"I have this." Simon opened his palm to reveal the cuff link. "I also have you on disc driving the Rolls from Stefanie's apartment building thirty minutes before she died. I suppose that's something."

Dragan looked at the cuff link and swallowed, his eyes suddenly blinking far too rapidly.

"Is everything all right?" It was André Solier, the president of the Monaco Rally Club. "Is he bothering you, Dov?"

"Am I?" asked Simon.

"Mr. Riske," Solier continued. "This is no place for personal disputes. I'm afraid I'll have to ask you to leave."

"You heard him," said Dragan. "Leave."

When Simon didn't move, Solier said, "Should I get the police?"

"Be my guest," said Simon.

"This man is crazy," said Dragan. "I have no idea what he's talking about."

"No?" said Simon. "Maybe this will jog your memory. Account five one five point seven eight eight ZZ." Simon spoke each number as if counting down a launch. "Banque Pictet. Geneva. Tell me again that I'm crazy."

Dragan's face drained of color. He shook his head, swallowing dryly, a man who had received a terminal diagnosis.

"And you're right," added Simon. "It is the finest private bank in the world."

Dragan lashed out with his wrench, clubbing Simon across the face, knocking him to the ground.

When Simon was able to stand, he saw that Dragan had reached his car and was driving rapidly through the crowd, men and women jumping aside, crying out, banging on his chassis.

Brushing aside offers of help, Simon ran back to the Daytona. He put a hand to his face and it came away covered with blood. He felt nothing, only rage and the will to avenge. He fell into the driver's seat and fired the engine. Dragan and the Bugatti had a lane clear to the starting area and passed beneath the official time clock, accelerating madly as the race officials ran after him, shouting and waving for him to stop.

Simon nosed the car forward, hemmed in on all sides by the race competitors and their support teams. He rode the horn, window down, calling "Out of the way! Emergency." People recoiled at the sight of him.

Finally, Simon entered the starting area. A band of race stewards blocked his path. Burned once by Dragan, they maintained a solid front, standing with arms akimbo on the starting line. Simon waved them away, to no avail. When they refused to move, he threw the car into first, swore at the top of his lungs, and accelerated as if they weren't there, knocking the men aside like bowling pins. The man positioned in front of the car rolled onto the bonnet, his face pressed against the windscreen. After fifty meters, Simon braked hard and the man rolled off the car onto the pavement. Simon decided he'd never liked race stewards to begin with.

Simon rounded the first bend and caught sight of Dragan's silver-blue Bugatti half a mile ahead. It was a two-lane road, following the contours of the ridgeline with plenty of curves and a few straightaways. A light rain was falling, with darker clouds spilling over the mountaintop. Simon drove the car as hard as he knew how, keeping the rpms high, using the engine to decelerate, rarely lifting his foot off the accelerator. He knew where Dragan was headed: to the north side of the mountains, where there was an on-ramp to the A4 superhighway. If Dragan made it, Simon would never see him again. Dragan would slip out of the country. Harry had made the car faster, but not fast enough.

Simon flew past a sign for the Grande Corniche and braked, searching for Dragan's car on the feeder road snaking up the hillside. He had a clear view of the road to the top of the mountain. There was no sign of the Bugatti and he brought the car back up to speed. The speedometer read 130 kilometers per hour—well over eighty miles per hour. Too fast. A burst of rain blurred the windscreen, forcing Simon to brake.

But Dragan suffered the same obstacles. The rain was playing havoc with his skills. He over-accelerated on the short straightaways and braked too early and too long on the curves. Despite driving the fastest production car on the planet, he couldn't get out of Simon's sights.

The road climbed a hill, the first long straightaway on the course, and Simon pushed the pedal to the floor. The Ferrari growled magnificently and he picked up speed faster than he could have imagined. A tall stone wall ran to his right, a field strewn with rocks and gravel to his left. There were few houses or structures of any kind on this part of the course. Simon reached the crest of the mountain. The road narrowed considerably. He braked and downshifted, preparing for a ninety-degree left-hand turn. He slowed, only a little, and touched his foot to the gas as he completed the turn. He was a moment too soon. The car traversed a slick patch of asphalt and began to slide out behind him. Ahead stood a squat weathered mile marker on the side of the road: a block of immovable stone. He turned the wheel in the direction of the skid and pumped the gas. The car straightened and missed the marker by a finger's width.

Simon was headed west toward Villefranche and Nice. The road flattened out and began a ten-kilometer stretch hewing to the contours of the mountains, a procession of bends, straightaways, and near hairpin turns that allowed the driver to view the road far ahead. A gentle curve and the Bugatti came into view. Dragan was closer than Simon had expected, his brake lights flaring before he disappeared around a jagged escarpment.

Simon threw caution to the wind, attacking the corners, selecting the fastest line, daring the car to lose its purchase on the wet asphalt. The course departed the Grande Corniche and shot down a dizzyingly steep feeder road onto a less used track, barely wide enough for a single vehicle. Small pitted-stone homes alternated with towering hedges, the pavement in lamentable condition: potholes, crumbling borders, depressions where the asphalt had been dug up and not properly repaired. The road dipped and rose and dipped and rose, making Simon feel as if he were riding out a rising sea. The hedges dropped away. No more houses now, just open territory, the mountainside diving vertically to his left. Only rocks and more rocks and the ocean below. Dragan's lead had dwindled to less than a hundred meters. He disappeared again, hidden by the next curve. Simon chose his moment. He pressed the accelerator to the floor, waiting, waiting as the bend neared, then downshifting a second too late, braking, spinning the wheel, feathering the gas as he came out of the turn.

Dragan was right there, nearly stopped after apparently losing control in the turn. Simon's fist slammed the horn. He braked. His nose touched Dragan's bumper. Dragan leered at him in the wing mirror. In a flash, the Bugatti sped away, so fast it seemed an illusion, as if it hadn't been just an arm's length away. A blink and it was fifty meters down the road.

But Simon knew he was the better driver. He had him. It was a matter of time.

Faster.

Faster.

Dov Dragan spun the wheel, keeping his foot on the accelerator, feeling the tires tear into the crumbling asphalt as he rounded the bend. He glanced into the rearview mirror. The bonnet of Riske's Ferrari looked like the snout of a marauding shark. Closer and closer it came, no matter what he might do. The man was relentless. First interfering with the princess, and now discovering Cutter.

Cutter.

He'd given the name to his card-counting program because it was when the player was given the cutting card that the casino made itself vulnerable.

Dragan had been a gambler his entire life. He'd played pinochle with his father on their farm in the Negev and poker with his barracks mates while doing his national service. In his forties he developed a taste for blackjack. He taught himself to count cards, but at his peak his skill gave him only a two percent advantage over the house. It required playing (and counting) for hour upon hour to win any real money. Even then, Lady Luck could double-cross you. Baccarat had been Toby's suggestion, almost as a dare. After all, how can one cheat at a game of pure chance?

It was a year ago. They'd taken to meeting for drinks at the Bar Américain every afternoon at five. Two expats in Monaco. Billionaires once. Bachelors. In his cups, Dragan had complained to Toby about his run of bad investments. To his surprise, Toby had an even longer list of his own. A far longer list, as it turned out. Dragan had seen something in Toby's eye. Maybe Toby had seen something in his. It wasn't long before they began discussing ways to scratch back their fortunes. By hook or by crook.

It was on a damp December day that Toby first mentioned the von Tiefen und Tassises and how he would be better off without them. He floated the idea as a kind of wild "What if?," almost as a joke. Only three of them left. Kill 'em all and take their money. Toby wouldn't really inherit it all, would he? He'd separated from Stefanie ten years earlier. It couldn't be. But of course Toby had studied the matter. He knew the law to a T. He had a plan all worked out. The killing was the easy part. The hard part was gathering money to pay the death duties.

"You're the smart one," Toby had said over a glass of his favorite grappa. "I own the casino. You figure it out."

So Dragan had. As Riske had said, he was a mathematical genius.

Dragan had no compunction about breaking the law. He had lost his soul years before. For a spell in the nineties, he'd run his government's targeted assassination program. It was difficult to order the deaths of people day in, day out, without sacrificing a portion of one's humanity, even if the people were the enemy. They deserved it. But did their wives deserve it, too? Their kids? And what had it accomplished, anyway? He was a murderer. Fact.

So when Toby Stonewood offered his hand and said "Shall we give it a go?," Dragan shook it and said "Why not?" A little theft and murder was nothing compared to the crimes that already tormented him. It wasn't even a question. It was a challenge.

Looking back, Dragan realized now that none of it had been Toby's idea, or his own. It had come from Ratka, and from his daughter, Elisabeth, who was smarter than all of them. She'd been screwing Toby for a year by then, long enough to have learned that he wasn't the rich man he claimed to be. She was the one who'd suggested that Toby kill off his family.

Dragan was thinking about all this, along with Cutter and the princess and that maniac, Ratka, when he noticed the curve approaching much too quickly. Ahead, the strip of pavement made a sharp turn to the right. Beyond the curve was sky, ocean, and a five-hundred-foot vertical drop.

Dragan slammed his foot on the brake. The Bugatti decelerated violently, propelling him into his safety belt, his head ricocheting off the steering wheel. For a second or two, the car held its line. Dragan realized he didn't have enough space. He yanked the wheel hard to the right. The Bugatti's massive V12 engine was mounted in the rear of the vehicle. By far the heaviest part of the automobile, the engine block's forward velocity overruled the grip of the car's sticky low-profile tires. The Bugatti entered an uncontrolled spin. The rear of the car slid out from its center of gravity, striking the flimsy guardrail. Frantic, Dragan forgot everything he'd been taught and steered against the skid. Instead of straightening out, the car continued its wild, uncontrolled slide. Dragan touched his foot to the gas, compounding his error. The car's course was set.

The chassis collided with the strip of metal, the force of the impact bending it into a convex curve. Bolts popped. The guardrail broke free. One section separated from another and boomeranged off the cliff. The right front wheel left the pavement and skidded across the shoulder. The car yawed left. Dragan saw blue sky, the rugged cliffside, and, far below, a stand of sharp rock rising out of the sea. All to an earsplitting chorus of metal scraping metal. He grasped the wheel with both hands. The passenger seat was suddenly above his shoulder, looking down on him. He cried out.

The car stopped.

Dov Dragan stared out the window.

He was a dead man.

"I wouldn't move if I were you."

Simon stood ten paces from the Bugatti, arms crossed over his chest. He'd watched the car spin out and was amazed that it hadn't plummeted off the mountainside. It was the first piece of luck he'd had all day.

The passenger window was open. Dragan stared up at Simon, eyes wide, hands trembling on the wheel. "Riske, get me out of here."

"Where is Victoria Brandenburg?"

"Just get me out. I'll tell you everything."

"You're safe," said Simon. "For the moment." He sidestepped down the escarpment and set his foot on the Bugatti's front tire, leaning on it.

The chassis groaned.

"Riske!"

"Talk."

"She's in Switzerland."

"I'm listening."

"Somewhere in the mountains. Her family has a chalet there."

"That's not good enough."

"How should I know where? That part of the operation doesn't concern me."

"Not buying it. I have you figured for a details kind of guy." Simon gave the car a shove. Dirt shifted. The Bugatti slid a foot farther down the slope, a foot closer to the rocks below. "Where in the mountains, Dragan?"

"If you kill me, you won't find her."

"You willing to bet your life on that?" Simon bent at the waist and placed both hands on the Bugatti's hood and began to push. The car was heavier than he'd expected, but the loose terrain and the angled slope helped greatly. Dragan begged for him to stop. Simon continued to shove the car closer to the precipice. "Where?"

"Pontresina. It's called the Chesa Madrun. Five kilometers off the main highway. There's a private road. It's the only place within miles."

Simon saw himself standing at Vika's back as she searched her keys to open her mother's apartment. One color for each of her homes. *Paris, Manhattan, Pontresina.*

And later, inside her mother's apartment, the picture of a boy, thin and pale, wearing a rugby jersey, with Vika's straight nose, a thatch of curly blond hair, and blue eyes that looked right through you.

"Fritz?"

"Well, that's what we call him. His full name is Robert Frederick Maximillian. He's away at school in Switzerland."

Zuoz.

The name came to Simon in a flash. He had a few clients at the bank who either had graduated or had a child in school there. Lyceum Alpinum Zuoz. Located a stone's throw from Pontresina.

"And the boy?"

"They've got him, too. He's already there."

"Who's got him?"

"Ratka's men. Toby Stonewood."

"He's a kid."

"It wouldn't work without him. Toby's the surviving heir by marriage. The estate goes to him."

"Why two hundred million?"

"To pay the death duties," said Dragan. "The taxes owed to the German government due on transfer of the estate. Otherwise, it all ends up in probate for years. The judge decides which assets to sell off to pay the taxes."

"So you decided to kill them all?"

"It's the only way."

"What are you going to do to them?"

"Explosion. A gas leak. It has to look like an accident. There can't appear to be any foul play or the court will get involved. That means a delay. Toby's not getting any younger. Neither am I. We can get our hands on the estate in ninety days." Dragan gazed at Simon, eyes wide, confident. "We can cut you in…a hundred million…That's real money, Riske…Just get me out. A hundred million."

"Cut me in?" Simon saw red. He leaned against the hood, pushing with all his might. The car slid and slid some more. Simon could nearly see its underside. A back tire dropped over the edge. The car teetered dangerously. Dragan screamed for him to stop.

Simon lifted his hands off the car. Dragan said "Thank you" over and over, hyperventilating.

"What were you looking for in the apartment?"

"A ring," said Dragan. "A family heirloom. We had to have it."

"Why?"

"Same reason. To keep the administration of the estate out of the hands of a judge. All part of the ancient protocol from God knows when. The ring signifies a lawful succession. No questions asked. A load of horseshit, but that's the way it is."

"So you killed Stefanie."

"Ratka killed her. He brained her with an old glass vase. Thing shattered and made a mess of the bathroom. I got her drunk before. She didn't know what was going on."

"You brought her the grappa?"

Dragan nodded. "Toby arranged for me to meet her one day at that Italian place she always went to. She was a lush. I took her out a few times after."

"But you scared her. You didn't know she was borderline paranoid. She guessed what you were after and hid the ring."

"That's enough of this," said Dragan. He'd gone white with terror. Tears streamed down his cheeks. "Help me, Riske." Timidly, he removed a hand from the wheel and extended it toward Simon. "Get me out. Please."

Simon looked at the Israeli spymaster in his blue racing suit and silver helmet. He'd never seen anyone so frightened.

"Get yourself out."

Chapter 70

Simon walked away from the car. He checked his watch. It was 9:45. Switzerland was a five-hour drive. He gazed up at the sky. An armada of black clouds approached from the north. The rain was falling harder by the minute. If it was raining here, it was snowing in the Alps. A sturdy helicopter with a very good pilot might be able to make it, but that wasn't going to happen. Simon couldn't show his face at the heliport. He was a wanted man.

He considered calling the Swiss police…and saying what? Victoria and her son had been kidnapped and were being held captive in their chalet…or that a team of Serbian criminals along with Victoria's stepfather planned on killing them to get their hands on the family's twelve-billion-dollar fortune? The first piece of information the police would require was Simon's name. Who was he to make such an accusation? It would end there. Simon had no doubt that Toby and his man, Le Juste, had seen to it that the name Simon Riske, escaped murderer, was on every police blotter across the European continent.

Going to the Swiss police was out.

Before Simon had a chance to think of anything else, a late-model Audi rounded the curve and accelerated straight at him. It was déjà vu all over again. He backed up a step before the car braked hard and came to a halt. The doors opened. Two men climbed out and came at him. One held a pistol and it was aimed at Simon's face. Simon recognized him. It was Goran, one of the Croats who'd been following him the other day. The second man, recognizable by the flexicast on his left wrist, had to be Ivan.

"What are you doing?" said Goran. "You're not supposed to leave until five minutes after the Bugatti. The starting times were posted online. We waited all night and you ruin it."

"What is this all about?" demanded Simon. "We've never crossed paths. I'm not in your line of work. What exactly do you want?"

"We're here for the car," said Ivan. Then he hit Simon hard across the face, staggering him. "I owe you," he said. "For breaking my hand."

Ivan walked past Simon and looked at the Bugatti, perched precariously on the mountainside. He looked over his shoulder at Simon. "You run him off the road, too?"

"He did it himself," replied Simon, confused.

"Why don't you help him?"

"I'm busy."

Ivan looked at Goran, who barked out instructions in a language Simon didn't understand. Ivan sidestepped down the slope to the Bugatti. Dragan was shouting for help. Ivan told him to unbuckle his safety belt, then reached into the cockpit and pulled Dragan out through the passenger window. It helped that Dragan weighed 140 pounds sopping wet.

Dragan scrambled up the hillside. He saw Goran and the gun and was quick to appraise the situation. "Look who's in the shit now," he said to Simon. "You should have taken my offer." He turned to Goran. "You… What's your name?"

"What's your name?" retorted Goran.

"He's Dragan," said Ivan. "I remember him from the starting list."

"I'm a friend." Dragan took off his helmet. "A friend who is going to offer you a lot of money."

"Really? What for?"

"Shoot him. Shoot Riske. I'll pay you."

"You are serious?" said Goran. He added, "You two really don't like each other."

"How much?" asked Ivan.

"Take my car," said Dragan. "It's the finest sports car in the world. A Bugatti Veyron. A V12 engine. Zero to sixty in two point three seconds.

Alcantara leather seats. Only fifty in the whole world. It's worth two million dollars."

"I'd say it's worth more," said Simon. "Two million five, easy. But he doesn't own it. The bank does. For that kind of money, they'll come looking. Like Mr. Dragan said, only fifty of them in the world. Hard enough to drive without being noticed. Forget about selling it."

"Don't listen to him. He's a thief. He used to be a gangster. A criminal." Dragan approached Simon, breaching his personal space. "I don't care what you think you have: no one will believe you. You're a murderer. You killed all the men in the drop house. Le Juste is with us. Anyway, Ratka will take care of you. I'll see to it. We know where to find you, Riske. I'm not the one in trouble. You are."

At the mention of Ratka, Goran stepped closer. "What did you say about Ratka?"

"He's my partner," said Dragan. "A close friend. He's from your part of the world. Know him?"

"We're talking about same Ratka…Zoltan Mikhailovic from Belgrade?"

"The very same," said Dragan. "A very good businessman. You have my word I will speak highly of you to him. Maybe you two can work for him one day."

"Me?" said Goran. "Work for Ratka?"

"Why not? I can see you are intelligent. You and your friend can become two of his lieutenants. I assume that is your line of work?"

Simon noticed that Ivan was no longer interested in him. Instead, his attention had shifted to Dov Dragan. Ivan was staring at the Israeli in a way that Simon hoped no one would ever stare at him.

Goran noticed this, too. "See my friend Ivan?" he said to Dragan. "He knows Ratka."

"You do?" said Dragan. "Perfect. I'm still happy to reintroduce you."

Simon retreated a step.

"Yes," Goran continued. "He knows Ratka very well. Ivan is from Srebrenica. You know it? When he was a boy, Ratka visited his town. It was during the civil war. Ratka is a Serb. Ivan and me, we are Croats. Ivan's father was Muslim, his mother Orthodox Church. Back then, no one cared about religion. Ratka came with his soldiers and took over the town. He built a camp outside—a concentration camp—and rounded up all the men and boys. Took them there. Also, Ivan's father and three brothers. Ivan was too small, just three years old. Anyway, Ratka, he cared about religion. He didn't like Muslims. He and his Silver Tigers…they killed all the men and boys. He made them dig their graves, then shot them. Five thousand. More, maybe. Yes, we know Ratka very well."

Dragan listened intently, eyes shifting among Goran and Ivan and Simon, as if analyzing where he stood, calculating the probabilities of his next move. Simon didn't think his mathematical skills were going to be of much assistance.

"He's your friend, eh?" asked Ivan. "A close friend."

"I mean…we are working on something together," said Dragan. "I'm not sure he's really a *friend*. More of an associate."

Ivan looked at Goran. "Friend, associate, whatever of Ratka wants to give us car he doesn't own. Asks us to work for Ratka. Be lieutenant. What do you say, Goran? You want to work for Ratka?"

Goran shook his head. "No, thank you, Ivan."

"Me neither." Ivan turned back to Dragan. "You going to see him soon?"

"Possibly."

"Yes or no? After all, you have to give him message about your friend, Riske."

"I believe so," said Dragan, haltingly.

"Good. Because I have message for you to give Ratka. 'Fuck you.'"

Two stiff fingers to the chest emphasized the final words. Dragan backed up a step. "I'll tell him."

"I want to make sure he gets the message."

"I promise."

"What do you think, Goran…you think he tell Ratka 'Fuck you' from us, from Goran and Ivan?"

Goran shook his head. "No chance."

"Me neither. I think better we send message ourselves."

"I'll tell him," Dragan insisted. "You can believe me."

Ivan was holding a pistol in his right hand. A nickel-plated .45. He raised it. "What you going to tell him?"

"'Fuck you,'" said Dragan.

"What?"

"'Fuck you.'" Louder this time. Dragan was red in the face.

Ivan lowered the gun. "Good. I think he gets it."

Dragan nodded earnestly as Ivan looked at Goran.

A moment later, Ivan raised the pistol and emptied the clip into Dov Dragan, the final shot sending the Israeli over the precipice. Ivan wiped off the pistol with his shirttail and threw it over the cliff. "That was for my papa," he said, walking past Simon.

"Him...the driver...bad guy?" asked Goran.

"Very."

Goran put his hand on Simon's shoulder. "I'm sorry, but we have to take the Ferrari. Martin Harriri owed us a lot of money. He gave us the car as payment. That's why you saw us the other day. We didn't know you were one of us."

Simon didn't think it necessary to tell him that he'd been out of that side of the game for twenty years.

Goran looked at the Bugatti. "You don't have a car anymore. You want that one? I don't know what to do with it."

"Sure," said Simon. "Give me a hand?"

"Ivan, come here!" shouted Goran. "We gotta move this car back on the road."

CHAPTER 71

The *Luftschutzbunker* was located on the farthest corner of the first underground floor, just off the Chesa Madrun's parking garage. A two-foot-thick vault door governed entry and exit. Inside were two rooms: a bedroom with bunk beds, a couch, a television, and all the usual necessities, and a workroom housing auxiliary power units as well as the water and power hookups for the chalet.

At exactly ten a.m., two men—both compact, dark-haired, and possessed of serious intent—entered the shelter, carrying with them a set of blueprints for the Chesa Madrun, as well as a canvas satchel holding a less prosaic item: a two-kilogram brick of Semtex plastic explosive.

Both men were veterans of the Serbian Armed Forces. Unlike Ratka and his paramilitary brigade, the Silver Tigers, they had served in official units. One was a trained civil engineer who had spent his time in the army building barracks, shoring up bridges, and, most important, demolishing them. The other was a commando who had served with distinction in the army's elite counterterrorist units. Between the two of them, they could blow up any structure conceived and/or built by man.

"The problem," the civil engineer was saying as he examined the pipe bringing natural gas to the heating unit, "is that if we blow the main here, the force of the blast will be largely contained belowground."

"So cut the line and let gas leak throughout the house."

"A place this size? It will take hours—a day, even. The risk is that it might go off on its own before we're ready."

"Then we have no choice," said the commando. "We use the *plastique*."

"Any halfway decent investigator will find residue," said the engineer. "Not to mention evidence of detonators."

"What's to investigate?" asked the commando. "A gas leak blows a chalet to kingdom come. There are such explosions every day."

"Not this chalet. Besides, this is Switzerland. They investigate a blown automobile tire. And don't forget…there will be victims."

"And so?"

"It can be done," said the engineer. "It's a question of placing the *plastique* in the correct place where it and the detonators will likely be incinerated."

"Where pockets of gas will accumulate," added the commando.

"Precisely. At those points, the amount of explosive left over will be minute and nearly impossible to find."

The engineer spread a copy of the chalet's blueprints on a table and in rapid succession banged his finger on spots at every corner of the structure. "Here, here, here, and here." He looked to his colleague. "Are we agreed?"

The commando nodded. "Agreed."

"Let's get to it, then," said the engineer.

He rolled up the blueprints and put them under his arm. "When we are finished," he said, "there won't be a stick or stone of this entire place left standing. Pity, actually."

Chapter 72

Simon drove east on the coast highway past Menton, San Remo, and San Lorenzo al Mare, one town melting into the next, all silent and sullen beneath the pewter sky. Apart from cosmetic damage to the driver's side of the car, the Bugatti had not suffered from its collision. Simon drove as fast as conditions allowed, dodging in and out of traffic, the speedometer yo-yoing between 250 kilometers per hour and the legal limit of 120. If he had passed a police car, he hadn't seen it. Should a blue and white strobe appear in his rearview, his strategy was to drive faster. Once an outlaw, always an outlaw.

He experienced the first slowdown in Savona, and he cursed the city's favorite son, Christopher Columbus. A prayer to the seaman did no good. The three lanes of traffic moved in unison well below the speed limit. Simon was just one more car in a sea of metal and exhaust.

Salvation came at the town of Voltri as he left the coastal road and headed inland on the A26, passing beneath a sign for Alessandria and Milano. In minutes, he was traversing the fertile Piedmont countryside, three lanes of wide-open highway, the rolling hills and fields of saffron but blurs of green and yellow at near three hundred kilometers per hour.

At the two-hour mark, traffic picked up as he approached Milan, the industrial capital of the north, a city of three million whose suburbs stretched for miles in every direction. Factories and warehouses and quarries lined the motorway. It was a barren, unloved landscape made more unpalatable by the unceasing curtain of rain.

Simon fought to keep from imagining the worst. Dragan's recounting of the plans to kill Vika and her son played over and over as Simon racked his brain about whom he might call for help. The answer came back the same every time. There was no one. It was up to Simon and Simon alone.

And then, finally, he was free of the metropolitan sprawl. The highway turned north. The weather worsened, cloud and mist sitting low on the ground, rain turning to sleet. He was swallowed by an endless tunnel and spat out in the lake district, long home to Italy's wealthiest families. Lake Como, slate gray and forbidding, lay along the left side of the road, his brooding companion for the final stretch to the Swiss border. He paid no attention to the string of palazzi and lakeside villas decorating the shoreline.

For an hour he made good time, growing to respect the Bugatti more than he would have liked, its narrow bucket seats and strangely small pedals, more suited to Dov Dragan than to himself. The road was slick; spray from vehicles soaked Simon's windscreen, leaving him essentially blind for seconds at a time. He gave all his attention to the band of asphalt before him, forbidding himself from slowing. Somewhere inside him he heard a clock ticking, and its relentless rhythm became his own.

An incoming call broke his trance. He recognized the number as belonging to Roger Jenkins at MI5. "Talk to me."

"We've got your friend on the radar."

"In Switzerland?"

"Why, yes, did you speak with her? Near the town of Pontresina. Her coordinates put her inside a chalet, actually more of a hunting lodge. No other structures within a few kilometers."

"Can you get me a picture?"

"As a matter of fact, I already checked. I'll send it straightaway."

"Thank you, Roger," said Simon. "I need one more thing. I don't have time to explain. Can you track another number?"

"You're pushing it. We do keep records, you know. This will have to be all."

Simon read off a number with a London area code.

A pause, then an explosion. "Do you know whose number that is?" demanded Jenkins. Then, calmer: "Of course you do. It belongs to Toby Stonewood, the Duke of Suffolk."

"You don't say."

"This isn't some sort of love triangle, is it?" asked Jenkins. "We don't do that kind of thing. MI5 isn't *The Sun*."

"Why are you asking?"

"Because Toby Stonewood, or whoever is holding that phone right now, is at precisely the same location as the woman you're concerned about."

Just then, Simon spotted a tall red flag snapping to attention in the near distance. He ended the call and slid past the Swiss border control with a show of his passport.

Rising in front of him, dark and never more forbidding, the Alps beckoned.

Something was up.

Robby could tell by the voices outside the library and the footsteps tramping up and down the hall. He felt the floor shudder and knew that meant the door to the underground garage was opening and closing. Someone had arrived. The house grew quiet again. He put his ear to the door. He heard something slam, then nothing. The silence was worse than the burst of activity.

Robby remembered Elisabeth telling him that they were bringing his mother to be with him. He didn't know how to feel. More than anything he wanted to see her, but more than anything he didn't. He couldn't bear to think that he'd failed to warn her. If she was really here, it was his fault. What more could he have done?

A man's voice echoed down the hall. Robby tucked in his shirt and brushed his hair with his fingers. Then he went to the bookshelf and selected a title at random. He took the book and sat down at the desk. He opened it and pretended to read.

The door opened and his mother stepped into the library. Robby struggled to keep his head down, eyes on the page.

"Fritz," she said, crossing the room. "Oh Fritz, I'm sorry."

Robby looked up, then calmly rose and came around the desk. He allowed himself to be hugged, and even put his arms around his mother and hugged her back.

"Are you all right?" she asked, clasping his arms. "What happened to your hand? Is that a cut? And your face… Your eye is swollen."

"Don't worry," he said, his voice steady, much too confident given the circumstances. A man's voice, she realized. "I'm fine." Then he put his mouth to her ear and whispered, "I'm going to get us out of here."

CHAPTER 73

The Chesa Madrun appeared slowly out of the snow and cloud, a hulking timbered giant with sharp eaves and sloping roofs, girdled by a gray stone retaining wall and dominated by a square tower, darker than the rest, rising from its center, a picture window at the top like an all-seeing eye. The Brothers Grimm had left the Black Forest and come south to the Swiss Alps.

Simon Riske ran down the hillside behind the lodge, his loafers punching holes in the snow. A navy parka and a watch cap, both purchased at a roadside store, shielded him from the elements but stopped short of keeping him warm. It had been a two-kilometer sprint from the car. Somewhere along the line, he'd lost all feeling in his feet. With difficulty, he slowed, grabbing on to a tree trunk to halt his descent. He closed his eyes, needing time to regain his breath, then edged close to the forest line.

The snow was falling harder at altitude. Though it was barely two, the day was colored a dark dishwater gray. Nary a breath disturbed the boughs. A trail of snow fell onto his shoulder. He glanced up to see a black squirrel dash across a branch.

Simon broke from the forest and ran to the rear of the house. He had only scant knowledge of its layout. An Internet search had turned up several articles about the Swiss mountain retreat. A piece from an old architecture journal offered photographs of the interior, as well as of the facade and summer garden. An article from *Blick,* the Swiss daily tabloid, showcased a party thrown at the Chesa Madrun to celebrate the marriage of Lord Toby Stonewood and Princess Stefanie and included color photographs of the happy couple taken inside the house. It wasn't much, but Simon had some idea what to expect once he got inside.

He reached the back terrace. All the windows were shuttered, the *rollladen* lowered and in place. A stout door was locked. Simon put his ear to the frame and caught a raised voice. He pulled his set of picks from his pocket. His hands were shaking from the cold. The lock was brand-new and beyond his skills. There was a picnic table with an umbrella, lowered and protected by a canvas cover, poking through its middle. He freed the umbrella and held it under his arm like a knight preparing to joust. He took a bold step, then rethought his actions.

The fact was, he didn't know how many people were inside. Regardless of the number, they would be armed. He wasn't. Making matters more difficult, he had no idea if Vika's son was also inside. He laid the umbrella on the terrace.

There had to be another way in.

"Everything's wired," said the engineer. "She's ready to blow."

"How long?" asked Ratka.

"An hour after we rupture the gas line, then…" The engineer made the sign of an explosion with his hands.

Ratka stood in the great hall at the front of the house. The room was two stories at least, a fireplace big enough to drive a tank through, lots of old furniture. A wild boar's head was mounted above the fireplace—the biggest, meanest, hairiest boar Ratka had ever seen, with tusks like a Saracen's battle swords. A stag's head hung from another wall, eighteen points. And facing it, a majestic hawk in flight, wings spread, talons curled to grasp its prey. In the dim light, the animals looked more alive than dead, waiting to spring from the walls and exact their revenge.

Ratka took in his surroundings. He'd never set foot in such a place. His presence stirred a sense of destiny deep inside him. He was here for a reason. He was meant to retake his place atop the Belgrade business world. Once there, he intended to stay. A man with a billion euros did not go to prison.

And yet it wasn't done yet, he warned himself. His mind went back to the Serbian Cup, the final penalty kick. An hour earlier, he'd received an anguished call from Le Juste. Somehow Riske had managed to escape custody. Le Juste mentioned a botched suicide, breaking out of a hospital, then a sighting of Riske at the time trial being held high on the mountain. Le Juste was speaking too quickly for Ratka to make sense of it all. In the end, the only thing that mattered was that Riske was running free.

Possessed of a new urgency, Ratka instructed the engineer to cut the gas lines immediately.

"Best if you kill them first," said the engineer. "Take them downstairs. Shut them in the bunker. Ten minutes, fifteen tops, is enough. Like sticking your head in an oven. Afterward, you put on the mask, put the bodies where you want. Ground floor is best. You want we can get them now."

"No," said Ratka. "I need to have a talk with the lady first. Face-to-face." He had unfinished business with the princess.

"Take this." The engineer handed him a metal box the size and shape of a pack of cigarettes. It was an electronic detonator. "Turn it on. Wait for the green light. Hit the red button. All fuses are set to the same frequency. When they receive the signal, they will simultaneously ignite the blasting caps and detonate the charges. Remember: wait one hour. By that time, there will be enough gas inside the house to provoke a large explosion. Afterward, the gas will continue to flow, sparking a conflagration. I'd suggest getting as far away as possible. There will be debris as well as a significant shock wave."

"I fought in the war, too," said Ratka. "Remember?" He slipped the detonator into his pocket. "Cut the gas lines. Then get out of here."

Toby Stonewood dumped the contents of the satchel onto the bed. He separated the cash from the checks in two piles. He looked upon the money contentedly, picking up his tumbler of gin and enjoying a celebratory swallow. He sat down and counted it all. The cash came to eight hundred thousand euros, the checks to nineteen million. They were two hundred thousand short. He looked at some of the artwork on the walls. Dramatic pastorals of windblown lakes and violent thunderstorms. One was a Caspar David Friedrich. That one alone should cover the difference. Pity about the rest of the furnishings in the lodge, but it couldn't be helped.

Toby gathered the money into neat piles and put it back in the satchel. Ratka had tried to warn him off coming, but he'd insisted. He didn't like the idea of being far away when the accident took place. With so much money at stake, there would be an investigation into his finances. He didn't want his innocence to be questioned, lest there be delays in the transfer of the estate to his control.

He preferred the mantle of sole survivor. He'd come with Vika to the Chesa Madrun to arrange her mother's—his wife's—services. People had seen them together the night before at the Sporting Club in Monaco. Returning to the Hôtel de Paris, Vika had held his arm as they'd crossed the lobby. They would comment on how beautiful she looked and how attentive he was. If ever there had been disagreements between them, they were past. Princess Stefanie's death had brought them closer than they'd ever been.

As for Robert, they'd taken him from school to make it a family weekend. No one would ever find his appointed bodyguard. Coach Norman MacAndrews's disappearance would forever remain a mystery.

Toby had it all planned out. If he was on a hike when the place went up, they would count him lucky. He'd need a suitable scar, of course. A piece of debris striking his cheek, something he could dine out on for the rest of his life.

He finished his gin as Ratka entered the room.

"We're ready," said the Serb. "My men are cutting the gas lines right now."

"Well, then," said Toby. "Let's."

Simon rounded the corner of the house, hunting for a way inside. The windows were shuttered, the doors locked. Growing desperate, he observed a rectangular hatch built low into the stone retaining wall. The hatch had a metal handle and appeared to open outward. Simon took it to be a coal chute from the days when a furnace warmed the house. He pulled on it, but rust and decades of disuse had welded it closed. He ran up the hill and broke off a sturdy branch. He returned and thrust one end inside the handle and leaned on the other. Leverage did its job. The hatch opened. Simon peered inside. A metal chute, filthy with age, descended to the storm cellar. He'd been correct. He removed his parka, arranged it on the chute's flat surface, then lay down headfirst and slid to the bottom.

In the cellar, he got his bearings. Except for the light from the hatch, it was pitch-dark and the blackness appeared to go on forever. He activated his phone's flashlight and located the stairs. Several coal pokers lay at his feet. He picked one up. Heavy, iron, with a spade-shaped prod at one end. It wasn't a SIG Sauer, but it was better than nothing. He climbed the stairs one at a time, the old rotting wood groaning under his weight. He had no choice but to go slowly. Should he give himself away, he was a sitting duck. Even Tommy couldn't miss him here.

Simon reached the top of the stairs two minutes later. An eternity. Gingerly, he pressed down on the door's handle. It was locked.

From deep inside the house, there was a gunshot.

He was too late.

Simon placed the sharp end of the poker into the doorjamb and forced the rod to the left. With a crack, the door flew open. He entered the house and found himself at the junction of two corridors. The light was dim, the ceilings low. He stood still for a moment, listening. He heard heavy footsteps descending a flight of stairs. Then silence. He advanced toward the sound, poker held at the ready. He had no idea what part of the giant house he was in. The doors on both sides of the hall were closed. He felt as if he were in a maze. He heard muffled voices somewhere ahead of him. A door slammed. More footsteps. Someone was running…coming his way. Simon raised the poker, holding it like a baseball player ready to swing for the fences.

A figure rounded the corner.

He swung.

*   *   *

They'd moved Robby and his mother to the cardroom downstairs. It was a small, dark room, the smoke from a thousand cigars seared into the arolla pine walls, maroon throw rugs over the parquet floor. Elisabeth played solitaire at the table. Viktor sat behind her, eyes trained on Robby, his gun resting on his leg, the barrel pointed directly at him.

"What are you going to do with us?" asked Robby.

"What do you think?" said Elisabeth.

"You're going to kill us. Tell me why."

"Your family is very rich. We want your money."

"How will you get it if we're dead?"

"From your grandfather," said Elisabeth.

"Both of my grandpapas died a long time ago. I never knew them."

"Toby's still alive. He's your grandfather."

"Not my real grandfather."

"Real enough."

"Is it true, mother?" Robby asked.

Vika didn't answer. She didn't know how to lie to her son. "May we use the bathroom?" she asked. "You've had us in here far too long."

"You can wait," said Elisabeth, offering a cruel smile. "Soon it won't be a problem anyway." She played another card, then rearranged a few. She was cheating.

Robby saw his mother looking at him strangely. She mouthed several words. He shook his head, and she did it again. "Hide-and-seek." Robby understood at once. He looked at Viktor and his gun, then thought of Coach MacAndrews. When they'd turned him over in the snow, his eyes were open and unafraid. One second he was alive, the next dead. Robby nodded to his mother. All his life he'd been trained to act like a prince. It had come to this. He wouldn't disappoint her.

His mother glanced at the ceiling. She was telling him to go upstairs to the shooting room. There were lots of guns in the house. He'd gone hunting with his mother and a guide last summer. He hadn't killed anything. He'd wanted to miss, but he'd learned how to load a shotgun and how to fire one.

"I need to use the bathroom," said Robby.

"I told you to wait," responded Elisabeth, still engrossed in her cards.

"I can't," said Robby. "Or I'll make a dirty, smelly mess."

"Aren't we demanding?" said Elisabeth.

"Now," he said.

"You are a little prince," she said, as if proud of him. "Fine. Let's go. But if you even think of doing anything you shouldn't, I'll hurt your mother. Understand?"

Robby nodded.

Elisabeth stood from the card table and walked to the door. "And you," she said to Vika. "Stay."

Elisabeth opened the door.

"It's this way." Robby turned left and walked down the hall. There was a closer bathroom, but it wasn't the right one. He turned a corner and stopped at the first door. "Wait here," he said.

"Stop!" Elisabeth marched past him and poked her head into the bathroom. It was small, no windows, just a toilet and large marble sink atop a cabinet with feet like a lion's paws. As in every other room in the house, the walls were made from arolla pine. These walls were different, however. They hid a secret.

Elisabeth came back out and told him to go inside and to hurry up.

Robby went in, shut the door, and locked it. He pretended to unzip his pants and made a pained, groaning noise.

Years had passed since he'd played hide-and-seek inside the house. The last time, he'd gotten stuck in the attic and had suffered a panic attack when he saw all the dead rats caught in their traps. He was braver now.

He took off his belt and used the buckle to pry open a special panel. He had to run the buckle's tongue along both sides before it came off. He put the panel on the floor and crawled into the opening. It was dusty. His nose itched and he needed to sneeze. Somehow he didn't. He squinted and made out the passage that ran to the other side of the house. There were lots of them like it. Over the years, Robby, and his mother and her father before him, had played in the house and fashioned their own entries and exits. He knew them all.

"Robert, open the door."

"Just a moment," he said, sticking his head back into the bathroom. "I'm busy."

"I said now."

"I'm not finished."

"Hurry up."

Robby pulled the panel back into place. Scooting backward, he scraped his knee on an exposed nail. He cried out. He couldn't help it.

"Robert!" Then: "Viktor. Come! Quickly!"

Robby skittered backward and the panel fell in the opposite direction, onto the bathroom floor.

There was an earsplitting explosion and he saw a jagged hole in the door where the lock used to be. Viktor's blue eyes peered through the opening.

"Run, Fritz, run!" shouted his mother louder than she'd ever shouted before.

Robby started up the narrow passage, stepping over joists and ducking under beams. The shooting room was upstairs on the far side of the house.

He knew exactly how to get there.

Chapter 74

Ratka reached the bathroom and found Elisabeth peering inside a rectangular opening where a panel had been. "What happened?" he asked. "Was it you who fired?"

"The boy," said Elisabeth. "He went in there. I sent Viktor after him."

Ratka bent and stuck his head inside the panel. He saw only a dark, confined passage much too narrow for a man of his size to fit into. "Where's the princess?"

"In the cardroom."

"No, she isn't. I was just there." Ratka took hold of his daughter's hair and yanked her closer to him. "Damn you."

"Take your hands off of her," said Toby, arriving a moment later.

Ratka released Elisabeth, turned, and shoved Toby against the wall. "Quiet." He pointed to Elisabeth. "Find the boy. Kill him."

"Don't shoot him," said Toby. "It will spoil everything."

"Do as I say," said Ratka. "We'll fix it later."

"Wait," said Toby. "I know where he's going. It's where I'd go if I were him."

"Where?" asked Ratka.

"The gun room. All kinds of rifles and shotguns. It is a hunting lodge, you know."

"Where is it?"

"Upstairs. In the old wing. Far side of the house."

"Go," said Ratka. "Take Elisabeth."

"And you?"

"I'll find the princess."

*   *   *

Robby felt his way forward in the dark, hands seeking out the rough tim-
bers, feet moving cautiously, one step at a time. It was pitch-dark, the
light from the bathroom no longer a help. When he was little and played
hide-and-seek, they'd all carried flashlights, the old-fashioned kind with
batteries. He didn't have that or a phone. He had to rely on touch and
memory. He came to a wall blocking his path. He turned to the left and
slid sideways into a narrow gap, his back pressed against a sheet of ply-
wood. They had called this part the cliff, because you had to get past it
as if traversing a knife's edge. A cobweb covered his face. He grimaced,
stopping to raise a hand and wipe it off.

"Boy! You there? Viktor is coming for you. You're dead. Hear me?
Dead."

The bad man sounded as though he was close enough to reach out
and grab Robby. It was an illusion. Either because it was dark or because
everything was so tight, every noise sounded as though it was an inch
from Robby's face. He could hear Viktor grunt and groan.

Robby kept moving, relieved when the wall behind him fell away right
when it should. He had more room now. He knelt down and ran his fingers along the wall facing him. He detected a depression in the wood the
shape of a large square. He was in the right place. He pressed against the
panel. It didn't budge.

Out of the corner of his eye, he detected a ray of light. His breath
caught. It was Viktor's flashlight. He'd reached the cliff. Robby was directly in his line of sight. Without thinking, Robby made a fist and
slugged the panel. He felt something crack in his hand; a sharp pain re-
verberated along his forearm. He moaned. The panel fell onto the floor
of a closet.

Robby dropped to his hands and knees and pulled himself inside just
as a gunshot exploded in the dark. He bit back a scream. Shaking with
fear, he stood, only to be suffocated by an army of musty woolen coats.
He found the doorknob and escaped the closet, collapsing onto the floor.
He was in the old part of the house, the original cabin built over a hun-

362

dred years ago. He was standing in a small, stinky room with hooks hanging from the ceiling and the walls. It was called the drying room. It was here that hunters hung up the carcasses of the game they'd shot so the dead animals would cure. Stairs ran up the opposite wall to a landing. The door on the landing led to the loft. On the other side of the loft was the gun room.

Robby closed the closet door and ran up the stairs. He turned the knob and found the door locked. Hope turned to desperation. He rammed his shoulder against the door, but it was old and sturdy. He ran back down the stairs, searching for something to break the lock. He found a pile of chains in one corner. On top of them was a large steel hook twice the size of his hand. He picked it up and returned to the landing. Over and over, he struck the hook against the door handle until finally it broke off and the door swung open.

"Boy!"

Robby checked over his shoulder and saw the closet door swing open, Viktor's blond head appear.

Robby ran.

He was almost there.

Simon stopped the poker an inch from Vika's face as she ran into him, nearly knocking him over. "Simon."

"What happened? I heard a gunshot."

She was breathing hard, but she appeared unhurt. "What…How?" she asked haltingly.

Simon took hold of her arms. "Who fired the gun?" he asked.

"Elisabeth. Ratka's daughter. I told Fritz to get away."

"Get away…where?"

"This is an old house. There are passages no one uses anymore. Some have been walled off. I told him to get to the shooting room."

"Can you take us there?"

Vika nodded. "Of course." Then: "How did you find us?"

"Don't worry about that. I'm here. That's what matters." Simon saw that her hands were bound. He took his set of picks and selected the sharpest among them, using it to slice through the plastic cuffs. "Who else is inside the house?"

"Toby and Ratka and one of his men."

"Where?"

"Back there," said Vika, throwing a glance toward where she'd come from. "Ratka's man went after Robby."

It was then that Simon caught a whiff of something noxious. He remembered Dragan's words about Ratka's plans. "Can you smell it? Gas. Ratka's cut the lines. He's going to blow the place. He wants to make it look like an accident."

Vika led Simon across the great room and up a broad flight of stairs hugging the walls. As they reached the top, Ratka appeared on the floor below. He fired at them. The bullet struck the wall behind Vika. She stumbled and Simon guided her to the corridor, out of Ratka's sight. "Go on," he said. "Help your son. I'll be right behind you."

Vika ran down the hall leading to the oldest part of the lodge. The corridors were narrower still, a forest-green runner covering the flooring, the walls lined with bleached steinbock horns, the local mountain sheep. She came to a junction. The oncoming hall led from the back of the house, where she'd been held with Fritz. She heard footsteps approaching and raced to the end of the hall, throwing open the door to every room, hoping this might prove a distraction. She mounted a half flight of stairs and threw open the door to the shooting room.

Fritz faced her, holding a double-barreled shotgun. "Mother."

Vika crossed the room. "They're coming. Give me the gun."

"No." Fritz put the shotgun to his shoulder. His eyes darted to the doorway. "Get down," he said.

Elisabeth entered the room, Toby Stonewood at her shoulder. She raised her pistol. Her hand never made it past her waist before the shotgun fired. Two shells of twelve-gauge buckshot struck her in the chest and neck, lifting her off her feet and slamming her into the wall, nearly decapitating her. She was dead instantly.

Toby looked at the body, then at the boy. "I believe you're all out," he said, advancing on him.

Robby split the barrels, hurriedly replacing the spent shells. Toby tried to wrestle the gun from his hands. As they struggled, Vika picked up Elisabeth's pistol. She didn't dare shoot for fear of striking her son. She ran at Toby, gripping the pistol by its barrel, and struck him in the back of the skull. Toby crumpled to a knee. Fritz freed the shotgun, closed the breach, and struck Toby across his jaw, sending him to the floor unconscious.

"Kill him," said Fritz. "Kill him, Mother."

Vika aimed the gun at Toby. Behind her, Viktor came into the room, eyes on Robby. Viktor raised the pistol, then noticed Vika. He hesitated, looking between them. She shot him twice and he fell to the ground.

Fritz set the shotgun against the wall. Vika hugged him. He laid his head on her shoulder. He'd grown in the weeks since she'd last seen him. "I love you," she whispered.

Fritz nodded. "We got them."

Simon entered the first room he came to. There wasn't adequate space to swing the poker as Ratka went past, so he knelt and waited, the poker held low in both hands. He heard Ratka's labored breathing, felt his heavy step advance down the hall. As the Serb ran past, Simon thrust the rod out of the doorway, tripping him. Ratka fell onto his belly. Simon jumped into the hall. Standing above Ratka, he drove the ball of the poker into his neck. The blow had little effect. Simon brought the poker down again as Ratka spun onto his side and grabbed the rod. His other hand brought the pistol to bear. Simon kicked it from his grip. Ratka took hold of Simon's ankle and wrenched it to one side. He was a strong man. Simon lost his balance and fell against the wall.

Ratka released him and, unhurt, sprang to his feet. He slugged Simon in the stomach, striking him inches below the wound. The pain was excruciating. Simon tried to swing but could not. Ratka struck him again and again, vicious jabs to the sternum, the chest. Simon felt the staples inside him tear. Unable to deflect the blows, he fell back, retreating down the hall. He was utterly powerless. His back struck the railing and he could retreat no farther. He looked over his shoulder. It was a twenty-foot drop to the flagstone floor. Ratka regarded him from five steps away, bloodlust in his eyes.

"Riske," he said. "Enough of you."

He came at Simon rapidly, arms extended, looking to throw him over the railing. Simon timed his approach and at the last instant spun, taking hold of Ratka's jacket in one hand, thrusting his hip into the Serb's waist, and using all that was left of his strength and the other man's momentum to flip him over the railing.

There was a sickening crunch and an agonizing scream. Ratka lay impaled on the antlers of the stuffed stag, a sharp, curved horn protruding from his neck and another from his belly. He stared at Simon, eyes wide. The stag's head sagged beneath his weight, coming loose from its mount.

From a far corner of the house came a blast of gunfire. Simon staggered down the hall, picking up Ratka's pistol. "Vika!" he shouted. "Hold on."

"We're all right," she replied as he neared the shooting room.

Simon saw a woman's body extending from the doorway, blond hair obscuring her face. "His daughter?" he asked.

"I shot her," said a thin, pale boy with blond hair. "She was going to hurt us."

"Are you Robert?"

The boy nodded.

"I'm Simon. I'm a friend of your mother's."

"Pleased to meet you, Simon." The two shook hands.

"Brave man."

"You're bleeding," said Robby.

Simon looked down at his shirt. "I'll be all right."

Vika touched Simon's arm. "Where is he?"

Simon shook his head. "We have to get out of the house," he said. "I can smell the gas more strongly now. Anything might set it off."

"What about Toby?"

Simon looked at the prostrate figure. He knelt beside Toby and slapped his cheek. Toby made no sign of regaining consciousness. "I can't carry him out."

"Leave him," said Robby. "He's evil."

"Yes," said Simon. "To the core."

"Just a minute." Vika went to Toby and searched his pockets. She held up the ring, then slipped it on her finger.

Simon put his arm around Vika.

Together, the three left the house.

CHAPTER 75

Toby Stonewood came to.

His jaw was broken. He knew that. His head throbbed terribly where Victoria had struck him. He pushed himself to his knees and managed to stand. He staggered into the hall, nearly tripping over Elisabeth's body. He stared at her for a moment, feeling nothing, then stepped over her and walked toward the front of the house. The sweet-sour odor of natural gas was overwhelming. More than anything, he felt nauseated. He had to get outside.

Suddenly, he stopped.

The money. It was in the master bedroom. How much had there been? Sixteen million euros? Seventeen? Far too much to leave behind. He turned back and navigated the warren of corridors until he reached the bedroom and saw the satchel where he'd left it.

He picked it up and looked inside. The money was all there.

He breathed a sigh of relief.

He made his way to the front of the house and down the grand staircase into the great room. With shock, he saw Ratka draped across the stag's head, impaled on its antlers. A terrible keening noise came from his lips. The man was alive.

Ratka noted some movement from the corner of his eye. He shifted his gaze and saw a man walking down the stairs. It was the Englishman. It was Toby!

Ratka raised an arm. He tried to speak. He might even have moved.

The motion was enough to sever the century-old wall mount.

The stag's head dropped ten feet to the flagstone floor. One of its points sliced through Ratka's back, angled off his pelvis, and struck the metallic box in his pocket. The electronic detonator sent a signal to the expertly placed explosives in all four corners of the house. The half-kilogram packets of *plastique* exploded simultaneously, igniting the invisible cloud of natural gas that by now filled the Chesa Madrun.

Toby Stonewood felt a blast of hot air, a fire hotter than imaginable. He was flying inside a cloud of flame.

And then he wasn't.

Chapter 76

So this is your schloss?" said Simon.

"I prefer to think of it as home," said Vika.

It was a cool, sunny autumn afternoon. The leaves in the vast forest surrounding the Schloss Brandenburg were colored every shade of red, orange, and yellow. Simon gazed at the imposing gray stone fortress.

"You don't ever feel funny living in a castle?"

"Of course not. I was born here. And actually, it's a palace."

"You have a moat. That makes it a castle."

"If you say so."

"I don't suppose you have to do the windows?"

"No."

"Or the floors?"

Vika shook her head. "The floors will be your job."

"Don't forget," said Simon. "I'm recovering from life-threatening injuries."

"When you're better, then."

"I plan on a long convalescence."

"Do you?" Vika looked at him, smiling. "Then it will give me time to teach you German."

Simon stopped and took her in his arms. "Are you sure you're ready for a commoner?"

"Are you sure you're ready for a princess?"

Simon kissed her. "I'm going to need to think about that."

ACKNOWLEDGMENTS

At Mulholland Books / Little, Brown, my thanks to Reagan Arthur, Pam Brown, Anna Goodlett, Karen Landry, and, of course, my editor nonpareil, Josh Kendall.

At InkWell Management, thank you to Eliza Rothstein, Lyndsey Blessing, Jenny Witherell, Michael Carlisle, and, last but not least, my agent of twenty years and counting, Richard Pine.

And finally, a special hello, hug, and thank you to my daughters, Noelle and Katja, neither of whom was born when I ditched my corporate career and set off on this crazy adventure way back in May 1995. When I wrote the last page of *Crown Jewel,* both (for the first time) were thousands of miles away at college. Over these years, they have grown into smart, beautiful, caring human beings who have enriched and brightened my life in ways I could never have imagined. I am proud beyond measure to call myself their father.

CHRISTOPHER REICH is the *New York Times* bestselling author of *The Take, Numbered Account, Rules of Deception, Rules of Vengeance, Rules of Betrayal,* and many other thrillers. His novel *The Patriots Club* won the International Thriller Writers Award for Best Novel in 2006. He is currently traveling the world and writing the next Simon Riske adventure.

MULHOLLAND BOOKS

You won't be able to put down these Mulholland books.

Visit mulhollandbooks.com for
your daily suspense fix.